THE OLD SCHOOL

Fresh from an Arts degree, P. M. Newton joined the New South Wales police force in 1982. She spent the next thirteen years working in and around Sydney in various departments – Drug Enforcement, Sexual Assault, Major Crime – first as an officer, then as a detective. When she had eventually had enough of meeting people for the first time on the worst day of their lives, Newton resigned from the Job to travel and live overseas, before returning to Sydney, where she works as a librarian and writes. *The Old School* is her first novel.

pmnewton.blogspot.com

THE OLD SCHOOL

P. M. NEWTON

PENGUIN BOOKS

PENGUIN BOOKS

Published by the Penguin Group
Penguin Group (Australia)
250 Camberwell Road, Camberwell, Victoria 3124, Australia
(a division of Pearson Australia Group Pty Ltd)
Penguin Group (USA) Inc.
375 Hudson Street, New York, New York 10014, USA
Penguin Group (Canada)
90 Eglinton Avenue East, Suite 700, Toronto, Canada ON M4P 2Y3
(a division of Pearson Penguin Canada Inc.)
Penguin Books Ltd
80 Strand, London WC2R 0RL, England
Penguin Ireland
25 St Stephen's Green, Dublin 2, Ireland
(a division of Penguin Books Ltd)
Penguin Books India Pvt Ltd
11 Community Centre, Panchsheel Park, New Delhi – 110 017, India
Penguin Group (NZ)
67 Apollo Drive, Rosedale, North Shore 0632, New Zealand
(a division of Pearson New Zealand Ltd)
Penguin Books (South Africa) (Pty) Ltd
24 Sturdee Avenue, Rosebank, Johannesburg 2196, South Africa

Penguin Books Ltd, Registered Offices: 80 Strand, London WC2R 0RL, England

First published by Penguin Group (Australia), 2010
This edition published by Penguin Group (Australia), 2011

Text copyright © Pamela Newton 2010

The moral right of the author has been asserted

All rights reserved. Without limiting the rights under copyright reserved above, no part of this
publication may be reproduced, stored in or introduced into a retrieval system, or transmitted, in
any form or by any means (electronic, mechanical, photocopying, recording or otherwise), without
the prior written permission of both the copyright owner and the above publisher of this book.

Cover design by Dave Altheim © Penguin Group (Australia)
Cover image © Gabrielle Ewart / Andresr / Shutterstock
Text design by Cameron Midson © Penguin Group (Australia)
Typeset in 12/16pt Adobe Garamond Pro by Post Pre-press Group, Brisbane, Queensland
Printed and bound in Australia by Griffin Press

Quote from interview with George Pelecanos on p.vii – quoted with permission from
Robert Birnbaum. http://www.identitytheory.com/interviews/birnbaum100.html
Posted: April 21, 2003 © 2003 Robert Birnbaum.
Quote on p.244 from Historical Records of New South Wales. [HRNSW] Sydney:
Government Printer, 1892–1901, 7 vols.

National Library of Australia
Cataloguing-in-Publication data:

    Newton, P.M.
    The old school / P.M. Newton.
    9780143204015 (pbk.)

    A823.4

penguin.com.au

To Mum, with love and gratitude.

In memory of my father and my eldest brother,
two good men
both named Noel.

There is no solving murders, you know. Not unless the dead are going to rise up out of the earth. Once somebody is killed, it's forever for their loved ones and their family and the community.

– George Pelecanos

Acres of sheep, an arctic wind that barrelled through town, and a colonial red-brick gaol with a reputation to match the mean winters. That pretty much summed up Goulburn as far as the young woman by the jukebox at the rear of the Empire Hotel was concerned. She stared around at what Friday night had to offer: sweat, smoke and sodden beer mats. Any half-decent Sydney pub would have had a Friday the thirteenth theme, bar staff in black at least. But instead of Thai food on King Street and a band at the Brasserie she was stuck in this toilet-break town on the Hume Highway.

All night long, convoys of trucks vibrated through Goulburn's main street, their red running lights reflecting in the windows of the all-night cafés with heart-attack mixed-grill menus. In a month, just in time for Christmas, the new stretch of the Hume would open and turn Goulburn into a bypassed town. No more queues for petrol, pies and a piss at the Big Merino. The gift shop in the giant cement sheep's belly would have to rely on the connoisseurs of kitsch, ticking off stops on their list of the 'big things' that small towns specialised in: the Big Prawn at Ballina, the Big Banana at Coffs, the Big Cheese at Bodalla.

The Empire wasn't big. It was a locals' pub with a dress code of flannelette shirts, dirty jeans and ugg boots. She knew they stood out. Her companion's T-shirt and jeans said surf, not sheep. He was heading back from the bar, drinks in hand, a scotch for her and a beer for him.

She'd have to watch that. Couldn't go drink for drink with those odds.

The pub TV was on mute. Clinton flashed his telegenic smile but no one showed any interest in the new US president, with his Southern drawl and way with women. In the Empire it was Cold Chisel and AC/DC on high rotation on the jukebox and a row of gold coins along the green baize cushion of the pool table pledging challengers to the reigning champ. Between shots and schooners, local eyes slid to the back table.

She ignored them. Let them think they were lovers. She dipped her head to catch the words of the man who sat down opposite her.

'It's good gear, girlie. Jump on it four times.'

'At that price? I want to trampoline on it.'

'Hey – four times your investment, straight up. Can't ask for more. Happy campers, you'll see. You'll be happy, I'll be happy, punters'll be happy.' The man smiled. Tanned skin stretched over sharp cheekbones, knitting up the edges of stark blue eyes.

'So when do I get to see all this happiness?' She drummed her fingers against her cheek, looked bored.

'Money first. Ya know, still can't get me head round it. Little girlie like you, running this all on her own.'

'Been outa the loop, mate. Sisters are doin' it for themselves these days.'

'Not everything, I bet?' His thumb rasped away on his cigarette lighter, leg jiggling against her bar stool in time with the spark and snuff of the flame. 'Just thought your lot were more, ya know, traditional? Bit of badness in you though, eh?'

She drained the last of her scotch, pushed the empty glass towards him. 'We're done.'

'Aw, Lily – don't be like that. Ya know the way things go.'

'I know we're done.'

A sharp ceramic smack signalled a fresh break on the pool table. A couple of balls found pockets and trundled woodenly through endless tunnels.

She flattened her forearms across the table, leant forward, blew her words into his ear. 'We coulda done business, coulda made some money.' She curved closer, forcing small moons to rise beneath her T-shirt. Blue eyes and brown swam out of focus. 'Had some fun. But you don't know enough to recognise a real deal and a real partnership when it's under your nose.'

His ankles, hooked around the legs of the stool, anchored him in place even as he arced towards her. 'Money first. It's not up to me.'

'Well, if it's not up to you, maybe I need to see your boss.'

'Look, just – it's all about trust.' His smile unravelled, features sharpening, a spider web of untanned lines appeared around his eyes. 'Yer not an Islander, are ya? Got a bunch of brick shithouses waiting to jump me outside, eh?'

'Jesus, Sam, give it a rest . . .'

'Nah, nah – not an Islander, more like one of those Hong Kong chicky-babes. Action gal! Good with ya feet, are ya?' Fire darted from his fingers. She closed her hand around his, stilling his fingers, smothering the lighter.

'Why? We dancing?'

'Ya sound like an Aussie. Born here? Lob up in a boat? Boat baby, eh?'

When it came to insults, this bloke was an amateur; she'd heard worse on her way to the bar. 'Sam, you said you had product, but I reckon you're just full of —'

'Lily, I swear it's good, it's great – I swear on, um . . .' He sputtered to a halt. His fingers began ripping a beer coaster to atoms.

Her laugh rumbled in her throat. She swung forward. 'OK, Sam, OK. Bit of trust. I'll get the money here . . .' He nodded enthusiastically until she cupped his chin to stillness in the palm of her hand. 'But just for a look, OK? Touch it, feel it, sniff it, count it – fuck it for all I care. You just can't keep it. It goes away. You get my gear here and it's as bouncy as you say, the money comes back, we all live happily ever after. OK?'

'Lily and Sam.' He reached up, fingers tracing the line of her cheekbone, pushing a strand of hair behind her ear. 'I feel like carving it in a tree.'

Carve it in bloody stone, she thought. Won't make it any more real.

She slid off her stool. He scrambled off his and followed her

3

to the back door of the pub. They had to shove through a knot of boots and beer by the cigarette machine. Voices were muffled by Barnsey hammering out 'Khe Sanh', but she still heard them, just like she was meant to.

'Ever humped a wok-jockey? Reckon you're horny again half-hour later.'

Male laughter followed her out into the night.

The car sat at the end of a row of utes and bush-bashed sedans, its unblemished panels and paintwork unique among its neighbours. A man loomed out from the driver's seat and opened the back passenger-side door. No interior light came on. The waning moon, still swollen and slow, had climbed far enough above the tree line to illuminate the sports bag on the back seat. It gaped open, spilling out a dull, grey glow. Sam came closer, drawn in by the metallic sheen of hundred-dollar bills, neatly bound in elastic.

'Get in. Give it a feel. It's all real,' she said, smoothing her arms, soothing the goosebumps.

The moonlight was feeble, accentuated the darkness beyond the space of the car. Mid-November but the Goulburn night still carried the bite of winter. After the smoke of the pub the air tasted almost green – damp and earthy, a feral, animal tang.

'Tell him to piss off.' Sam was shifting from foot to foot. 'I'm not getting in till he's away from the car.'

She shrugged at the driver, who hesitated then stepped back into the shadows.

Trucks slogged down the main street, the deep drawl of their engines only slightly dampened by the pub's bulk. An air horn sounded, brakes compressed abruptly. They leapt at the sound, instinctive, then embarrassed as they identified it, eliminated it – no threat.

Sam slid along the back seat, dipped his hands into the open bag.

'So. We doing business?' She leant in, caught the odour of

4

thousands of sweaty palms rising from the notes flicking through his fingers.

'Why not,' he mumbled, curling over the bag, burying his face in it.

He straightened up, a shaft of moonlight fusing into something solid, metallic, in his hand. A gun. The barrel yawned, a round, black vacuum. Time and light fell into it.

The pale moon waxed yellow, as Lily fell away. The ground fell open beneath her, the moon drenched in red, as she spiralled back, in a swirl of colour and sound, to a flash of light in the dark of night a lifetime ago.

Then the Goulburn night splintered into voices shouting 'Police!', shouting obscenities, shouting her name – *her* name, not Lily's.

Suspended between the open jaws of the car door, no longer Lily but not yet herself, she hung on, fingers drilling into the roof, finding reality in the pain of her nails snapping against the cold, metal resistance.

NSW POLICE SERVICE
Goulburn Police Academy

UNDERCOVER TRAINING COURSE: #32 November 1992

Situation Report of training operation held in conjunction with Undercover Training Course No. 32.

Course Supervisor:	Det. Insp. D. Fowles, OIC Undercover Unit, DEA
	Call Sign – Uniform 1
Name of Operation:	**Tiger Lily**
Date:	13 November 1992
Officer in Charge:	Det. Sgt P. Robotham (Lismore Detectives)
	Call Sign – Foxtrot 1
Undercover Officer:	*Lily* – Det. Con. N. Kelly (Bankstown Detectives)
	Call Sign – Lily
Target:	*Sam* – Det. Sgt S. Murphy (Undercover Unit, DEA)
Money car:	Det. Con. J. Mathews (Bankstown Detectives)
	Call Sign – Foxtrot 2
Situation:	A controlled buy of prohibited drugs and the arrest of target.
Means:	UC Officer 'Lily' to meet and arrange to buy half a kilo of heroin from target 'Sam'.
Location:	Meet to take place in main bar of Empire Hotel, Auburn St, Goulburn, at 8 p.m. Buy-bust to take place in car park of hotel.
Result:	Operation unsuccessful.
Details:	Soon after the money was brought to the scene, the target, 'Sam', produced an undetected firearm and 'shot' the UC, 'Lily', and the money-car driver. Operation aborted by Det. Insp. Fowles at 9.45 p.m. Debrief at Goulburn Police Academy.

'Ned?'

A hand on her arm. A voice saying her name.

The nickname belonged to her more truly than the name she'd been given twenty-four years ago by a mother she barely remembered. Few ever got their tongues successfully around her birth name, Nhu, but it had taken cops to fully exploit the irony of her surname – Kelly.

Her eyes unsealed to a familiar world. No blood, though memories lingered in the odour of exhaust fumes and the hum of car engines. Instead, the Goulburn night was filled with familiar heads shining in torchlight and headlights. Strangers two weeks ago, they had been forged into solidarity by the intensity of the New South Wales Police Undercover training course.

And now, they were angry.

'You OK, Ned?'

Pete Robotham was patting her arm like she was an animal in need of calming. She couldn't be sure if the tremors running over her skin were hers, his, or a mutual charge of adrenalin. As the officer in charge of *Operation Tiger Lily*, Pete would be wearing his share of the blame. She nodded, not trusting her voice yet, not trusting herself to let go of the car door.

Other voices, mutinous and angry as only the truly conned can be, pinged back and forth. Ned lost track of who said what; the night was fluid around her, resentment a rising tide.

'This the UCs' idea of a joke?'

'Not fuckin funny, if ya ask me.'

'Yeah, well, undercovers are different, mate.'

'Yeah – they're wankers.'

'And here comes the chief wanker.'

A nondescript panel van was bumping slowly into the car park, the headlights blinding the group as it swung towards them.

Detective Inspector Swiss Fowles, head of the Undercover Unit, course supervisor and all-round mind-fucking bastard, climbed out of the driver's seat.

'Well, who wants to start?'

He wore his silver hair long, symbolic of the special status of the UCs. No ponytail tonight, it spread over his shoulders like he was Jesus. Long-limbed, with a once-fit body growing soft as he approached fifty, he folded his arms, leant back against the car door. Swiss Fowles – ringmaster of his own private twisted circus.

Ned heard Figgy, her workmate from Bankstown and her money-car driver for the training operation, clear his throat, begin to make an excuse. The ringmaster shut him down with a stare, included her in it.

'You're dead, remember, Mathews? Both you and Detective Constable Kelly. You're nothing but evidence. In the real world you're on the ground with the GMO pronouncing life extinct and jamming a thermometer up your arse while Physical Evidence take the photos. I want to know from your colleagues just where you both fucked up. Anyone got any suggestions?'

'How about snuff films next, Swiss?' shot back another voice from the edge of the group. 'This how you get your jollies?'

Fowles had earnt the nickname Swiss after he'd been shot on an undercover operation back in the seventies. He'd ended up with more than one hole in him. Miracle he survived, the official story went. 'Miracle he's only ever been shot once' had become the UC course motto. Naked hostility didn't seem to upset him. He gazed around at the faces, assessing them like prey. Ned dropped her eyes to her hands. She lifted them, mesmerised by the speed of their shaking. Ashamed, she hid them, made white-knuckled fists around the car window sill.

'It was a set-up.' Pete Robotham's voice wore all the weariness of two weeks of late nights, early starts and excessive alcohol. 'And you got Murph down here to do a job on her. On us.'

A rumble of agreement came from the rest of the class. Input ignored, Swiss lectured as if an audience was optional, analysing precisely how she had let 'Lily' die.

'Lily doesn't look like a cop but that can be a risk too. She was so busy flirting Sam into a money-show she missed all the clues. All that chat about what she is, kung-fu, getting jumped – he was doing a threat assessment on her and she missed it.'

Threat assessment. The rubber window seal buckled under her grip. Thought Sam was bantering, baiting her, not measuring her as a risk.

'And what could she do about it? Demand a search? She's wearing a wire, she could hardly volunteer for a mutual pat down.' Robotham was asking the questions, out of a sense of duty maybe; it was clear his heart wasn't in it.

'Walk away,' Fowles replied.

A roar of disbelief.

'Bullshit, then we'd be bitching about *that*,' came a voice from the back.

'Sometimes you need to walk away.' Detective Sergeant Sean Murphy circled around the car to stand between Swiss and the group of cranky cops. Swiss might run the UCs, but Murph *was* a UC. He did for real what they'd been doing in training. His words were met with silence and grudging respect. 'It's just a job. Remember that. Could save someone's life one day.'

For the last couple of hours his voice – 'Sam's' voice – full of edge and aggro, was all Ned had heard. He sounded different now, spoke slowly like he was dealing with fractious children who required patience.

'Walk away. It's always an option. Worth screwing over a colleague to prove it.' Murphy stuck out his hand towards Ned.

She'd been playing A-grade, and A-graders played without rules. Up to her to be a good scout now, shake his hand, even though she'd rather kick him in the balls. But she couldn't even let go of the car.

'Anyway, I like to shoot one trainee a course.' Murphy extended his unshaken hand further and clapped her on the shoulder. 'Especially the good ones. I don't like competition.'

At that the group broke away, chuckling back to their cars. Show over, honour restored, no harm done.

'Debrief in fifteen minutes and I want to hear more than whingeing and excuses,' Swiss ordered over the laughter.

'C'mon, Detective Kelly. Let me give you a ride back.' Sean Murphy opened the front door of the car. Her hands were locked around the window frame, tears of anger and shame spiking. She couldn't move.

'Breathe – they've gone now. Just breathe, deep and slow.'

Beneath car doors slamming and engines revving, the words were almost subliminal; only the warmth of his breath in her ear made them real.

He stroked a lock of her hair behind her ear. His fingertip trailed warmth, retracing the journey Sam's had made, only this time Murphy's continued down the side of her throat, along her shoulder. He stepped closer, his body radiating heat on a cold night. Then his hand fast-tracked down the curve of her ribs, ran along her belt, slipped beneath her shirt. A sharp sting as he ripped the listening device from the small of her back. He held it in front of her, Elastoplast dangling from it, her skin still stinging as he broke the connection.

'Welcome to the UCs, Ned. This is what we do. We get close, we win trust, we let people think we're their best friend, right up to the moment we fuck them over. And this is how they feel at that moment: murderous. Right?'

He was right. She'd never felt so enraged, but it wasn't just about *Operation Tiger Lily*. He tossed the Nagra into the car and turned back to her, a hand on each shoulder, firm, reassuring, keeping her at a distance.

'Befriend and betray, Detective Kelly. We do bad things to dangerous people, but we never fuck over our own. Each other's all we have.'

Her spine tingled where the tape had ripped free. It earthed her.

She reached around him, one hand on his waist, one running down his spine. Knew he'd feel them trembling.

'What did I just say? But hey . . .' He lifted both arms and pivoted around. 'Go ahead, Ned, search me. No wire. You were the UC.'

He was fit, torso hard beneath his T-shirt. She felt muscles sliding over bone as his arms rose higher. Thirties, maybe older, hard to tell. An Aussie face, the kind that wore the lines of sun damage like a badge of honour.

Sam had been a jangle of twitching limbs and jerky movements, but with Murph, one languid gesture flowed into another. Time slowed down around him as it sped up around her. Ned began to shake so violently her teeth chattered. She plunged her hands into the back pockets of her jeans, grazing her knuckles on the seams.

'We're going to be late for Swiss's debrief, Sarge.'

'He can't start without us.' He swung the front passenger door open. 'And call me Murph. You'll have to when we work together.'

'We won't be.' Brittle as glass, she packed herself into the car.

'For the record, you did a good job. Think on your feet,' he said, settling behind the wheel.

She yanked at the seatbelt. It locked, refusing to unfurl. He drifted across her, she sensed the weight of him above her, caught the scent of the sea. His hand closed over hers, coaxing the belt from the wall. She pressed back into her seat, forcing dead air between them.

Abruptly Murphy was back in his own seat, keys in the ignition.

'Where are you from, anyway?'

'Bankstown.'

'Very funny. What's your background – Chinese? Islander? Like Swiss said, you've got a good face for UC work.'

'It's my face, not a fucking job application.'

He started the car. The tape player came on. Music wound out, sinuous and sinister.

'Very fucking funny.' She ejected the cassette before it hit the chorus. 'Breaking the Girl'.

'Not – my – car.' Murphy dropped the words slowly like she needed time to catch them. 'Not my tape.'

He was right. It was Bankstown Detectives' car, the one Figgy had used for the money show. He'd been sitting alone out here in the night, waiting, listening – to her bloody Chili Peppers tape. She pitched the cassette into the back seat.

'Adrenalin's gotta go somewhere, Ned. Better work out a way of using it.' His reflection hovered in the windscreen, bathed in the green light of the dashboard, watching her. 'Ride the buzz.'

'Yeah? What do you do then, Sarge?'

'Well . . .' He threw the car into reverse, swung out of the space, hands moving hypnotically around the steering wheel. 'There's always sex.'

NED TURNED OFF LIVERPOOL ROAD into Stacey Street and stopped. Monday morning peak-hour traffic made Goulburn Police Academy, the Undercover course and *Operation Tiger Lily* fade safely into the past. Sydney Harbour lay thirty kilometres and an hour's drive back east. A good five degrees cooler there too. Down the slope of Stacey Street, Bankstown was a pool of concrete, shimmering in the heat haze of a thousand idling car exhausts.

The Cumberland Plain rolled out south and west, a mat of streets, suburbs and red-tiled roofs dissected by a fuzzy green line twisting through the middle distance. The Georges River. A river named after a dead English king and a town named after a dead English botanist, now peopled by Australians with distinctly un-English names. The suburbs out here reflected the course of distant wars: Eastern Europe in the fifties, Vietnam and Lebanon two decades later.

Traffic inched forward. There were overpasses, underpasses, one-ways, pedestrian malls and a train line up the middle, but all roads into Bankstown seemed designed to deliver cars to the expanding shopping mecca at its heart. Bankstown Square. Each year it ate up a little more of its surroundings. The excavation for its next car park had already claimed a set of traffic lights along with the corner they'd occupied, and demolition on a block of flats was well under-way. The billboards promised four new levels of parking spaces. No pictures of the traffic jams you'd sit in trying to get one.

Scrolling through breakfast radio, Ned heard one subject

dominating the chat and squawk-back: the opening day of *Operation Milloo*, the Independent Commission Against Corruption's hearings into relationships between police and criminals. Ned had no appetite to hear Neddy Smith's performance on *60 Minutes* being parsed by the pointy-heads. He'd teased like a cheap stripper, hinting at dirty secrets about stick-ups and rorts and Roger. Arthur Stanley 'Neddy' Smith. ICAC's star witness. It was going to be a long week to be a copper – even longer with Ned for a nickname. She changed channels.

The familiar guitar riff slithered out. Ned's skin tightened. She punched a cassette in, one of her sister Linh's oldies. Light reggae and a rich voice replaced the Chili Peppers. 'Down to Zero'. Could've been *Operation Tiger Lily*'s theme song. She joined Joan Armatrading on the chorus – loud.

Coming up on the intersection Ned finally saw the reason for the worse-than-usual bottleneck. A man on his back in the middle of the road, fists raised, cursing in the blurry patois of the chronic alcoholic. Cars performed a clumsy dance around him.

'Jeez, Mabo, anybody else'd be dead by now.'

For a man with no home, he had a lot of names. The older coppers called him Black Charlie, after Black Charlie's Hill. But the younger cohort of cops knew that the hill was Condell Park now, so they'd taken to calling him Mabo after the long-running Indigenous Land Rights case. Still a funny nickname, they reasoned, but more 'cutting edge'. Only magistrates called him by his birth name – Patrick Arthur Murray.

Up ahead the revolving blue lights of a police paddy wagon drew closer. She lowered the window, leant out.

'Get up before you get flattened, you silly bugger.'

Mabo was a dero, he stank and she didn't want him in her car, poor old bastard. Not so old, really – forties maybe, but prematurely pickled by decades of booze and rough living.

'Oh, sis.' Mabo propped up on an elbow. 'Bad land, sis – sad land. Whitefellas been no good to this land.'

Sis. From the first day he'd set his bloodshot eyes on her, she'd been sis. Maybe because hers was the only non-white face in the cop shop, a place where Mabo spent too much time. His face crumpled under the weight of tears. Getting drunk was meant to *dull* the pain but whatever his pain was, it seemed beyond treatment.

'Plenty of other places to go, mate.' She gestured at the half-demolished block of flats.

Mabo had haunted that place, sleeping rough among the bins, howling under clotheslines, dancing and digging in the scabby squares of dead grass.

'Bad place, sis. Sad, bad place.'

'Yeah, well, Mabo, this won't help, you know?'

The paddy wagon was bumping down the median strip. At the wheel was a fresh-faced probationer one month in the Job; the other half of the cab was filled by a big blue box, simian outline of head, neck and shoulders interrupted by a large set of ears.

'Shit. C'mon, Mabo, fuck off.' Ned spoke sharply.

Car horns bleated from behind as the traffic in front moved off but she stayed where she was. A pair of watery brown eyes blinked slowly, red-rimmed and yellow, like runny eggs where they should have been white. The paddy wagon's siren whooped, close enough to hurt.

Mabo jumped. Terror replaced pain. 'Ugly!'

The ink was barely dry on the Royal Commission's report into why Aboriginal people in police custody died like flies, but its recommendations had just made some cops more cunning. Hadn't made them any less mean. Mabo spent a lot of time getting arrested. Offensive language, usually – code for being drunk. But somehow, whenever Sergeant Ugly was involved it was always the trifecta: offensive language, resist arrest and assault police. Ugly was an equal-opportunity racist; he served up 'power point' or 'slope-head' to Ned but, like Mabo's alleged assault police incidents, never in front of witnesses.

'Yeah, it's Sergeant Ugly. Piss off.' Ned rapped the side of the car, trying to gee him up.

The skinny black man gathered up a couple of shopping bags and weaved off through the traffic backed up behind her, pursued by taunts and snatches of abuse. The paddy wagon loomed up, the probationer working the radio handset and trying to make a U-turn while Ugly glared at Ned. She wound up her window as it rolled past, then turned at the dull thud of Ugly's fist thumping the roof of her car. Despite the safety of glass she flinched, snapped back against the headrest as a wad of brown, viscous phlegm spattered onto the window.

'Prick.'

Bankstown Square might be getting a new car park but Bankstown Police Station wasn't. Even finding a spot for a police car sometimes meant a hike from car space to workplace. It took her through the Old Town Plaza, against the flow of city-bound office slaves running for their trains. She bought coffee from a Greek café and a pastry from the Vietnamese bakery. Heading up the stairs of the police station, she inhaled the familiar Bankstown Detectives perfume of stale cigarettes, spilt beer, fast food and running shoes. Not so much an office as a warren of rooms, with doorways knocked through walls that circled back to where you began. From her desk Ned could clock the traffic on the stairs, so part of her job was to tip off those who didn't want to be found. Her place. Imagine, trading all this glamour for the UCs? She must've been nuts.

Paperwork had spawned new generations on her desk during her absence. She ignored it and headed past empty desks to the inner sanctum. Deep in one corner of the furthest room, in a small, glass cubicle, TC was bent over his desk, bald head shining under the electric light. The glass reminded her that some things had changed in the last two years. Detective Sergeant Trevor Charlton,

Top Cat, had been her buddy, her mentor, when she'd arrived on the A-list. Day one hadn't kicked off too well. Patrol Commander Morgenstrom had let her know he'd requested her, had plans for her. Wanted to beef up Community Liaison. When he'd asked about her language skills, a semester of English Lit at uni hadn't been the expected answer. His smooth, managerial demeanour had slipped further when Ned had knocked back the offer of paid Vietnamese language classes. Failed French in Year Eight, she'd said. Monolingual brain.

But by failing Morgenstrom's test, she'd passed TC's. He'd taken her on as his partner, trained her. Little buddy and big buddy. They'd arrested baddies, got roaring drunk after court results good and bad. She'd sat in his backyard on Gunnamatta Bay watching him barbecue chops while his wife, Lorraine, showed off photos of the first grandchild. Maybe Ned had filled a void their grown-up children had left, she didn't care. They'd filled a void in her life she'd forgotten was even there.

Now, two years later, she had her detective's designation and TC had been promoted into the fishbowl at the pointy end of the ship. Detective Inspector. One hand propping up his head, the other wielding a fat blue pencil as he checked the duty books. He looked like a large, prematurely bald schoolboy applying himself to a difficult bit of homework.

'Hey, TC.'

'Little buddy.' He looked up, pushed the books aside, settled back in his chair. Ready, as always, to chat. 'So, was I right? Or was I right?'

'You were right. They can hide behind a corkscrew.'

'How'd Figgy go?'

'Figgy by name, Figgy by nature,' she said, recalling his detailed defence of his role in *Operation Tiger Lily* during the long drive back from Goulburn. It had been a relief to finally reach the Shire and tip him out into the arms of his wife and kids.

TC had christened Detective Constable James Mathews shortly after the ambitious young detective had arrived at Bankstown. 'Figjam': Fuck I'm Good, Just Ask Me.

'And you?'

'Got ripped off – lost the money, never even saw the drugs.'

Figgy could fill in all the gory details. With his form, the audience would divide everything in half, then subtract.

'Ripped off, eh? Who was your target?' TC settled back in his chair, hands behind his head.

'Detective Sergeant Murphy.'

'Murph? Turning up for a training op . . .' TC whistled. 'Well, little buddy, no shame in that. He's been undercover so long he probably pins a note to his pillow to remind him who he is when he wakes up. Murph's smarter than any druggie you'll ever meet, smarter than his boss too.'

'Well, he was smarter than me.'

That last night in Goulburn replayed in drunken flashes; the compulsory drinking session after the debrief then, later, somewhere in that swirl of alcohol and need, Sean Murphy breathing warm words against her throat. Ned jolted back to Bankstown, shook it loose.

'Practised liars who love practising lying. How'd ya find Swiss?'

'Lives up to all his publicity. Makes my current boss look pretty good.'

'Damned with faint praise.' TC's grin widened.

He had the easy confidence of a man who commanded the respect of an office full of detectives who'd still willingly drink with him at the end of the day. What TC knew about managing people didn't come from a book, and it showed.

'Swiss just thinks he runs the UCs, little buddy. And Murph lets him.'

'Worth taking a look, but I don't reckon I'm cut out for the UCs after all.'

'Nah,' he said, riding the vowel. 'Why spend your life palling around with druggies and dropkicks? That's not real police work.'

'Not like Banky, eh? What'd I miss?'

'Had a rape we could have done with your touch on.'

A flash of irritation that was close to anger caught her. She didn't want to do it anymore: sit opposite demolished women and tear out of them all the details they longed to forget. The better she did her job, the worse she felt afterwards. *Oh God, I'd forgotten that . . . Yes, he did . . . oh God . . .* Refreshing each ugly, intimate agony. Not just a spectator, she got in there, stuck her fingers into open wounds. And recorded it, page after page of neat, closely typed trauma. Then she cajoled the victims to bare themselves again before impartial justice in a cold courtroom where, often as not, they were done over once more by a well-dressed barrister who was paid handsomely to do what the offender did for kicks. All that crap about closure – she wasn't convinced.

'Rather interview the baddies.' That, at least, felt like clean, honest work.

'Yeah, little buddy, but no statement, no victim, no case.' TC shrugged.

'Hand-holder, eh? I've had enough of rapes. You can only keep caring for so long.'

'Not if you do it right.' He leant forward, sad-dog eyes. 'Keep your distance. As long as it looks right from their side.'

To the outside world TC seemed a soft touch, but many a crook had discovered the hard way that he concealed a steel core.

'They're not your friends, Ned. They're your job.'

'Another commandment for the list, eh? Does it come before or after "Never screw a target"?'

'I'm just saying sometimes you need to pretend. The UCs forget that it's *all* just pretend.'

'Yeah?'

'Yeah.'

'War stories?'

TC had been around the block and back so many times that there were few people, or places, in the New South Wales Police that he didn't know about, have an opinion – or a brief – on. People trusted TC, told him things. He also had a sixth sense about people. His brown eyes drilled.

'Anyone in particular you want to hear stories about?'

The phone saved her from further interrogation.

'Bankstown Detectives, Detective Inspector – oh it's you. Yeah, what's up?'

She turned to leave but he gestured her to stay, then began writing. An old-school D, he still took down details in shorthand.

'Uh-huh, who's there now? Ugly . . .' He glanced up at Ned and winked. 'Yeah, well, tell him to stay put.'

The one-sided conversation went on, TC scribbling his jagged shorthand, rapping out a series of directions: Physical Evidence, the GMO, Police Rescue. He hung up.

'Come on, little buddy, grab your notebook. We've got a dead'un.'

Her stomach fluttered. Coffee and pastry ebbed and flowed. 'How dead?' She checked her bag for her notebooks, brown for official biz, yellow spiral-back for the fresh and unfiltered.

'Very.' He scrawled a large note on the in-and-out board that theoretically kept tabs on the office members.

Ned's nose wrinkled. She backtracked, scrabbling in her drawer for her tube of Vicks. She didn't do smelly, messy dead'uns well.

'Bones, little buddy, bones in concrete. You won't need that.'

'Better safe than sorry.' She popped the small blue tube in her pocket. 'I passed Ugly on the way in. What's the story?'

'Bulldozer's just uncovered someone's nasty little secret in Bankstown Square's new car park.'

'Maybe Mabo had a point.'

'Huh?'

'He was conducting a one-man protest against life, the universe and everything down there.'

'These bones are in concrete. No land claim for Black Charlie here.'

'Black Charlie' had never gone out of style for TC and now it was making a bit of a comeback. Not so many laughs in 'Mabo' after the High Court decided Australia's faith in terra nullius was unfounded. TC's opinion of Bankstown's most arrested Indigenous local was one of benign contempt. Ned preferred not be reminded of it. Instead, she settled behind the wheel of TC's Commodore and turned her attention to driving, darting in and out of lanes, reading the traffic flow. When she ran an orange light TC chided her.

'No hurry, little buddy. Been waiting a few years by the sound of it. Couple more minutes won't matter.'

TC fiddled with the radio, tuning to *Hits and Memories*. Couldn't hear 'Hotel California' too often, in TC's opinion. He was at his most phlegmatic when everyone else spun in circles. His view on murder, gleaned from fifteen years on the Homicide Squad, was that it was just an assault with a coroner's report attached.

Ned had discovered for herself that murders generally solved themselves. Like accidents, they happened at home, committed by someone you knew and maybe loved and who loved you – once. An iron-wielding wife who'd taken thirty years to fight back. A teenager smashing in an uncle's head with a brick, retribution for a childhood burst open by sexual abuse. A new mum with the blues seeking one uninterrupted night's sleep. All different in execution, all appallingly similar.

Strangers rarely killed strangers. Killers usually killed because they knew someone far too well.

TC's duet with The Righteous Brothers was ended abruptly by a newsbreak. Neddy Smith's *60 Minutes* interview, alleging corruption everywhere from Police Commissioner to cleaner, led the bulletin.

'Did you see it?' Ned asked.

'Wouldn't waste the electricity.'

He rummaged in the glove box, came up with one of Ned's cassettes and popped it in. Salif Keita's wails and beats leapt from the speakers.

'Jesus, girl. What the hell is this shit?'

'It's African.'

'African bloody bonking music, if you ask me.'

'Ever come across them? Roger, Neddy?'

'Hard to avoid back then,' TC said as one foot began tapping in time with the *djembe* drum. 'Two things you want to remember about the good old days, Ned. They weren't that good and they're not that old.'

HALF AN HOUR EARLIER THE SITE had been buzzing, machines devouring stone and steel, dismantling the old block of units. It was quiet now, though traffic was racing past again, normal service resumed since Mabo had cleared off. A knot of workers, silent, smoking, watched the police through narrow, suspicious eyes. Sergeant Ugly was in the paddy wagon reading the morning tabloid, while the young probationer scuffed his boots on a half-demolished wall.

Ugly had once held the rank and place TC now did – boss of Bankstown Ds. His fall from grace, according to legend, had been spectacular, though the details of the badness had not been shared. Transfer, loss of rank, stripped of his detective's designation, fortunate to avoid gaol time; he'd gravitated back to Bankstown, in uniform, eventually regaining a set of sergeant's stripes. But in the new police service, where promotion required a passing acquaintance with EEO and anti-discrimination, that was as far as he was likely to go. Still in his early fifties, Ugly had a decade or more to kill before retirement.

Ned rolled to a stop. 'How long have these units been there?'

'Dunno,' TC said. 'Before my time. Ugly'll have a better idea.'

Ugly was still valued, by some, as the ultimate source of local knowledge.

'Ever had one like this? So old?' she asked, dropping the thought of Ugly into the same vat as the UC course and the black void of a gun barrel in the moonlight.

'We don't know what this is yet,' TC pointed out, then started to organise the troops over the police radio. 'Tell Gumby we'll be on a portable, channel five. Hope he's got some ideas on how to get a body out of concrete.' TC replaced the radio handset.

A man with a face the colour of cement stood beside an excavator, holding his hard hat by the rim, turning it between his hands.

'You're the police?' He looked uncertainly at them as they approached.

Ned was used to the double-takes; TC bear-like, big and bald, the contrast making her seem smaller, more alien. 'Detective Inspector Charlton and Detective Constable Kelly. You're Mr Lalor – site manager?'

'Yes, that's right.' He looked anxiously from TC to Ned then back again.

No one ever rehearsed how to behave if they found a body and had to call the police. Well, not innocent people, anyway. Most people lost the ability to think once the police arrived. As if coppers miraculously knew exactly what was going on, without ever actually being told.

'Perhaps you could show us?' Ned prompted.

'Yes, yes – of course. Ah, over here – it's, um . . .' He stumbled as he led them around the digger. 'Um, it was Petro, actually, pile driver, he was breaking up these footings, and um, he – well, he thought he saw something, so he stopped and, well . . . that's it really. He stopped, called some blokes over and they weren't sure, so, he jumped in, had a look and, well, they called me over and I called you. That's it.'

Lalor finished with a jab at a large, rough, deep hole in the rubble at their feet. It was unremarkable at first glance. Then Ned saw it. Poking out through the wall of the hole, about six feet below ground level.

The machine had shattered the building's footings, smashing through old pipes, sheering through the reo that ran like arteries through the concrete, leaving a twisted tangle of steel and mesh

24

protruding from the edge of the excavation. Towards the bottom of the hole, the blade of the excavator had snapped off the ends of something that looked like a bundle of dry sticks, organic amidst the man-made ruins. Tattered flags of sinewy dark material hung from the jagged ends that jutted just beyond the face of concrete wall.

At the bottom of the pit on top of the rubble lay a few strips of brightly coloured cloth, some long splinters of bone and the thick sole of a woman's platform-heeled shoe.

TC went down on his haunches, big baby face alive with curiosity.

'Well now, this one's a bit different, eh?'

Ned crouched beside him, then knelt, and finally got onto her belly and inched forward, glad it wasn't a court day and she wasn't in her truth suit. As she focused, the details began to clarify. The bones seemed shrink-wrapped by their own skin, suspended in a concrete cavity that tunnelled back into the darkness.

'TC, I reckon —'

'I should put you two in overalls.'

The dry voice came from above and a pair of size-eleven gum-boots passed her nose as she wriggled backwards.

'Jeez, Gumby!' Dust clouds rose as she beat her jeans and shirt. 'Gumby' Glashon was kitted out in his regulation overalls and flanked by a wall of large metallic cases, the sacred talismans of the Physical Evidence section.

'So, what do you reckon then, Embryo-Detective Kelly?' Gumby said, crouching in the spot she'd just vacated.

'I think there's more than one set of legs.'

Gumby grunted, and walked around the pit, first clockwise then back again, round and round the hole in the ground like a dog looking to lie down.

'Could be right,' Gumby said eventually. When he turned back to TC there was almost approval in his voice. 'Interesting – haven't had one of these before. In for a treat.'

Ned saw her chance. 'How are we going to get them out?'

There was a long silence during which everyone took a step or two closer to the pit and peered in.

Gumby broke the silence. 'Carefully.'

They burst into laughter.

'Fuckin ghouls!' The voice came from behind. 'Someone dead down there, and you're all up here, laughing. Show some fuckin respect, why dontchya.'

A large man in an orange safety vest bore down. His workmates flapped from his massive arms as they tried to hold him back. 'Settle down, Petro, settle . . .'

TC stepped forward, apologised instantly. His lack of defensiveness, acceptance of blame, seemed to baffle Petro. Ned felt the heat of embarrassment.

Dead'uns. Always *someone's* precious.

Sergeant Vik 'Ugly' Urganchich was slumped in the passenger seat of the paddy wagon, newspaper folded over his chest, snoring resonating from within.

'Wakey, wakey, hand off snakey.' TC banged the side of the truck.

Ugly made a sound that could've been 'Fuck off' or just a wad of phlegm clearing from his throat.

'When am I getting my driver back? My shift finished half an hour ago.'

'He's busy – Gumby's got him on exhibits. You're stuck here,' TC said.

'Fuck that.' Ugly began to slide over to the driver's seat. A cloud of dust rose at the site entrance as the Police Rescue truck rolled in. 'Be a cast of thousands here soon. I don't need to be one of them.' He started gunning the engine.

'Local knowledge, Vik.' TC opened the passenger door, placed a foot up on the running board and leant in. Ned stood a few paces back and watched the tableau unfolding. Members of Police Rescue gathered around the pit with Gumby. TC could deal with Ugly. She'd rather read five years' worth of old occurrence-pad entries to get local knowledge than get it from him.

'Can you remember when this lot went up?'

'No idea.' Ugly pumped the clutch a few times. Turned the engine over. 'Before my time.'

'Not going to have a gander then? This one's a bit different.'

'Seen one dead'un, seen 'em all.' Ugly shifted into reverse. 'I'm not a fuckin tourist and I'm not a fuckin D. So it's not my fuckin problem.'

TC stepped off the running board and let the door fly back. Ugly barely waited for it to shut before he spun the wheel, spraying them with dust. Ned had half-turned in anticipation but TC was left spitting out dirt-laced expletives as they walked to the site office.

'Prick,' she said.

'Yeah, well, he gets tired carrying the world's biggest bloody chip on his shoulder.'

'Did he earn it? The chip?'

'All a long time ago, Neddie. He was a good D – once.'

Like most of the old school, TC was closed-mouthed about the nature of the hurdle Ugly had hit all those years ago. The badness had been big enough to demote him, but not big enough to earn him the sack or a forced resignation. Mind you, it took a lot of badness to get sacked back then.

By the time they rattled up the rickety aluminium stairs to the site office, Lalor had boiled a kettle, made three strong teas and found a DA number and approval dates on a set of old plans. He pointed at the faint pencil marks in one corner. 'Even got the name of the mob that put 'em up.'

'That'll make things easier.' TC sipped his tea, decanted more sugar from the pourer. 'Your eyes are younger than mine, Neddie.'

She leant over the fading diagrams, noting down every figure.

Her pencil paused at the date, 1976, then the name of the building firm. *Bushrangers.* She stared at the neat printing, and for a moment couldn't remember why she was there, or what she was meant do with the information in front of her.

Bushrangers.

Lalor was expanding to TC. 'Old firm did the original job. Not around now.'

'What can you remember about 'em?'

'Jeez, it's a while back now, I was just starting out. They folded in a hurry, can't remember why . . . Hang on, let me have another squiz at those plans.'

Ned stepped away from the unfurled papers while Lalor puzzled over the pencil marks.

'Hall, Brian Hall – that's him. I worked for him just after I got my Clerk of Works. He was freelancing then. Ended up with SydneyPlex – think he might still be there.'

'Very helpful, Mr Lalor.' TC rolled up the plans, tucked them under his arm. 'You won't need these for a few days.'

Ned followed TC down the steps and back into the dust. The day was starting to bite, another Sydney stinker on the way. She reeled slightly. Her notebook itched in her palm.

They ducked under the blue-and-white checked tape corralling the dusty pit and transforming it into a crime scene. Professional, that's how it looked to Ned. Under control, subject to the attentions of experts. The name she'd written in her notebook threatened her membership. What with Neddy and Roger and ICAC turning up the heat, everything would be done by the book. She turned to TC, found him staring down at her, began to say it but her words disappeared beneath the shrill scream of a huge concrete saw.

The mix of dust and sound drove them back to their car. Gumby followed, leant in through the window. 'Big job, TC. Getting imaging equipment in before we go deep. We'll need smaller drills and hand tools to preserve any evidence in the concrete. Rescue's setting up lights – be a long day and a late night.'

'Whatever you need, Gumby,' TC said.

'Well, for starters I need a uniform crew to secure the place. We're getting screens up but that'll only attract the buggers.' He nodded over his shoulder at the gates, where the local newspaper's photographer and reporter were hovering. 'Like flies to shit.'

'No worries. Stay in touch.' TC rolled up the window and settled back in his seat.

As Ned drew level with the pressmen at the exit, TC stopped her. 'Wait a sec. Open your window.'

The reporter's dust-smeared face immediately filled the space, sweat soaking into the collar of his shirt. 'Lot of activity for an old building, TC. What've they found?'

'You know the score. You'll be told when there's something to tell.'

'C'mon, TC. We've already spoken to the workers – they reckon it's Juanita Nielsen.'

'Got a scoop, then. For what it's worth, I don't know what it is, let alone who.'

'Jeez, TC. Gimme a break – something to get me back to the office. Gunna top thirty degrees today.'

'I'd take it in shifts, then,' TC advised, leaning back into his seat to adjust the air-conditioning.

Ned took it as a signal to drive on. She gripped the wheel, resolute now. 'Bushrangers. Bit of a coincidence, that.'

'What is?' TC sounded distracted, flicking through his notebook.

'Bushrangers. My dad was a partner. Kelly and Hall, you know.' She swallowed.

'I know.' TC didn't raise his eyes from the notebook. Sounded unperturbed. Ned was buoyant with relief.

'Wondered if you'd remembered,' TC went on. 'You were pretty young.'

'Seven. The name made me find out about Ned Kelly and Ben Hall and what bushrangers were. And I remember Dad worked a lot. Up early, home late, covered in dust. Muddy boots outside on the verandah.'

'Remember much about Hall?' TC closed his notebook.

She shook her head. 'Might remember Hall's kids if he had any.'

'You going to be all right with this? I can put you on something else, if —'

'Be the burglar's clerk, while you solve the disappearance of Juanita Nielsen? No way. I was a kid, TC. I barely remember them.'

Her parents belonged where they'd left her: in the past.

'Well, Hall probably remembers you and it never hurts to flatter, Ned. Let's find him, then you can pretend you remember him and we'll see what he says.'

'Back to base?' The wheel spun through her cupped hand.

'Yup. Things to do, people to see.' *Hits and Memories* oozed from the speakers.

'Juanita Nielsen?' TC broke the companionable silence with a deep guffaw as if he'd only just got the joke. 'Probably end up being a bunch of medical students playing silly buggers with their anatomy skeletons.'

Seasoned hide sucked in tight around white, splintered bone swam behind her eyes. It wasn't students.

THE BANKSTOWN DETECTIVES OFFICE WAS in Monday-morning mode. A weekend's worth of break-and-enters to follow up, losses to tally, court cases to attend, witnesses to marshal, paperwork and exhibits to be lost and found; the wheel didn't stop turning just because bones turned up in concrete.

Only the dozen long-stemmed red roses on her desk were out of place. Ned picked them up, inhaled. All show and no scent. The note was handwritten.

Je suis si désolé. Comparé à toi, l'Indochine pâlit.

Her French was limited to perfume and pastry but even so, she knew they were from Sean Murphy. 'Desolate' seemed a bit over the top. 'Debacle' was a better description.

Over post-debrief drinks, her classmates had proclaimed the UCs a bunch of wankers, Swiss a fuckwit, Murph a shithead and *Operation Tiger Lily* a set-up. Everyone had shared in the humiliation, even if it was second-hand. Relief it had been her, not them, made them generous. She recalled passing around the room like a parcel, each drink, each slap on the back unpeeling her a little more, until it had become too hot, too noisy, too full of drunken bonding. She'd slipped outside into the chilly Goulburn night. And Sean Murphy had followed her.

Sitting at her desk in Bankstown, the noise of the office around her, she flushed. If anyone needed to apologise, it was her – to him. Flipping over the card, she saw a phone number followed by four digits. Connect pagers, same company she used. The detective sergeant was a careful man.

There was a whistle. 'Whatchya do to earn them, then?'

Troy Wood, trainee detective and fully qualified nuisance, stood at her desk, sniffing her roses. Her age but still only an A-lister, he was desperate for his designation and dirty that Ned had got a run at the UC course instead of him.

'What goes on tour stays on tour, isn't that right, Neddie?' Figgy, always good for a cliché, appeared beside Troy, trying to read the card.

She slid the note into her back pocket. 'Ever thought there might be a reason you can't keep a girlfriend, Toyboy?'

'He's so pretty,' Figgy chipped in. 'They all get jealous.'

With the big Three-O looming and his hairline retreating, Figgy never missed a shot at the younger A-lister with the headful of thick, curly hair and the ever-changing array of girlfriends.

TC broke up the entertainment.

'Council, Figgy. Get anything and everything they've got on this place. Toy, go make yourself useful and give Whitey a hand. He's heading into Missing Persons. Neddie, see what you can dig up about Brian Hall and make a start on the running sheets.'

Ned pushed aside the roses to get at her notebook, then picked up the phone on impulse. She read out the pager number from the back of the card.

'I don't speak French,' she said to the Connect operator. 'No, nothing else, that's the message. No name.'

Criminal investigations often consisted of foot leather and phone time in mundane and methodical paper chases. Collating running sheets was a lowly position, recording every job assigned along with its result, but it gave remarkable access. No one knew the brief better than the running-sheet officer.

Securing a phone and a coffee, Ned began the present task: trawling through business and building licences in search of one half of the old building partnership. She hadn't been lying when she'd told

TC she had no memory of Brian Hall. To a kid, he'd have been a pair of hairy legs in stubbies passing by at eye level.

The driver's licence database was slow and unwieldy. The blue text crawled slowly up the black screen as she tabbed down. There were Brian Halls all over the state. Then one address stopped her. This Brian Hall had been living at the same place for over thirty years. Cheviot Street, Ashbury.

She closed her eyes and the smell returned, grassy and sweet. Lucerne hay. That smell *was* Cheviot Street, Ashbury. From a memory she didn't know she had came the image of a wide, tree-lined street running alongside Canterbury racecourse, stables behind some of the houses. She couldn't say whose house it was or why she'd been there, but an afternoon glistened photographically. A parade – well, that's how it had seemed. Nothing like that had ever passed their house in Bankstown. She'd peered up through iron gates at the massive animals walking by. Yards of glossy hide would suddenly twitch, like a full-body blink, to shake off flies. Metal striking the road as the racehorses were led past.

'You look a long way away.'

She hadn't heard TC approach. The scent of hay and horse dissipated, leaving the unsettling ache of longing. She jotted down the address, speaking without looking up.

'Address is ringing a few bells. Could be him.'

'Good. Take a run past on your way home, see if it looks familiar.'

'Want me to —'

'Just take a gander at the outside, Neddie. This has been waiting a long time, won't suffer for waiting a bit longer. Right now, you can give Figgy a hand.'

Figgy had returned from the council offices with more than anyone had bargained on. Identifying who had access to the site in 1976 was important, but it meant generating lists of companies that no longer existed, with directors identified only by an initial and a surname.

A murder was a chance to shine – and Figgy knew it – but to shine through this much paper he'd have to burst into flames.

Ned scrupulously recorded the information the records offered up. The company paying for the construction was Erimar Pty Ltd. Their address was a long-expired post-office box in Bankstown. Phone calls to government departments set checks in motion, wheels within wheels; movement was infinitesimal. The afternoon disappeared under snowdrifts of paper.

TC sent the day mob home with instructions to stay sober, contactable and be back bright-eyed and bushy-tailed. The afternoon and night crews could look forward to watching concrete and dirt shift under lights.

Ned couldn't resist one more look at the site. The transformation into crime scene was complete. Hard to see it as a grave, it was all too busy. Now it was just a problem to be solved. Whoever lay in that concrete hadn't come home a long time ago. Was anyone still waiting? Hoping? Knowing by now that the news, when it came, wouldn't be good.

A cast of experts she didn't recognise was moving about beyond the fence, but the bored constable on the gate knew her and waved her through. Inclusion. Still a thrill passing through barriers into places others were craning their necks to see.

Any thrill the constables helping Gumby might've felt had been sweated out of them. Coated in a fine grey dust, they were shaking pulverised concrete through sieves like a pair of old prospectors, but the treasures they sought were bone, teeth and fibre. It was shift-change and their replacements, still clean and cool, looked doleful. Murder could become mundane, excitement turned into a process, discovery nothing but a long, drawn-out procedure. No urgency. No life at stake here. Attentiveness, not haste, was all that was owed now.

The excavation had extended down, so that at ground level only the disembodied heads of the forensic team could be seen bobbing about.

'Thirsty?' Ned's voice caused the excavators to look up, see the bottle she'd brought for them.

With a grateful nod Gumby climbed out and took the cold bottle of Coke from her. He drained a third, capped it and tossed it into the pit, where his colleagues emptied it. He looked even hotter and dustier than the sifting crew.

'TC thought it might be a prank – uni students,' Ned said.

'No chance, they're fair dinks.'

'They?'

'Yeah, definitely two sets of legs. That's about it, though. Bodies or body parts, not sure.' He grinned, rubbing his fingertips together in the universal signal of overtime.

'Who's that?' said one of Gumby's companions, resting his elbows on the edge of the hole and squinting across the site towards the fence that backed onto the existing Bankstown Square car park.

A lone figure leant into the chicken wire, plastic bags in a crumbled heap at his ankles. The western sun at his back rendered him in outline.

'That's Mabo. He used to sleep rough here,' Ned told them.

'Traditional owner, eh?' said Gumby, rejoining his companions. 'A member of the famous platform-heel-wearing tribe.' His team received him with laughter.

Ned twisted in discomfort as she drove out onto Stacey Street. Mabo was a silhouette against the setting sun in her rear-view mirror. Gumby's crack was nothing special. Since the Mabo ruling, bad jokes were the norm, along with predictions of land claims on backyards and swimming pools and the Opera House. Talkback and opinion pieces tapped into barely buried national resentments and kept the spite alive. Casual displays of racism from cops, that was nothing special either. Still unsettled her, though. A test, was that it? To gauge her reaction, see if she was a good scout. Or was it to remind her that she too was a potential target, but one who could buy immunity with silence? All the way down Georges River Road, Ned composed a series of put-downs she knew she'd never have the guts to use.

Ashbury was smaller yet more luxurious than she remembered. Only ten Ks to the city, the old inner-west suburb was prospering. Sydney's passion for renovation was on display, before-and-after shots: old, brick single-storey bungalows sat next door to multi-colonnaded marijuana mansions. A handful of old houses had retained their large backyards, and stables still stood in a few.

Hall's place looked like its last renovation was a long time ago. The fibro attic and extension out the back didn't match each other or the rest of the house. The driveway was empty, the garden filled with established shrubs and old roses, thirsty in the dry earth. Without Hall's street number she would never have recognised the house, though that had more to do with memory than refurbishment. Now she was actually here, the memory of the horses and the scent of lucerne found no resonance.

But then, reality and memory rarely matched up. Two years ago, as a new trainee detective, she'd grabbed her first shoppie in Bankstown Square. Back then she'd feared running into reminders around every corner. Ned guessed her mother had probably taken her shopping there when she was just a wide-eyed toddler. But it could have been any shopping mall, anywhere. Her memories had found no purchase on those slick, faux-marble floors.

After one more run past Hall's home, Ned turned for home. In the racecourse car park a couple of strappers were grazing horses, their coats hidden beneath matching coloured rugs. It wasn't until she was rising over the swell of the Gladesville Bridge that she remembered Sean Murphy's roses, wilting on her desk.

THE INDUSTRIAL RUBBISH SKIP SITTING in Ned's usual parking space outside View Street proved that renovations were no less popular in Greenwich than in Ashbury. Tall gums masked the front of the low Federation cottage in deep green shade. Its windows, slick and black, betrayed no sign of life. Ned sat in the last of the car's artificial chill studying the glossy forest of camellias guarding the front path of her aunt's home. Even on a heat-struck day, Ned knew legions of mosquitoes lay in wait in the damp moss. She swung out of the car into the steamy evening, slapping away the attack on her ankles.

The screen door was unlocked, the front door wide open. From somewhere out the back her aunt's voice floated, clear and warm as the golden light slanting up the long hallway. A familiar melody. Mary Margaret might sometimes have trouble naming common household implements, but the aria still came to her, lush, full and perfect. No hint of an ageing voice. Ned stopped and listened to a few phrases of 'O Mio Babbino Caro'.

She passed through the front of the house and the gloomy damp rooms where the sun never reached, out into the dry heat of the back deck. The view, across the neck of the harbour where it narrowed to split into two rivers, never grew stale. Limp-sailed yachts rocked, sluggish, off Longnose Point, as a small green and yellow ferry unzipped a white wake between them.

Mary Margaret was in full voice on the raised deck, standing astride the rays of the setting sun, arms raised towards it. She was stark naked, in full view of the neighbours' backyard pool, which was filled with goggle-eyed, giggling kids.

'Aw, shit!' Ned dumped her bag and grabbed her aunt by her spongy shoulders. God alone knew how long the concert had been going on. 'Come on, MM. Show's over.' She tried to turn the woman back towards the door.

Mary Margaret twitched as if shrugging off an insect. 'Not yet. I have my encore.'

Getting her through the back door was just the first part of the battle; MM was merely between acts.

'Where's my death scene costume? What have you done with it, you foolish girl?'

The woman rounded on Ned, fierce, eyes wide, teeth bared, hand raised. Ned ducked the slap easily but resisting the instinct to hit back was harder. This was new. It must be new, or it would have been high on the list of 'things' Linh had to report. Ned wondered for a guilty instant if her sister had mentioned MM becoming aggressive but she hadn't been paying attention. It was likely.

'Come on, MM, your costume's in here.'

She hated indulging MM's fantasies; she felt manipulated. Linh might buy MM's performances – Ned didn't. She knew MM regarded the Freyers next door as 'gauche', 'nouveau riche'. That naked show was just as likely a stunt to embarrass them, as a symptom of dementia or Alzheimer's.

Mary Margaret muttered, stalking down the hall towards her room.

'I told Michael and I was right. Bad enough he brought one back, now we're overrun with them.'

Ned held out underwear for her aunt to step into. Mary Margaret steadied herself on her shoulder nonchalantly, as if her niece were a chair.

'Not that one – *that* one – the purple.' Snap, snap. Manicured nails glittered, ordering her 'dresser' about.

Ned took the silk kimono from its hanger. MM stood, arms outstretched, as if requiring only a cross to be nailed upon. Ned slipped a capacious sleeve along one arm, then the other, wrapping the kimono across MM's body, securing the wide sash. Only then did the woman drop her arms with an impatient sigh, and glide out the door.

Ned sat heavily on the bed. She was exhausted and just at that moment didn't particularly care if the bitch went and cavorted naked with the neighbourhood dog.

Ned had no love for her aunt, not really. Linh had supplied information leaflets and Ned read them, but she didn't see fear or confusion on MM's face – just sheer bloody-mindedness. Even if her racist shit could be written off to some disease, then it had just eroded the walls of reserve that had concealed it all these years.

Resentments both old and fresh rose in her. MM's career had kept Ned and Linh fringe dwellers in her life. And now, Ned couldn't help her shameful, spiteful pleasure that the Job was all-consuming, important, the ultimate excuse for not being around more or caring more. But just as their father's sister had unwillingly inherited them, now it appeared they were destined to inherit her.

'Nhu?'

Only her little sister still called her Nhu.

'In here.'

'What are you doing?' Linh's round face mixed curiosity and concern.

Ned heard singing, light and cheerful, coming from the kitchen. MM was rattling pots and pans with focused purpose.

'Has she ever tried to hit you?' Ned asked it, blunt.

Linh's look of horror was answer enough.

'No! Nhu, what's happened?' Instantly Linh slipped onto the bed beside her taller, older sibling. One hand running over Ned's face, checking for marks, the other stroking her arm. A warm, sweet scent drifted from the sandalwood beads of the *mala* wrapped around Linh's wrist.

Ned made her story brief, editing out her own desire to hit back.

'We have to do something. All right? Her doctor. We'll see her, together, tell her what's going on.' Linh switched to organisational mode seamlessly. In Linh's scientific world, problems were identified then solved. Cause and effect. Simple. 'Then tomorrow maybe we can go to a few nursing homes, find out about waiting lists.'

'Tomorrow?'

'This weekend.'

A sharp rap on the wire screen door at the front of the house interrupted Linh's planning.

'Linn? Noo? I need to speak to you.'

When the Freyers first moved in five years ago, they'd been thrilled to have a minor celebrity for a neighbour. Ned guessed the novelty had worn off.

'I'll go.' Linh got up, arranging her face into diplomatically humble embarrassment.

Ned had moved in and out of View Street more times than she could number, starting with boarding school. But once she'd joined the cops she'd never imagined coming back. She could have ridden out a flatmate who'd decamped leaving behind three months' unpaid rent, but coupled with the panel beater's bill after a dickhead rear-ended her, she'd been left with no option.

It was View Street or having her wages garnisheed. TC had pointed out that being garnisheed wasn't a good look for a copper. She'd been 'home' two months but already she was climbing the walls.

Greenwich Baths at high tide was a suburban secret. The netted harbour pool lay in a curve of sand at the foot of Greenwich Point, overlooked by large old homes with leadlight windows and sandstone walls. A boat builder flanked one side, the Flying Squadron the other; across the water Balmain was deceptively close. Ned jogged down the steep stairs and saw the regular lap-swimmers working their lanes. She heeled off her shoes, the warm sandstone of the sea wall scuffing the soles of her feet before she arced and dived into the dark, deep water.

Engulfed, transported in an instant from the world of dust and heat and family into a cool, liquid dimension. Surfacing, she rolled her shoulders and settled into her laps, the rhythm of breath and the churn of water. Tonight she would go home and eat dinner with her sister and her aunt and get an early night. Tomorrow she would go to work and play her role, criminal investigator on a murder inquiry. Today would become a memory. Another one.

She slipped through the water, her body loose and light. A passing RiverCat sent its wake through the pool. It washed over her.

Goulburn washed over her.

Not *Operation Tiger Lily*, but afterwards. 'Sam and Lily' had been role-playing, but then, later, alone with Sean, when he'd drawn closer, she didn't care if it wasn't real. She'd just wanted to feel flesh warming her lengths and depths, anticipating that unrepeatable excitement of discovery; a new body. Exploring its texture, unearthing its secrets, learning its scent. She'd inhaled his, salt spiked with citrus.

Attraction and impulse. Her reckless recipe.

At the end of the lap, she plunged into a tumble turn. Eyes open behind her goggles, light flashed green and white through the chop while she imagined his body spanning hers, the tang of his sweat on her tongue. She turned her head, took a breath, salt water rushing over her lips.

If they'd stayed silent, that taste of him would be memory, instead of imagination. But they hadn't stayed silent.

'I can't keep calling you Neddie. What's your real name?'

'Nhu.'

She extends her hand. He takes it, leans across the divide and kisses her. Tries out her name, whispers it across the skin of her throat.

'What's it mean?'

'Way you're saying it? Means stupid.'

'A trap for young players. What's the right meaning?'

He cradles her head, fingers thread through her hair.

'Gentle, peaceful.'

'Chinese?'

'Vietnamese.'

'You're from Vietnam?' His head draws back, tilts to one side. She feels herself freshly assessed.

'No. Bankstown.' True enough.

'*Indochine,*' he murmurs, dropping his head back down towards her neck as if to sip this newly discovered country. '*L'Indochine – tu as toute la beauté exotique de l'Orient.*'

Her forearm shoots up, belts his arm away.

'I'm not a fuckin place.'

His eyes narrow, the hand cupping her head tightens.

In the time it takes to contract a muscle they're poised, snarling.

'Don't reckon you're that fucking gentle, either.'

'Want an exotic adventure, mate? Take a holiday.'

And that had been that. She batted a jellyfish out of her lane. Harmless, but she still flinched.

She ran back to View Street but the memories nipped at her heels. Under the fluorescent glare of the bathroom light, two weeks of stress, too little sleep and too much alcohol was cruelly evident. Sallow and drawn. Dark rings orbited the half moons of her eyes. She knew that look. Couldn't blame it all on Goulburn.

They'd called the dreams 'night terrors' when she was a child. But she'd never told anyone about the ones that happened while she was wide awake, those moments when the past sliced through the present. It hadn't happened for years. Until Goulburn. Until Sean had said that word, *Indochine*, and her parents' voices, loud and angry, exploded into the Goulburn night.

One word had caused an argument. But whose argument? Mum and Dad didn't fight.

It had become a habit – not remembering them. Now she tried to. *Indochine.* The weatherboard house in Bankstown, she and Linh sharing a room, thin walls.

From her bed, she hears them.

Low voices, Mum's laugh, like she's smothering giggles at school.

The couch breathes beneath them, floorboards stretch underfoot, the door to their bedroom sighs shut.

As she falls asleep, she follows the flow of sound that is her parents at night.

A BATTLE OF THE BEL CANTOS was raging when Ned got out of the shower. MM was slugging it out with Joan Sutherland via the CD player. She found Linh in the kitchen, preparing dinner.

'Mum and Dad fight much?'

'Fight?' Linh stopped chopping. Ned uncorked a bottle from the fridge, poured two glasses of wine, handed one to her sister.

'Yeah, fight. You know – arguing, yelling, tears, chucking things?'

'No.' Linh ignored the wine and returned to chopping onions.

'Perfect marriage, was it?' An edge that a mouthful of wine couldn't soften.

'It was a marriage. I don't know that any of them are perfect. But fight? No, I don't think so. Possibly I'm no judge.'

Ned winced. Linh had lived with Mary Margaret for the past two years, ever since the night she'd run out of the house she'd shared with Baxter, wearing nothing but her nightie and the scars he'd given her. A bad, brief marriage, beginning at nineteen and ending in stiches and blood before her twenty-first.

Another night Ned had trained herself to forget.

'Didn't think you wanted to think about them,' Linh said.

'I don't. Not really. Just – sometimes things come to me. Like a word or a . . .'

Linh put down the knife and turned her full attention on her sister. She had to look up at Ned to do it.

'What's happened, Nhu?'

'Nothing.'

44

'Nightmares?' Linh had lived through her own night terrors. Ned had held her when Linh had woken up screaming.

'No. No. Just . . . Oh, I don't know. Someone said something and it felt like deja vu. Like a memory of an argument they'd had.'

'Why do you always want to think the worst of them, Nhu? You weren't like this before.'

Before you joined the police. Unsaid. Linh turned back to the stove, away from her sister and the familiar conflict. Just one topic on the list of things they didn't talk about.

'It's not that, it's . . .' Ned took a different tack. 'You know, when I think back, I can't even remember what language we used to speak together. I remember words and I don't even know what they mean.'

Linh faced her sister, eyes wary.

'They spoke English to each other,' Linh said without emotion. 'A few words of French when they didn't want us to understand. They both spoke English to us – Mum's rule. Guess she wanted us to fit in. No accent. I don't know if Dad even knew Vietnamese.'

'And they were happy?'

'Yes.' Linh tipped the onions into a pan and the rush of sharp heat and flavour made their eyes water. 'Why the sudden interest?'

'I thought I remembered them having a fight. Well, I think I remembered it. I don't know. That's why I asked.'

'You just remembered. Something like that? All of a sudden?'

They didn't have conversations anymore, Ned realised. Maybe Linh didn't like the Job, but at times like this Ned wondered if interrogation might be a family trait.

'I told you. I heard something and it reminded me.'

'What?'

'A word.'

'A word?'

'Yeah.'

Linh could spin a silence till it was taut. She captured Ned in a stare as level and flat as any battle-weary old detective sergeant.

Ned cracked first, like always. '*Indochine.*'

'That's it?' Linh looked disappointed.

'Yeah. They were fighting, but not in English. I couldn't under-stand. Then something smashed.'

'Smash things? Mum and Dad? No, Nhu. Never.'

Linh went back to tending the stir-fry. Tofu again. Linh's embrace of Buddhism was getting hard to stomach. Ned felt a strong craving for flesh. 'Gotta see how you handle yourselves with too little sleep and too much piss,' Swiss had said. Her body was calling in the debt now. Tofu wasn't going to pay it.

'So, you had to speak French on this course, then?' Linh said.

Ned sipped her wine, tried to order her thoughts as they lurched between Goulburn, Bankstown and the kitchen.

'Nah, just came up in conversation. Spent most of the time lis-tening to Swiss Fowles talk —' Talk shit, she'd nearly said.

'Swiss?'

'As in cheese, full of holes. He's actually only ever been shot once, but that's the joke, you see. He's such an obnoxious dick that it's a miracle he's only been shot the once.'

'I see.' Linh's mouth tightened.

Ned knew that look. 'Think I might go and buy some chook to put with that stir-fry. Looks great.' She escaped before she could say anything else to confirm Linh's view of her career.

Eyes open, mind whirring, Ned listened to the house grow silent. She knew she had an early start but that only made sleep more elu-sive. Eventually she gave up and surrendered to the question nagging her. The good sitting room was a shrine to MM's career, extravagant gifts of crystal dotted about on ornate tables, walls adorned with photographs of MM with celebrities, in costume on stage, weighed down by bouquets. Ned opened the lower drawer of the old oak dresser, stiff from lack of use. Inside, stacked one on top of the other were old, plastic-coated photo albums – a cheap, suburban touch in this room of frivolous expense. She hadn't looked at them in at least a decade. From the look of the film of dust clinging to the album covers, neither had Linh. She opened one up; the pages pulled apart like bandaids.

A fat-faced, black-haired baby grinned out of polaroids. Linh, in Mum's arms. Linh on Dad's knee – Dad a giant, his hand swamping his baby daughter's waist, propping her upright. Faces beaming. A background of nappies flapping from a Hills hoist like a ragged circus tent pitched over bare patches in a dry lawn.

Ned picked up another volume, older, not plastic-coated. Photos pasted in. Lots of empty spaces, the images missing, the glue now crystalline and useless on the page. Black-and-white backgrounds of street stalls, striped awnings and cyclos filling narrow streets. Tourist snaps of a moat, filled with lilies and lotus, lined by dark, tall walls. A young, curly-haired giant sat in some of these scenes. Even in the grainy monochrome the man looked flushed and freckled, rings of sweat under his arms. He was encircled by Vietnamese women of different ages, all of them wearing *ao dai,* bodices hugging and skimming across their curves before flaring modestly over their trousers. They all had the same long hair, almond eyes, oval faces, but smiled at the camera with varying degrees of confidence. The quality of the images was poor. So poor she couldn't pick her mother from among that handful of serious young women with tiny waists and secretive, seedling smiles.

Ned opened another album – colour photos. It was as if one of those carbon-copied young women had been plucked from black and white to burst into life. Her mother stared directly at the camera, her smile broad and bold, Ned as a baby clasped to her. Ned turned the pages, her mother in a bikini, head thrown back, laughing as she dangled Linh in the small waves at the edge of the sand. Her parents, Mick and Ngoc, sitting together on the beach, her head on his shoulder. Her long, wet hair was plastered across his chest, his fingers splayed around her waist, hers curved around his neck, their legs entwined. Looking at each other, their lips almost brushing.

She closed the albums and slid them back. The oak drawer resisted and she had to stand up to shove it back into place. She trod on something – a loose photo – peeled it away from the sole of her foot.

Lunch at Manly. She and Linh with plates of fish and chips and milkshakes in frosty metal containers before them, the pines tall behind them. Two little girls grinning at the stranger pointing the family camera. Mum and Dad bookending their daughters, staring past each other like strangers who had stumbled into the same photo, sharing nothing but space between them.

But Mum and Dad didn't fight.

Hottest October long weekend in decades. She remembered the car radio as they trekked across Sydney, waited for the bridge to swing shut over The Spit, bowled down the hill past the man built out of rubber tyres to Manly Beach, she and Linh singing 'Summer Breeze'.

Linh's broken arm was a white blob in a cast. She'd had to put it in a plastic bag and could only paddle on the edge while Ned rode out to the big waves on Dad's back. She drew in a breath and smelt salt water. High on Dad's shoulders, his skin freckled and white against her brown legs.

Then there'd been the long drive home in the hot, sticky car. The fat, yellow moon rolling along the telephone wires, keeping pace with them up the highway. The bump as they turned into the driveway. The figure on the footpath.

She nursed the picture in her hand, cool in the heat of her palm. Ned tried to read her parents' faces, as if the years since that day, years denied to them, gave her some insight.

But her parents remained mute.

By nightfall, they were dead.

MORNING RADIO'S THOROUGH SUMMARY OF *Operation Milloo*'s opening day at ICAC kept Ned occupied on the drive from Greenwich to Bankstown. An hour to listen to Arthur Stanley Smith and Graeme John Henry making their journey from criminals to celebrities. Only mothers and courts ever used middle names, so these two had become Neddy and Abo to their new audience, just as ex-detective sergeant Roger Caleb Rogerson was now just Roger or, in the media's more colourful moments, 'the Dodger'. Neddy Smith reckoned he'd been given the green light from the Stick-ups to do, well, to do stick-ups, with Roger and his mob aiding and abetting – for a fee.

It was a world Ned could barely believe existed. Outrageous. Fantastical. This was the nineties; these guys were relics of the seventies, the eighties. But from the whispers, the winks and the war stories told in pubs, in clubs, over boozy, smoky sessions in offices after midnight, from the cracks and throw-away lines uttered by lips loosened by alcohol, from the way more sober heads cut them off and changed subjects, she'd sensed that the badness still existed parallel to the world she knew. With these scandals occupying the headlines, the news of what they'd discovered at Bankstown barely broke the surface.

The police station was buzzing with morning activity as she walked up. Prison vans backing into the rear yard, cops heading out to peak-hour prangs. The normality of a suburban cop shop was a good antidote to ICAC.

A blue station wagon pulled up at the entrance, the back window lined with bumper stickers for various dog associations. The blonde woman in the driver's seat leant across to hug her passenger, ran a hand over the back of his red neck, tickling the grey spiky line of his short back and sides. The passenger returned the embrace, lifted something from his lap. A puppy wriggled between his large hands as he handed it to the woman. Sergeant Ugly got out, pulled a cardigan over his blue shirt and wandered off towards Chapel Road.

'Looking for a phone he can trust,' said a voice over her shoulder. Figgy, with Toy in tow.

ICAC had become a bit of a standing joke among the younger cops, who noted how many of their senior officers had started taking a stroll to public phone boxes whenever they wanted to make personal calls. There'd been sightings as far away as the Hume Highway.

'Why? He never worked in Stick-ups, did he?' Toy said.

'Never worked, full stop,' Figgy replied.

'They should call you Fife, not Figgy,' Ned said. 'Fuck I'm Funny, Eh.'

They watched as the blue station wagon pulled out into traffic. The German shepherd puppy was on his hind legs, head out the window, over-large ears flapping as he balanced on the woman's lap.

'Good sort,' Toy mused. 'In a Mrs Robinson kind of way.'

'Can't be too smart though. She married Ugly,' Ned said as they watched the square-headed sergeant lumber around the corner and out of sight.

'Erika's no dumb blonde,' Figgy said, opening the station door. 'She makes a motza out of selling those dogs.'

Ned followed him in. 'Animal lover, eh? Ah well, that explains the attraction.'

Ned reached her desk to find a pile of fresh running sheets. She read each one hungrily. It was mid-morning when TC came in, crooked a finger at her and headed downstairs. She caught up with him in the station foyer; he dropped the car keys in her hand.

'They're out.'

With a jolt of excitement, Ned crushed the keys in the palm of her hand. A real murder inquiry now, with real bodies, above ground and about to give up their secrets. It was hard not to run to the car. TC followed her down the stairs at a more sedate pace, stopping to have a yarn with the station sergeant on his way out.

Ned was waiting in the car, engine running, when TC finally flopped into the passenger seat. At the intersection, she indicated a right-hand turn towards the building site. TC leant over, flicked the indicator to left.

'No time for sightseeing, little buddy,' he said. 'We've got police work to do.'

The longing to go to the site, to see what Gumby and his team had unearthed, was overwhelming. She hid her disappointment, became a professional. 'Where to, boss?'

'Time to catch up with a Bushranger, I reckon.' TC laughed. 'Couldn't get away with a name like that these days.'

Ned had found Brian Hall's current workplace easily enough after she'd hinted to SydneyPlex's personnel clerk that they needed to see him about a personal matter. Her sombre tone and reticence implied a death message and she let him assume it. As a result, he'd been helpful, discreet, no doubt hanging up with a shiver of relief – *Not me, not mine.* Hall was overseeing a construction in the heart of Sydney. She and TC picked up kebabs and drinks for lunch in the car and headed into town. Even with a park-anywhere pass, Ned had to make ever-widening sweeps before she found a space. They walked down Liverpool Street, past the old sandstone courthouse towards the bus-clogged artery of George Street. It seemed every other corner had a hoarding around it. Sydney's building boom defied both gravity and a recession that was as deep as the planned skyscrapers were high. But for every building going up, there was an equally big hole in the ground that was going nowhere.

Ned read out the copy on the billboard wrapped around the site entrance on George Street. '*City Living: Lifestyle choices for the new millennium.* Getting in early, aren't they?'

'Depends which millennium.' TC shaded his eyes and tilted his head back to look up at the tower that was finally rising from one of Sydney's most notorious holes in the ground. 'Hmm. We could ask him to come down.'

'What happened to the element of surprise? Come on, think of the view. At these prices, it'll be the only chance we'll ever get. Anyway, you might get lucky – his office could be on the ground floor.'

Five minutes later they were both in hard hats travelling up the outside of the building in a construction lift with wire for walls. TC stood with his back to the view, studying the open floors as they flickered past. Ned watched Sydney unfurl at her feet, midday, blazing with light and heat from glass and steel in every direction. They rose higher, and there it was. The harbour. That big blue bowl of cool promise at the city's heart. To the north, rounded headlands and finger peninsulas, most clotted with buildings, butted out into waterways busy with boat life. Blues Point Tower stood out like a single digit raised in bad taste. Beyond the tower, North Sydney's skyline mirrored the CBD in shape if not in size. Though Blues Point had been sacrificed on the altar of property development, some of the harbour headlands had been spared. Bradleys Head, Balls Head and Berry Island were still thick with bushland, dense green and shady even in the heat. A whisper of what had once been.

The lift bumped to a stop. Ned turned back to work.

TC led with a handshake. 'Detective Inspector Charlton, Bankstown Detectives. This is Detective Kelly. Brian Hall?' The man waiting found his hand being pumped as he nodded.

'Yes. That's right. What's this about?' Despite TC's genial greeting, Hall wore a face that feared the worst – like every other face that got an unexpected visit from the police.

'Perhaps your office?'

'Yes, of course.'

They followed him through the skeleton of the building, rough concrete walls, exposed steel ribs and a mechanical drone that muted the sound of the city far below. His office was a flimsy pre-fab.

'We'd like to talk to you about your company, Bushrangers,' TC said.

'Bushrangers? Jeez. Haven't heard that name in yonks.' Hall looked baffled.

TC glanced at Ned and inclined his head towards Hall.

'It's about a building in Bankstown that Bushrangers worked on in the seventies, Mr Hall,' Ned began. 'But I should introduce myself properly first – I'm Mick Kelly's daughter, Nhu.'

Hall's eyes magnified behind his glasses.

'One of Mick's little girls?' Embarrassment followed hard on his look of surprise. Ned had learnt to hate that look. 'Jeez. Little Noo.'

'Call me Ned. It kind of stuck.'

'Ned? A second generation Bushranger, eh? Look at you. A detective? I wouldn't have recognised you, you were just a little girl last time I —'

'No, no, no. I wouldn't expect you to – all a long time ago.' She smiled and tried to remember something, anything about him. 'I remember the racehorses. They used to walk past your place in the afternoons.'

'Still do. By God, you've got a good memory. Mick came around when I was doing the extension, only brought you girls a couple of times though.'

'Family good?'

'Yeah, yeah. All grown up, left home.' He shook his head, tried a laugh. It was a sad gesture, the smile forced. 'Small world, eh?'

'Yeah. Did a bit of a double-take myself when I saw the old name on the papers. You're still in the construction game, then?'

'Well, you know, after Mick . . . died . . .' The pause was brief, but Ned had learnt to listen for it. 'Well, the business just wasn't . . . the business world changed. No room for the little guy. Couldn't beat 'em so I had to join 'em.' He gestured around the office where everything was branded with the interlocked initials *SP*. He lowered his voice. 'Don't know why we're bothering. Another building no one can afford to rent. It's just a job – slapping up crap. Looks swish on the outside but not the workmanship like in our day. We built 'em to last.'

An uneasy silence followed. Hall's eyes flicked from Ned to TC, then back again. 'They did last, didn't they?' he said. 'That's not why you're here, is it? I'd hate to think something Bushrangers built fell down.'

'No, this building lasted. It's being demolished. We're here about what was underneath it.'

Hall looked confused.

'Block of units, corner of Stacey Street and Rickard Road,' Ned prompted.

'Stacey Street . . . Can't say I remember it. What do you mean, "underneath" it?'

'A couple of dead bodies in the footings,' TC chimed back in. 'Any ideas how they could've got there?'

Hall blinked, swallowed and sat down. 'Shit.'

Ned and TC settled into chairs and watched him. He looked at them in turn. He'd gone pale and clammy but she didn't automatically read guilt into that; her arrival and the memories it dredged up, on top of the news of the bodies, would've been enough.

'Bodies . . .' Hall broke the silence. 'That's awful. I'm not sure I can help you. I'm not even sure I remember the project. Who are – were – they?'

'We don't know yet,' Ned answered.

TC unrolled the building plans across the desk. Hall stared at them, swallowing.

'Yeah. That's one of ours.'

'We know that, Mr Hall,' TC said.

'Yeah, of course you do. Brian, call me Brian.'

'We're after as much information about the site as we can get. Who worked on it, who might know about the concrete pour schedules, any problems during the construction.' Ned opened her notebook as she spoke.

'Who worked on it? It's so long ago. When the business folded I kept what I had to, legally – you know, seven years. But I pitched it all out years ago.'

'Well, let's start by seeing if we can't narrow down a time for when those footings would've been poured. We're getting paperwork together from the council, maybe you can estimate when the concrete went in?' Ned encouraged.

'I can try. Where was it again?'

Ned described the flats, drew a rough map of the intersection in her notebook. She turned it around to show him. Hall's eyes flickered.

'Oh, yeah. I *do* remember it. We were flat out. Had a few sites on the hop. Mick had that one. Pig of a location.' He smiled up at Ned, apologetic. 'I remember him getting the shits about trucks banking up waiting for a right-hand turn out of Stacey Street.'

'Yeah, the traffic's only got worse,' she said, proving to him he could talk about it, that she wasn't going to dissolve into tears.

'I had another one up on Liverpool Road. It was a real bitch too, but . . .' He stopped. The blood returned to his face in angry patches, staining his cheeks, his throat, his forehead, like a series of vivid birthmarks.

'I remember now. Aw, shit. It was while we were on that site, um, in the middle of it all, that was when Mick . . . Mick and Ngoc . . . died.'

In the silence, metal struck metal, machinery ground against gravity and a shadow passed over the window. Through the small porthole, Ned saw the prehensile arm of a crane sweep out into the empty blue of the sky.

'I didn't get down to Stacey Street for a week or two after it,' he continued. 'The foreman – aw, what was his name . . . Stan – Stan Lucas, he kept it all ticking over. When I finally got down there to go through the office, clean out Mick's desk, the footings were in and the brickies had already started. There ya go, sometime in early October '76.' The hand he raised to his mouth shook. 'Jeez, what a way to remember.'

Ned detached. She listened to Hall like a professional, one whose only interest was establishing the time of burial for two bodies. As if the event he relied on to pinpoint that moment held no personal significance to her. She studied him. He looked older than he had ten minutes ago.

'That certainly gives us something to work with, Brian.' She wrote as she spoke. 'The foreman, Stan Lucas – any ideas where he is these days?'

'He used to live in Panania. Heard he had an accident. Not sure, might be dead.'

'What kind of accident?'

'Building, industrial, fell off a roof or something. I heard it third-hand, not sure of the details.'

Ned finished writing and lifted her eyes to find TC staring at her. She gazed back, unblinking, then turned to Hall. 'That's great, Brian. You've been very helpful.'

TC got to his feet. 'Thanks, Brian. When we get the paperwork together you can come up to Bankstown, make a statement. Meanwhile, have a think about any names you can remember from those days, contractors you might've used, that sort of thing.'

They left him sitting at his desk studying the liver spots on the backs of his hands and rode the lift down in silence. TC's face wore the same look as Hall's. She recognised it. It was the face people adopted when they said 'I'm sorry' about her parents, as if they were somehow responsible, guilty, if not for their deaths then for making her remember. She felt guilty, too, but for a different reason. For not feeling anything.

Goulburn had been an aberration. She was a cop, not a victim. She'd proved that interviewing Hall.

Clouds were piling up beyond the city, messy, bruised green with hail. An early-afternoon southerly buster brewing down over the Illawarra. A few hours off yet, but the tang of the sea was already in the wind. The lift plunged back into the humid soup of the city, the floors rattling past in ever-increasing stages of completeness. They clattered to a stop and waited for the operator to open the cage gate. The pager on her waistband vibrated, and she twisted its face up, shading the screen from the glare with her hand.

I'll translate over dinner.

She took a deep breath and felt herself draw together in anticipation, torn between being flattered and scornful at such a cop stereotype: romance by pager, no overheard conversations, no names, no pack drill.

'Good news?'

TC was standing by the gate waiting for her before she realised she was still staring at her pager and suppressing a grin.

'Maybe,' she replied and tossed the car keys upwards; they spiralled, glittering through shafts of sunlight before she caught them.

'TWO DAYS IN A ROW.'

'Huh?' Ned stopped at the foot of the stairs at the sound of Sergeant Ugly's voice. Traffic had been heavy on the trip back from the city, she had a list of jobs to do and was running out of hours to do them in.

'These came for you.' The sergeant nodded at a bunch of flamboyant tiger lilies taking up half the charge counter like an explosion of orange fireworks. 'No card.'

'Nice of you to check.' The scent was rich and sweet and strong enough to overwhelm the usual charge-room stink of sweat mixed with the faint trace of vomit and a hint of industrial-strength disinfectant.

'Going to take them home this time? If you're not, the wife could do with some sweetening.'

Ned raised a finger behind her as she walked out.

No secrets in the Job.

No card, either.

Never put anything in writing. No paper trail. Nothing cops liked more than getting briefs on one another. A macho name for gossip. She took the stairs slowly, inhaling the sweet perfume. A memento of *Operation Tiger Lily*.

Wouldn't have occurred to anyone to call it *Operation Irish Rose*; no one ever seemed to get past the fifty percent of her genetic inheritance that shaped her eyes and coloured her skin. She didn't feel any more part-Vietnamese than she did part-Irish. In fact, she didn't feel part-anything, just herself. Born and bred in Sydney, she reckoned she belonged in it anywhere she bloody well wanted.

Undercover cops with their cover stories, their mind games and their covert ways. Suddenly she felt angry at covert. If he wanted to see her, he could ring her up and ask her out. Overt. Just like a real human being would, not like a copper. She breathed in the lilies again. Unlike yesterday's roses, these had show and scent.

Stan Lucas wasn't an uncommon name and this time Ned had no childhood memories to draw on. An industrial accident would mean a record somewhere: unions, government departments, compo, maybe a death certificate. So she called and called, waited and got shuffled, repeated the same spiel over and over, left messages, took notes of names and contacts. In between outward calls she got an incoming from Linh.

'I've been on to her doctor.'

'Whose doctor?' Ned tried hard to pull her mind in from multiple threads and focus on her sister.

'Whose doctor?' Linh's voice changed from urgent to exasperated. 'Mary Margaret's doctor. Your aunt. Honestly, Nhu.'

'Right, right, sorry. Been talking to doctors all day.'

'You have? About Mary Margaret?'

'Well, no. Work.'

'I see.' Linh could go icy faster than a freezer. 'So no chance of you getting away to come with me?'

TC appeared beside her desk. She put her hand over the mouthpiece, aware of Linh's voice but not listening to it.

'Want to get away from the phones and go see Stan Lucas?' He slipped an address in front of her.

'How did you get this?'

'You did. Workers' Comp just returned your call.'

She uncovered the mouthpiece. 'Sorry, Linh, I'll be working till I don't know when. I'll talk to you about it when I get home. Got to go, bye.' She hung up.

'Hey, if you've got something to do I can get Toy to go. It's just an interview.'

'No, no, it's nothing.' She was on her feet, hooking car keys off the rack before TC could change his mind. 'Meet you back at the pub.'

He gave the lilies a sniff. 'Nice.'

'Thought I'd give myself a treat.'

His look said he didn't believe her.

Thunder rumbled somewhere but the southerly, if it was coming, was hours away. Ned walked across the street to the car. Bankstown was pungent in the afternoon sun: onions and roasting lamb flavoured the air around the kebab shop, the frenetic driving beat of a Bollywood soundtrack blasted from the Indian spice and video shop next door. On the pavement, the Vietnamese greengrocer was putting up shade cloth and stacking green vegetables with names she couldn't say beneath signs she couldn't read. It was a family business; the kids turned up after school in their uniforms, helping out in between homework, slipping from flat-vowelled Strine into Vietnamese when they spoke to their parents.

During her first week at Bankstown, Figgy had paraded her in front of Mr Dinh, looking for a discount. When dropping the handcuffs hadn't worked he'd tried dropping the ethnic instead. For the next few months Mr and Mrs Dinh had turned each visit into an impromptu and unsought language lesson. Mr Dinh would proffer some slender greens, narrow-leafed, roots attached, saying '*Rau muống, rau muống*', while she'd smile and mumble sounds that she couldn't repeat ten minutes later. These days they just smiled at her and she smiled back, both sides going through the motions of politeness.

Massive Attack's opening track, blowing Bristol cool through the speakers, only emphasised how baking hot the car was. She pumped up the air-conditioner and the volume. Eventually the air cooled and the music soothed, sheltering her from the full assault of noise and heat and truck exhaust. The drive to Greenacre would've been a few minutes without traffic. As it was she had time to contemplate the mix of service stations and shopfronts along Liverpool Road and sing along with 'Unfinished Sympathy' four times in a row.

Dry heat arrowed up from the wide cement driveway of the Boronia Rehabilitation and Respite Care Facility. Ned's shins itched. Inside reception her nostrils shrank. The antiseptic aroma pumping out of the cooling system couldn't mask the odour of baby powder, urine and boiled vegies. Before she had a chance to ask for Lucas, a voice filled the corridor.

'You the detective? Don't look old enough to supervise school crossings.'

A man rolled up the passageway. He was upright and broad through the chest. The bright, crocheted rug covering his lower body dropped abruptly at the lip of the seat where his legs should have been.

'Mr Lucas, I'm Detective Kelly —'

'Makes no difference to me who you are, love. Suppose you tell me what this is all about, then?'

'It's about a building site you worked on —'

'Well, it's about bloody time. Crappy scaffolding,' he said, slapping his wheelchair. 'That bastard Ferguson told me, "Go up or sling your hook." Locked out the unions before he got those contractors to put up the scaf – cowboys. Criminal bloody cowboys. So, you coppers have taken your time. He must've killed someone this time, eh?'

'Um, no, Mr Lucas, I'm afraid I'm here to talk about another building site you worked on. Before you had your accident.'

'Not an accident, girlie, a crime. And that's the only site I'm interested in talking about.' He spun his wheels backwards.

'Mr Lucas, this is important. It's a building you worked on in 1976. You were foreman, for Bushrangers – corner of Stacey Street and Rickard Road.' Ned spoke quickly, trying to arrest his departure with words. It worked better than she'd expected. He stopped and stared hard at her.

'I worked on a few jobs for Bushrangers. What's special about this one?'

'Mr Lucas, perhaps we could talk about this somewhere.'

He remained immobile, staring at her, then jerked his head. 'Follow me.'

He rolled into an activities room, deserted but for half-finished crocheted squares and piles of jigsaw pieces. Ned gave him the barest minimum of information: address of the job, time period, scanty details of what they'd found. Nothing more.

'Block of units, the Stacey Street job. I remember. Built a lot back then, and built 'em better then than now, if you ask me.'

'You have a clear memory of this particular job. Why is that?'

'I lost me legs, not me brains, love.' Stan Lucas's eyes were bright; they looked her up and down. 'You married?'

Ned wondered if despite his protests he might be losing the plot, just a little. Before she could respond, he went on.

'Kelly? That your married name?'

'No, no it's not.'

'Local girl, then? Born round here?'

'Mr Lucas, about the site, can you remember —'

'I remember Mick Kelly. You look a bit like him.' He crossed his arms, waiting her out.

'You have a keen eye, Mr Lucas. My father was one of the owners of Bushrangers. You remember him, then?'

'Didn't I just say so?' He narrowed his eyes. 'Just something about you. Same chin and mouth, that's it.'

She felt her father all over her face. Her lips pressed together, eyes wanted to. She hung on to her pen to stop her hand from rising up to push away the warm wet past. She'd been ready for Brian Hall. But Lucas, he'd taken her by surprise. Queasiness mingled with the institutional food smells; much longer and she'd have to excuse herself and find a toilet.

'He was a hard man, your dad, but he never took short cuts with safety, I'll give him that. Often wondered what happened to his kids.'

'Well, now you know.' She forced a smile and moved her pen over her notebook. 'Can you tell me what you can remember about this job in particular?'

'Already did. The boss – your dad. He and your mum died in the middle of it. Don't forget a thing like that. Fucking terrible.'

'Do you remember anything else unusual about the project, Mr Lucas?'

'Nah. Normal bloody job. Hurry up to stand still – usual thing with building. Can't get the brickies in till the foundation's down – can't have them hanging about getting paid to watch concrete set. Waste of time having concrete ready and no brickies to work it. Always a balancing act; always blokes, contractors, coming and going on a site, trying to work out when their job's going to start.'

'What was the security like on the site, at night?'

'What you'd expect. Pay a security mob to send a bloke round every hour, leave a card as evidence. He comes round once, leaves all his cards in one hit. Our problem at night was same as always: stuff being nicked, not stuff being dumped.'

'Can you remember who did the concrete pour? A big company or sub-contractors?'

'Contractor – Pete Stillman. Bushrangers used the same mob for all their jobs. Don't bother writing it down, love. Pete's dead. Arse fell out of the building industry, small operator like him got out, sold his mixer, bought a semi. Tipped it one night outside Coffs. Had to scrape him off the road, so I was told.'

Ned started to fold up her notebook. Another running sheet

to put in, another name to tick off. Nothing to follow up. Good conscience caused her to ask one more question.

'I know it's a long time ago, but we need to track down anyone who worked there; could you put together a list? Any chance the union might —'

'You've got Buckley's of getting anything that old, but I'll have a think.'

'Give me a call if you do.' She handed him her card.

He took her hand, squeezed it.

'Tough bloke, your dad, but he didn't deserve . . . Well, I served too, you see. Vietnam. Didn't know him, over there, he never talked about it, neither did I. Suited us both. Didn't even know his wife was, you know, Vietnamese, till later.'

Lucas and her dad, two young men who'd won the worst kind of lottery, a wooden ball with their birth date on it that sent them off to war.

'Thanks, Mr Lucas.' Ned smiled automatically, longing to escape. She was about to walk out when the thought struck her. 'You can't remember anyone taking an interest in the site before the concrete pour, but how about after it? Brian Hall says you ran the site afterwards for, what was it, a week or two, before he got down there to clear out the office?'

'That what he said, was it? He didn't clear out the office for a week or two, eh?'

'That's what he says, Mr Lucas.'

'Yeah? I think he's forgotten how I found out.'

'Found out?'

'Yeah, about your mum and dad. He told me, morning after it happened.'

'What, by phone?'

'Nah, I was early. Had to get the brickies into gear. Tuesday after the long weekend, I was going to give your dad a bit of stick for being late, then Hallsy turned up and told me . . .'

'You had to supervise the brickies? That means the concrete pour must've —'

'That's right. Pour must've gone in a few days earlier at least, maybe a week. Would've depended on the weather.'

He didn't realise the significance of his recollection. He'd just focused their murder inquiry to a week in late September 1976, during which two bodies had been hidden under that concrete pour. One question answered. Another took its place.

'And Brian Hall was definitely down at the site that morning?' Probably nothing but TC noticed discrepancies, expected his detectives to notice them too.

'Yeah, he was on his way out of the office, had a box full of papers, stuck it in the car boot. Told me about Mick. Left me in charge till he could get back. I took a look at Mick's desk – he'd cleaned it out.' Stan's eyes glinted like two bits of blue metal in a hard road.

The skin at the back of her neck knitted tighter under the hard, blue gaze. 'OK, thanks, Mr Lucas. You've been a big help.'

'Terrible fucking thing, terrible. Bloody unfair, you know, for your dad, after what we'd been through, over there.' Lucas looked both sad and angry. 'Funny how things turn out, though.' He winked up at Ned. 'You turned out OK – for a copper.'

The pub had a real name, but no one ever used it. It was known as Court Five for the good reason that Bankstown Courthouse only had four and the pub was right next door to the last one. The unofficial debrief was in full swing by the time Ned arrived. To the untrained ear it sounded like a brawl was about to erupt at any moment. The back bar had a pool table, booths against one wall and, today, a row of tall bar tables pulled into a chain, around which the full complement of Bankstown detectives were drinking, shouting and laughing along with a handful of cops in part uniform. There were a few unfamiliar faces as well: Police Rescue, she guessed, and some of the Firies, the ones who'd done the hot, hard yards opening up the concrete. Civilian regulars had ceded the room to the cops and faded into the front bar. Ned ordered a gin and tonic, adding a middy of light when she spotted TC making his way over to her.

'Lucas can narrow down the date for the concrete pour, sometime in the week or so before the October long weekend of 1976, and he's given us a few questions for Brian Hall to answer.'

'Hall's not going to be answering any questions,' TC said, sipping his beer.

'What?'

'Had a stroke not long after we left. He's in Vinnies on life support.'

'Jeez.' Ned sat down on a bar stool, not sure if it was shock or disappointment she felt. She took a good mouthful of the icy, astringent liquid. 'They're not saying we caused it . . .'

She saw Lucas's sharp blue stare again, his certainty that Brian Hall had taken something from the site before the police had come. She gave a brief summary to TC. 'What do you reckon? Could be Hall has a guilty conscience, about something?'

'Don't know.' TC was a centre of calm. 'Had – has – a dicky ticker. Could be a combination of things, or bad luck.'

'Hall could've just forgotten the date and time, though? Can't expect him to remember every little detail after all this time.' A professional, she tested the evidence, anticipated defences.

'Yeah, that's probably it,' TC said in the same way he told juvenile offenders' parents their kids would probably get a bond, when he knew they'd probably go inside.

She found herself wondering about Hall's look of despair when she'd announced herself. *Little Noo.* What had she heard in Hall's voice? Affection? Regret? Hall and her father had been business partners, but had they also been friends? They sat silently at the bar, away from the long, crowded table. TC finished his beer, turned down a refill.

'Heading off – early start,' he said, dropping the keys to one of the office cars into her hand. 'See you at the morgue at nine, OK?'

'OK.' She tried to be nonchalant, but the pride that TC still chose her as a workmate was mixing with stomach flutters at the thought of the morgue. The gin stiffened her spine and if she hadn't needed to drive she'd have downed another one, just to be sure.

HALFWAY DOWN GREENWICH ROAD Ned saw Linh stamping along the footpath, bags of files under her arms. She pulled over, leant across to open the passenger-side door, started apologising before Linh got in.

'Sorry, we had a —'

'Yeah, right. You always have a something.' Linh picked up the lilies and tossed them into the back seat.

'A murder, Linh. It'll be all over the news tonight, probably already on the radio.' Ned tuned to a news station, caught another IRA bombing attempt in London. Bankstown would be well down this bulletin.

'You'd hardly be making it up, Nhu.' Linh turned the radio off.

'So what was the . . .' She almost said *verdict* – not the right word.

'Paperwork, assessments, waiting lists, appointments, waiting lists, places in nursing homes, waiting lists.' Linh reeled off the obstacles.

'I detect a pattern.' The Boronia nursing home was still fresh in Ned's mind, the aroma of industrial-strength care stagnant in her nostrils. She risked a glance at her sister.

Linh looked fed up. Her short, black hair was plastered against the back of her neck, fine lines arched downwards around her mouth. The late-afternoon sun caught the thin scar at her eye. Baxter's handiwork. Ned's palms tingled and she gripped the steering wheel. Not the time to share nursing-home horror stories with Linh.

'We knew it wouldn't happen in a hurry,' Ned said. 'I mean, we'd have to get her scheduled to get her into a place overnight and that wouldn't be . . .'

Linh's glare was like a slap and Ned turned back to the road. Scheduling someone under the Mental Health Act was the kind of professional advice you gave strangers looking to lock up troublesome relatives, not your sister.

'No. It won't happen quickly but you're not the only one with a schedule, Nhu.'

'You got the nod, then?'

'Unofficially, yes. We've got three months at Arecibo. Start in February.'

As far as Ned understood it, this part of Linh's doctorate entailed three months locked inside a giant radio telescope somewhere unpronounceable, looking for something incomprehensible. But Ned had picked up enough to know that Arecibo was the big one and that her sister and her colleagues would have to go to Puerto Rico to use it.

'Great,' Ned lied. She realised she was doing a shitty job at sounding thrilled. 'Really, fantastic.'

They turned into their street.

'Where'll you be in February, Nhu? Not that it really matters – even when you're here, you're not. Whose car's that?'

A silver Celica, low slung, swift lines, was parked in the driveway. Ned didn't recognise it.

From the front door, they heard Mary Margaret giggling in the kitchen.

Ned swore quietly. Not another incident like the one with the plumber; she didn't know if she could stomach finding another young tradesman pinned up against the fridge, fending off a kimono-clad, cocktail-wielding MM. The plumber had been more understanding than they'd had a right to expect, mumbling something about having a gran with 'Oldtimer's' as he'd made his escape.

Linh had seen it as more evidence but Ned had suspected that MM just had a taste for tradies and only pleaded Alzheimer's if she got a knock-back.

Halfway down the hall Ned caught a male voice and stopped dead.

'Of course I remember. You sold out the Opera House with Pavarotti.' His voice dropped, confidential. 'So, tell me, your Mimi – that kiss was all just an act? I seem to remember rumours?'

'Ah, naughty, naughty. One can't reveal the secrets of the stage,' Mary Margaret trilled – her bel canto belly laugh, she called it. 'I'm working on my memoir, you know. There'll be a few secrets told there.'

'Do you need a proofreader? Maybe a sneak preview? I wouldn't tell a soul.'

'Well, let me just say —'

'Mary Margaret, we're home.' Linh called ahead, her entrance interrupting any further indiscretion. 'Who's this?'

Ned hung back in the hall, curious how Detective Sergeant Sean Murphy would introduce himself.

Mary Margaret glided over to Linh. 'My niece, Linh, and . . . where is she? New? This is . . .' MM faltered, the recently acquired name gone.

'Sean Murphy. A friend of your sister's.'

Ned came to the doorway just as they were shaking hands. Murphy's eyes travelled over Linh's shoulder and he smiled. He could have been a CEO instead of a surfie. The scruffy jeans and T-shirt of Goulburn had been replaced with a charcoal suit, its weave so fine it rippled as he moved; a chalk-white shirt and deep turquoise tie completed the transformation.

'We were just going to have a cup of tea,' he said. 'Weren't we, Mary Margaret?'

'Yes, that's right. I was just getting the kettle.'

He turned to Ned. 'Quick word first, perhaps?'

He was past her, collecting her in his slipstream and heading up the hallway in one movement.

'No, no, no,' MM protested. 'The mozzies will eat you alive.'

Sean closed the front door. Ned immediately felt the airy brush of the insects around her ankles.

'What do you think you're doing here?'

'Picking you up for dinner.'

'I didn't say yes.'

'Didn't say no.'

'Didn't think I had to. How'd you know I'm not going out somewhere?'

'I don't. Took a punt – had to see you again, to apologise.'

'For what? Just doing your job in Goulburn, weren't you? Set up the trainee – shoot them, steal the drugs and money. Valuable lesson for all.'

'Let me make it up to you.'

'Didn't tell you what the lesson I learnt was – never trust a UC. Look, forget it. Nothing to apologise for. You did your job, I fucked up mine, then we got drunk. Same old same old.' She stamped her feet to shake off the mozzies.

'No.' His face softened. 'Not same old same old.'

'I'm getting eaten alive here.'

'Then say yes. Have dinner, we can talk, then you can tell me to piss off if you want to.'

Pride made her obstinate and curious to see how hard he'd work. She rubbed one ankle against the back of her legs and then the other. At this rate pride was going to cost her a bath in calamine lotion.

'Ringing up to ask me out like a normal person wasn't possible because . . . ?'

'I've rung your office five times today – you're never in it.' His grin flashed, eyes disappeared again. 'Could've left a message with Figgy, I suppose.'

Checkmate. She scratched an ankle with her toes.

'Come on, it'll cost you a couple of hours,' he continued. 'Worst that can happen is you have a fabulous meal. I'll have a cup of tea with your aunt and your sister, you get ready, and we can start again. What do you reckon?'

She pushed the door open. 'If you can survive tea with MM, I can survive dinner with you.'

'Frock up, it'll be worth it.' He grinned and loped up the hall towards the sound of china.

He didn't move like a cop. Most of the detectives she knew might as well have worn uniforms, so clearly did their arms-akimbo, loose-legged roll identify them. Sean Murphy moved like he had all the time in the world and the ability to do with it whatever he pleased.

Ned was wriggling into a silk dress when Linh walked in without knocking.

'He's married, isn't he.' It wasn't a question.

Ned hadn't asked, hadn't cared. He was a copper, thirties – early, late, hard to tell. Be a miracle if he hadn't been married at least once. She zipped up and turned her back on Linh.

'Dunno, Linh. Just a work colleague.'

'Wear your black lace bra and knickers for TC, too, do you?'

'It's dinner.' Ned sprayed a cloud of Diorissimo over herself; it settled like a mist on her bare shoulders. 'Anyway, we're all above the age of consent.'

She hunted out her stilettos, wincing as they enclosed her toes. Foot binding. After having been outrun by a dealer in Bankstown Square, Ned now limited high heels to court attendance and nights out that didn't involve dancing.

Linh stood by the wardrobe watching Ned assemble her but-you-don't-*look*-like-a-cop camouflage. Linh didn't do 'dates', or not that Ned knew of, anyway. Her sister's life seemed to consist of tutoring at uni, working on her doctorate, and marking endless student assignments. She had added Buddhist classes to the mix, but even that was something Ned had only glimpsed – not something Linh had shared.

'Linh, just . . .'

Ned held her sister's gaze. It wasn't like her to take this much interest in one of Ned's jaunts. Perhaps Linh picked up the same vibe around Murph: enigmatic, carnal, risky. If so, like in most things, Linh's reaction was the polar opposite of Ned's.

Linh shook her head. 'Hooked on the new, that's your problem.'

On impulse, Ned leant down, kissed her sister on the cheek. 'Don't wait up.'

Operation Tiger Lily chaperoned them onto the Warringah Expressway.

'You did well,' he began.

'At what? You shot me.'

'I had to.'

'Always do what Swiss tells you?'

'Neddie, if I was a dealer I'd have sold you everything I had and then stolen what I needed to sell you more. You were good. I think you have a flair.'

'A flair?'

'For deception.'

'Like you?'

'I've been at it a long time.'

'You have a flair —'

'Ned, you have no idea —'

'For not answering questions.'

'See. You are good.'

'If I was that good – if Lily was that convincing – why'd you shoot her – me?'

'And I'm sorry I did. Shouldn't be. It was just a job.'

'Not a very professional attitude, Sergeant Murphy.'

'You're unprofessionalising me.'

'I find that hard to believe.'

'OK then. I'm not sorry. I like asking attractive women out at gunpoint.'

The peak-hour traffic was bumper to bumper on the bridge approach. Just past the Berry Street on-ramp he took his eyes off the road.

'I haven't told you how lovely you look.'

'I was just going to say the same thing about you,' she said, reaching over and running the lapel of the suit between her fingers. 'I didn't know Billabong did suits.'

He caught her fingers, bringing them to his lips, watching her. 'I'm sorry if I hurt your feelings. You handled yourself well in the op. Didn't rise to the bait.'

'Yeah, well, it wasn't very original.'

'Get the oriental shit a bit, eh?'

'A bit. I was born in Bankstown, never been to Vietnam, don't speak Vietnamese, Chinese – or French. Whereas, you?'

'Marianne's French.'

'Ah.'

He didn't need to spell it out. She'd guessed married and now married had a name. But was it once married – or still married? His hand went back to the wheel, no telltale band of untanned skin, no ring. He uncurled his fingers, waggled them.

'Never wear one.'

'Fashion choice?'

'They break your fingers when you hit people.'

Not *if*, she noted.

He went on, raconteur now. 'My last year of high school was big. Marianne was the foreign exchange student from Paris. She was a bit of a hit in Narrabeen. By the HSC she was pregnant, by Christmas we were married, by New Year I was in the police cadets, by Easter I was a dad.'

Ned digested this in silence as the traffic funnelled into one lane. She had expected evasion, not honesty.

'Been together a while then.'

'Long enough to have four boys and an understanding – we both need space.'

'Space.' Ned heard echoes of Linh in herself.

'Yeah.'

'An understanding.'

'Yeah.'

'Very French.'

'It works.'

They reached the merge point, entered the flow, rolled over the apron of the harbour bridge. Dusk. The red glow of sunset to the west and a row of grey cloud-mountains to the east. Ned tilted her head back and stared up through the sunroof at the web of iron arching above them. The spotlights that turned those heavy steel spans into insubstantial traceries of shadow and light were coming on. She looked at Sean's profile, the fine white sunburst of lines fanning from the corner of his eye.

'So, I'm guessing you got a lot of jokes about failing your "French orals".'

He accelerated into a space, laugh lines creasing his cheeks.

'Oh, yeah. One "French oral" cancels one *Indochine*. Square now?'

Smiling, she sat back and stared back up. Already seagulls were swarming about the girders and struts of the bridge, flocking in to feed on the insects drawn in by the hot, bright lights.

A table by the window, Opera House framed like a postcard, attentive service – a waiter who seemed well-acquainted with monsieur and beamed indulgently at mademoiselle. Ned wasn't sure if it was forward planning or routine that made the evening run so smoothly. By the end of the entrée she'd decided she didn't care.

Over the years she'd so refined her lines that she didn't have to think twice. 'My parents died when I was young, I hardly remember them' was a smooth transition on to other subjects. 'In a car' usually satisfied even the most curious. There was always the off-chance, with older coppers, that they might put the name and age together but Sean only registered the look demanded by such a sad, but distant, event.

Main courses delivered, wine topped up, the waiter melted away. A new figure approached the table. Ned looked up at a man, early thirties, Chinese, wearing a dark suit. He wasn't a waiter.

'Sam.' His accent was broad Strine. It matched his manner, that blokey blend of business and mateship.

Sean responded with an open hand and a gesture towards Ned.

'Sunny. I didn't know you were back. I'd like you to meet Lily. Lily – Sunny.'

Ned's face fixed as they shook hands. They were a long way from Goulburn but an identical sensation ran over her skin. She gave a meek smile, needn't have bothered. Sunny glanced her way, seeming to calculate her height, weight, clothes and face in an instant and find her wanting. He turned and spoke to Sean.

'Got back a couple of days ago. We need to catch up.'

'Perfect,' Sean said, nodding.

'I'll call you.'

And he was gone.

'Sam? Lily?' Ned's hands were alive with adrenalin; she held them tightly in her lap.

'Hazard of the job. People don't know you're off duty. Far as they know, it isn't duty, it's just business.'

'And he is?'

Surprise sharpened Sean's face. 'If I told you, I'd have to kill you – again.' Only the grin removed the sting.

Coffee and golden glasses of Frangelico came and went. The glasses stood empty, the last ferries were pulling out of Circular Quay.

'Walk?' Sean offered.

Down under the bridge the water was black and loud, slapping at the sandstone sea walls, showering the path in droplets. They walked into the cool, sticky mist. The southerly had skirted the city, leaving a humid night behind. Out to sea, an electrical storm was putting on a show between the clouds. Sean wrapped his arms around her, wrists clasped across her belly. Ned drew him on as easily as a favourite coat. Her cheek against his throat, his voice quiet, conspiratorial, vibrating through her skin like thoughts. She rode the rise and fall of his chest. Inhaled salt and citrus.

'So, should you be running away about now?' He hugged her to him. 'I am a married man, you know.'

'I don't want to marry you.'

Ned pressed her palm against artificially chilled glass. Far below, the harbour was an absence between lights strung around and above it.

'Confident, weren't you?'

The room had been pre-booked in the name of Sam Murray.

'Not confident, Nhu. Hopeful.'

Her name. Pitch perfect. His reflection hung before her, pale hair glowing in the dark glass, eyes seeking hers in the refraction.

'Least I could do was learn how to say your name.'

She turned to him. Her hands slid beneath his suit coat, finding the slopes and narrows of his back and waist. His hands cupped her head, tilted it back, brown eyes and blue too close to focus. Their scents and bodies mingled beyond any need for names.

The vibration of Sean's pager woke her. That instant of disorientation. Strange room, strange bed, drenched in a stranger's smell; then surfacing, recognising it. Sean. No longer a stranger. He rolled over and picked up the shimmying little object. The digital clock showed a quarter to three. He was swinging his legs out of bed when the hotel phone rang, loud, intrusive.

'Yeah. Just got it.' He sounded alert in contrast to the fog that lay over her. The voice coming through the earpiece was muffled but familiar. She wrote off the paranoia and sank back onto her stomach, absorbed by her body's memory of his. With one finger she reached out and traced the tan line that glowed white across his hips, followed the long diagonal of his back up to his shoulder. The muscles bunched as he held the phone to his ear. She rocked her hips deeper into the bed.

'Well, he won't be able to, will he? You're on the bloody line.'

She hadn't been paranoid. This time she heard him. The slow drawl of Swiss Fowles. Not clear enough to make out what was said, but clear enough to be sure. Her hand fell back to the sheets. Discovered in all the wrong ways.

'Yeah, sure – soon as he's gone.' He hung up. 'Sorry.' Swung back, an easy movement, brushing her hair from the nape of her neck. 'Business – flexible hours.'

Then he was up, pulling suit trousers over his bare backside, zipping up carefully, reaching for his shirt.

'Swiss likely to pop in for a debrief? Maybe I should go?' She made no movement to back up the offer.

The hotel phone pierced and he peeled away.

'Yeah, same place?' He laughed the way men do when they think women won't understand it. She did and rolled onto her side to study his face. He was tucking his shirt in, phone hooked under his chin. 'Very funny . . . Yeah, the usual. See you shortly.' He dropped the phone into the cradle, picked up his wallet, his watch.

'How'd Swiss know to ring you here, Murph?'

'He knew we were here because the target knew.' He strapped on his watch, preoccupied.

'The target?' She remembered the young Asian guy who'd arrived along with their main course.

'Sunny's got eyes all over town but we've got his phone off. They heard him ringing around the traps, tracking me down, then calling

Connect to —' He was suddenly all process. The detective sergeant lecturing the troops in a car park on a Goulburn night. He turned back to the bed, gauging her. 'You don't know who Sunny is, do you?'

'No. Should I?' She felt defensive.

Sunny, Swiss, the UCs – she wondered how long the gossip would take to spread. Yesterday she'd been cranky about UCs playing covert games. Now she wished Sean had been more discreet.

'Sunny Liu. You've heard of his father?' Sean sat back on the side of the bed, ran a finger along her jaw, gently tilting her head back towards him. 'Albert Liu?'

She'd heard that name, all of Sydney had. Albert Liu, reputed head of the Golden Dragon – a triad. It made the young man in the restaurant the son of a man who was rich, powerful, dangerous. She nodded and turned away, feeling like a ridiculous suburban plod.

'Liu . . . yeah, well, you better get going. I'll get a cab.'

'Don't you dare.' He kissed her, open-mouthed, the taste of shared skin.

Then his pager beeped again and he was up, moving towards the door. The man whose body she'd just explored, whose tang still lingered on her tongue, fell away a little more with each step.

The door closed and the room immediately felt hollow. A perky chime as the lift arrived, then silence. Lightning strobed in the east, anvil-shaped clouds illuminated in a flash then erased by darkness. Time to think, to consider, to question what had just happened. Time to get up, get dressed and get out. Instead, she rode waves of remembered pleasure back into sleep.

He slipped into bed at dawn, with the early fog still clinging to his body. He spooled around her, damp and cool against her bed-warm skin.

'Good fit.'

'Makes me sound like a shoe,' she murmured, waking slowly.

'Don't deny it. One night's definitely not enough.' His hands moved over her, reminding her.

'Shame you weren't here for most of it.'

He nuzzled her neck. 'Not by choice.'

'Swiss be up with our breakfast trays soon?'

'Nhu, don't do this.' He rolled over her, straddled her, looked down into her face.

'Do what?'

He slipped his arms beneath her shoulders and rocked her to his chest. His naked body stretched around hers, she was suddenly shy. In this room wrapped in fog, with no sense of time or light, she felt cocooned.

'Not just pillow talk here, Nhu. I want to see you again. Not sure how, not sure when, just sure I want to. You up for that?' His breath in her ear, hands between her thighs, reacquainting themselves with her.

A mutual attraction: that was as far ahead as she'd thought. Now she wasn't sure what he was asking. Her body answered while her head wrestled with the proposition. In the intense moments that followed she abandoned herself and the question entirely.

NED COULD'VE LIVED WITHOUT POST-MORTEMS. She crept up on the morgue from the rear, through the narrow streets of Glebe, avoiding Parramatta Road, where the morning traffic ebbed and flowed past the front doors of the low-key building marked *Coroner's Court*. Drivers who knew what lay in the basement averted their eyes, drumming their fingers on the steering wheel if they caught the red traffic light outside. Like the loading bay in the rear lane or the understated grey panel vans driven by the grey-suited government contractors – once identified, never forgotten. She parked, wound the seat back and the window down, then closed her eyes. She'd beaten TC and earnt a short nap. Her belt began to vibrate. The message on her pager was unsigned.

Surf's up – wish you were here.

She squinted north, in the direction of the harbour and beaches beyond. Close, but hidden by geography and buildings it could've been a world away. Her hangover was tiptoeing up and settling over her. She needed a Coke – full strength, no diet shit. The black aspro. A horn blasted beside her. Figgy and TC grinned at her.

'You look a bit green, little buddy.'

'Just the anticipation of *eau de morgue*.'

Figgy let TC out then chucked a squealing U-turn. They watched him skid through a right-hand turn before they walked through the loading dock and into the cloying chemical odour of the morgue. TC dropped a friendly hand on her shoulder.

'Mummified, so they shouldn't stink. Just imagine you're

watching an episode of that grumpy Pommy copper.'

From what Ned had seen, Inspector Morse always looked queasy around dead bodies, gazing at the ceiling.

'You're here.' Doc Deakin barged out through a set of plastic swing doors. 'Good. Let's get started.' The doors slapped closed but not before a frigid draught stood the hairs of Ned's arms on end, a physical reminder of what lay behind them: rows of trolleys and walls of shining steel, the refrigerated units.

The forensic pathologist shepherded them onwards, no time for anticipation to turn into nausea. He led them past another doorway that Ned recognised – the entrance to a long, numbing room with metal tables strung like ribs from a central walkway. Gowned figures were already hard at work at most of them.

Four years ago on her first walk along that icy aisle – standard initiation for all probationary constables – she'd fastened her eyes to the floor, concentrating on her sensible black shoes creeping across the tiles. Even so, in her peripheral vision she'd caught sight of two tiny bare feet, dwarfed by their obscene surroundings. And nothing blocked out the sound of an electric saw on bone. Now she trod down the memories of all who'd been brought here, to be trolleyed, stored and pawed; focused instead on TC's brown leather shoes pacing along in front of her.

They pressed on through sets of plastic doors that opened reluctantly then clung on grimly as they passed. Deeper into the labyrinth, past small, glassed rooms that she was tempted to call operating theatres, except none of these patients ever got better. They finally stopped. Mummified bodies were rare enough to draw a crowd. Outside the room, peering through the glass, a small audience of medical students had formed. Inside, five surgically sealed figures were studying a series of photographs on the wall by the door. Deakin tossed gloves, boots, gowns, masks and caps to Ned and TC, then stood to one side, ushering them in like a real estate agent showing a property.

Ned stopped by the door to look at the photographs. They showed something that looked like a sediment-coated, petrified log on a white plastic sheet. She recognised Gumby in one frame, leaning down and pointing at an exposed knee that had erupted from a crack in the hard shell encasing it. Other shots showed him indicating a glimpse of an arm, part of a shoulder, a flash of clothing. So this was how the bodies had looked when they had emerged from their hidden graves, fused together, swaddled in concrete.

'We'll do them one at a time. The other one's next door, haven't made much progress. But here, we lifted prints and got a hit. Our job just got easier, but I think yours just got a little harder. Detectives, meet Dawn Jarrett.' Doc Deakin's voice summoned Ned from her study of the photographs, forced her to turn and confront the reality lying on the steel table at the centre of the room.

Stripped of concrete, the body was naked, dark and desiccated. It seemed clad in leather, not flesh.

TC swore quietly. Ned looked at him in surprise; early identification on such an old murder was a good thing, surely.

'This is going to be big, Neddie,' TC said. 'Big and ugly. Deak, you sure about this? A hundred percent?'

Deakin nodded, arms folded, apparently enjoying the fallout from his news.

'You knew her, then?' Ned asked TC.

'Everyone knew Dawnie, or knew about her. She disappeared back in the seventies. Never got the sort of publicity Juanita Nielsen did when she disappeared. Dawnie wasn't an heiress, she was just a . . .' TC shook his head.

'We're showing our age, TC,' Deakin sighed.

'Yeah, but there'll be enough people who remember Dawn to cause a lot of grief.'

'Why? Who was she?' Ned said.

'A big name. Aboriginal land rights, Black Power, that sort of thing.' TC pulled out his yellow notebook. 'Disappeared a year after

Juanita. No one was really sure if she'd gone missing or just buggered off.'

Ned turned back to the table. The corpse now had a name and a history.

Dawn.

A name full of beginnings had ended up on a slab. On the table, in the space where the lower legs had been snapped off by the digger, shards of bone lay alongside a pair of thick-soled platform shoes, their once-vibrant colours sucked out. The visible joints looked monstrous, the whole body misshapen, the legs twisted at strange angles, the foreshortened shins skewed from the knees, thighs corkscrewed from the hips.

Deakin looked from Ned to the body, nodding. 'You noticed, eh? She was busted up pretty bad before she got buried.'

The skull seemed too big to have ever been held erect by the shrivelled neck. Then Ned realised why. It was wider than it was deep, the face smeared and twisted. Her stomach heaved. She looked away.

Better to think of what the woman had been, not what she was now.

'We're definitely talking murder here, Deak?' TC asked as he wrote.

Ned stared at her boss. He sounded like he was clutching at straws. Two bodies buried in concrete – what else could it be?

'Well, that's for your lot to say, but I'm guessing she didn't bury herself.' Ned reckoned she could hear Deakin grinning under his mask. 'All I can tell you is that it was an unnatural death – a particularly nasty one. She's been run over, and not just once. Looks like someone tried to obliterate her face, used a car to do it. Left her fingers on, though. That was a mistake.'

'Cause of death, take your pick?'

'X-ray showed fractured pelvis, multiple fractures of both legs, compound fracture of the right arm, multiple fractures of the left, ribs crushed, spine broken in three places, skull fractured and displaced. Be easier to tell you what wasn't broken.' He handed TC a file. 'Someone turned her into road kill.'

Deakin handed Ned an evidence bag. The polaroid accompanying it showed a twist of fabric: three colours braided into a bracelet. Black, red, yellow – skin, blood, sun. The colours of the Aboriginal flag.

'How old was she?' Ned said.

'According to the Missing Persons report, twenty-eight.'

'Forensics?' TC asked.

'Rich. Only just started, but sooner you get this lot out to Lidcombe the better. There'll be more.'

'Ned can do a run now.'

'Her clothes've been bagged and tagged. There's soil, broken glass, paint flakes, rubber, metal. Lots to work on. We may get a car, make, model.'

'Probably gone to wrecker's heaven years ago.' Ned saw Deakin's eyebrows lower. The pathologist didn't take kindly to having his painstakingly collected clues dismissed too lightly. 'Could build a circumstantial case against someone, though.'

'Well, that's more than we have on number two. It's been a slow process, stripping off all detritus without flaying them. Don't want to lose any evidence on that dermal layer. Might not get anything, but we have a few advantages – whoever buried them back then didn't know what we can do in the lab now.'

In the next room a group of pathologists were at work with tweezers and brushes on the second skin of dirt and rock and concrete still coating the corpse. The face and upper body had been released. Pinched nose, great concave slopes beneath wide cheekbones. The wizened breasts marked it as a woman. Like something from the Valley of the Kings, not someone who'd lived and died in Bankstown sixteen years ago. The absence of life in a body was an elusive quality; somehow they seemed more dead when the skin was marbled and cool, when they looked as if they'd been interrupted in the middle of living. This one looked like she'd been dead forever. The nose was nothing but a narrow ridge of dark cartilage, with enlarged, ragged holes to mark the nostrils. A few strands of long, dark hair were still attached to the skull, stuck there by some process of desiccation Ned didn't want to hear explained.

'Ran her through X-ray. Only two fresh injuries here. Skull fracture – someone hit her hard enough to stop her in her tracks, but not to kill her.' Deakin picked up a ruler, pointed at the withered neck. 'This is what killed her. Snapped at C3. Paralysed. She wouldn't have been able to breathe.'

'Maybe they'd run out of cars,' Ned murmured, thinking about Dawn's distorted face. 'Is she Aboriginal too? Any record Dawn Jarrett went missing with a friend, a relation?'

'You lot'll have more information about that, but this woman was Mongoloid – hard to narrow it down further yet.' At the look on Ned's face, he interrupted his speculation. 'Mongoloid as in Caucasoid, Negroid, Australoid. Talking about broad racial types, Detective, as identified by skeletal remains. She's had a rough time, from the look of these old injuries.'

'Old injuries?' Ned and TC stepped closer.

'X-rays show an old bullet wound to the right shoulder, healed, but it carved out a good bit of bone on its way through.' Deakin's hands moved over the body with the familiarity of a family doctor. 'There's a bullet still in her back. Whoever treated her at the time made a wise choice and left it there.'

'Jeez, a one-woman Rambo,' TC said.

'And that's not the really interesting stuff. Both collarbones have been broken and healed. Both shoulders show signs of significant trauma. She has a mass of healed fractures in both feet and all her fingers have been broken and healed.' He pointed to a series of pockmarks forming circular patterns in the dark, dead hide around the woman's breasts. 'See these? Old scars from cigarette burns. Her back's covered with them too. Well healed over by the time she died, but . . .'

'Shit.' Ned's mouth went dry.

'Yes, tortured.' He handed TC another file. 'No closer to an ID, I'm afraid. We'll re-hydrate the fingers and try for prints. Still got a lot of work to do, but she had this on her. Might be useful once it's cleaned up.' He handed Ned another bag and a polaroid of a concrete-encrusted lump. It took a good, long look to distinguish a thin chain, stiff with concrete, and a tarnished bauble of some kind.

'We've taken samples of the dirt around them both, lifted whatever was under their fingernails. You could be in for a bit of an adventure trying to get a name for her.'

The woman lay on the table like a strip of dried meat. Ned shivered. To have suffered what she'd suffered and survived. What a will to live. All that, just to end up chucked in a hole.

The Division of Analytical Laboratories was a high-tech outpost on the corner of a six-lane thoroughfare linking Bankstown to Lidcombe, but it looked more like a bush clinic. Though surrounded by trees, the DAL building itself was an ugly concrete example of what had passed for modern in the seventies.

Ned carted her box of exhibits into the lift, then along the beige and grey linoleum corridors to the reception area. A couple of uniformed constables from the country were ahead of her, collecting exhibits for what seemed to be every police station between Newcastle and Dorrigo. She sat down and wished she had something to read besides the latest newsletter from the Association of Forensic Anthropologists.

'Ned?'

A familiar face appeared at the counter. Ben Torres. They'd met over seven hundred cannabis plants in a chook shed at Windsor on a stinking hot February day. Ned had been in charge of exhibits and Ben had been sent out from DAL to certify the crop on site. Unlike the analytical scientists Ned had previously known, Ben wasn't pale, dull or pissed off. They'd gone out for almost a year, even got to the point of having toothbrushes and favourite clothes at one another's places before Ben had discovered triathlons and Ned had discovered that when a man who trained eight hours a day on weekends said he was going to bed, he meant he was going to sleep.

'Ned. I wasn't sure it was you. Different hair?' he said, flipping up the counter and leaving his workmate to continue the great north-coast exhibit run.

'Yeah,' Ned replied. 'Thought I'd let it grow a bit.'

In uniform she'd worn her hair short and, at one point, white-blonde – not that any hairstyle survived a policewoman's hat. Now it bounced down past her shoulders, red and gold highlights trumpeting freedom from uniform regulations. Ben looked like he was still in training, whipcord muscles braiding his forearms, almost gaunt in the face.

They traded the usual catch-ups – his triathlon schedule and finish times in Foster and Hawaii, her first place in the detectives course. It segued smoothly into the current job. Ben read Deakin's notes with obvious interest and set about entering them into the ledgers. Nothing happened quickly here. Court cases could be won and lost over the chain of evidence of an exhibit. Who handed what to who and when. It all had to be noted and Ned had a bundle of exhibits. Once the last evidence bag had completed its journey across the counter, Ben turned back with a long cotton bud and a test tube.

'One more thing,' he said. 'Open wide.'

'Why?' she asked, at which he popped in the stick and ran it around the cheeks of her mouth.

'DNA. Deak wants us to try and work up some profiles on the victims and on samples he's taken from them – you know, under nails, clothing, hairs.'

'What's that got to do with me?'

'DNA's opening up a whole range of possibilities, Ned. The Poms and the Yanks have had a few convictions using it. We're just starting but mitochondrial DNA for example can show us —'

'Jeez, you're like kids with a new toy.'

'Can't be too careful, cross-contamination. You've handled the exhibits so I'd better add a hair sample just to be sure.' He reached across the counter and plucked one out.

'Ow!'

'Got to get the root, Ned.'

BY THE TIME NED GOT BACK to Bankstown, organised chaos had broken out. TC had called in the cavalry before he'd left the morgue. Dawn Jarrett's murder was too big to stay a suburban brief, so the Homicide Squad had moved in. The police radio was thick with chat and crackle: a car accident blocking Marion Street, fire brigade in attendance, a suspicious person in the vicinity of Bankstown Public School and a hold-up alarm at the Caltex in Condell Park. Local life went on.

The door to TC's fishbowl was closed and so were the venetian blinds. Strangers in power suits were reading files at desks that didn't belong to them, and a new face wearing the feminine version – pencil skirt, padded shoulders and four-inch heels – was collating the running sheets at Ned's desk. Ned looked at the pristine stilettos. Obviously not much call for chasing baddies at Homicide. Her hangover was dissipating; she needed a dose of fried food and sugar before the 2 p.m. briefing to finish it off.

Murders pulled crowds: those with roles to play, those who'd have to answer hard questions if it all went wrong and those who were just curious. The cast for this one included the Patrol Commander, the Area Superintendent, a party from Police Media, some high-ups and heavies from Headquarters and the boss of Homicide, with as many of his mob as they'd been able to fit into four cars at short notice. Uniforms crusty with pips and braid, sharp, dark suits, eyes and attitude filled the meal room – the only place in the rabbit warren of Bankstown that could fit them all in for a briefing. With fifteen years in Homicide, TC had probably run more murder investigations than the rest of the room put together. He looked unfazed by both the audience and the victim's identity.

A Missing Persons poster of Dawn Jarrett was blu-tacked to the whiteboard. It showed a woman with a wide, smiling face, freckles spread liberally over coffee-coloured skin, and eyes bright with optimism. Posters of the missing often featured discordantly merry faces, unaware of their fates, too happy to go missing. Ned couldn't stop staring at Dawn's smile, trying to reconcile it with the mashed-up features lying in the dark at Glebe.

TC was succinct. The handover to Homicide would follow his briefing.

'Dental records and prints say we've found Dawn Jarrett. For those still at preschool in the seventies, the significance of this might be lost on you. Dawn went missing sometime between late August and October 1976. She was up to her armpits in the Land Rights movement, the Tent Embassy in Canberra, setting up the Redfern legal service, Green Bans, Springboks, Moratorium. If there was a ruckus, you could count on Dawnie being somewhere near the centre of it. Fair to say she pissed off a lot of people.

'Never got a confirmed last sighting. Late September had her leaving a pub in Chinatown, pissed as a fart according to one, sober as a judge according to another. Witnesses couldn't even agree on a date. Then a sighting of her early October hitching north, another hitching west – we never pinned down exactly when, or even if, she'd gone missing. Officially reported by the family at the end of October. Inquiries at the time heard she'd buggered off to New Zealand with a Maori boyfriend, or gone to America to join the Black Panthers. Today we can safely say those theories were bullshit, but until now we never had any evidence she was dead.

'Detective Inspector Zervos and the Homicide Squad South will have carriage of the investigation; don't need to remind anyone here that when this does get out, the shit is truly going to hit the fan. You'll report to Detective Inspector Zervos and you won't be talking to anyone else. Understood?'

The muttering that had been building during the last part of TC's speech grew louder. Hard to say who was copping the bigger serve from the locals – Dawn or the squad called in to solve her murder. TC ignored it.

'Now just in case anyone's forgotten, we have two bodies to concern ourselves with.' He scrawled a circle with a question mark in it next to Dawn's poster. 'Detective Kelly will brief you on the autopsy results so far for both victims.'

Ned went to the whiteboard and stood with Dawn Jarrett grinning over one shoulder and TC's rudimentary symbol hovering over the other. Modelling her delivery on TC's, she kept it concise, not pausing at the reactions to the grisly list of injuries. As she finished, Zervos, dark-haired, dark-suited, took her place at the whiteboard. He smelt of stale tobacco and began his monologue in the husky voice of the heavy smoker. Ned was about to sit down when she noticed Sergeant Urganchich leaning against the sink at the rear of the meal room, one arm draped over a cardboard box. He was tapping the box, the label beneath his fingers clearly visible, even from the front of the room.

Homicide:
Kelly: Michael & Ngoc
4 October 1976
Bankstown
CRN 76/54

Her mouth, her throat and her mind dried up. Zervos's voice was white noise. Her focus narrowed to the cardboard box, its yellowing label and the meaty fingers drumming against it. She started moving towards Ugly but TC beat her there, jerked his thumb at the door, then followed the uniformed sergeant, who picked up the box and walked out.

TC's voice was raised by the time she got to his office.

'I told Lennox, my office. How did you get a hold of —'

'Lennox had an AVO walk in, I told him I'd look after this.'

'And what the fuck did you think you were playing at, swanning in there —'

'No one in your office. Didn't want to leave it unattended.' Ugly stared at Ned. 'Not secure, leaving a murder brief around. Even an old one. Someone might tamper with it.'

'Just fuck off.' TC's voice was almost unrecognisable. Ugly made a mock salute and left.

'No point asking him to keep it quiet. Only give him more pleasure when he ignores it,' TC said. 'Look, I didn't want you to find out like this, Neddie, but I wouldn't be doing my job if I didn't pull this brief, have a look. Two murders within days of each other, a common connection through Bushrangers, unsolved . . .'

'I've never thought to ask to see the brief.' She felt she was observing the office, TC and herself from a distance.

'Sit down, Neddie.' TC shut the office door. He sat on the front of his desk, leant forward, hand hovering to pat her on the knee before shifting to her shoulder. Seeing him awkward, indecisive, just added to the sense of unreality.

'Can you believe it? Been in the Job four years and I've never thought to ask for a look at the brief.' Her stupidity seemed wondrous to her. All that brooding over what her parents had done to get themselves killed but she'd never had the guts to find out. A real detective would've asked. Would have discovered that this thing that had shaped her life was nothing but a cardboard box and some papers.

'Look, it's a shock but I didn't want you getting your hopes up, little buddy.' TC's voice matched the rhythm of his hand on her shoulder, half a pat, half a clap, caught somewhere between soothing and heartening. She blinked up at him, at this weird version of TC with concern corrugating his forehead. 'We'll do our best,' he continued. 'If there's any link, between this and what happened to . . . It's a long shot, but if we can finally find the bastard we will.'

Her skin contracted. 'Linked?' Adrenalin charged through her body as the meaning of TC's words finally sank in.

A child could accept the simplicity of tragedy. A 'bad man' had killed Mum and Dad. But an adult – a detective – knew better. There was always a reason, a motive. But what was it? Why had her parents been murdered? Who had hated them enough to kill them? What had they done, Mick and Ngoc, to give someone a reason for that much hate?

The Job had soured her memories – rendered the murdered as guilty as the murderer.

She stood up and placed a hand on top of the box. 'I want to —'

'Let me go through it first.' TC got to his feet. 'There's stuff here that's —'

'Told Homicide?'

'Not yet. Zervos'll ask for it eventually, when he gets his head around the brief and the background. Planned to get a head start, have a geek at it myself and then . . .' He shrugged.

'Better let you get on with it, then.' Her hand came away from the box, dusty.

TC opened a lower drawer of his filing cabinet, pulled out a tatty jumper, an old pair of shoes, a mouldy holster and a bottle of scotch, and put the box in. He closed the drawer, locked it and dropped the keys in his pocket. She was like an addict watching a chemist closing a drug cabinet.

'You need to take some time off?'

'Why? I'll be fine. It was all a long time ago, TC. I'm used to not knowing. Just came as a bit of a surprise, that's all. Ugly, you know, he presses my buttons.'

Her mind made connections as she spoke. Any links, even slight, and she was off this case – if she wasn't already. ICAC had everyone jumpy.

From the sound of Zervos's voice down the corridor things were wrapping up. 'He won't be impressed – I walked out on his briefing.'

'Forget it, it's covered. I've got a job for you.' TC tore off a page with an address and phone number.

'Aboriginal Legal Service?'

'Dawn's little boy, Marcus Martin Jarrett. He's all grown up now and a solicitor with the ALS.' TC grinned. 'He's not your standard ALS easybeat, either. He fights dirty, he flings shit, and even though he doesn't win many he knows how to inflict maximum damage on the way down. IA, Ombudsman, the usual round of crap. Jarrett never heard an allegation against police that he didn't believe. I told Zervos you did sensitive better than anyone here. Go, break the news, and arrange for a DNA sample and a statement.'

'Sensitive new age cop, that's me.'

'Look, Neddie, if you don't feel . . .'

She replied by getting to her feet.

THE RED, BLACK AND YELLOW flag in the window of the old shop-front marked it out as the current home of the Aboriginal Legal Service. An old corner store, perhaps a butcher's shop with those big glass panes and prized location at the junction of Cleveland and Abercrombie. Would've been walking distance for the working-class occupants of the tightly packed terraces of Chippendale and Redfern. Losing track of the street numbers as she drove down Abercrombie, Ned had already crossed the intersection before she caught the flag's colours in her rear-view mirror. She took the first left she could and found herself in Dangar Place, a quiet, narrow lane with a noisy, bloody history. Back in the early eighties, Detective Sergeant Rogerson had shot and killed an ambitious drug dealer, Warren Lanfranchi, here. A coroner's court jury hadn't recommended charges but it hadn't vindicated him, either. Lanfranchi's career certainly ended on the spot but the old school agreed that the Dodger's had begun its death dive that day as well.

Ned parked the car and walked out of the shadows lengthening into the laneway. Might've been only a decade ago but it felt like another age, as remote as when street hawkers called out 'Rabbitoh!' meaning they had a bunny for the cooking pot, and people had wandered down to corner stores instead of driving up to the supermarket at Surry Hills.

Marcus Martin Jarrett's office left no doubt as to whose son he was. Framed news stories with his mother's face – that same, smiling image from the Missing Persons poster – hung on the walls. The man sitting behind the desk was an echo of her: broad-featured, freckles that only stood out up close. But no smile, even though the face seemed designed to wear one. His receding hairline was masked by a buzz-cut that accentuated the roundness of his head.

'Detective Kelly.' He neither rose from his seat nor extended a hand. 'Here on a personal matter? I don't have personal matters with the police, Detective Kelly, just professional ones.'

'Mr Jarrett, this is a matter that concerns you personally . . .'

'If you've been sent here to make a special pleading on behalf of a colleague, you're wasting your time. Tell 'em they'll have to cop it sweet.' His smile wasn't friendly.

Cop it Sweet, the documentary about police in Redfern, had aired earlier in the year. The careless racism it captured had triggered a furore but, to its subjects, was more a confirmation than revelation. Most of the cops she'd heard discussing it were shocked, not by its content but by the stupidity of saying it on camera.

Ned took a breath. 'Mr Jarrett. I'm not here in connection with any of your current cases. I'm from Bankstown Detectives and we have information about your mother.'

So much for sensitive.

Marcus Jarrett stopped. His mouth opened slightly to speak but nothing came. His eyes rested briefly on Ned, then went to the framed picture on his desk. A small boy with a white rabbit on his football guernsey and skinny legs poking out of a pair of shorts, reluctant in the embrace of a woman with a huge afro. Her long, knitted coat hung down in the mud despite the platform soles of her shoes. Though the hair was different, Ned recognised Dawn's take-on-the-world-and-win smile.

'What information?' The scourge of arresting police from Redfern to Revesby now spoke so softly Ned had to lean forward to hear him.

'Mr Jarrett, we believe we have located your mother's remains.

I'm sorry it's not good news, but I doubt after all these years you were expecting any.'

His eyes remained on the photograph. They filled with the swift tears of a boy but the tears were blinked away before they could spill. Whatever he was remembering of that day, he had momentarily forgotten she was there, just like Ned herself had forgotten TC's presence when confronted with that box with her parents' names on it. Years of knowing, expecting, accepting – they all blew away in the face of facts.

'I'm sorry.' The hated, hypocrite words sprang out.

When he looked up, his face was filled with open grief, unashamed love and confusion, as if unsure who she was – why she was there. He shook his head, took a tissue from a box on the table and blew his nose. Ned looked away, embarrassed. There'd be a price to pay for that glimpse of the boy the man had been.

'Never thought she'd be found. How sure are you?'

'Very. We'd like to do DNA as well, with your cooperation.'

He nodded silently, his face settling back into its professional lines and frown.

'How was she – what happened?'

'The coroner's report isn't complete yet, but it looks like she was run over. There were severe injuries.'

He was quiet for a while. The sound of Cleveland Street intruded into the space. A semitrailer coming down the rise caught the red light, the air brakes applied in a series of controlled explosions.

'Death was probably instantaneous,' Ned improvised to break the silence.

'An accident, after all this time? A car accident?' Then, the look of a lawyer sharpened his eyes, as if by testing the evidence he could rebuild himself. 'So, where's she been all these years?'

'She was buried, probably pretty soon after she was hit —'

'Someone buried her? Not an accident, then. Where?' And Marcus Jarrett hard man of the ALS was back.

'Bankstown.' Ned paused, thought, then spoke. 'The bodies were found in the footings of a demolished building, covered in concrete.'

'Bodies?' Grief and shock hadn't clouded his attention to detail; he started taking notes on a yellow legal pad.

'We've found two bodies, Mr Jarrett. Two women, buried together.'

'Who is it, the other one?'

'Well, we were wondering if you might have an idea. Can you remember if your mother had a friend, an Asian woman?'

He shook his head, a slow deliberate action, thought behind it.

'None I remember. Name'd help.'

'Not yet.'

His eyes fell back to the picture. Weariness crept into his voice. 'So somewhere, there's someone still missing her, then.'

'Maybe, maybe not.' Ned opened the file she'd brought with her.

'What do you mean?'

'Could be she was floating below the radar. Maybe some of your mother's friends might help us identify her.'

He ignored the suggestion, reading her file upside down. She spun it towards him. The top statement was only two paragraphs long.

'Your original statement. I thought it might jog your memory.'

'My memory don't need no jogging, Detective.'

His language slid seamlessly from lawyer to street, both sounding equally natural. Ned suspected it was a tool, one he used to calm or confront as required. Right now she felt a confrontation building.

'Oh, I remember all right. Had to go up the cop shop at Redfern 'bout five times before those bastards would even take a report. Spotty little shit who took this statement knew nothing about Mum, nothing about why we were there. Didn't want to know neither, just got it done as quick as he could and pissed us off out of there.'

'So, there's more you could add to this statement? We can do another one now.' Ned tapped the computer at her side.

'Make a full and detailed statement sixteen years too late? You telling me you've got a suspect?' He sneered at her.

'No, Mr Jarrett. The inquiry's still at —'

'Yeah, right. Tell you what – you charge someone, I'll give you a statement. Otherwise, I'll make mine in public, to the Coroner, at Mum's inquest. You can see yourself out, Detective Kelly.'

'Fine. You can expect a couple of Homicide detectives to turn up shortly asking what you're hiding – about yourself and your mother.' She picked up the three kilos of useless notebook computer she'd lugged up the stairs. Jarrett had opened a file on his desk, ignoring her. 'Get over yourself, Mr Jarrett. From what I've read about your mum she deserves better.'

'Yeah? And what have you read about her, Detective?'

'She made waves, trod on toes, got things done and deserved to be around to see the Mabo case get up.'

'My mum travelled all over this bloody country, working for people just like Eddie Mabo. People you've never heard of – and never will.'

'I reckon it's her turn, then. Don't you?'

'What?'

Ned sat down, dumped the portable computer on her lap, leant her yellow spiral notepad on it and opened it. 'About time someone worked as hard for her as she did for everyone else?'

His face changed, anger fading into sadness. Ned felt a momentary guilt that faded when Jarrett began to speak.

'We . . . we didn't really know she was missing for a while. Not till she missed my birthday. The cops . . .' He spat the last syllable. 'They just said she's scarpered, she's left you, shacked up with someone else.'

'What did you think had happened?'

'We knew she was dead. Too many people hated her. Landowners, politicians and the cops. Special Branch, ASIO – they were always sniffing about when she was alive but when she was missing, when she needed help, they couldn't give a shit. We knew. We've always known.'

'You still in contact with her friends, colleagues, from back then?'

'Reckon they'll talk to you? Been fighting your mob since before we were born.'

'My mob?' Ned laughed. She might battle for inclusion, acceptance within the Job, but to outsiders, it was instantaneous. Uniform or no uniform she was part of that amorphous group – she was a cop. 'I'd have thought they'd care that she's finally been found. Want to help us find out what happened.'

'Oh, they'll care. They just won't care to help you.'

'There's other ways to track people down, you know. My boss won't settle for lack of recall. He'll have to rattle those old Special Branch files, I guess, start knocking on doors.'

'Same shit, different century.' He shrugged. 'I'll talk to them. I'll decide if there's anything significant, and what to do with it.'

'You don't get to decide what is and isn't significant, Mr Jarrett. You can't go around interviewing witnesses —'

'You still don't get it. They're not witnesses, they're my family, my extended family, and the minute they hear what's happened they'll come to me, but they won't speak to you. They don't like the police, they don't trust the police, they won't talk to the police. Not even police who look like you, Detective Kelly.'

'Ned,' she said.

'What?'

'Ned,' she repeated. 'Detective Kelly – you know, no need for that.'

'That can't be your real name,' he said, thrown, as she'd hoped.

'It isn't but that's what I'm called.' Satisfied to have broken the tension even a little. 'What is it you're afraid of finding out about your mum, Mr Jarrett?'

He looked at her, surprise widening his eyes.

'Afraid?' His voice grew strident. 'What would I be afraid of? I want to know who the bastard was who reckoned they could just run down a Wallamba woman, chuck her in a hole like she was rubbish and think they'd get away with it.'

'Then we want the same thing. So, how are we going to get it?' she said.

His eyes narrowed. 'You're not bad at your job, are you, Detective Kelly?'

'They send me for the stuff they think needs a bit of hand-holding. I get to break a lot of bad news.'

'I don't need you to hold my hand.' Jarrett stood up, picked up his backpack. 'Office hours are over. You've broken your bad news; go back to Bankstown, Detective Kelly.'

Ned saw herself turning up back at Banky, explaining to some heavy from Homicide how the interview had gone sour because she couldn't resist a smart-arsed crack. The laptop seemed to weigh more on the way out.

Jarrett led the way through the empty outer office, posters for Survival Day concerts on the walls between filing cabinets. They walked down the stairs and through the waiting room, where mismatched chairs lined the walls around a table stacked with back copies of the *Koori Mail* and leaflets with titles such as 'What to expect at your first court appearance' and 'Bail – your rights and responsibilities'. A toy box sat in one corner, plastic shapes in garish colours poking out of the top. He coded an alarm, locked the door and they were back into the noise of the intersection.

TC had steered this job her way, a job that would get her noticed by Zervos if she did it right. She addressed the solicitor's broad back.

'This isn't just about your mum, Mr Jarrett. Her friends are the best shot we have of identifying the other woman. They might remember her; she had some pretty distinctive scars, cigarette burns —'

He turned on her, big and swift. 'How could you see cigarette burns? The bodies must've . . . It's been years, they're just bones, surely?'

'They were covered in concrete. Mummified.'

'Jeez.' He slumped hard against a light pole, hand covering his face. Then gruffly: 'I want to see her.'

'Well, that's your decision, of course, but —'

'But?' His voice rose. Passers-by stared. He was upright now, shoulders bracing back, finger pointing at her chest. 'You telling me I can't?'

'Of course not, it's just . . .' Ned hesitated, no kindly way to say Dawn looked like Pharaoh's mum, not his. 'She's not really recognisable.'

'I want to see her.' His face settling into stubborn lines. 'Tomorrow.'

COURT FIVE HELD MOST OF Bankstown's Ds, but no Homicide Squad – something Ned was quietly thankful for. Usual suspects at the usual tables; Toy was picking the brains of Bankstown's two detective sergeants, who looked happy to tell war stories all night if the audience was appreciative. The television on the wall and the jukebox were competing to make the most useless contribution to the noise level. The television had a momentary triumph with a news story about the planned Hong Kong handover. General consensus in Court Five was that as long as Honkers remained open for cheap package holidays and duty-free shopping, it didn't really matter who ended up running the show.

She met TC at the bar.

'I'll see Jarrett at the morgue in the morning. Finish the interview afterwards – ran out of time this arvo.' She concentrated on her drink, avoiding TC's eye.

'So you got him talking, did you?' TC looked surprised. 'Well done. Told Zervos to expect a summons from Jarrett, not a statement.'

'Well, got him talking – nothing on paper, though,' she admitted. 'Haven't put in the running sheet yet.'

'Sounds more like Jarrett.' TC looked thoughtful, one hand rubbing his pate, the other holding a beer. 'I'll tell Zervos you're taking the son to view the body in the morning; he and his lot won't want to go anywhere near that.' TC kept rubbing. 'They're all at a media orgy down at the site now.'

'Bit late for the evening news.'

'Yeah, well ICAC was lead story tonight anyway. It's going feral down there. But I guess with cameras and concrete and a hole in the ground, Zervos'll get some good pictures. Might stir the possum a bit. He's set up a number and some uniforms to man the phones.'

TC stopped rubbing and leant forward.

'Knock out a running sheet, stick it on my desk, then piss off home. I'll hang on to it, and if they ask for it I'll give it to them. Think Jarrett might change his mind after you spend a bit more quality time with him?'

'Doubt it.' She sipped her drink. 'He's pretty dirty. Understandable, really.'

'Wait till you come up against him in court, see if you still feel like that.'

'He says the cops back then told them to piss off when they tried to report Dawn missing.'

'Yeah, well, the original Missing Persons report was a pretty piss-poor effort all round. A few retirees will get their cages rattled over that. Lesson in this, little buddy: do a good job the first time, makes life easier in the long run.'

'Speaking of old briefs . . .'

He shook his head. 'Been flat out here. Zervos reckons that until we know who the other woman is, we're like a one-legged man in a bum-kicking contest. Deak got her prints, now Zervos wants them checked everywhere all at once – other states, Immigration, Fedpol, Interpol, ASIO. Chasing up government departments I didn't even know existed. Maxwell-fucking-Smart territory.'

Ned laughed. 'Want me to make some of the calls?'

'Nah, if you can't put "Inspector" in front of your name you won't get past the front desk. Get your sheet in and head home. Not made of overtime, you know.'

Dawn Jarrett's disappearance had been marked by disregard. In death though, she had the benefit of all the latest technology the police could provide, including a running-sheet database tended by Miss Heels from Homicide. Ned had hoped for an empty office; she didn't want to answer any tricky questions from Homicide about her interview with Marcus Jarrett. She needn't have worried. Miss Heels was too busy flirting with Figgy to notice Ned or her missing sheet. They paid no attention to her, while she wrote up the results of her job and slipped it onto TC's desk. Figgy was perched on the edge of the running-sheet desk, displaying his local knowledge to Miss Heels, promising her 'the best Vietnamese meal this side of Saigon' as Ned made her getaway. She was halfway down the stairs when Figgy called after her.

'Ned? Phone!'

She retraced her steps, weary from a day that had started in the best way, with the thrill of a new lover, but had spiralled rapidly down since, to include morgues and old briefs and the re-awakened grief of a son for his mother. She'd lost count of the distances she'd driven – Glebe, Bankstown, the DAL, the city, back to Bankstown – the forms she'd filled in, the notes she'd taken. She needed bed. Her own and, much as she hated to admit it, alone.

Ned picked up the phone. 'Yes.' Terse and tired.

'That's not how protocol says we should introduce ourselves now, is it, Detective? I could've been the Commissioner.'

Her skin changed shape at the sound of his voice. She stood without responding for a moment, just taking pleasure in the way her flesh flickered and warmed. That empty bed no longer held appeal.

'Or someone ringing up with a big break on your murder,' Sean Murphy continued.

'Yeah, right.' Ned's tone was neutral. She pretended to study a file on her desk, as Figgy leant in closer to Miss Heels and whispered something that made the woman giggle and glance over at Ned.

'You're not encouraging me to open up and give you that vital clue, Detective.' Sean laughed. His voice echoed slightly, as if he was calling from a cave. 'Got an audience there, eh?'

'Yeah.' *Listen to yourself*, she chided silently, *sounding like a mono-syllabic moron*. Figgy was hard at work on Miss Heels – his kids and the wife tucked away safely in the Shire for the night. So why should she be coy?

'Or maybe you're ashamed of me.' Sean seemed to be enjoying himself. 'I feel so used.'

Figgy and Miss Heels stood up, keys and briefcases in hand. 'Say hi to Murph,' Figgy said, grinning, as they headed out.

'Figgy's appointed himself liaison to Homicide, I think.' Ned flopped into her chair, swinging her legs up on the desk, the office hers.

Sean laughed. 'Caitlin must be doing the running sheets.'

Miss Heels had a name.

'I think Figgy's hoping she'll do him as well.' The glance and the giggle from Caitlin had got under her skin. A reminder of what a small, incestuous world the cops lived in. She twisted the phone cord between her fingers, wondering how many similar conversations she and Sean Murphy would fuel.

'Gotta have hope,' Sean said. His voice changed, the bantering tone replaced by something else. 'I just hope you'll want to see me again.'

She stopped herself from blurting out *When?* 'Your life looks a little full.'

'Oh, you'll be surprised how well I can fit in the things I care about.' She could hear the grin. She wasn't sure she liked the idea of being fitted in.

'Maybe you're too busy? How's it going, your murder?' he said when she didn't answer.

'Same old same old. Back at the morgue tomorrow morning to show a son his dead mum – you know, all the glamorous stuff, just like on telly. You?' She weighed the word – *You?* Frisked it for any trace of neediness.

There were doors opening and slamming at his end, voices echoing; the cave was filling with action and sound. His tone changed from banter to business in a beat. 'Won't be around for a few days, but as soon as I can, we'll catch up.'

Her warm skin twitched and cooled. In that instant she realised she'd got it bad, much badder than was good.

Before she could reply, Swiss called out. His voice loud, distinct, near the phone: 'Gotta go, Murph. Tell your tart ta-ta.'

'That's my cue.' Sharp-edged, aggro. Sam the jumpy druggie. 'See ya.'

Gone. The phone buzzed in her ear, goosebumps parcelling her up. She replaced the receiver and retook the stairs. They seemed steeper on the way back down, the charge room and muster rooms too full of fluorescent light and lively coppers, joking, laughing and yelling out orders for junk food to the designated meal crew.

At knock-off, a general exodus of cops headed south to the Sutherland Shire – God's Own Country. Reality, as far as she could see, was a heavily mortgaged home, stocked with wife and kids and bills. Ned was too junior to score a work car to herself very often and generally a lift home wasn't worth the whingeing that accompanied it. Her own car was starting to leak oil and blow smoke; she was rationing it, hoping it would at least outlast her debts. So Ned routinely rode the eighty-wheeler out of Bankstown.

A train journey drew a line beneath the day. Listening to a soundtrack of Massive Attack on her Discman, Ned watched the day draw down in the homes that lined the track as the train ran east to the city. Out here the Australian dream of the quarter-acre block had taken root in brick-veneer and fibro homes. Some still stood on large, flat backyards that were sown with sheds, swings, vegie patches and clotheslines. But they were being weeded out, replaced with bought-off-the-plan brick-and-concrete palaces that bloated out into every inch of their blocks.

The post-war baby boom and immigration had propelled the suburban sprawl along the railway lines deep into south-west Sydney. Now, the signage on the shopfronts of the railway-station centres mapped the paths of migration. The Vietnamese flourishes and Chinese characters of Bankstown blended with Arabic curls in Punchbowl until, by Lakemba, all signs of South-East Asia had disappeared.

By the time older suburbs of the inner west rattled by, a melange of languages adorned the shopfronts: new boxy Korean characters jostling out older Arabic signs in Campsie, Vietnamese back alongside the Greek alphabet in Marrickville. Rows of turn-of-the-century terrace houses in various states of renovation, restoration and rescue backed onto the tracks through St Peters and Erskineville. Closer to the city, the rail network widened out as the streets flanking it grew narrower. An XPT burst past, rattling the windows of the suburban train.

There was a map of the Sydney rail system at the end of her carriage. Tubes of colour mapped the urban sprawl, abstracting it into a neat, ordered shape, the western edges rounded off to fit into the compact rectangle. Those railway lines plotted the disordered timeline of her life. Since she'd been in the Job she'd lived and worked in different corners of that map: probation in the heart of the city, then plain-clothes training in the eastern suburbs. But it was the Bankstown line that took her from one end of her childhood to another.

Now, years after leaving Bankstown for the harbour, she oscillated between the two each day. Her earliest memories of Bankstown remained the faint sensory impressions of childhood. The smell of cestrum through a bedroom window on a hot night, the dusty driveway running down the side of a house, warm and prickly under bare feet, the voices of her parents quietly singing along to records in the night. They were fragments that dissolved at the touch of reality to become even more imaginary than before.

Daylight was fading as the train passed through Redfern. Ned looked with sharper interest at the area surrounding The Block, that infamous rollcall of streets: Eveleigh, Caroline, Hugo, Louis. They sounded like the names of a bunch of delinquent young European royals. She'd had her share of calls to The Block during her probation in the city. Marcus Jarrett had grown up somewhere in there. A motherless child. She wondered if he'd had a big mob of relations who'd rallied round.

Lights were coming on in some terrace houses along Eveleigh. The doors stood open in the heat of the evening, figures moving down hallways. Others were dark caves, fire-blackened bricks ringing windows and doors. Once heroin had hit The Block, the place had started to come apart at the seams.

According to her probation training buddy – an old-school cop who still called it 'The County' – Redfern had gone to shit after 21 Division had been disbanded. Once upon a time 21 Division would lob into the Empress Hotel on Regent Street and restore order the old-fashioned way – before any trouble had broken out. *That*, the old warhorses would harrumph over their beers, was proactive policing.

She remembered the faded graffiti on the Redfern railway bridge.

First 20,000 years a Dreamtime
Last 200 a nightmare

Leaving Wollstonecraft Station, Ned followed the path through Smoothey Park, under eucalypts and over the footbridge onto the Greenwich peninsula. She dawdled through the quiet streets. It was dark by the time she headed down Greenwich Road, past the lights of Gore Cove oil terminal, a remnant of a time when the harbour housed industry, not views.

A Toyota panel van that had seen better days was parked in MM's driveway. Maybe Sean had a down-market cover story and had swapped the Celica for this. Her leap of excitement confirmed her descent into adolescence. She leant against the bonnet to give herself a stern talking to, when violence erupted from the back seat. A large German shepherd hurled itself at the windscreen.

'Shit!' She leapt back.

She wasn't scared of dogs, but this thing was terrifying. Berserk. It looked ready to tear out her throat if it could get free. A handsome animal, black muzzle, thick coat, perfection marred by the missing tip of one ear. In three strides she was up the front stairs and through the door, still shaking when she heard his voice.

'Ned?'

'Newie, look. Your friend brought me some utterly glorious tiger lilies. How did he know? My utter, utter favourites!'

Sean came down the hallway, gave a hapless shrug. 'Got time for a walk?'

'Couldn't go without saying goodbye, properly.' They lay side by side on the headland at Manns Point, the sandstone still warm beneath their backs with a whole ten minutes before Sean had to head up the coast. Somewhere close by, a brush-tail possum coughed and hissed, claiming territory. Leaves shook as something smaller fled.

'Nice thought – the lilies.'

'Your aunt certainly appreciated them. I think she's got me confused with some other policeman, though.'

'Yeah, well, she's confused about a lot of things. When do you think you'll be back?'

'When the job's done.' He kissed her throat. 'Do my best to conclude business in a hurry. I'm very motivated.'

'You let that dog near your kids?'

'Nero's a working dog, not a pet.'

'Didn't think the Dog Squad would let you borrow their dogs.'

His hand slipped under her shirt, cupped her breast. 'He's under-cover, like me.'

NED PULLED UP OUT THE back of the morgue. Late. She hustled through the loading bay and saw Marcus Jarrett through the waiting room window. Alone, sitting rigid on the edge of the lounge, his features sagging with sadness. By the time she opened the door he was on his feet, face stiff and closed.

'Mr Jarrett, sorry, the bridge was . . .'

His expression didn't change.

'Someone seen you, for the DNA samples?'

'Yeah, taken them.' Brusque, but not with the aggression she'd heard yesterday; more like apprehension, suppressed, but not far beneath the surface. Morgues did that.

'Then, if you're sure . . .' Offer him a way out, no shame in it.

'Wouldn't be here if I wasn't.'

A morgue attendant led them into a narrow room: one wall, all window, curtain on the other side of the glass. It reminded Ned of those old images of maternity wing nurseries, visitors gathering for a showing, pressed up against the glass, the curtain drawing back to reveal baskets of babies. This room represented the full circle.

Jarrett was having none of it. 'What's this?' He rapped a knuckle on the glass. 'May as well be looking at a picture.'

'It's standard procedure for a viewing, sir,' the morgue attendant said.

'I'm not here to "view" her – she's not some fucking house I'm thinking of buying.' He stopped. Ned saw him exert control, a deliberate action, jaw working from side to side as he spoke. His delivery steady. 'I'm here to say goodbye. Face to face.'

'Any reason Mr Jarrett can't go in there?'

The attendant shrugged. They filed into the room beyond the curtain, bigger, with a set of steel sliding doors. Bare but for a second attendant and a hospital gurney with a white sheet covering a longish shape.

Jarrett hesitated, looked unsure which end to go to. The second attendant lifted the sheet and folded it back under the chin of Dawn Jarrett's mummified face.

He made a sound. Not so much a word, or even a cry, just a sound that came from somewhere deep in his chest. It keened up into his throat. Hesitant but drawn forward, he reached out to his mother. One hand hovered above her face, vibrating before sinking down, resting there as if checking for fever in that dark, parchment skin. He stroked her forehead, wider than it had been in life. The injuries she'd absorbed had set it forever, like the concrete she'd been part of all those years while he'd been growing, wondering. Missing her.

He bent over her, one hand on her head, the other stroking the sheet covering the gnarled length of her arm, his lips moving, his breath stirring the wispy hair that clung to her scalp in isolated clumps. He leant further forward, eyes closed, until his lips rested on the dry terrain of her brow. He kissed her.

Ned stepped back into the corridor, away from his quiet sorrow. She pressed her spine against the wall, hands clasped behind her. Rocking back and forth on her heels, she tried to beat the tremors out, palms slapping against the back of her thighs in a haphazard pattern. She couldn't have done what Jarrett was doing. She barely wanted to look at Dawn Jarrett or that other, unknown woman. The more she knew about the dead, the more real they became, and the less she wanted to deal with their remains. Touching, kissing – she couldn't imagine caring so deeply about another human being that it could transcend the rank aspect of death.

The dead didn't linger and the carcasses they left behind were evidence, nothing more. Bodies held clues, putrefied, made her want to throw up but she refused to sentimentalise remains. Maybe others could afford that luxury; she was a professional. Her hands had finally found a rhythm. She concentrated on the beat.

A few moments later the door clicked. Jarrett was wiping his eyes with a handkerchief, blowing his nose, steadying himself with deep breaths.

'Call yourself a hand-holder?' His voice was phlegmy with tears. He gave his nose a last, angry wipe and folded the cloth back into his pocket.

'The ones who want hand-holding would still be out in the car park,' she said, irritated by her failure to match his courage, stand beside him.

'Yeah, well,' he said. 'All I want is the bastard who did that.'

Jarrett told Ned he had someone for her to meet, and got into her car without comment. It smelt of chlorine and coffee; the back seat was scattered with training bags, towels, swimmers, running shoes and last weekend's *Sydney Morning Herald*. He didn't expand, just directed her on the short drive from Glebe to Redfern. The one-ways and no-right-turns made it a roundabout journey through back lanes and side streets, down Abercrombie, past the pub, right into Vine, right into Hugo. Into the heart of The Block. Despite wearing jeans and T-shirt and driving her tatty old Mazda, she still felt as obvious as if she was wearing the blue suit. Driving past a burnt-out car shell, she gripped the steering wheel that little bit tighter.

'Don't worry, Detective, I'll look after you.'

'You could call me Ned. Or are you worried what people might think?'

Two could play the sarcasm game, even if her face was hot and guilty. She was angry with herself and now, twice in half an hour, unfairly angry with him. He read her too easily, caught her stereo-typing. She resented stereotyping, hated it when it happened to her, but she did it too, like most of the coppers she knew. There were degrees. TC was no Ugly, but when shit came to shove most of them reverted to instinct. Instinct was cruel but it worked just often enough to make it useful.

Just the tips of the city skyline were visible from down here at street level, where a sofa was disintegrating on a footpath outside a terrace, and glass shone like a thousand tiny teeth along the pave-ment. A group of school-age boys tumbled out of a doorway then skidded into hostile silence, watching her get out of the car. Like a cloud passing from the face of the sun, the hostility puttered into recognition, then naked curiosity, when they saw Jarrett. Ned reached into the back seat and hauled out the notebook computer.

Jarrett shook his head. 'Won't need that, Detective.'

Ned took it anyway, deciding she'd rather cop Jarrett's mock-ery than have to explain to Zervos how she'd let his brand-new 120-megabyte hard-disk baby get snatched from the back seat of her car at The Block. She followed Jarrett, who was leading the way towards one of the terraces.

Its front door was wide open. A Koori flag hung across an upstairs window and part of a rainbow serpent slithered across the front wall. Next door, the colour of its belly glowed despite the fresh coat of white paint covering it. It snaked down the street, reappearing in full splendour one house beyond. The freshly painted house was shuttered up tight, window grilles and a security door all glittering and new. Two ceramic planters stood in the tiled front courtyard, two dead somethings in them, both thickly mulched with cigarette butts. The *For Sale* sign on the iron railings offered polished floor-boards, contrasting coloured ceilings and cornices. Someone had scrawled beneath the auction date: *Can't sell what you don't own. Always was – always will be – Aboriginal Land.*

'Marcus.' A head of curly brown hair emerged through an open front window then disappeared, reappearing at the front door. The woman looked familiar, and when she smiled Ned realised why. Dawn Jarrett's smile, same full face. Even fuller than Dawn's, as this woman was spreading magnificently into middle age. The smile turned off like a light switch when she examined Ned.

'This the one you told me about, then?'

'Yep. Aunty Pat, this is Detective Constable Kelly – she likes to be called Ned.'

'Yeah? Well, I suppose anything'd be better than Constable.' She stressed the first syllable. 'Better bring her in. Whole world'll know who she is and why she's here before the kettle's boiled.'

Ned decided her best approach was mute amiability. They went down the long, narrow hallway to the kitchen at the back of the house. It looked out over a yard bristling with vegetables.

Aunty Pat followed her gaze. 'You garden?' she asked.

'Nah. Pot-plant killer, that's about it,' Ned said.

'Should. Good for the soul, getting your hands in the dirt, eating food you grow yourself.' Aunty Pat clattered a kettle onto the gas stove as she spoke. 'Want to get a community garden happening out there, most of these places haven't got fences anyway. Could get a buncha plots happening, maybe some chooks.'

Jarrett feigned a look at his watch. 'Must be a record, Aunty Pat. Under one minute and you've got the soapbox out.'

Aunty Pat folded her arms around him, tilted him backward in his chair and kissed his forehead.

'My house, my soapbox,' she said, releasing him, running her hands over his shaved skull. 'Detective Ned, what you reckon?'

Ned opened her mouth to answer but Aunty Pat picked up a copy of the daily tabloid and tossed it onto the kitchen table. She wasn't talking about vegetables anymore.

'You lot going to find out what happened to his mum – my little sister? Or we gunna have to swallow this kind of shit, all over again?'

It was an inner-page spread on the discovery of the bodies.

Dawn smiled from the page, condemned to perpetual cheerfulness by that Missing Persons poster. There was some background – a crash course in seventies politics for a new generation of readers – while another piece focused on the technical details, grisly thrills for the commuters: mummification, excavation, identification, complete with artist's impressions. It took Ned a few seconds to see it. A small, breakout piece, bottom of the page, quoted an unnamed police source.

Brothel battle may be key

A battle of the brothels from the mid-seventies may be the vital clue in the murder and interment of two women, found in Bankstown. A police source believes, 'It's possible these women were prostitutes caught up in a battle between brothel bosses and murdered as a warning.' The source speculated that the discovery of an Asian woman with an Aboriginal woman was significant: 'Offering these "ethnic" services could have been attracting clientele from the more established brothels.'

Feeling like she'd just been handed a shit sandwich, she looked up from the tabloid. If she felt that way, her companions must have felt like they were eating it without the benefit of bread.

'News to me. Though I'd use the word "news" pretty loosely with this rag, wouldn't you?'

'Who's the source?'

Jarrett was the cold-eyed legal inquisitor again and Ned started to feel the jaws of a set-up closing around her.

'Fucked if I know. There's always greedy buggers who'll make up shit to sell and there's always bloody reporters who'll pay 'em. Look, for what it's worth, I'm sorry.' She spread her hands wide, palms up. 'I don't know who did it and as far as I know, there's no line of inquiry about this. I can make a call back to base and see what's going on?'

They stared at her while the kettle rose to a shriek.

'You want me to leave, I will. Homicide will have to talk to you both anyway.' She got up. 'Like I said, I'm sorry.'

'Sit down, Ned,' Jarrett said. 'It's not ideal but we've all got to work with what we have, don't we.'

Aunty Pat lifted the kettle from the flame, pacifying the kitchen in an instant.

'So where do we go from here?' Ned said.

'To the back step, I reckon,' said Aunty Pat, handing Ned a mug of steaming tea. 'Think better when I'm weeding.'

Aunty Pat slapped on a wide straw hat then crouched between rows of tomatoes and heads of lettuce, plucking out the green invaders.

'When Dawn disappeared, well, we knew. We knew straight off it was bad. But not knowing when or where or how – that made it hard to know who'd done it. Been thinking a lot since yesterday, her turning up in Bankstown, with some Asian woman. It just doesn't make any sense. Dawn didn't know any of your mob, you know, it was different back then. Not so many about. But why Bankstown? I reckon she'd have been out there a handful of times in her whole life.'

'She was buried in Bankstown,' Ned said. 'Doesn't mean she was killed there. Could be it was just a convenient spot to hide her body.'

Aunt and nephew exchanged a look.

'Many come round after I left last night?' Jarrett asked her.

'Just who you'd expect.' Aunty Pat stopped weeding. Sweat ringed her hat.

'And?' Jarrett turned the mug between his hands.

'Asked a lot of questions, didn't answer many.'

'OK, you going to let me in on this, or should I leave?' Ned placed her tea on the step and looked from aunt to nephew.

'It's not all happy families in this community, you know,' Aunty Pat said.

Ned stared into her tea. *Not on your Pat Malone there.*

'Wasn't back then, either,' Aunty Pat continued.

'Go on.'

'Tough times, tough lives, Limited resources, limited opportunities – gets competitive. Then throw politics into the mix.'

'Politics?' Ned echoed, but Aunty Pat kept weeding. Ned turned to Jarrett.

He shrugged. 'People look at us and think it's Black this, Aboriginal that, Koori whatever – like we all speak with one voice, think with one mind. It's not like that.'

Aunty Pat stood up, bitterness slicing through her voice. 'People get so caught up fighting their corner, they end up fighting each other.'

Ned chose her words with care, uncertain where this tale was leading, sensing her right to hear it was still being gauged. 'You've seen a lot I guess, living here?'

'Yeah. Compared to what's going on out there,' she replied, sweeping her hand toward the street, 'the garden's an easy thing – you dig, you plant, you grow, you eat. It's simple.'

'It's fabulous.' The longer Ned sat there, the more the full depth of the garden revealed itself to her. Innumerable shades of green, under-plantings and over-plantings; the rich, loamy smell of soil and sharper scent of foliage under sunlight grew stronger.

'I'll tell you what's fabulous,' Aunty Pat said, seeming to have come to a decision. The words tumbled out now. 'Taking a stand, getting involved, fighting for change – that's hard. That's what Dawn did. *She* was fabulous. But having to fight her own people? She wasn't expecting that.'

Ned felt goose pimples rising despite the warmth of the back step. 'What are you saying?'

'Long story,' Aunty Pat said, squatting back down.

'Better get started then. Who was Dawn fighting?'

'Phil Walker.' The name came out together with a weed.

Ned knew that name. Walker was the current head of the Housing Authority that controlled most of the suburb they were sitting in, and the newly pre-selected Labor candidate for a plum inner-city seat in Federal Parliament. TC was going to hand this to Homicide with asbestos gloves and a huge sigh of relief. 'I've read the original Missing Person report. Phil Walker's name's not in them.'

Jarrett seemed absorbed by his tea, and Aunty Pat had found rich pickings beneath the broccoli. She didn't look up from her swiftly moving hands. 'He's family. My cousin – Dawn's and my cousin.'

'So?' Ned's voice was cold.

Aunty Pat left it to her nephew.

'Over the years, you look back, you remember things, you see things more clearly.' Jarrett the legal attack dog had disappeared.

'Or you look back and you see what you want to see and remember what you want to remember,' Ned observed dryly.

'Sounds like experience talking.' Aunty Pat didn't look up from her task. Her voice was hard. 'Dawn and Phil had a major falling out. These days, Jarretts and Walkers – well, you'll find Jarretts in the ALS and Walkers all over Housing, but not vice versa. It started over that bloody trip to America to meet Black Power groups. One place left and Dawn and Phil both wanted it. Dawn got it – deserved it, but you wouldn't think so, way Phil went on. Never forgave her.'

'When was this?' Ned had her notebook out.

'Late sixties, can't be sure. He was only a little fella.' She looked up at Jarrett from beneath her hat, smiled. 'First time I ever came down to Sydney was to look after him.'

'Long time to nurse a grudge,' Ned said. 'Why wait till 1976 to do something about it?'

'Who says he waited?' Aunty Pat went on. 'There were other things. When she got to America, Dawn had big problems with Immigration – reckoned they had a tip-off. Drugs. You'd know what happens when Customs do a cavity search?'

Ned nodded. Spiteful.

'When she gets back from the States, same thing at this end. Then the rumours start. She's joined the Black Panthers, the Weathermen, she's trying to set up a violent radical organisation, she's carrying Huey Newton's baby. Somehow they always surfaced whenever she was up for a place on a board or a committee. That federal seat he's just landed – Dawn was in the running for that back in '74. Photo of her shaking hands with Huey Newton turns up and Gough gets cold feet. A private photo. She went looking for it – missing, along with the rest of the photos from the trip. Whole album – gone.'

'And no one told the police about this when —'

'No.' Aunty Pat placed both hands on her thighs and straightened up.

'You still don't get it, do you, Detective?' Jarrett said, irritation driving him to his feet. 'But you should. Bar's higher for us. Can't be good enough, or just as good. Got to be better – gets in your own head as much as other people's, doesn't it?'

Ned put down her mug, didn't take her eyes off Jarrett, knowing the truth of what he said.

'Can't be like any other local council, or most politicians with their hands in the till, not allowed to have people who stuff up, or are greedy or corrupt. So we don't parade our shit in public. And people aren't going to want to tell police about this now, let alone back then.'

'People like me have a pretty high bar, Mr Jarrett. It's called proof. Got any proof?' Ned said, also rising.

'No.' He looked at his watch. 'But it might interest you to know that in the mid-seventies Phil Walker lived in Bankstown. Would've known where he could hide a body if he wanted to.'

THE COUNTRY PLATFORMS OF CENTRAL STATION seemed glazed in the midday heat. Empty now, but somewhere beyond sight and sound, spread out across the state, long-haul trains traversed the spaces between Sydney and the bush. The corrugated-iron roof arching overhead was home to a host of pigeons, living fat on fast food. Could've still been World War Two up there; everything had a washed-out tone – the birds, the clock, the iron ribs. At ground level the present announced itself in garishly coloured food franchises. An array of people waited for trains, lifts or nothing much at all. Some nursed pillows on their knees for a drooling trip against a window back to their home towns. A very black, very old woman with a cloud of lamb's-wool-white hair sat in the station café, her hands turning out something bright from the blur of her knitting needles.

'Detective Kelly, Essie Freeman.' Jarrett made the introduction.

'Mrs Freeman.' Ned took the old woman's hand. It was marble-smooth and cool.

'Detective.'

Ned felt herself appraised by a pair of bird-bright eyes.

'What good do you see, Detective? What good in raking up the past? What would it change?'

Not a question Ned had expected. She considered her answer under the scrutiny of the sharp-eyed old lady.

'Well, nothing can change the past. But the past can change the present and the future.'

'Dawn Jarrett believed the past should shape the future. She didn't get much support for that point of view when she was alive. What's changed now she's dead?'

'Maybe nothing.' And nothing to lose by speaking plainly to this old inquisitor. Those unremitting eyes were probably reading her thoughts before they came out of her mouth, anyway. 'I'm not a politician, I'm a police officer. I can only talk about my job. Dawn and another woman were murdered in 1976. We've found them and now we want to find out who killed them. Maybe we can. Maybe we can't. But we're going to try.'

'How hard?' Essie's needles were clicking and clacking in reproof.

'Look, I'm a local detective from Bankstown. Suburban, you know. I'm not a TV cop, I'm not going to stand here and swear to you that I'll personally get to the bottom of it. That'd be bull—' She chose another word. '. . . silly. But I'll do my part of the job as well as I can and I trust my colleagues will as well. Murder's as serious as it gets. The Homicide Squad are on this. If we don't arrest anyone, the whole thing goes to the Coroner – a public inquest. One way or another, Dawn's going to get her day in court.'

'Dawn reckoned she was a one-woman homicide squad, you know that?' Essie's fingers moved across the needle, counting stitches. 'Only, the victims she was interested in had no names, no graves, no records of when and where they were killed. We all know who did it, though, don't we? They disappeared. Look up there – see what I mean?'

Ned turned in her seat, following the line of Essie's pointed needle. High above them, etched into the faux marble of the café walls, were a pair of matching images dated a year apart. The picture marked *1787* showed naked natives making fire, trailing through the bush, spears and children in tow. In *1788* men dressed in work clothes laboured to bring barrels, sacks and tools ashore from a small boat in the background. No savages – or shackles – marred the industry of the scene.

'Terra nullius,' Essie continued. 'Latin for one bloody big grave,

Dawn used to say. She reckoned her job was to remember them. Make the gubbas remember them. Prove that they'd lived, prove it was their land, get it back, and do it all in the gubbas' own bloody courtrooms. Then Dawn disappeared too.'

'Only now she's been found, she has a name, a grave – and a killer. Would she want you to do something about that?'

Counting finished, the needles began their march again. Essie answered Ned's question by ignoring it.

'She wanted to be around more, for Marcus. Felt like she'd sac-rificed him for the cause, the struggle, whatever you want to call it. That last year, she was tired – tired of travelling, fighting – wanted to do something closer to home. Have a job where she could come home every night, have tea with her son before he was a man and she lost him to the world. Course she never told *you* that . . .' Essie flicked a needle towards Jarrett. 'Didn't want to disappoint you. With what she knew about land issues, well, natural fit was the MLC.' At Ned's blank look she spelt it out. 'Metropolitan Land Council, Sydney-based. Meant she could do the same work, but she could do it local, not have to travel all over the bloody place. But Phil Walker was making a play for the same job. She was going to try and line up a meeting at his pub. Work out their problems. She wanted to meet, in public.'

'Why? She think he was violent?' Ned wrote as she spoke.

'Never to her, but there was talk,' Essie said. 'Just think she wanted it all out in the open, you know. Nothing to hide.'

'Where, when, was this meeting?'

'Can't tell you, don't know. She visited me in Tuncurry in winter '76, on her way back from Queensland. Told me Phil used to drink at a place in Chinatown, lots of Labor movers and shakers. I asked her about it when I came down to Sydney for the footy carnival.' She smiled at Jarrett, her skin rippling into dark folds. 'But she still hadn't done anything about it. She'd been on the go in the Western Desert and then she'd had problems at home.'

'What problems?'

'Her bloke – forget his name, one of the Balgarrys – been playing up while she was away. She was fed up.'

'What —'

'We didn't go into it. She was about to, then Bill, her brother, turned up.'

'And?' There was a pause. Ned found herself tapping her notebook in time with the knitting needles.

'My Uncle Bill was an alcoholic and a drug addict,' Jarrett finally said, his voice tight. 'He's dead. Mum and Aunty Pat, they decided, for my sake, to bar him from our place. It was a hard thing to do.'

'Probably heard it's a weakness, family? We let relations drag us down,' Essie said calmly.

Ned's cheeks grew warm. Oh yeah, she'd heard that before. Those words, in some shape or another, when her colleagues were justifying their conviction that none of 'them' would ever amount to much. She stayed silent, pen poised, eyes fixed on the pages of her notebook as Essie resumed her story.

'Dawn and Pat, they used to see Bill, used to try and look after him, get him into accommodation, got him onto the 'done, used to give him money, bail him when they had to. He wasn't cut off. Anyway, Bill was there at the carnival, wanted to watch Marcus. Seemed pretty straight, for Bill. Said he needed to talk to Dawn, in private, said he had her ticket into the MLC – something big, something he could've told Phil but he wanted to give to his sister, as a gift. He was a talker, Bill, couldn't help it, comes from not having much of anything. He'd big-note himself when he could. I left them to it. Last time I ever saw or spoke to Dawn or Bill.'

'Don't suppose the police were told any of this when Dawn went missing? A boyfriend she was blueing with, a brother with a habit and a promise?' Ned asked the question, knowing she wouldn't be the last one to do so. They all might as well get used to it.

'Detective Kelly, when Dawn was murdered, the police insisted she'd run off with any of a hundred mystery boyfriends. That Balgarry boy took off because someone told him the coppers were going to pin something on him if we kept on stirring up trouble about Dawn. He didn't do anything to Dawn, he loved her. More than she loved him, but that wasn't his fault. He died in a police cell, Detective, so he didn't run far.'

'It's routine, to look at the husband, boyfriend,' Ned murmured.

'Not from where we were standing it wasn't. You don't know what those times were like. Think it's bad now – well, the hate back then, it was real, it was dangerous. Did you know, there were *Wanted Dead or Alive* posters of Dawn out in the Western Desert, on fences, sides of bores, along the cattle routes? We thought she'd been murdered somewhere out there, not around here.'

Ned wondered what those posters had looked like. Had Dawn smiled out into the dust, until the sun scorched her into brittle sepia?

'Sorry, I didn't realise . . .' She ducked her head, then started making more notes as she spoke. 'We need to find who Bill was palling around with, see if he told anyone else about this big news. If he was such a big-noter, maybe he did.'

'I've got time for another cup of tea before my train goes. I'll see who I can remember from those days.'

'It's a long haul back to Tuncurry. You're not staying overnight?' Ned asked.

The old woman looked out onto the concourse, beyond the barriers, to the railway lines that ran out of Sydney.

'Not here, sister. Sad place, this. One bloody big grave.'

'Can I give you a lift?' Ned asked Jarrett.

'Nah. I'll walk.'

'Productive day – a suspect who's a high-profile, respected leader about to go into Parliament, against whom we have no evidence, and a vital witness who's dead.' She shook her head, leant against the car, tossing the keys from hand to hand.

'If it was easy, everyone'd do it, eh?' Jarrett said.

'None of which explains why your mum ended up buried with a woman no one seems to know anything about.'

In her back pocket she had a spiral notebook with the names of Bill Jarrett's old mates and confirmation from Essie that she had no recollection of Dawn ever having met, spoken about or known an Asian woman.

'Yeah, well, maybe Bill's mates will remember something. I'll see if I can turn any of them up.' Jarrett began to walk away.

'His mates aren't likely to be travelling too well, are they?' Ned called after him. 'How many do you reckon are even still alive?'

Jarrett shrugged.

'I'll stay in touch then,' she promised to his broad back.

Ned watched him pass through the cursory patch of park in front of the train station, stopping and exchanging a few words with the small group of regulars who camped there. His hand went to his pocket, then folded a note into a black, gnarled hand that reached up to him. His gait seemed to be fighting the ground as he turned and headed back towards Redfern.

Weariness was infectious. She yawned and slumped back into the car. The Homicide Squad's portable computer remained unsullied by any statement from Jarrett. Once he'd started talking and introducing her around, she hadn't dared risk putting him off. It seemed logical at the time, but now she had to face up to a long drive back to Bankstown, empty-handed and bearing unwelcome news.

'COURT FIVE.' SERGEANT UGLY DIDN'T look up from his newspaper, arms folded, leaning on the front counter of the station. Anger at rest. Any member of the public walking in off the street with a query would think twice before stirring him into activity.

The noise from the pub slopped out onto Chapel Road, the deep roar of male bonding. Most of the Bankstown Ds were in session, talking loud and fast, drinking deep and swift. For a change, a few of the junior suits from Homicide were present, but not Zervos or his sergeants. Figgy and Toy had Detective Constable Running Sheets and her sidekick on the pool table, where local knowledge was paying dividends. Suit coats hung off bar stools, ties spilt from pockets.

TC was at the bar. He turned, fists around a brace of schooners, saw Ned weaving through tables and tossed her order at the barman. Ned collected her scotch and ice and followed him.

'Missed a big day here, Neddie.' Toyboy was flushed by beer or excitement or both, Ned couldn't tell. She had a vision of him in his fifties, propping up a bar somewhere, telling war stories, red veins star-bursting over his nose and cheeks.

'Yeah? Lock someone up when I wasn't looking?' she asked.

'Nah, but —'

'I'll give Ned the sit-rep, thanks Toy,' TC said, depositing the shout, retaining his own and heading towards a corner booth. Ned followed, scanning the room more closely. The conversations were animated, but not euphoric. Perhaps the locals had been knocked off the job early – maybe permanently.

'So? Big news?'

TC shook his head, 'Only in Toy's world. I want to hear what you got first.'

He listened while Ned recounted the day. He frowned at her lack of Jarrett on paper but when she said Phil Walker's name his eyebrows shot up.

'Interesting. Phil Walker's our news. Rang the information line this morning. Homicide's only just finished taking his statement.'

'And?'

'Provided every scrap of gossip connected to Dawn Jarrett since the doctor held her upside down and spanked her bottom: lovers, drugs, radical politics, power-crazed, power-hungry, loose with the truth, loose with funds. According to him, there'd have been a queue to bump Dawnie off.'

'Any particular person or reason in mind?'

'Not that he could say.'

Ned groaned. 'Mirror image of the Jarrett mob – lots of innuendo, no facts.'

'Well, when pressed, he most reluctantly obliged.' TC's lip curled in contempt.

'Yeah?'

'Reckoned it was a domestic. Dawn had a boyfriend round then, violent bloke by the name of Darren —'

'Balgarry.'

Ned said the surname at the same time. TC took a swallow of beer and waited.

'Essie Freeman mentioned him. Didn't mention violence.'

'She tell you he hit the toe after the family reported Dawn missing? Maybe he didn't want to talk to the cops. Anyway, turned up dead in a lockup in the Kimberleys about eight months later. Royal Commission looked at it. Death in custody.'

'Essie Freeman says he took off because a copper threatened to load him to shut the family up about Dawn.'

'What copper?'

'Couldn't say – third-hand by the time she got it.'

Bill Jarrett, Darren Balgarry – more persons of interest dead than living. She rubbed her eyes. They felt red-raw, unpaid sleep debts catching up.

'It's bullshit. No way a domestic ends up in a concrete grave in Bankstown next to Madame X,' Ned said.

'Nope,' TC agreed, slumping.

'And I don't buy the "whore wars" line, do you?'

'Surprised you didn't hear Zervos all the way over there at Red-fern.' TC shook his head. 'Swears his team's too professional to leak. Between you and me, don't reckon ours have the imagination.'

'So, Zervos still digging for the leak?'

'Nah. Waste of time. Dawn Jarrett in a brothel? Sounds like someone with a fat and a fantasy.'

'Marcus and Dawn's sister weren't too impressed.'

TC sucked air through clenched teeth. 'How'd you go?'

'Apologised. They let me stay – devil you know, I think.' Ned paused. Too proud to look needy, she kept hoping TC would men-tion her parents' brief. 'So, where to from here?'

'What we're already doing. Pin any half-baked suspects down to a few provable things – where they lived, what cars they had access to, where they were around September and October '76, when they last saw or spoke to Dawn. Then sweat on Deak and the DAL extracting some miracles.'

'How does Phil Walker stack up?'

'Lived out near the aerodrome, owned a Falcon, had access to a Holden through work, gave us a DNA sample like an innocent man.'

'Any joy yet on the other woman's prints?'

TC tipped back his beer, drained it. 'She's not on our records.'

'What about Immigration? She probably wasn't born here. Those marks on her, she'd been through some bad shit somewhere —'

'Yeah, yeah,' TC interrupted, looking as tired as she felt. 'Immigration have records all right, lots of records. All that paper, means a manual search. They don't have anyone qualified to compare thousands of prints, so we'll have to send one of ours over to do it. That's serious man hours, and print experts don't grow on trees.'

'Jeez.' Ned leant back.

Investigations got to a point where the only things left to throw at them were time and people. It was about then that the budget usually ran out, and theirs would run out long before Homicide's did.

'Anything interesting on the phone-in, apart from Phil Walker?'

'Snapshot of this case: five "Throw her back"s, a couple of "Black bitch deserved it"s and about a dozen "She had it coming"s. Been a long time but Dawnie's not forgotten.'

'Nice.' Ned sipped her scotch. Its bitterness at least had purpose. 'Any news about Hall?'

'Still in intensive care, stable. He'll live, but . . .' TC's shoulders lifted. 'Zervos executed a search warrant on his place, looking for that box Stan Lucas told you about.'

'Fuck.' A good one to have missed, serving a warrant on Mrs Hall while her husband lay in intensive care. That would've been nasty. 'And?'

'Nothing there that shouldn't have been. His wife didn't know what we were talking about. Said Hall and your dad were ex-army buddies, exchanged the odd letter and postcard, but nothing he hung on to.'

'So . . .' She rolled her glass between her palms, watching the oily liquid ooze over the ice.

'Something else?' TC tilted his beer back, watching her over the rim.

'Had a look at the brief yet? The old one?'

Before he could answer, the barman called his name, phone in hand. TC lumbered over to the bar, Ned following again. The office was settling in for a drink and more than a few were avoiding eye contact with the boss. Toyboy, ever vigilant, bobbed up beside them.

TC hung up, turned to his audience of two. 'Gumby's recovered a couple of pics from the mystery woman's locket. He's faxing them through to Zervos now. Want to have a look?' Casual, like he was asking them to come and check out his new car-seat covers.

Ugly hadn't moved.

'Expecting a fax.' TC began. 'Has it —'

'Not yet,' Ugly grunted in reply. 'Told him I'll ring when it —'

'Bring it up.' TC, normally affable, now curt.

'Can't leave the desk, offsider's sick. Here on me own.' Ugly turned a page, made it look heavy.

Toyboy was already out of sight, up the stairs two at a time, homing in on Zervos. He'd established himself as gopher to the Homicide boss, making his coffee, doing his photocopying, filling up his car.

'No worries, I'll get it,' Ned offered, as TC tackled the stairs at a more sedate pace. She went into the back room where the fax had started singing.

The paper fed out, pixel by pixel. A cover sheet, a three-page typed report. She tore them off, reading Gumby's account of the DAL's work on opening the heart-shaped locket, the discovery of the two images it contained: fragile original portraits of a man and a woman. The dead woman's parents, perhaps. Ned frowned.

The first face crept out. A dark hairline, then space between the dots, forming a forehead, faint, thin eyebrows, serious almond eyes peering from the lip of the machine. The face floated on the filmy paper, the shape of the woman's hair lost to the oval cropping of the portrait.

Ned scanned through Gumby's report, past the details of his restoration of the photos, back to the description of the locket. Gold heart. Engraved with an intricate pattern of interlocking fleurs-de-lis and, on the back, an inscription: *Toujours dimanche avec toi.* Gumby had provided a translation. Always Sunday with you. Intimate. Not something you wrapped your parents in.

Ned looked into the ink-dot eyes. Disappointment sank through her. It was a whisper of a woman. She'd emerged from the locket enlarged by technology, but any detail that might define her as an individual had been lost.

'Huh. A power point. Looks like you – then again, don't they all?' Ugly materialised behind her, poked a nicotine-stained finger at the woman's face.

Empty office, no witnesses, so of course now he'd come to life. Fighting him was tiring; he could out-swear her, out-insult her. Hating him in silence seemed the easiest option.

She watched as the next face spooled out. A tousled hairline, lighter in colour than the woman's, a broader expanse of nothing as the forehead grew. She willed the image out faster.

The buzzer over the public-access front door sounded. Someone at the desk with a story to tell and only Ugly to tell it to, poor bastards. At least it meant he'd have to bugger off and leave her alone.

Ugly yawned, scratched under his armpit, showed no sign of attending to the desk.

The paper crept out a line at a time. Wide forehead. Curly hair. Male. A pair of thick eyebrows emerged.

Even though the image was pixelated and distorted, Ned could tell from the shade and texture of the hair, the shape of the forehead, the round eyes that were beginning to form, that the man was Caucasian, not Asian.

'Well, look at that. Here comes the plug for the power point,' Ugly laughed, standing so close she felt the heat of his body.

She stepped away from him as the buzzer at the desk sounded again, followed by a nervous voice calling out, 'Hello. I need to see the police. Hello?'

'You're wanted, Sarge.'

'Nothing that can't wait,' he grunted, eyes fixed on the fax. 'Well, well, well. Wonder who lover boy was, then? Suspect number one, I'd say – wouldn't you, Detective?'

Ugly leant in closer. He smelt of tobacco and aftershave.

She turned back and saw that the top half of the man's photo had resolved, smiling and merry-eyed. This face was as indistinct as the other but as familiar to Ned as her own.

They were only half-formed, but she knew those eyes. She followed the progress of the nose – long, narrow, a slight bend to the left – spat out in rows of dots by the machine. She didn't need to see the rest but it was unstoppable. The machine was ruthless, chattering out the image until finally, dangling from the tray of the fax, her father, Mick Kelly, smiled up at her.

TC HANDLED NED LIKE SHE had a terminal illness after he'd found her in the ladies', throwing up. He pressed a cold can of Coke into her hand, pulling back the flip-top for her when her fingers failed to grip it. She no longer held the faxed pages. He must have retrieved them from the floor. Together they climbed the long narrow staircase up to the Detectives office, through the warren towards TC's fishbowl. She could see Zervos at the desk, a dark mass of suits filling the space around him.

Zervos was studying the two faxed faces on TC's desk. She didn't want to go through the doorway, but TC's bulk behind her blocked her retreat.

'So, if that's Mick Kelly, then who's she?' Zervos was saying.

'Mrs Kelly?' A dark suit in the corner, small, wiry, tossed in a hand grenade.

'Hope to fuck it isn't.' Another dark suit, back to the door, tall, leaning over, arms braced on the desk, outline like a giraffe drinking.

'Why?'

The rest of the Homicide troops silently followed the serve and volley of their senior officers. Head down, eyes half-closed, Zervos listened to his two sergeants fielding theories. Under the fluorescent light his sleek, black hair shone. Was he old-school enough for Brylcreem? Ned's mind sought refuge in the banal.

'Cos that'd take us nowhere,' the tall suit argued.

'Why do you say that?'

'Because Mrs Kelly was shot dead with her husband. October

long weekend. Our victims went under the concrete sometime in the week leading up to that weekend. Mind you,' he continued, tapping the woman's picture with his forefinger, 'if this is victim number two, not a bad motive for someone to come after Kelly.'

'Unless the woman shot dead wasn't Mrs Kelly . . .' The small suit came forward to the desk and stabbed at the picture. 'Might explain a bit more about both murders if *this* is Mrs Kelly and —'

'Let's try not to make things more complicated,' Zervos said calmly, adjusting his glasses as he peered at the woman's face. 'Got eyewitnesses to the Kelly murders, remember. This could be our victim. Hard to be sure, she's not looking her best these days. We'll do DNA anyway . . .'

'But it could be —'

'That's *not* my mother.'

Steel rods drove along Ned's limbs, tightening giant screws at the back of her knees. She felt bolted together. Angry at these men in their suits with their suspicious eyes, and most of all at the man with the grin and the curly hair, whose picture was being spat out of the photocopier along with the woman's, to be stapled together by Toyboy.

The tall detective spun around and had the grace to blush. The smaller one just looked at her harder.

Zervos beckoned her in. His action, asserting ownership over who entered TC's fishbowl, turned the bolts further.

'You sure?'

'Of course.'

'It's a bit fuzzy, maybe —'

'It's not her.'

'Take a closer look. That photo's probably old – before you were born, maybe.'

'I know what my mother looked like.'

Zervos fell silent.

'Have you seen this woman before?'

'No.'

'What about the man – you sure it's your father?'

'Yes.'

'Seen that photo before?'

'Yes.' It was out of focus, a melted outline, but it didn't matter. She recognised the little pieces of herself trapped there. Her stomach lurched. She swallowed the Coke, washing down the phlegm that tasted of scotch and bile. She felt them lean in, imagined their breath against her neck, their interest sharp against her skin. Zervos's stare compelled answers.

'Where?'

'My sister has it, in a frame.' All through school, on Linh's bedside table. A second frame beside it – Mum, proud, holding Linh, a bundle of white. 'Bigger, not just the face. This one's been cut down.'

'We'll get it. What do you know about it? When was it taken? Where?'

'It's Linh's, you'll . . .'

Embarrassment brought silence. Zervos's eyes flicked past Ned. She felt TC somewhere behind her, a hand edging her towards a chair.

'I'd rather stand.'

'All right, Detective Kelly, it's been a shock, but we need some answers.' His perfunctory nod to empathy made, Zervos resumed. 'What do you know about that photo?'

'Nothing, really. I think it was taken in Vietnam, but I don't really know. I mean, in the background of Linh's, there's palm trees – I just thought . . .'

'How old is your father in the picture?'

'I don't know.'

'Think – is that how he looks in his wedding photo? In later photos?'

'I – I can't say, I don't know.'

Ned realised that all her photos of her father seemed to be the same. As if he had only ever had one decade of life. He was suspended forever somewhere in his thirties, or was it his forties? He was tall Dad of the long legs, strong arms, deep voice, never growing older. For all his familiarity, he was a stranger. He'd existed for less than a third of her life. That fraction shrank each year.

'We'll look at all the other photos – try and narrow it down.'

Ned realised these asides were not for her. They were for the two dark suits, to take note of, to add to their list of things to do, things to retrieve, items to nominate on warrants. Her back was so rigid, it ached.

'Now, the woman, Detective. Maybe someone you saw as a kid?'

'No.'

'Met, maybe, at a family do?'

'We didn't have —'

'No family dos? No extended family thing?'

'No. My mother's family stayed behind – they died, disappeared, lost. No family, no dos, no get-togethers.'

'What about your dad's family?'

'My aunt was overseas a lot. My grandma and grandpa, I don't remember them. He was in the navy, they retired to Darwin. Then Cyclone Tracy – they were killed.'

'Unlucky mob.' The short suit whispered, not meant for her ears.

'OK. What about in photos, then – have you seen this woman in family photos?'

'No. No. I . . .'

'What?'

She thought about the family albums, those glowing girls, tried to place the face. Zervos's expectation like a wave about to break over her. The three Homicide detectives watched her; from behind she felt TC's hand on her upper arm, pressing gently.

'No – I'm not sure.'

She waited for the next question then understood that Zervos was talking to his troops, ignoring her. The investigation had extracted what it could from her, and was rolling on – without her.

'Check out the car – make, model – should be in the original brief, he died in it.'

'Deak got scrapings under her nails, could be his. It'd put him at the scene if they are.'

The small one turned to Ned, 'Your mum and dad – where are they buried?'

'They . . . why?' Whatever was holding her together was starting to fail, the bolts grew icy, so cold she was shaking from the inside out, shattering the struts holding her up. Her parents had a grave. She'd never visited it. Couldn't give it a name or a place.

'We might need to exhume – check —'

TC spoke. 'They were cremated.'

Zervos glanced at him and nodded. 'OK. We'll need to get comparison samples, then, from both the daughters. Mick Kelly's sister too.'

'Already got Detective Kelly's.' The tall one was looking at a report. 'DAL did her when she took in the exhibits.'

Zervos nodded, absorbing information, processing it and generating actions.

'Photos are key – family albums.' He addressed Ned again. 'Get them together. We'll get a warrant, of course, it'll all be legal. No need for strife with your sister or your aunty down the track.'

A search warrant for her home. Her covert suspicions finally bearing fruit. No sense of vindication, she just felt ill. Her life and Linh's and Mary Margaret's, with all their innocent, pathetic little secrets, to be turned over by the hands of strangers – worse, by the hands of workmates looking for clues to her father's past. The murdered had no right to privacy. Their mysteries were barriers to break down. All the niceties of normal life suspended; where eyes might be averted out of respect, or tact, or kindness, the investigator gazed harder, dug deeper. Remorseless, detached, relentless.

'Neddie.' TC was at her side, arm around her shoulder, guiding her out of the office.

Zervos was still talking, but not to her. Toyboy sidled in from his vantage point in the hall to fill the space she'd vacated, waiting to be tasked like a dog waits for someone to chuck a stick.

'Think she knows who it is?' the wiry one asked Zervos. 'Can't see how she could be so definite about a fuzzy fucking image like that. Could be any-bloody-one, eh?'

TC tightened his grip around her arm, kept her going forward.

'Neddie, Zervos and his mob are just doing their job. No people skills – that's why they work with the dead. There's a million reasons your dad's photo could be there.'

Looking up at TC, his face filled with concern, his mouth filled with kind lies, she felt acceptance settle over her. Peace. After all this time, answers – whatever they were – would be found.

TC led her through the office. It was like the Luna Park house of mirrors. Everywhere she looked her father was smiling back at her, alongside him the sad, faint outline of the woman. They dangled from detectives' hands, and had already been blu-tacked to their whiteboard.

The phones were ringing, the light on hers winking. She ignored both it and her bag. TC swung the leather strap over his shoulder.

'Come on, little buddy. I'm taking you home.'

They'd barely left Bankstown when the pager on Ned's belt began to vibrate. A nervous heart beating against her waist, it felt comforting. Legs curled, eyes closed, rocking with the stop and start and sway, suspended in the capsule of the car.

'Coming up on Strathie. Which bridge?' TC had been silent till then.

'Gladesville,' Ned replied, eyes opening to an intersection choked with traffic. She closed them again, slipping her hands between her knees and burrowing her cheek into the seat back, but her legs grew stiff, her hands cold. She unfolded, gripped the door handle, turned to look at TC.

'How did you know my parents were cremated?'

His throat moved, one swallow, two, then a tilt of the head, away from her, as if ducking the flight of the question.

'I made inquiries.'

'Why? Did you think you might want to look at their bodies?'

His fingers chased each other around the steering wheel. Stopping when he began to speak again, decision made.

'I worked the brief, first time round. In '76. Brand-new detective constable at Homicide, came in at the end, to do the donkey work – chase up loose ends, file running sheets, make sure they were all ticked off, signed off. Put the thing to bed, really. After the Coroner's inquest I remember that the sister – your aunt – made a request for the bodies to be cremated and interred when released. She wasn't around – in Europe somewhere – and the two kids, er, you and Linh, were too young. She had some legal firm deal with it. I was pretty new to Homicide, to the cleaning up. I remember thinking how it all seemed so sad. No funeral, no family.'

The familiar suburbs rolled past, TC running the back streets. Outside was all banality, inside all brutally new.

'And you didn't think to mention any of this?'

'When you came to Bankstown, at first I didn't make the connection, but once I did, well, you never seemed to want it advertised. Didn't think you'd appreciate being reminded of it.'

'But once all this started?' She was twisting in her seat, trying to look him full in the face. He was concentrating on the road. 'You got the brief, never thought to say, "Hey, little buddy – I remember this one"? Didn't think it was worth mentioning?'

'To be honest, I got the brief because I needed to refresh my memory —'

'You're talking to me, TC, not some barrister under cross. Refresh my fuckin' memory . . . jeez.' She balled her fist, struck the dashboard, enjoyed being briefly lost in the concentration of pain. Beat back the urge to do the same to TC.

'It was one unsolved case that I was on the edge of a long time ago. I can remember the details of every person I've ever locked up for murder. I see their faces, their names, everything. Maybe it's just me, but the ones we don't get, well, they kind of fade. Like bad memories.'

They didn't speak for a few kilometres, up the hump of the Gladesville Bridge, staring at sky, then down the other side into the green of the bushland suburbs of the Lane Cove River. Water flashed beneath the elevated roads, expanses of glass from homes buried deep among the gums, flamed in the evening sun. A rowing eight sculled over the dark, still water, their snapping backward rhythm fusing into fluid forward motion. The air-conditioning masked the silence between Ned and TC in an ambient hum.

They pulled up outside View Street. TC held out a plastic folder, the faint-faced woman swam behind the clear cover.

'If this is our victim, Ned, then —'

'If?' Ned sat and stared at it, not wanting to take it from him.

'Nothing's certain yet, but they'll have to be shown, be asked if they recognise her. Your aunt particularly. You want Zervos to do that – cold – tomorrow morning?'

'Why don't you come in, TC, do it yourself right now?'

'Neddie,' he sounded tired and disappointed and hurt. 'I thought you'd want to break it to them. But —'

'Break what? What am I breaking to them? Tell me.'

Silence.

'So, go on, you've got the inside knowledge here – so what do you think, eh? What's my dad's face doing round the neck of a dead woman – no, no, not just a dead woman, a murdered woman? You tell me. Then maybe I can tell them.'

'Neddie, I don't know. It's too soon to say, there could be any number of explanations. If we can ID her then —'

'Any number of explanations – yeah, there could be, couldn't there? But we both know what the real one is, don't we. If this wasn't my dad, what would we be saying right now?'

'Same thing, Neddie.'

'Bullshit. We'd be saying, she's wearing this prick round her neck; she's not his wife, she's not his sister, so who else would have his picture in her locket, eh? A lover, that's who. And who's the most likely suspect to knock off a lover? Who'd want to get rid of the lover of a married man? *He* would. That's what we'd be saying.'

'Maybe, maybe, but we'd also be saying that without any proof it's all just speculation.' The more tightly wound Ned became, the more doggedly TC argued for the defence. 'And we'd also be asking what the hell Dawn Jarrett was doing in the same grave if this was just a domestic.'

Ned took a breath. Her day had begun focused on Dawn Jarrett but she'd been overwhelmed by events. Twelve hours ago the problem exercising her mind was how an Asian woman had wound up dead beside Dawn Jarrett, a woman whose death didn't seem to lack for motives. Now the situation had inverted.

'You going to tell Marcus Jarrett about this?' Ned took the folder, stepped out of the car.

'We'll be re-interviewing witnesses, yeah,' TC said.

'If they don't remember an Asian woman, maybe they'll remember Mick Kelly?'

'Ned . . .'

She leant against the car door and asked the question that had been germinating.

'So, once you refreshed your memory, what did you find in that brief? Who did they think did it? They always have a theory. What was it?'

TC wouldn't look at her. His profile was set.

'Ned, I was the filing clerk – no theory.'

'You were Homicide. What was it?'

TC chewed his lip before darting a look at her face. His answer came on the release of a breath, as if the strain of holding it in was finally too much.

'The war. They reckoned it had something to do with the war. Your dad had been into some clandestine stuff – your mum too. Messy, never could quite get a grip on him, or her, what he did, what she did, just that it was ugly. Then they both get killed – in something that looks like an execution a year after Saigon falls and the boat people start turning up here. Never a shred of proof – our army wasn't helpful, the US Army even less; Vietnam was still a shitfight. But that's it – the theory was that somebody had a score to settle with them both, and did.'

The earth tilted. She steadied herself against the door, the humidity of the evening draped around her. The folder slipped out of her fingers.

'Clandestine?' Mick Kelly had been conscripted, just one in a lottery of unlucky men. 'What's that supposed to mean?'

'Special Ops. He was attached to something the CIA was running.'

'He was conscripted. Since when do —'

'Neddie, he was regular army. A captain. He was in Intelligence. He spent a long time in Vietnam.'

'We – I'd always thought . . .' Voice fluttering, she heard herself, pathetic. A swell of anger towards the dead moved through her. She picked up the folder. The woman gazed through the plastic.

'You need to talk to your aunt, Ned.'

'I need to see the brief.'

TC shook his head. 'Not now. It's not possible. After, maybe —'

'After what?'

'After this is . . . over.'

'Am I suspended?'

'No, of course not, but —'

'Yeah, "but" I can do shitty jobs – like this one.' She slammed the door.

NED TRIED TO RECALL HOW she'd absorbed the knowledge that her father had been one of the young men Australia had conscripted to go 'all the way with LBJ'. She couldn't. The nuns at school had talked in general terms about Vietnam, the war, the men called up and the sadness. MM had rarely mentioned her brother or the military, but when she did it was with heavy sighs about a 'quagmire' and 'having no choice'. Ned realised she'd put these elements together and created a history based on what she'd learnt about Vietnam, rather than on what she actually knew.

Her father and mother had never talked about the army, and they were dead before she was old enough to ask them how they met. They'd appeared eternal, together because that was how it was, that was how it always must have been. There was no time before.

Standing in the driveway looking through the front window, she saw Linh and MM at work in the Shrine, MM supervising the rearrangement of her gallery. They existed in a parallel universe, uncontaminated by the knowledge she held. She would change that reality – change them – in seconds, just by the act of telling. She gripped the folder tighter and climbed the stairs.

'Yes, yes, that's the spot.' MM was directing operations from the depths of a plush, red velvet armchair dripping with gold braid, tassels and embroidery. A piece of the set from a long-ago performance of *La Traviata*, a throne fit for a high-class hooker.

Ned punctured the scene, no greetings. 'What did Dad do in Vietnam, Mary Margaret?'

'Hmm, dear?' MM sounded distracted but her eyes sparkled.

'You always implied he was a low-level nobody, just another conscript. He wasn't though, was he?'

'New, New, New, always questions.' MM shook her head sadly, smiled at Ned as if humouring her niece's whims. 'You have to remember dear, the times. That was not a popular war and the men who came back, well . . . Called "baby-killers", spat on – you learnt about it all at school. At least the conscripts, they had no choice. It was easier on you girls to think that.'

'Nhu.' Linh's voice sounded a warning, the tone taken with a toddler reaching out to a hot stove.

'No, Linh. No more lies. There can't be anymore – it's not just me asking.'

'Oh, you're not the first to have asked, dear. Last time, they'd dug about and found it all out before I got back. But at least I could protect you both.'

Linh turned on Ned. 'What do you mean, not just *you* asking?'

'Don't worry, Linh,' MM soothed. 'You know what she's like. The little detective, never knew a child more suited for her career. So like her father.'

'Shut up.' Ned spun back to her aunt, who was lounging in her ridiculous chair, diamonds and manicured nails glinting, waving questions away like flies.

'So like her father,' MM sighed. 'Like a dog with a bone. Some bones should stay buried, New. No good comes of digging them up, collecting them.'

'Nhu, what's going on?' Linh's face was a white disc. 'What's Dad's army service got to do with anything?'

Ned flipped open the folder. The woman's features floated on the white paper, curiously disconnected from each other.

'Who is she, Mary Margaret? Seen her before? With Dad maybe?' Ned pushed the image forward.

'Really, New . . .'

'Look. Who is she?'

'Nhu . . .' Linh's voice was cracking.

MM took the piece of paper, made a show of examining it, Linh at her side, looking from the image, to Ned, and back again.

'I don't know, dear. Is it your mother? Terrible photo – taken over there, of course, look at the quality. Hard enough trying to tell them apart in a *good* photo.'

Linh anticipated her sister's move, placing herself between them, taking the image from her aunt. She held it in both hands, studying the woman's face, shaking her head.

'This isn't Mum. Who is this?'

Ned took out the second photo – Mick Kelly's smiling face. Held it up like a Wanted poster.

'Her picture and his – in a locket, round the neck of a murdered woman. I want to know who she is – *they* want to know who she is.'

Linh flinched. The scar that ran from her eye to her temple puckered, deepened. She gazed down at the fuzzy photocopy in her hands. 'Who is she?'

'Probably the same woman we dug out of the concrete in Bankstown. I don't know, but I want to – and *they* want to know who she is.'

'They?'

'The police. Homicide Squad. A woman was *murdered*, Linh. Sixteen years ago someone broke her neck, threw her in the ground and covered her with concrete. She was wearing his face round her neck when it happened.'

'Mikey, Mikey, Mikey – what did he bring home with him? Knew it'd be trouble, soon as I heard about it, we all knew, but . . .' MM shook her head. A smile, simultaneously indulgent and sad, dimpled her cheeks. 'Souvenirs, badges, knives, helmets, bullets and bones – war souvenirs. That's all she was, all any of them were. Whores and wars, as my father used to say.'

Ned felt her sister's hand resting on her forearm, restraining.

'She can't help it, Nhu. She's sick.'

'She's not sick.' Ned shook off Linh's hand. 'Is this woman a whore, then? How do you know? Or are all women who look like this whores?'

'Your father was very gallant, very discreet, but really, we all knew. I suppose she was pretty – never did take to that look myself. No definition, no distinctive features —'

'What are you talking about?' Ned shouted at MM.

'Newie, Newie. That's your father's temper, right there. Soldiers, police – violent. Such a violent streak in both of you.'

'This isn't Mum. Who is she?'

'Newie, dear, if you say it's not Ngoc, then I take your word for it. You'll never know my relief when you grew so tall, New – used to dread I'd mix you two up.'

Linh lurched towards her sister, the edge of the picture crumpling in her hand.

'Do the police think it's the same killer? What's going on?'

'Linh, this woman died before Mum and Dad.'

'So, the same person . . .'

Ned didn't want to have to spell it out. She wanted her sister to put it together.

'Why do you think his face is there? A woman was killed, buried on a building site he was overseeing. You think that's a coincidence? They don't.'

'Nhu, what have you done?' Linh's voice had almost disappeared.

'What have *I* done? What do you think I did? Planted his face in some woman's locket just before someone broke her neck sixteen years ago? What did *he* do?'

Linh crumpled the photo into a ball, threw it into the corner of the room and pushed roughly past Ned, who swayed away from her sister's small, sturdy form. The bedroom door slammed shut like a rifle shot.

Ned flinched, eyes screwed shut against the sound, fists clenched,

nails biting into palms to keep the blood-red moon of her memory
at bay. When she opened them again, MM was re-organising her
display of Lalique figurines and the house was silent.

Ned opened her sister's door after a discreet knock and a second,
louder knock had been ignored. Linh was on her cushion, legs
folded under her, toe pads upturned in the fold of her knees. A
wooden rosary turned under the barely discernible movement of
thumb rolling against forefinger. Her eyes were half closed, focused
on the low table in front of her and the text that lay open on it.
Only a few hours earlier, Ned had told Essie Freeman that the past
could change the present and now it had.

'Linh, things are going to happen. I can't stop it – wouldn't, even
if I could.' Ned spoke softly.

'No, no, you wouldn't, would you. You're not interested in
remembering them, loving them, accepting them for what they
were, when we had them.' Linh's voice quivered. 'You just want to
convict them – of something.'

'The truth, Linh. I just want to know the truth.'

'And then what? Gunna set you free, is it? No "thing" is going
to set you free. Truth, lies, him – blondie, whatever his name is . . .'
Linh reached the end of her rosary. The wooden string clattered
onto the table; she cupped her shaky hands in her lap.

'Linh, I don't need your zen crap about freedom and truth
and —'

'You don't know what you need, Nhu, apart from some sick
compulsion to convict your parents of their own murder. What do
you expect's going to happen?'

'I don't expect anything. I just want to know – need to know –
why. When I know that, I'll find out what happens next.'

'And what if you don't? What if there aren't any answers this
time, like the first time? What if there are never any answers?'

'Then I'll know I tried. Anyway, this isn't just about us anymore,

Linh. It's a murder inquiry. That means Homicide Squad, here, tomorrow morning, with a warrant. They can search and take anything to do with Dad. They'll take samples for DNA that may prove she and Dad had a fight, that she scratched him up and now she's dead and he's dead – and maybe that's all we'll know. But it's more than we knew before.' Ned tried to keep her voice low, reasonable, pushing her breath deep into her guts before she let it go. 'Do you know who that woman is, Linh?'

'No.' Linh remained folded on her cushion, hands gripping each other. 'Tell me, Nhu. Did you love them – him? Ever?'

'How can you love someone you never knew?'

'They were your parents – your mother, your father.'

'You love an idea, the idea, of them. I can't. It's not real.'

'Loving your parents isn't something you should have to think about, Nhu. It's natural.'

'It's a fantasy.'

'Listen to yourself. Is this how you're expected to be in the cops?' Linh was on her feet, unable to contain her rage in lotus position. 'Is this all part of "the Job"? Your bloody, fucking job. It's fucked you up, well and truly, it —'

'No, you listen. You don't like my job – fine. You don't have to.'

'No. I don't. I don't like what it does to you. I don't understand, why do you want a job where you spend your life meeting people for the first time on the worst day of their lives? Why? Have you thought about that?'

'Maybe for the same reason you want a job that is as far away from all human life as possible – deep space. Fuck, couldn't get more remote than that, could you? Have you thought about that? Have you?'

They stopped, panting. Took deep breaths, trying to decide just how hurtful they'd got, whether they'd gone over the abyss this time or still just teetered on the brink.

'Linh, is there anything about Mum and Dad, about their death, that you've kept a secret from me? If there is, then tell me now, before it comes out through someone else.'

'Secrets? You ask *me* about secrets?'

'Linh, I just —'

'You don't care about the truth, Nhu. You want revenge – just like you did with Baxter.'

'I wanted justice, Linh. He put you in hospital, he deserved —'

'What, Nhu? What did he deserve? Before you start asking me if I have any secrets, why don't you tell me the truth about what happened to him?'

Ned backed away from her sister. Linh was unrecognisable in her rage.

'I don't know who killed our parents, Nhu – or why. But I do wonder what you'd have in your life if someone hadn't.'

'I knocked, but I don't think anyone heard . . .' Sean Murphy stood in the hallway, a bottle of wine in one hand, car keys and a barbecued chicken in a plastic bag dangling from the other, his face impassive.

THE AIR PARTED OVERHEAD, fruit bats beating a flight path out of the city. Ned led Sean up and down the hills, through the quiet streets of Greenwich. Sean listened, mostly quietly, an occasional question for clarification as they walked side by side. Hand in hand as she stripped off her story. A simple gesture that was more intimate than sex. When he'd arrived she'd wanted to hurtle across the room, like some heroine in a bad romance with a knight fantasy: strong arms, broad chest, world falling away. She'd wanted it so badly she was ashamed.

They reached the end of the point, sat on one of the picnic tables, thigh to thigh. An oil tanker thrummed in Gore Cove like a mechanical cicada.

'What happened up the coast? Didn't think you'd be back for days.'

'Job fell through. Supplier got ripped off. I paged you.'

She remembered the little throbbing heart at her waist as TC drove her home. Sean pulled her closer, warm, solid and real – even if the world didn't fall away.

'What happens now?' he said.

'Zervos turns up with a warrant, takes away anything I give him, pokes around for anything else he wants. Scrapes MM and Linh for DNA.'

'What do they want DNA for?'

'Scrapings under the woman's nails. Reckon she put up a bit of a fight. They can get a profile, see if what's under there matches . . . him.'

'Want someone here?'

She softened against him with weary relief. 'Haven't you got —'

'Don't want to intrude. Just thought, you know, you might . . .'

'I do, but what about work?'

'I'd say Figgy's blown your cover there, don't you think?' He kissed the top of her head. 'But if you're embarrassed, I'll rack off before they show up.'

She tried to cover up her apprehension. 'I meant *your* work – you must have jobs on?'

He smiled. 'I can always come up with a good reason.'

Lies. So easily. Lies for a living. Lies to be with me. She closed her eyes, turned her face into his shoulder to hide the thoughts running through her head.

'Always include kids in a cover story – great reason to break a meeting. Kids sick, wife's frantic, maaaaate. Not many jib at that – don't like it, but they accept it and that's the main thing. Good excuse for never bringing them "home", either.'

They walked back down into View Street. The panel van had been replaced and the low-slung Celica was parked in MM's driveway again.

'I better go make some calls,' Sean said, opening the car door.

'You can use the phone here.'

'Nah, best to keep the number consistent when I call targets.' He plugged a power lead into the cigarette lighter and turned on the ignition as he spoke. A portable phone lay between the front seats, positively svelte compared to the back-breaking brick they hauled around at Bankstown.

'Had anything to eat yet?' he said, punching a number in to the handset.

'No, but I don't really feel like —'

'You know what they say: if you don't eat, you don't shit, and if you don't shit . . .'

'You die.'

She was still smiling at the pathetic joke as he pulled the door shut, his voice slipping seamlessly back to Sam.

'Maaaaate, not going to happen – not tonight. Something's come up.'

With the offer of a chat and a drink, Sean managed to keep MM on the deck after dinner. Their voices carried into MM's bedroom as Ned opened drawers and cupboards, growing hotter than the night warranted. Prying through her aunt's silken knickers for secret, hidden things about her father: letters, photos, anything beyond the old photo albums she'd grown up with. Her embarrassment was matched by anxious anticipation. Zervos could do the same tomorrow, to all of them if he chose.

MM was recounting her roles and lovers, her enemies and triumphs to Sean, who was displaying infinite patience. Old women, old crims, establishing rapport, making it look genuine – that was his job. Same as hers. Interviewing strangers. Engaging in the foreplay preceding a confession: justification, self-serving pity, sometimes pure pain. Maintaining the confection of concern. So much easier with strangers.

A giggle filtered in from the deck where, under Sean's attentive empathy, MM was blossoming.

'A shock – yes, it must have been. Inheriting a ready-made family, just like that, when your art was your life. It must've been —'

'Well, it was a huge disruption. A tragedy, of course, but I mean *me*, suddenly saddled with two young children . . .'

'Two traumatised young children . . .'

'Exactly. They weren't easy to deal with.'

'How did you cope?'

'I had to cancel an audition – Milan – drop everything and head back here. The Maori got it, you know.'

'Dame Kiri?'

'Missing that role, I don't know if my career ever really recovered.

La Scala. I lost seasons – the whole winter season in Europe, the New Year performances – all lost, all great opportunities. And you know, it's true, opportunity knocks and if you're not there, it moves on.'

'Great sacrifices – you've made great sacrifices. Alone, too? No other family to help out?'

'None.'

'You had to deal with the house, sort it all out yourself?'

'Exactly – I mean, it wasn't practical. I wasn't in Sydney very often. It had to be emptied. Sold. I had to buy this place – interview nannies, get the girls into a school that could look after them.'

'And with no one to help.' Sean's tongue clicked in sympathy. 'I guess you got rid of most of Mick and Ngoc's things.'

'Some memories weren't good – aren't good – for the girls, you know. A fresh start, while they were both young enough to make one.' MM's voice was brisk, no trace of Alzheimer's or even woolliness now. 'The psychologists were all giving different advice. So I used my own judgment. Clean slate.'

'So everything got pitched out?'

'What good could possibly come from trying to remember the Vietnam War? Tell me that. It's not as if the girls even have any memory of it. They were born here. There's nothing for them there.'

'Well, it might've made things a little easier now, I guess. But who was to know then, eh?'

If MM picked up on Sean's gentle probe she ignored it.

'A few photos so they know what they looked like, but beyond that? It's bad enough people make these ghastly films about it all, and now, God help me, *musicals.* Can you believe it? *Miss Saigon* – bastardising *Madama Butterfly.* Comparing a geisha with some Saigon slut – really! Movies, TV, books. Who wants to read about that war?'

'Mick never put anything down? That's a shame. What about the memoir?'

Ned's search was finished and fruitless, but she sat quietly on MM's bed, listening as Sean drew more from MM than she and Linh had ever managed.

'I'll have to mention it in my book, of course – but only as back-drop. Tragedy should be understated, I feel.'

'His papers would've been helpful, though.'

'What papers?' she snapped. 'He was a soldier, not a novelist. This is *my* story. It's bad enough having to put such ugliness in it; I have no intention of dwelling on it.'

'No, no, I see. Can't wait to read it. Remember, if you need a proofreader . . .'

MM giggled.

'So he wasn't much of a letter-writer, then – Mick?'

'He knew I wouldn't be interested in reading anything about that dreadful place and that dreadful war. It was everywhere, any-way – on TV every night, front pages of newspapers, magazines.'

'Yes, I remember.'

Ned came out onto the deck. Zervos would no doubt confirm the lack of anything useful for himself in the morning.

'Newie, I thought you'd gone to bed.' MM swivelled around in her seat. 'I thought I'd be entertaining our guest all night myself.'

Ned avoided Sean's eye. To the south, behind the city skyline, sheet lightning backlit massing clouds. Thunder shifted the air pres-sure. Another southerly. Maybe this one would deliver.

'I'd better head off to bed.' MM rose from her seat, draped an arm across Sean's shoulder, leant in to press her cheek to his. 'Well, young man, it's been delightful to talk to someone so compassion-ate and understanding. Nice to see some things haven't changed after all these years. The police were just wonderful back then, too. So considerate, couldn't have done enough to help me.' She ran a finger along his jawline as she straightened. 'Handsome, too. *Plus ça change, plus c'est la même chose.*'

'*Dormez bien, ma belle dame,*' Sean responded.

His fluency reminded Ned again of its origin and the wife and children who were tucked up in another suburb, somewhere by the sea. In the space MM left behind, Ned felt shy with him, this stranger who'd plunged into the centre of her life.

'You look like you need a drink,' Sean said and headed back into the kitchen. He came out with a bottle of Dimple, poured generous measures. Handing one to Ned, he slid a photo album covered with cracked plastic from the stack.

'Come on. You don't want to do this cold tomorrow.'

He was right. So, side by side they sat, turning the pages. She'd looked at them recently but now she scanned each image of her father for clues, for some hint of violence – past, present or possible. Sean was another set of eyes, asking the right questions, looking as carefully as she at the rare photos from Vietnam, none of them showing her father in uniform, just those groups of women, faces hidden by the shade of an umbrella, leaving only their white *ao dai* to dazzle in the sunlight. If the dead woman's face was one of these, it was impossible to say.

The level of the bottle dropped and the ice trays emptied.

'These gaps – your aunt's hoovered out the war. These could be holiday snaps,' Sean said finally, slight sibilance the only evidence of the alcohol. 'Not bad going, considering that's where your dad met your mum. Did you never ask how they met? Weren't you curious?'

Ned thought back.

'It seemed normal – it *was* normal. And then later, well, be like asking how Santa and Mrs Claus got together after you've stopped believing in them. And there wasn't really anyone to ask.'

He propped his chin up with the palm of his hand, eyes sleepy-lidded, a flash of deep blue between his lashes.

'But you've had a suspicion, haven't you, that something wasn't right?'

Ned tipped back her glass, let an ice cube float into her mouth, sucked the whisky from it. Lightning forked down somewhere beyond Balmain, followed by a thump of thunder. She crushed the ice between her teeth.

'It's mainly since I joined the Job. You know how it is. The motive for murder, always something to do with the victim. Guilty or innocent, the trigger's in them somehow. Even if it's just because they're blonde or they remind someone of their mother. Let's face it, people usually get killed by someone they know. Got me wondering, and now . . .'

'You've found your trigger?' He touched the crumpled fax of the woman's face, then reached out and stroked the crook of Ned's arm. 'Did you see who shot them? Did Linh? Could they have been Vietnamese?'

The scotch burned in her mouth. A flash blinded her, thunder rattled the windows and she wrapped her face in her arms, hearing things smashing somewhere, not caring, just wanting to block out the sound.

Then a set of hands were stroking her neck, easing away her forearms, touching her face, pushing her hair back behind her ears, following the shape of her forehead, cheeks, throat; tilting her head, opening her mouth with another mouth, sharing her breath.

'Sorry, Nhu, I'm sorry . . .' His words filled her. 'Come on, you're exhausted. Bed.'

She stood up and swayed, felt the scotch hit home, heard glass crunch underfoot. Her tumbler in slivers, surrounded by a pool of liquid and ice, on the tiled floor. He was on his haunches, sweeping it onto paper, wrapping it, binning it, while she watched from a spinning room.

He steered her to the sink and insisted on water.

'You'll thank me in the morning.'

'You're going to be here in the morning?'

'Said I would. You want me to?'

Did she? In front of TC, Zervos, the suits from Homicide, the inevitable smirks. They were already brief-of-the-week at the UCs. Did it matter anymore?

'Wouldn't blame you if . . .' She halted.

'I'm too drunk to drive. Guess I'll have to sleep in the car.'

She reached for him, wobbled a bit. 'Just thought it mightn't be very discreet?'

He laughed, drained a glass of water and poured her another one.

'You think I care what people think? I don't. Anyway, we have things to do tomorrow, after the circus has passed through.'

'What things?'

They stumbled down the hall, slurring words at each other in total understanding.

'Well, you can't keep working on the case.'

'Well, I, uh . . .' He was a copper; he'd worked it out for himself. 'Nuh, TC's already . . .' She motioned a rocky kick.

'So, we're going to get you a secondment to my playground.'

'We are?'

They'd made it to the bathroom door, where Sean gallantly stepped back to allow her access.

'We are.'

In that moment it seemed the most logical course of action.

'But, Swiss – I really don't like Swiss,' she pointed out.

'Who does?' he said reasonably.

Sean slid into her bed and for an instant she felt awkward, hyper-sensitive to the sound of the springs as he shifted beside her. She'd always been the one to sleep away from home, to slip into a strange bed and out again in the dark or the dawn. But when Sean closed around her, her back curving into his stomach, it didn't feel odd anymore. It felt safe. A bed filled with the warmth of a living being, a heart beating against her back, arms wrapping around her, the storm ripping outside. As the rain began, she fell asleep marvelling how simple acts – holding hands, being held, skin to skin – tendered comfort beyond expression.

The car is dark and cold as she waits. Adrenalin cures her hide into gooseflesh. Fingers wrap and unwrap around metal, the shaft round, thick, roughened to enhance grip. No radio to disturb the night.

Anger, righteous and pure, delivers her here. But now, alone, silent, it cools, leaving a void where anything is possible. Ahead, across the car park, lights blaze from the pub. Cars stopped turning up hours ago. Now, one by one, lights white and red blink into life, wheels turn, the parking bays empty.

She's in a laneway, windscreen framing the scene. The route he'll take – stumble-drunk feet, finding the shortest route home. A good spot: delivery lane between closed shops, large rubbish skips behind her.

When his shape cuts out the light through the pub door, her hands cease kneading. Calm. The observation clinical. He walks past. No recognition, no turn of the head. Self-absorbed, awash in the night.

She opens the car door, lifting the latch, silent, like a mother with a sleeping child on the back seat. Rubbish rot, trapped within the lane, soaks her senses. She leaves her door open, interior light switched off.

He doesn't hear her coming. Light, quick feet.

The first blow is textbook: legal, disabling, across the flesh of the calf. It spins him, doubles him over as instinct sends his hands down to confirm the pain. She's already drawn the baton back, like a tennis player weighing the next shot. It slices down – vicious backhand, lots of spin – but this time finds hands, fingers, shin.

She registers steel on bone; vibrations shudder up to her shoulder. She resumes the ready position, chooses the next stroke. Palms reverberating.

He's howling now, balling up on the ground. She finds his shoulder; her forearm absorbs the impact, his collarbone surrenders to it.

The baton throbs, alive in her grip; her arm tingles, nerves sing. She measures the arc, the back of his cowering head, a round magnet. She steps back, arms across her body. The baton draws back into the ready posture, tucked up behind her left shoulder, poised to swing down. A master-class position – primed but unexecuted.

A scuffle under the skip, a family of rats flee, breaking her trance.

She's back in her car, ignition, no lights till she's a street away, the baton rolling noisily on the back seat, chiming against the seatbelt buckles.

She's crossed Tom Uglys Bridge, is driving past Brighton-Le-Sands, before she remembers Linh. That last sight of her face: bruises, blood, stitches taut and spiky by her eye, skin straining against the black thread.

Tries to rediscover the rage that sent her to the lane.

Tries to conjure up the love she tells herself lies beneath it.

Wonders if Baxter blamed love too.

She's driving under the airport runways, the tunnel neon white, blistering the night, when the void finally begins to fill. Not with anger, satisfaction, justification – just fear. Of herself.

She jolted into consciousness.

'Whass . . . ?' Drowsy, half asleep, half scotch-soaked, Sean stirred beside her.

She was already halfway to the door, didn't want him to feel the clammy skin, the shakes. 'Nothing, go back to sleep.'

Cold water, on her face and in her mouth. Not a nightmare, a memory. One she didn't want to share with Sean. Or anyone. At least in the memory she stopped. In nightmares, she didn't. A wet crack as baton found bone and a skull caved in.

Wrapped in a towel, she went out onto the back deck. The storm had come and gone. She lay on the damp deckchair, eyes wide open to the sky, and waited for the tremors to pass.

The earth rolled beneath her; the stars were in motion, boring away through the blackness. Linh could name them. Scientific names, ancient names, constellations; Linh could draw a map of the sky with her fingertip, hidden figures leaping into being at her touch. She could wind myth and magic and maths into one wondrous vision of the night sky. Ned tried to remember the last time they had lain on their backs and stared up into the night. Certainly not since the night Linh had run for her life from her marriage.

View Street had been Linh's refuge. By coming back Ned had disturbed her sister's sanctuary and illuminated the tension between them. Each time the light caught that fine line that ran from Linh's eye into her temple, Ned felt a chasm yawn within. Even as she recoiled from the memory, her hands burned, just as they had that night. Sometimes, in the second before Linh turned away, Ned had seen the unasked question in her eyes. But she'd never confessed and, until tonight, Linh had never asked. It had just stretched between them, a canyon of unspoken suspicion, reproach and regret.

More than Baxter had been damaged that night. She knew what bone felt like when it crushed and splintered under a blow. She knew the sound it made. Had her father heard those same sounds, felt bone surrender in a shiver that ran along his arm? Had that woman who'd worn his face around her neck once cowered before him, as Baxter had before her?

One strike to her head. A neck snap. Then silence.

Had Mick Kelly loved Ngoc with the same violence that Ned loved Linh – a love that damaged anyone who threatened them?

'**PHOTO ALBUMS ARE ON THE** kitchen table. Can't see her in any of them.'

Ned led the parade up the hallway, hands flicking from side to side.

'My room, my sister's room, bathroom, my aunt's room.'

Zervos followed her, trailing a few yards of Homicide suits in his wake. Mercifully, TC was the only representative from Bankstown. He dropped her car keys on the table and gave her shoulder a squeeze. She marched the entourage into the kitchen where Linh, MM and Sean were arranged like Act 3 Scene 1 of some terrible farce: MM in place at the table, drinking coffee, examining studio portraits of herself in one of the albums; Linh standing, her back to the sink, fingers white-knuckled over the stainless steel; Sean at her side, arms folded, ankles crossed, an image of idle ease except for his eyes, which sliced from Zervos to TC.

Ned heard one of the suits take a sharp breath behind her. A sound that usually accompanied an initial visit to MM's kitchen, with its ceiling-to-floor glass doors, filled with the headlands of Balmain and Birchgrove and the swell of the harbour. After the overnight storm, the bushland glittered in the sunlight.

'Murph?' Zervos's acknowledgment was a question.

'Zorba.' Sean nodded.

The look on Zervos's face said he wasn't fond of nicknames.

'Friend of the family are you, Murph?'

'That a problem?'

'Not unless you get in the way.'

'Of what?' Sean's eyebrows rose.

'An investigation. You know, real police work – probably a bit out of practice on how it's done.'

'I'll look on this as one of life's learning experiences, Zorba.' He picked up his coffee and sat down.

'Can we get started?' Ned asked Zervos, avoiding TC's eye. 'My aunt and my sister would like to get this over with.'

Zervos nodded and one of the Homicide suits came forward, silver forensic case in hand. The process was painless but humiliating; MM seemed not to notice, but Linh wiped her mouth as if to remove the lingering touch of a latex glove.

'If that's all,' Linh mumbled.

'Not quite,' Zervos said, as his sergeants attached themselves, one apiece, to Linh and MM. 'Just a few more questions. Detective Kelly, with me, please.'

Zervos strolled onto the deck, while Linh and MM were led back down the hallway. The murder investigation was momentarily forgotten as Zervos was unmasked as a typical Sydneysider, seduced by real estate with a view.

'See why you live here.' He nodded approvingly.

'I don't, usually.'

'Known him long?' He gestured back to the kitchen where a silent movie played: TC talking to Sean, hands gesturing as Sean sat, sipping his coffee.

'What's that got to do with this?'

'You're a detective; you know everything has to do with everything.' He leant back against the railing and took out the makings of a cigarette. Delicately dropped tobacco into a paper cupped in his hand.

'Yeah, I'm a detective, and I know a good detective never passes up the chance to try and get a brief on someone.'

Zervos laughed, a noiseless movement of his mouth and throat.

'Murph's got more briefs than Bonds, girlie.'

'Well, if that's all.'

Through the glass doors, Sean now leant against the benchtop, TC against the table. Neither gave much away, studiously nonchalant body language. No hand gestures, barely any head movements, till on some signal she couldn't see they both turned and stared out the door, catching her studying them. Their mouths stilled.

'Sit down, Detective, and tell me what's in there. We'll want your dad's stuff – papers, letters, home movies.'

'There's photo albums,' Ned replied, still standing.

'Photos. Right. What else?'

'Nothing.'

Zervos stopped admiring the view and stared at Ned. 'What do you mean?'

'There's photo albums – that's it. No letters, no papers, no —'

'Bit odd, isn't it?'

'What?'

'You didn't keep anything – no little trinkets, knick-knacks, mementos. Why is that?'

'I was seven. I got to keep what other people gave me.'

Ned stared out at a ferry churning past the headland, ripping blue water open into white. She put her hands behind her, clasped them together, blamed the slight shaking on the nip of her hangover.

'What people?' Zervos broke the silence.

'Excuse me?'

'What people decided what you kept, what you didn't?'

Ned imagined MM on her knees, sweating over a cardboard box, folding Mick and Ngoc's clothes for Vinnies. She smiled. Absurd.

'Better ask my aunt. She did it – or organised to have it done, more likely.'

Zervos stubbed out his cigarette in the dirt of the closest pot plant, swearing as a bougainvillea thorn punctured his wrist. He sucked at the blood.

'What do you remember about him – your dad?'

'Patches, glimpses. Days at the beach, holidays.'

'In Asia?'

'Greenmount.'

'Liked the beach, eh?'

Ned squinted into the sun. The harbour at high tide bellied up at the old sea walls and crooked wharves of The Rocks. She remembered beach and sand and surf and her father. There must have been long, dull winter days, but they were lost.

'Ever hear him talk about moving there?'

'Where?'

'The beach.'

The look on her face answered his question.

'Never told you he'd put a deposit on a house? Going to move you all out of Bankstown and over to Curl Curl?'

'What?'

'Yeah. Bit of a step up, eh? From Banky to the northern beaches. He was renovating a house there. Never said a word about it?'

Ned shook her head, feeling in one blinding instant both the longing for and loss of another life, one she'd had no knowledge of. The life of a family who lived by the sea. She gave in and sat down.

'Perhaps your sister remembers more?' Zervos swamped the smell of the ocean with another cigarette. 'Your aunt?'

'My sister's younger than me and my aunt's senile. Go for your life,' she snarled.

'They ever talk about the war much? Your dad, your mum?'

'Not to me.'

'How about their friends? Remember them entertaining many Asians?'

'They didn't entertain much.'

'Pretty odd when you think about it.'

'I didn't think about it, I was a kid.'

'You're not a kid now, you're a detective. So what do you think about it?'

Ned thought her parents sounded cut-off, like people keeping a deliberately low profile. People hiding something, or from something – from someone. They sounded suspicious.

Antagonised, she didn't want to give Zervos the satisfaction of her agreement. She shrugged her shoulders again. 'I think a seven-year-old's memory is unreliable. Wouldn't make too much of it.'

'You're right. Only, the neighbours interviewed back then, when it happened, they noticed the same thing.'

'Wouldn't know, haven't seen the brief.' Skin icy despite the sun.

'Thought he might've shown you?' Zervos spoke in smoky puffs. Not bothering to indicate who. They both knew he meant TC and they both knew that even if TC had shown her, she wouldn't have told Zervos. They sat, watching the harbour busy itself at their feet, while the inspector rolled and smoked another cigarette.

Ned and TC stood on the footpath as the convoy drove off down the narrow Greenwich streets, photo albums and samples of spit safely stowed alongside the suits. Further down the street Figgy sat in a Bankstown car, sunnies on, not looking their way.

TC seemed to chew his next words. 'Murph says you're thinking about going to the UCs.'

TC lacked a hard-man face. His way was to befriend and beguile. Now he looked disappointed, faintly hurt, like he did when a crook lied to him. He stared back up the driveway where Sean sat in his car, the engine ticking over, talking on the car phone.

'Jeez, Neddie, you said you didn't think it was for you – the UCs? Don't rush into anything, OK? This won't last forever.'

'TC, after this, what's it going to be like back there? The cop whose dad was a killer? The local rag alone —'

'We don't know that, Ned.'

She tried to breathe out the tightness in her throat, but it came out as a sob instead.

Arms wrapped her up – fleshy, soft – a shoulder, TC's voice. 'It's OK, no rules against crying.'

Frustration, bitterness, shame, humiliation: numberless emotions, beyond comfort. Unable to pinpoint which one hurt the most, anger underpinning them all. Anger at Mick Kelly and whatever he'd done that had left four people dead.

'I'm sorry, your shirt,' she snuffled, trying to clean herself up, fingers slick, turning her head. Both of them backing away from the unexpected intimacy.

'Thought Zorba was playing bad cop, TC?' Sean stood behind them, packet of wipes at the ready.

'You came prepared.' Ned grabbed one and mopped her face.

'Live in a car, you lay in supplies,' Sean said. 'Glamorous world, the UCs, lots of surveillance along with the fun stuff.'

'Fun stuff? Talking shit to shitheads all night,' TC said, sponging his shirt.

'Good chance to get away from all this, slip into another skin. We take good care of our own there.'

'I'd end up shooting Swiss,' she said.

Sean nodded in agreement. 'Wouldn't be the first.'

Police were just an overgrown, inbred family. They absorbed you, then immediately split you up, pitted uniform against plain-clothes, city against country, coast against bush. Each layer you penetrated only revealed more cliques. Closed doors and whispered conversations were the bait, luring you to push for entry, become a detective. But plain-clothes concealed an even denser mosaic of interlocking groups: suburban Ds and specialists, suit-wearing Ds who chased white-collar criminals, and grungy, shifty, squadie Ds. Stick-ups, Breakers, Vice – named after those they pursued, they often grew to look more and more like their quarries. Then, hidden down a dark alley, unknown and unrecognised by most, were the UCs.

'Well, no need to rush into anything,' TC said. 'Think it over on the weekend. We'll talk about it on Monday before court.'

'Monday?' The week was losing shape.

'Dodgy Brothers' committal,' he said, opening his car.

'Shit. I haven't warned —'

'It's OK, I'll contact the witnesses.'

The wheels ground on regardless. Even a pair of incompetent car thieves caught waxing the evidence – a hot car – in their own back-yard deserved their day in court. Her life might have been up-ended but that wouldn't excuse her from a day of gathering witnesses and waiting to give evidence. That's what professionals did. That was what the Job demanded.

Sean slipped his arm around Ned as they watched TC drive away. He grimaced at the sound of his pager, hugging her in a hard, sudden movement.

'I've got to go,' he said, reading the message. 'Tag along, if you want? Come out and have a look at —'

'No.'

'Tag along' had done it. She wasn't turning up there as a tourist. Once he'd gone, she looked.

Her bedroom was as she'd left it – a little neater than usual, in anticipation of visitors. Then she saw the perfume bottles on her dresser, not quite where she'd left them, one lying on its side. Often happened when the bottom drawer stuck and she had to give it an extra-hard tug.

Which one of Zervos's sergeants had it been? The tall one who'd had the grace to blush, or the little one with the granite stare?

The corner of her left eye twitched, a pulse throbbing at her temple that her fingers couldn't smooth out.

FOR AN EMPTY HOUSE, View Street was remarkably noisy. After Ned had washed up the coffee cups, she gradually became aware of how the refrigerator engine would hum, then click, then shudder into a silence that exposed the sound of the electric clock. The second hand ticked forward in a series of audible shudders. She'd go mad listening to the day measured out like this.

Ned felt adrift. No job to hide in. No inquiry to lose herself in. Amazing how habituated to uncertainty she'd become; now, faced with confirmation of her suspicions, she was at a loss.

Sitting quietly on the back deck she watched the harbour going about its business and tried to think professionally about what had happened. There were any number of reasons that Dawn Jarrett may have been murdered, but she could think of none that related to her father. In what way could Dawn Jarrett and Mick Kelly have come in contact? The only connection was the grave Dawn had ended up in – the fact that it was on a building site her father was managing.

In the brutal parlance of criminal investigation, this gave him means, opportunity. But it still didn't answer motive.

Dawn had not been alone at her burial; it was the other woman who had dragged Mick Kelly right down into the concrete with them.

Then she was on her feet, pacing through the empty house, picking up her running shoes then casting them aside, searching for a swimming costume, turning over the question: who the fuck was this man?

Mick Kelly: career soldier, a background in dirty ops, murdered days after these women. Her father. A professional. Like her.

In the end it was simple. All it had required was the decision to do it. Bereft of her tools, the highly trained investigator turned her skills to the phone book and the number for Defence Headquarters in Sydney. A few transfers later she was talking to Second Lieutenant Chalmers, who was tasked to provide army records to curious family members – people just like her. If like most families she wanted the documents prettied up – something suitable for framing – it would take a few weeks. Ned assured the soldier she didn't need that. What she expected to discover were facts much uglier than any formatting could hide.

Ned left Linh a note. That was an act unusual enough in itself, but she guessed Linh would find her promise to return early, her desire to talk, even stranger.

Army bureaucracy lived in a tall building near Hyde Park, not far from the Sydney Police Centre. In the reception areas the mix of civilian and uniforms was pretty even. Young men and a few women waited for recruitment interviews, folders and numbered tickets in hand, surreptitiously eyeing the posters on the walls.

Ned recognised what the posters were selling. Adrenalin rush. Eyes wide, mouths open, hands clasped round weapons – movement and exhilaration. She felt it herself in the rush of lights with sirens blazing, flying through the traffic, near misses quickening the heartbeat. Leaving the mundane behind, bolting headfirst into something risky. Had her dad been seduced by this? Had she?

But they were faked, like all good advertising. Real war was that ramshackle convoy of Iraqi soldiers, last year's news. Incinerated from on high, along with their plunder on the road out of Kuwait: twisted tanks and cars, buses and oil tankers, charcoaled figures fused to the metal, stretching for miles through the desert. Real war packaged an entirely different message.

Second Lieutenant Chalmers was proof that some things had changed since her dad's army days. Chalmers was a woman, not much older than herself. Crisp and starched in khaki, razor-blade creases, hair shellacked back into a bun. Even without looking, Ned knew that the shoes would be spit-polished to perfection. If there were any slovenly grubs in the army, then they weren't on parade in places like this. Ned had failed spit-polishing – quite spectacularly – at the Police Academy. She'd ended up cheating, going for a paint-on product that dried shiny as glass. It ate shoe leather, but she didn't care; it had got her through the few months when such things mattered. She hadn't spat on a shoe since.

On Chalmers' desk lay a pile of computer sheets, folded along the perforation marks, small print in faint blue ink, track holes punched along their sides like lace. They looked like the criminal records and crime reports she got at work. The soldier was taking a final look, as if reluctant to give up custody now the moment had arrived.

'Is there a problem?'

'No.' Chalmers sounded doubtful. 'It's just, this record has been accessed lately. But then, I suppose you . . .'

Ned had used her police badge as proof of identity. Chalmers would know that, just as she'd know about the requests from Homicide.

'Yes, I know. I'm here as his daughter. Our family, they – we – weren't told too much about his service. My sister and I, we'd like to know for ourselves.'

Chalmers slid the printout into an envelope and handed it across the desk.

'He was caught up in Tet, your dad. It would've been pretty bad.'

Tet. Vietnamese Lunar New Year. Working at Bankstown had

taught her that much. It rang bells from school history as well. The word 'Offensive' was usually tagged after it.

'I guess it was all pretty bad, for everyone.'

'Worse for some. His record says he was listed as MIA behind enemy lines in Hué. Wounded too. That's his last service entry before he was discharged on medical grounds. Survived the siege of Hué . . . bit of a hero, eh?' A soldier's admiration coloured her voice.

That mark on his shoulder, where the freckled skin rippled white like whipped cream. He'd said a shark bit him when he was a little boy because he'd gone out too deep without his father. A tale told to make sure his daughters didn't slip off into the surf without him.

'Did you know he'd been wounded?'

Linh shook her head. They sat on the deck, backs to the western sun, Linh wary as Ned's finger ran down the computer printout. Sharing what she'd extracted from the report with her sister. It hadn't been easy but the shape of their father's progress from officer cadet to his discharge as a captain was there. Much of it was unintelligible; numbers and letters representing divisions, regiments, battalions. Another language, as Chalmers had warned. But their father had had a facility for languages; he'd come to the army with a degree from Sydney University. He'd studied humanities – the classics, languages.

Then he'd gone to Duntroon and done a second degree – in war.

One entry before Vietnam stuck out, because it was written in sentences and few acronyms. He'd spent most of 1963 and some of 1964 in France, at a place called Saint-Cyr. He'd studied languages, strategic operations, society and culture of Indochina, intelligence gathering and psychological warfare. His Vietnam service was an alphabet soup – MACV, JUSPAO, AATTV, CSD. In fact, if Second Lieutenant Chalmers hadn't told Ned about the Tet Offensive and Hué and his wounding, she would never have translated it.

Linh read and listened but had little to say. She shook her head when Ned suggested more research.

'I know what I remember about him, Nhu. That's enough.' She walked down the hallway to her room, closing the door quietly behind her.

Ned felt the tug of curiosity like the pull of an undertow around her legs and knew that for her, it wasn't enough.

BY MONDAY IT WAS A RELIEF to have a real reason to leave Greenwich, even if that reason was a day in court. Ned avoided the highways and freeways, preferring the suburban routes, criss-crossing the main roads that funnelled into Sydney, passing through suburbs with names that no longer matched their appearances; Haberfield, Ashfield and Belfield had little left in the way of fields, and Green-acre was now acres of red-tiled roofs. The wide brown land was in reality densely urban and tightly braided with traffic-choked roads.

She sat at the Frederick Street lights, waiting to cross Parramatta Road. A parade of heavy vehicles headed out of town: car carriers, semis dragging sea containers, refrigerated transports bound for the supermarkets of commuter suburbs and the rural regions beyond. But while the population centre of Sydney may have been shifting west, the early traffic snarls still reflected the city's old truths: the harbour was a magnet to money, and where money flowed, jobs followed. A numbing procession of cars poured from the distant suburbs towards town, driver after driver sat upright and alone at the wheel, windows up, locked into their own soundtrack, just like her. She gave Salif Keita a bit more volume.

Without consciously deciding, she swung off Stacey Street into the building site. Police tape still hung from the chain-wire fences, tattered streamers of blue and white, rouged by dust. The gates were open, though the earth-moving machines were still inert. A utility was parked in front of the demountable site office, but there was no sign of the workers. She was out of the car before she saw the pile of rags and rubbish, lying by the open ground of the crime scene.

'Mabo, you shouldn't be here.'

He shook himself awake. Dew had settled on him, amplifying the stink of his clothing. Summer or winter, the same heavy coat. The mark of the homeless: never wearing what the weather required, obliged instead to wear their wardrobe.

'Sad place this, sis. Sad place.'

'Yeah. It's a bad place, Mabo. No place to hang around. Construction'll be starting again soon.'

'Can't start – haven't finished.' He was getting to his feet, stumbling and swaying.

'They've finished, Mabo. It's all over.'

And it was. Police tape was resilient. Probably hang there until someone pulled it, or the fence, down. All the activity, the science and expertise had packed up and moved on. The work still went on. Out of sight. At Lidcombe, Ben and his colleagues would be reducing the dirt, concrete, bone, blood, hair and fibre extracted from the vast space here to samples and smears on glass slides.

'Can't finish. Haven't found 'em.'

'They did, Mabo. They found 'em, they found Dawn and . . .' And who? My dad's lover? She rummaged in her bag and came up with a five-dollar note. 'Why don't you go get some brekkie, eh? Get away from here, mate.'

'No, no.' He shook his head and pushed her hand away, gently. 'Something to tell you, sis. Sad place. Sad. My people. All my people. All bones. All dead. All gone. But still here – here in this sad place. Not gone. Not yet.'

Ned felt a lick of annoyance, her generosity spurned. Guilt, too, knowing her offer was motivated equally by wanting Mabo to shove off as well as hoping to soothe her conscience. Instead she was left feeling foolish, money in hand and an old warb still rambling on.

'Yeah, Mabo. It's a sad old world.'

'They still here – my people, our people.'

'Too right. Still standing, eh?'

Then he took her arm and turned with her, his other hand outstretched before them, tracing a circle through space as they slowly rotated. Ned saw concrete and brick and dirt churned together, three Hills hoists standing like strange, symmetrical metal trees still rooted in a concrete slab and, along the back fence, a large-barrelled gum, branches reaching out in all directions, blue sky filling the spaces between limb and leaf.

'Not finished. Dig. Dig more – you find 'em. He told me. He told her. Now I'm telling you: that mob, that old mob, they still here, sis. You find 'em.'

'Mabo. What are you talking about? Who told you? What —'

'Bill.'

The roar of traffic dimmed as the connections came back to her. 'Bill who?' Professional, don't lead the witness.

'Bill, Bill Jarrett, he told me.'

Dawn Jarrett's brother. Marcus Jarrett's uncle. Bill, the big-noter. Bill, the dead witness. Ned swallowed, throat dry, assessing Mabo afresh. He looked and smelt like a warb but, focusing his egg-yolk eyes on her, he was a man with a memory and a need to share it.

'Tell me about Bill, Mabo.'

'Bill had tough times. Was gunna turn it round here. Got a good job building this place. No worries. Reckoned he'd work, just use a bit, weekends.'

'Use what?'

'Smack. One big love in his life, that shit. Loved his sister, her little boy, but smack, it got him, in Nam. Got called up, got hooked.'

'What happened here? What did Bill want to tell Dawn about?'

'One arvo, I seen him at the pub, he's all het up. I did the garbo run them days, mornings on the truck, arvos in the pub.' Mabo's eyes glistened.

Must seem like glory days. Drinking as a social activity, not an anaesthetic applied in the gutter.

'Bill bounces in, says he's found something, on the site, something important.'

'What?' Ned asked. 'What did he find?'

'Brothers. Sisters,' Mabo said proudly, his chin rising.

'I don't understand.'

'My brothers, my sisters, my fathers, my mothers, my grandfathers, my grandmothers . . .' Mabo chanted a litany, his voice rising against the sound of a semi slowing to take the corner, tumbling down through the gears.

'But those bastards. Coppers said animals. Animals! But Bill knew, he knew. Told the boss too. And the boss – that Kelly bloke, he was a soldier – he knew, he says he'll look after it, be patient, just wait. But Bill, he couldn't wait. Says Kelly's taking too long – too busy, got something else on his mind. So he tells Dawn. Then Kelly's dead. Bill can't find Dawn, can't talk to Kelly, so he buggers off. Next time I see him, needle's got him something fierce, making no sense no more. Then one day, he takes enough, and . . .'

Up close, Ned could see how ravaged Mabo was. A different life would have produced a fit, healthy man with a future ahead of him. Instead, here was a man with a caved-in face, spaces between blackened teeth, and a scrawny neck that hinted at the undernourished body hidden beneath his coat. Her witness.

'What did Bill find, Mabo?'

A hand, fingers cracked, nails split and crusted in dirt, took her hand and pressed it to his chest; his yellowing eyes held hers.

'My people. Bones.' He began to stamp his feet, shifting his weight slowly, carefully, from side to side. One foot lifted up then stamped down. Then the other. Over and over. Dust rising and settling over his filthy runners. 'My people. Still here. Not finished. Still here, still here.'

NED WALKED PAST THE POLICE station and made straight for the courthouse. Mabo's claim rattled within her. She assessed her options.

Inspector Zervos, an informant claims there are more bodies on the site. Swiftly rejected.

TC, Mabo reckons there are more bones on the site. She saw TC's face as he repeated the name.

She ducked into the court police room, empty this early, phones all free. Marcus Jarrett listened to her without interruption, thanked her for the information then hung up. Buzzing phone in hand, Ned felt shamed and needy.

Bright sunlight lit the little patch of park in front of the court – scrabbling gums, a few benches, a war memorial with the names of Those Too Young to Die but had anyway. A standard suburban scene, only this one was occupied by a very particular cast and audience. Just before 10 a.m. the numbers swelled to the point where it was difficult to imagine how they would all be dealt with before 4 p.m., with time off for morning tea and lunch. There always seemed to be more people than any court could consume in a day.

The Dodgy Brothers were a pointless waste of both her time and the court's; Ned's irritation grew as the morning passed. The Job made demands. Court was just one of them. But today, with Mabo's words fresh in her mind, his warb stink still lingering in her nostrils, she decided 'court' was spelt wrong; should've been 'caught'. Summed it up better, described it from all sides. The guilty, the innocent, the bystanders, they were all trapped in amber, nothing to do but wait, worry, feel the bowels flex and turn in on themselves. Ned walked, up and down the corridors, out the front, around the gums, back up the stairs, rehearsing, not the case, not her evidence, but what she'd say to TC when she finally escaped.

From outside a brief, the activity of the Ds office seemed to move at a different pace. Ned saw her office with the eyes of a stranger. Toy was wedged between a phone in one ear and a suit from Homicide in the other. He nodded at Ned, briefest eye contact, then sought sanctuary with the speaker in the suit. Zervos was installed in TC's office, coat slung proprietarily over the back of the chair. TC sitting opposite made the room look the wrong shape. The wall of bodies lining the fishbowl, shoulders pressed one to the other, backs pressed against the glass, impeded their view of her.

'Well, it'd explain a bit – not everything, but a bit.' She heard Zervos as she drew near.

'Like supposedly not recognising her.' The short sergeant's voice.

'Nah, she was just a kid. Mate, you see more conspiracies than ICAC.'

'Ya reckon? How far would you go for your dad, then?'

'Boss . . .' A warning from one of the more sharp-eyed suits. Heads snapped her way.

TC was on his feet and at the door. 'Court done?'

'Never got started. Dodgy the Younger in hospital – whiplash.'

TC suggested lunch, all but pushing her ahead of him.

The whiteboards and Missing Persons posters were gone from the meal room. The investigation was contracting back into the detectives' office. Eventually, it would shrink all the way to the Homicide Squad office, leaving Bankstown to its diet of robbery, rape and reckless driving.

TC was attentive. After the tension of their last meetings he didn't give her a chance to ask questions, talking as they walked, all the way across the railway station, down South Terrace and into Uncle Pho's. He asked about Linh, about MM, about the Dodgy Brothers, but didn't say one word about what Zervos had been saying. Asking him would be pointless. TC was a professional and she wanted him to know she was one, too. So, she let him go on, pointing out all the reasons against joining the UCs and waited until they were sitting over their bowls of pho, inhaling the sweet scents of star-anise and cinnamon from the searing hot broth, before she began what she'd spent the morning rehearsing.

'Went past the building site this morning. All finished up, eh?'

'Yup,' TC slurped.

'Got everything or was it an overtime decision?'

'Two bodies, a shitload of bibs and bobs – be working that lot in the labs till next Christmas.' A noodle flipped him on the nose as he sucked it in, a drop of hot broth sparking his eye. 'Shit.' He scrabbled for his napkin and dabbed.

Behind him Ned saw Uncle Pho shaking his head. Disgust or pity, she wasn't sure. The restaurateur was seated, as always, at the cash register, from where he could lean into the kitchen and yell the orders to whichever of his family members were working the pots and woks that day. He never moved from his seat; she'd been dining there a year before she realised he had no legs beyond his thighs. He smiled politely but without enthusiasm when her workmates dropped the handcuffs. Just as he had never corrected their mangled pronunciation of his product, rhyming *pho* with *ho*. Ned only realised when she heard the Vietnamese diners ordering *fer*. But like Uncle Pho she maintained a fake smile when her workmates did it. Uncle Pho caught her looking at him; she turned back to TC.

'Saw Mabo down there.'

'He better not haunt that place once the car park goes in,' TC responded. 'He'll be . . .' He smacked the tabletop with the flat of his hand.

'He reckons there's more there.'

'Huh?' TC stopped busying himself with his eye and looked at her. 'More what?'

'Bodies.'

'Jeez, Neddie. You had me going there for a bit.'

'I'm serious.'

'What bodies? Been a serial killer out here, or what? I think we'd have noticed.'

'Aboriginal bodies. Bones. Old ones. Says a bloke who worked for, for my dad . . .' The words still choked her. 'This bloke saw them, back in '76, reckons he told Dad about them.'

TC captured a large piece of beef, rolled a wad of noodles around it with his chopsticks, then delivered the lot into his mouth. He chewed and looked steadily at Ned, one eye glowing like the Terminator.

'Say he saw anything himself?' he asked through his food.

'Nope. Says Bill Jarrett told him – that's Bill Jarrett as in Dawn Jarrett's brother. Says Bill told Dawn about it as well.'

TC continued to chew and then assembled another load. 'Nice touch – dead man told him, and not just any dead man but the dead woman's brother,' he finally said. 'What's he trying on? Land claim? Trying to live up to his name?'

'Could be true,' Ned replied.

'Could be a load of cods, too.'

'Might explain why Dawn was there?'

'But not why . . . the other woman was.'

Ned noticed the pause.

'Black Charlie know who your dad was?'

'I don't know. I mean, I haven't told him. He calls me sis.'

'Well, you're not – you're a cop, and for the time being you're still my cop,' TC said before he started listing objections, tapping his chopsticks against his fingers as he numbered them. 'Black Charlie's a warb, spends his days and nights drunk or passed out. Whatever he's got up there between his ears is pickled, has been for years. This isn't even hearsay, it's . . . it's *pissed*-say. That site's been combed by professional bloody combers; if there was anything else there they'd have found it. They moved a couple of ton of earth and sifted it good and fine. If anything pops up out at the labs then maybe – just maybe – there'd be a reason to go back and dig, but not on the say-so of an old alky.'

'But he's a witness. He knew Bill Jarrett. Essie Freeman says Bill had something important to tell Dawn. Last time she saw Dawn alive, Bill was about to tell her something – and if that something was about Aboriginal bones then that would involve the Metropolitan Land Council, and that means Phil Walker.' Ned sat back, satisfied she'd joined all the dots.

'Look, he's a witness, needs interviewing – I grant you that. But that's all.'

'So, I put in a running sheet and —'

'No.'

Ned sat back, thin pools of fat forming as the broth in her bowl cooled.

'Sorry, Ned. You can't be on the record on this anymore.'

She understood. He didn't need to spell it. ICAC, IA, IPSU, any combination of initials responsible for police integrity would demand she had nothing to do with this case.

'I'll see if Toy can —'

'Toy?'

'All right, I'll do it. Black Charlie's like a bloody hotel guest in the cells.'

'Not since Morgenstrom read Ugly the riot act,' Ned said.

Patrol Commander Morgenstrom had never had a death in custody under his watch and he planned to keep that record. Collecting the records for a death in custody that predated him was as close to the grinding wheels of a Royal Commission as Morgenstrom ever wanted to get. He'd let his troops know that the last thing he needed in his cells was a dead 'Indigenous local identity'. So the troops had

had to think up other ways of dealing with Mabo: driving him into another patrol, parking him under a tree or outside the Sallies or the Wesleys – they were pretty ecumenical on that count.

'I'll make you a deal. Hang off deciding about the UCs until I talk to him, OK?' TC pulled a note from his wallet to cover both meals, dropping it in front of Uncle Pho and waving Ned's hand away.

'I'll go and find him, bring him up —'

'I'll find him, Ned.'

They stood in front of the restaurant, its glass windows covered with images of soup and signs written in short words with flourishes over most of the letters.

'And until then, what am I meant to do? Come in and answer phones? Do the filing? Buy the coffees?'

'Neddie, take some time off. Do a bit of research. Go find out about your dad – for yourself, not for the brief.'

He pressed something into her hand. It was a card with a name on it: *John Simpson (Brig. Ret.), President, Queenscliff Surf Life Saving Club.* There was a phone number and an address on the northern beaches.

'*Brig. Ret.* What kind of wanker —'

But TC wasn't listening. He was staring over her shoulder, up the terrace. Ned turned and saw Zervos walking towards them, black hair glossy in the sunlight. He nodded to TC, not hello or an acknowledgment, more like the nod that unleashes a round of artillery.

'Neddie, there's been a development,' TC said, ushering her towards one of the picnic tables dotted along the terrace.

A group of elderly women glared as they joined them, then continued to speak in the rapid-fire language of their birth. Ned and TC sat down, backs against the table. Zervos stood, staring at her. It was feeling like an ambush.

'We've had a result on the second woman's prints,' TC continued.

This ranked as good news, so why was TC treating her like she was about to break? She felt trapped. TC at her side, Zervos in front, the old women at her back; their chatter intensified in the silence that followed.

'Well, who is she?' Ned finally asked.

'Nguyen Thi Phuong,' Zervos said. 'Ring any bells?'

'No.' Ned's scalp prickled. 'Why? Should it?'

'How about Cassandra – Cassie? She had a few names.' Zervos blew the names out in puffs of smoke. 'Kiều, Tiger Lady, or maybe you just remember her as Aunty?'

'What's he talking about?' Ned turned on TC. Certain now, he'd brought her here, had been keeping her occupied while he waited for Zervos.

'The Americans. They came up with a match on the prints,' he said. 'Those scars on her . . .'

'Your dad's name made the link,' Zervos said, moving in closer, one foot up on the bench beside Ned's thigh, arm resting across his knee. 'They dug out a file on Captain Mick Kelly from his time in Intelligence in Hué. Nguyen Phuong's name and prints were right there on the first page.'

Zervos's eyes transfixed her: dark brown, iris and pupil indistinguishable.

'Picture of her, too,' he continued. 'She's a few years older than in our photo, bit knocked about but —'

'Neddie, she's family.' TC spoke, drawing her gaze back to him. 'She's your mother's sister.'

Her questions, when they came, felt endless and humiliating. How unlike a 'family' her family had been – was now. The ultimate shame, having Zervos tell her about them. To be exposed as never having made any effort to find out.

'Probably in the first wave of boats, though I wouldn't put it past her to have slipped in earlier, undercover.' Zervos cleared some phlegm and spat. 'Sure you don't remember Mum and Dad ever talking about good old Aunty Phuong, or Aunty Cassie, or any other aunties and uncles from the old country?'

'No, never.'

'Sure about that? Like you've said, you were just a kid.'

'I . . . no. Never.' All she had was an absence of family, no aunties, no uncles. She clung to it.

'How about old Grandpa Nguyen? Your mum ever talk about her dad?'

'No. There was no one left,' she said. 'The war – they all died.'

'This one didn't,' Zervos corrected her. 'At least not in the war.'

Ned looked across at TC. He was staring at his hands, hanging big and useless between his knees.

'Those skin samples under her fingernails . . .' Zervos didn't finish.

Didn't have to. From somewhere in that family brew they'd be looking for the scientific proof that Nguyen Phuong had gone to her death clawing at Mick Kelly.

'THEY THINK HE MURDERED HIS own wife's sister? A refugee? A woman who'd been tortured by God-knows-who and came here, to escape, to be safe, to be with her family?'

Linh's right foot tapped the timber floor. A rapid, staccato beat. The bronze images of multi-armed, many-headed idols – some dancing, some locked in carnal conflict – gathered like witnesses in Linh's bedroom.

'If she came here to be with her family, then we'd remember her. Do you remember her, Linh? I don't.'

Linh's fingers jumped, grabbing at themselves. The tic, the active fingers – it was like the worst days of her marriage.

Ned knew she should just let it rest. Leave Linh in ignorance if it meant leaving her in peace. But she couldn't.

'Linh, she had his photo round her neck. Then she turns up —'

'So he kills her and then while he's at it he kills another woman because . . . why is that again? Oh, right – we don't know why. He must've just decided to start killing women one day. If this is the kind of logic you cops use, no wonder you end up having to verbal people.'

Ned flinched. 'Then come and speak to this guy with me, this brigadier. He knew Dad. Worked with him over there.'

'You can't stop playing detective, can you? They've sent you on leave, Nhu. They want you out of the way. But you can't let them convict your father on their own, can you?'

'I just want to know the truth. I want to know who he was.'

'He was my dad. That's who he was. He was your dad. He loved us.'

'Linh, you have to be prepared. Stuff's going to come up. Maybe he was having an affair with this woman; why else would she have his photo?'

Linh picked up her car keys, crunched them in her hand and went to the door. She didn't turn around but her words carried.

'I can't take this anymore. I've been offered a job working on the Very Large Array. I'm going to say yes. It's in New Mexico.'

Linh didn't slam the door behind her, didn't even bother to close it. They'd finally tumbled over that edge they'd teetered on for so long. Free fall now.

The overpriced shops along Military Road drifted by as Ned thought of all the things she could have said better and the things she shouldn't have said at all. Traffic was stationary at The Spit. The tip of a yacht's mast glided between the open jaws of the bridge. Seaforth rose steeply on the northern side, homes hanging from its slopes – sandstone originals and glass-and-concrete modernist – all with Sydney-dollar views of harbour, boats and beach. Ned uncurled her grip from the steering wheel and flexed her fingers, trying to pump blood back through them.

The brigadier's bungalow was high on a hill at Queenscliff, looking back down the golden stretch of sand that ran south all the way to Manly. She parked and got out of the car, stood for a moment watching the black shapes of surfers, then turned and looked north. Beyond the headlands of Queenscliff Bay and Freshwater Reserve lay Curl Curl, the place that could have been her home. Further north again were the sands of Dee Why, Collaroy and Narrabeen. Sean Murphy had grown up here, surfing these beaches, screwing his girlfriend, becoming a teenage dad. That had been his life. And she'd had a whole other life, a life that might have happened here if her parents had lived, if her father had moved them to the beach.

Ned turned back to the bungalow. The dwelling matched the brigadier's voice on the telephone. The lawn looked mown with the aid of a spirit level, hedges and edges at right angles, beds filled with ranks of symmetrical plants.

It was unmistakably Brigadier (Ret.) John Simpson who answered the front door. Tall, upright, a grey moustache with angles as sharp as the garden's, skin like a tight leather drum. He inspected Ned as she stood on the doorstep. She almost expected to be bawled out for a lack of spit polish, but he stood aside to let her in.

'Detective Kelly, go through. Study's on the right.'

The hallway featured pictures of surfboats and crews, Simpson front and centre in most, younger but just as lean. The study had a different ambience. Pictures on these walls were of men in uniforms carrying large weapons. One caught her eye.

On the verandah of a house, men in baggy shorts, some shirt-less, raised beers to the camera. They'd arranged themselves in rows, some squashed together on rattan lounges, others flanking beside and behind, as if unable to resist the tug of order even in relaxation. Her father stood in the back row, a broad, bare chest, dog tags, big smile. It looked hot, the men sweaty, strong but somehow adrift. A holiday snap, but one without women, children or any sense of joy. On the white wall of the building, some words in Vietnamese scrolled around black lettering in English: *Home of the Expendables.*

'Dead, dead, wounded . . .' The glass smudged as Simpson's finger stabbed the faces. 'Four VCs and thirty-three dead by the time we left. Australia House, Da Nang. The Team rarely got together, so Christmas Day and Anzac Day we did all the trappings: dawn parade, barbecue, two-up. Other than that you were on your Pat, in the boonies for months on end with a bunch of ARVN or paired up with a Yank.'

'Arvin?'

'Army of the Republic of Vietnam. Take a seat, Detective Kelly.'

'Call me Ned, please. I'm not here as a detective, I just wanted to talk to you about Mick Kelly – my dad – and Phuong . . . Nguyen Thi Phuong.' Little lies. She wasn't here officially, but she was still a detective.

Simpson loomed over her before finally sitting down in a wing-backed, upholstered chair.

'The things I can tell you about your father, you may not be happy to hear.'

'I didn't come here to be made happy.'

Breakfast still lingered in the house, bacon and eggs. She guessed the pan sat on the kitchen bench, fat congealing, awaiting Mrs Simpson. Brigadier Simpson clearly didn't pull punches or do the washing up.

'You mentioned "the Team". What was it?'

'Best of the best. All professionals, all experts. First in, last out.'

'And he was part of that?'

'Smart fella, Mick Kelly. Was going to run Psy Ops once our commitment increased.'

'Psy Ops?'

'Psychological Operations. Big picture stuff. Big future, till he let that bitch burn him.'

'Nguyen Thi Phuong?'

'Phuong, Cassandra, Cassie, Kiều. Whatever she called herself. "Treacherous bitch" covers it.'

'Treacherous?'

'You really don't know much, do you?' Simpson's lips stretched but Ned wouldn't have called it a smile. 'She was VC.'

'VC . . .' Ned echoed. CIA, VC, traitor, double agent; these were words from history lessons, documentaries, bad movies. They were also words that cracked real bones, burnt real scars into living skin – provided real motives for murder.

Fire leapt from a match-end as Simpson lit up a cigarette. Ned saw those scars on that leathered hide, imagined it pink and puckering around a burning ember. She felt her nipples contract, the flesh around her groin flinch as she watched the glowing tip of Simpson's cigarette travel from his fingers to his lips.

She tried to remember if her father had smoked.

'Did you know her?'

'Met her once. Knew all about her though, or I thought I did. Your dad and me had an agreement; he sent me unofficial reports – back channels, without the Yanks nitpicking. The duck's guts, I told him. And that's what he did. He told me about her, about the work she was doing – translation, cultural advice – she sounded too bloody good to be true. Turns out she was.'

'What was she like?'

'Beautiful, like all the others. But in that place you could pass fifteen princesses on bicycles before breakfast. That wasn't what made Cassie special. She was smart, educated – convent school, then uni in France. Spoke about four languages, excellent English. Canny too, advice was right on the money. Name was a joke between her and Mick – Cassandra, always predicting what would happen next. Good reason for that, eh?'

'And my dad – he never suspected?'

'First hint we had was she didn't come back from a trip to Saigon. There was a lot of kidnapping going on in those days.'

'How do you know she wasn't kidnapped? Sounds like the sort of person who —'

'She wasn't,' he laughed. Scornful. 'Our stuff starts turning up as anti-propaganda in VC leaflets. Little things, but it added up.'

'She'd been tortured. Maybe that's how they got the information out of her?' Leathered skin, seared into craters with smooth, melted centres, spun behind Ned's eyes.

Simpson's eyes narrowed, neck jutted forward. 'The VC didn't torture her. She jumped the fence. A Chiêu Hôi returnee told us he'd spotted her in Hanoi. She was strutting about in a bloody NVA colonel's outfit. She turned, all right. Maybe in France. He never admitted it but that's probably when she started screwing Mick, too.'

'They met in France? You're sure?' The French inscription on Phuong's locket – something about Sundays – clicked into place.

'She went to uni in Paris. Army sent Mick over for specialist training. She probably targeted him.'

From the house next door a screen door on a tight spring whined closed and a radio came on, the hectoring voice of talk-back. The study began to feel over-warm and stuffy. The odour of bacon fat was insinuating itself into her nostrils; she longed to open a window. A lawn mower sputtered and caught somewhere in the street.

'What skills did he learn in France?'

'The kind you needed in that place.'

'But he worked for the CIA, didn't he?'

Simpson's eyes never strayed from her face. 'What if he did? He had a job to do, but instead of doing it he got taken in by a bitch who should've been dead five times over. He was un-*pro*-fessional.' He pronounced it slowly, as if to magnify the shame.

There was anger there, still raw. Retirement hadn't settled comfortably on him. The AGMs down at the surf club must have been interesting affairs with him in the chair.

'What about Tet? Do you know how he was wounded?'

He glanced left, as if someone had just entered the room. Ned followed the look but saw only an empty hallway, dust motes falling through sunlight. Unfaded squares of wallpaper marked the outlines of missing pictures.

'He never told you about Tet?'

'Never said anything about the war. We – my sister and I – were too little.' Made it sound like he would have, one day when they were older.

'Trapped in Hué, during the siege. Three weeks behind enemy lines. Then when he comes out of the Citadel, he's wounded, dragging a young Vietnamese woman behind him, saying he wants out of the whole bloody thing. Out of Vietnam, out of the army – he's going to marry her, take her home to Australia. That'd be your mum, I guess.'

'My mum?'

'When we heard about it, back in Saigon, we thought it must've been Cassie. But it wasn't. It was Cassie's little sister – forget her name.'

'Ngoc.'

Sieges and citadels, it all sounded like some medieval fairytale. Her mum, the quiet woman with the rich laugh and low voice, singing along to the records she played on the stereo. Ned's memories shifted, trying to fit this new shape around Ngoc's slim shoulders.

'Shy little thing, didn't speak much English. He's wounded, she is too, so they're dusted off to Da Nang. When I get there, Mick's screaming for a monk, a mayor or a priest to marry them and wants to junk his commission.'

'What do you mean? He was medically discharged,' she said. 'His army records —'

'Records say what we want them to.'

'But he was wounded.'

'Not enough to be boarded out.'

He challenged her, hard-eyed. Facing that stare, the price of information.

'What happened?'

'Think it was easy bringing a Vietnamese wife here in 1968?' Simpson snarled. 'It wasn't. And the little sister of a VC traitor? Forget it. But Mick, he knew a few things by then, things that might've been embarrassing to the army, the government. So some gutless politician decided it was easier to let him go quietly – honourable discharge, medically unfit. We were going to give him a medal just for surviving Hué, but instead he shat on us all, fucking off to play happy families.'

'What things? What did he know?'

'You fight a war on the territory and the terms you're given.'

'Meaning what?'

'Meaning the locals fought dirty and we matched them. Things that needed doing got done, and force was met with equal force. The hippies lying around on George Street never got that basic fact.'

'Equal force?' Ned retorted. 'I don't remember the Vietnamese using napalm.'

'What they lacked in hardware they made up for in imagination.'

'And my father?'

'Was very imaginative.'

'In Psy Ops? What, like making ads?'

'You need to gather intel before you can disseminate it. Human intel. And after that treacherous bitch screwed him, Mick went into the field.'

Bright eyes. No thousand-yard stare, this one; his was an in-your-face, nose-to-nose, hands-around-the-throat look of someone who'd be happy to watch you die. Ned smoothed her arms.

'Did you stay in contact with him, after —'

'Never spoke to him again. Tried to never think about him again. We were at war, he was a soldier, he had responsibilities. You can't turn around and walk away from your duty. Not to pick up some . . .' He stopped, as if physically reminding himself that the child of the woman he was about to describe sat opposite him. 'Soldiers don't get to choose what they do. They're a team. We were *the Team* and he deserted us. It's called service for a reason. It demands sacrifice.' His eyes locked on hers. 'I never forgave him.'

Ned looked away. Across the hallway she could see a bedroom, double bed unmade, a wardrobe door ajar, suits crammed in on one side, the other half empty.

'So when they were murdered, what did you think?'

'I thought, well, the chickens have finally come home to roost. The police back then, they wanted to know about Vietnam and I told them, much as I could. I was still a serving officer and some things were still classified. They thought it was connected to the war and I agreed.'

'So, who did you think it was?'

'I said I *agreed*, I didn't say I knew. Who knows who Mick crossed back there – or her, for that matter. Bit too coincidental, first boatloads of reffos start to turn up here and he's knocked off. Had to be a connection.'

'Ever think it might've been someone from the Team?'

'No.' Sharp as a rifle bolt snapping shut.

'Why? You just said he was a traitor. You never forgave him.'

'Because I know those men and I know none of them would have done that.'

'Not in this country, anyway,' Ned fired back. 'Different rules in different places?'

'We're finished here, Detective.' Simpson was on his feet, at attention.

Ned stayed in her seat. They'd been assuming Vietnam had come and exacted revenge against Mick and Ngoc. Maybe the hate had been a whole lot closer.

'I'm not here as a detective,' she said again. 'I'm here because I'm their daughter and her niece.'

'Then find someone else to tell you family stories.'

'Who was it my father threatened to expose if the army didn't let him out?'

'You know, things that were secrets then are in bloody museums now. Go educate yourself, girlie.'

'But if someone thought he'd broken his word – were there rumours?'

'War *is* rumours. None of his old buddies would've pissed on him if he was on fire but they wouldn't have dignified him by killing him, either. We all sacrificed things, families. What made him think he deserved more?' He closed one eye, as if bisecting her through the cross-hairs of a gun sight. 'Of course, if we'd known then about what happened during the siege, then his little blackmail stunt mightn't have worked and . . . Well, let's just say you wouldn't be sitting there now.'

'What do you mean?'

'They caught up with Cassie, you know. Eventually.'

'I know someone did. I've seen the scars on her body – cigarette burns all over her. Who did that, do you think?'

'North, South, I told you they all used pretty similar methods,' he snapped. 'Don't be so sure those marks weren't from her own side.'

'Couldn't have been anyone from *our* side, then?'

'Or maybe little Cassie had some questions to answer after the siege.'

Ned smelt skin sizzling in the stink of fried bacon still clinging to the house. Her stomach lurched. The house reeked of the past, like a sad, empty memorial. Every photo featured a surfboat or a soldier. No kids, no women, no weddings or parties. The gaps on the wall, the empty wardrobe, the build-up of dust. Mrs Simpson wasn't coming home to wash up any time soon.

'Of course, if it'd been up to us, Cassie would never have made it to Australia.' Ned waited; he wanted to tell her. 'She'd have been shot dead while escaping – in reality, not just on paper.' His lips stretched again, a mix of pride and cruelty.

'What?'

'In 1972 Cassie was picked up by the Phoenix Program and shot while trying to escape. I'd always taken a bit of comfort in that. Justice.'

'Well, she wasn't. She died in 1976 in Bankstown when someone snapped her neck, chucked her in a hole and covered her in concrete.'

'Justice delayed, then. Couldn't have happened to a more deserving bitch.' His hands were leaving deep indentations in the leather of the chair. He unbent, peering down at her. 'So, Mick Kelly is the main suspect for her murder, then?'

'I'm not on the investigation.'

'Well, you know what? If he did it, then it was the only smart thing he ever did with the bitch.'

NED NURSED THE THINGS SIMPSON had said like fresh wounds on the drive home. The image of Ngoc and Mick emerging from the siege of Huế – maimed, bloodied and bound together by something unspeakable – haunted her journey. Imaginative. Phuong with her tortured skin, the result of someone like Simpson or her dad using their imagination to gather 'human intel'.

Secrets. What right did she have to know her parents' secrets? She harboured secrets, petty and small, large and profound. Alive she had a right to them, but dead? We accept we can't completely understand the living, yet we demand it of the dead. She was their daughter; and their secrets were all they had left her.

A police car flashed past as she sat at a red light on Military Road. The lights and sirens ignited a familiar buzz in her blood, even as they signalled her exclusion. She was good at her job: background-ing, profiling crooks, digging the dirt, finding the links, talking to people – human intel. But how to do that without access to profes-sional resources, and when the people with the answers were all dead? How to do it to your own family – a forgery of a family? Who the hell were these people?

An army captain who'd worked at the dirty end of the war. A career soldier, who'd known something big enough to blackmail his way out of that war with a wife and a new life. And then there was Phuong – Cassie, her mother's sister. Supposedly killed in Vietnam, four years before she died in Bankstown. They'd all started out together in Vietnam, and then they'd all died in Bankstown within a week of each other – along with an Aboriginal woman who'd been fighting an entirely different war.

The lights turned green and she rolled forward, bumper to bumper, to the next one. The western sun was low and blinding. Criminal investigations were like fires and information was oxygen. As long as information about Phuong poured in, Dawn Jarrett would just be a jigsaw piece that didn't fit – yet.

Driving down Greenwich Road, Ned was ashamed to catch herself wondering if Sean was at his home, with Marianne and their boys, enjoying a real life that didn't include her. For the past few days Ned's pager had conveyed a series of messages, none of which gave her any clue about where he was, nor when he'd next show up. The thought of another night with MM in View Street was unbearable. Ned headed back into the western sun towards Bankstown.

Last time she'd seen Mabo lugging his shopping bags around, she'd remembered the granny grocery trolley sitting veiled in cobwebs in MM's garage. She'd hauled it out and stuck it in the back of the car, thinking that Mabo could use it for whatever precious things he kept in his plastic bags. Delivering it was just distraction, but at least it was a useful one.

It was dusk when she started seriously looking. He'd be settling in for the night somewhere, Ned guessed. She started at the building site. The police tape was still up but there were no other signs of activity. It didn't look as if the demolition had resumed either; a flight of stairs rose to nowhere beside half-shattered brick walls. Red tail-lights flashed on the other side of the block. The Bankstown paddy wagon pulled out of the site's gates and trundled back onto Rickard Road. Still checking the place, then. Might be a sign that TC had spiked Zervos's interest if the locals were still lurking about.

No sign of Mabo.

She drove down towards South Terrace, along Olympic Parade, checking the embankments beside the railway line. A few mattresses and empty bottles scattered behind sagging chicken wire showed the place was used, but the mattresses weren't occupied yet. From Memorial Park to Apex Park she checked under shrubs and beside walls as darkness fell. She'd found a couple of local meth drinkers and a pair of teenagers with their pants down by the time she decided to give it away.

She was rolling home through the chicanes that skirted the mud flats of Dobroyd Point when her pager sounded. Driving one-handed, she read the message.

Your band at the Brasserie?

Bubaca were deep into their set when Sean and Ned arrived. The Senegalese singer was spinning on stage, the heavily embroidered cloth of his *boubou* billowing around him. The talking drum pulsated through a crowd that shimmered under a self-created heat haze. An eclectic bunch for a late-night, midweek gig: girls with Bali-braided hair, blokes in MC Hammer pants and dreads, and probably every African student in town.

Ned turned to Sean. 'I told you they were good,' she mouthed to him as they plunged into the mix.

The *djembe* drove the beat and Ned's hips picked up the rhythm.

The band had two dancers on stage – Senegalese guys, who leapt and spun, then gathered up the flowing material of their fisherman's pants in their hands in coordinated wide-legged displays. Dancers on the floor copied them, women sliding their dresses high onto their hips before letting them fall back, bodies alive with the beat.

'This isn't dancing,' Sean yelled in her ear as she coiled next to him. 'It's foreplay.' He grinned and rested his hands lightly on her hips, riding the rhythm of her movements.

By the time the band took a break, the whole room shone with sweat, and Ned felt she'd exorcised the day. They grabbed drinks from the bar and found a quiet place at the back of the room, in front of the large glass doors that faced the harbour. The

Harbourside Brasserie was aptly named, almost directly under the southern span of the bridge. Absolute waterfront and live bands compensated for the shabbiness of the venue by day. A container ship swung out from White Bay, so close it looked like it was about to plough straight through the back wall.

Ned took a large swallow of her gin and tonic, then rolled the tall, icy glass over her forehead and neck.

'You look happier now than an hour ago,' Sean said, sliding a hand along her arm, silky with sweat.

'Had better days.'

'The kind you want to talk about?'

She told him, all of it – the truth that lay in DNA, Linh's decision to leave, Simpson's ugly revelations.

'Told me I should go and educate myself,' she finished. 'Fucking prick.'

'Educate yourself, eh? Sounds like a challenge to me. You up for it?'

She leant into him, kissed him, open-mouthed and seeking.

THE ARCHIVE AT CANBERRA'S WAR Memorial was underground. Above it was the reflection pool, a dome, lists of the dead – a secular cathedral. Ned had ignored the galleries of dioramas, not interested in depictions of rugged little outcrops of Turkey or how they had been won and lost and at what cost. Below ground, in the archives, the sound of drilling echoed.

'Seventy-fifth anniversary of the end of World War One next year,' explained Sandra, the archivist who had unearthed the documents that now lay on the desk. At Ned's blank look she elaborated. 'They're bringing back the remains of an unknown soldier from the Western Front, to inter in the Hall of Memory. Got a bit of work to do first, hence the noise.'

Ned nodded. It had taken a bit of time and more than a few dead ends before she had been put in touch with Sandra. Now, after a lifetime of not knowing about her father and his war, she was surrounded by people who did nothing but think about such things, marking the days on the calendar in remembrance, tending to the paperwork that had surrounded the killing, digging up the dead.

'I've arranged the correspondence in chronological order rather than by subject – I thought that might make the most narrative sense to you?'

Ned nodded again, looking at the pile of letters with Australian Army letterheads that lay under Sandra's hand. They looked old and fragile, some carbon-copied. The archivist indicated another, much smaller pile that looked like various official documents.

'These are records relating to Nguyen Thi Phuong. They're quite patchy, certainly not a complete record by any means – the US Army would have that. They look like responses to requests for information by Brigadier – or Major, as he was then – Simpson.'

'Simpson? He donated his records?' Ned asked. 'I've met him, he didn't mention . . .'

Sandra's plump cheeks reddened as she explained the 'provenance' of the letters. The archivist was round, almost motherly, her soft dark curly hair in an unfashionable cut, with glasses on a cord around her neck, but she told the story with the unflinching gaze of a historian.

A clerk who'd worked for Simpson had kept meticulous records, along with a long-standing grudge against his old boss. Whether or not the man blamed Simpson alone for the troubles that had followed him home from Vietnam, he'd made it clear in his suicide note that he wished to bequeath his treasure trove of military correspondence to the Australian War Memorial. Ned reckoned that clerk couldn't have found a better way to avenge himself from the end of his rope.

'I'll just be out here if you need any help translating the jargon,' Sandra said and went back to her desk.

Ned picked up the first letter on the top of the pile, amazed by the flimsy paper. It looked incapable of surviving normal postage, let alone a war zone. Dated 1964, it was from Simpson to her father, thanking him for his report on the situation at a place called Phu Bai and encouraging him to cultivate his relationship with someone called Nguyen Duc Tran in Hué. The name Nguyen appeared with frustrating regularity. It wasn't just her mother's family name, it was the most common name in Vietnam. Ned made notes, unsure of who was being discussed and what relationship they had to Phuong.

It was slow going. Simpson's letters to her father were like hearing an answer without knowing the question. They were a mixture of military jargon and relaxed, comradely banter. The two men had been friends, but it was clear Major Simpson also valued his captain's advice.

Slowly it became obvious that Mick Kelly was backgrounding Phuong's family for Simpson. Ned caught a glimpse of her Vietnamese ancestry through the letters of two soldiers who regarded them as nothing more than human intel assets.

The list of names grew into a family tree. Her grandfather now had a name – Tran – and Simpson wrote about him with contempt. Tran had been a Hué Mandarin, a leftover from a vanished class, but one who'd still had clout with the current Emperor. Tran had been a collaborator for everyone, from the French colonial rulers to the Japanese invaders, and he was now in the pay of the Americans. Simpson mightn't have liked him, but Tran had been useful. *Hold your nose and remember – he's our monster*, Simpson had advised her father. Grandfather Tran. A monster. Ned glanced over at Sandra, then quickly looked away.

Another letter, another discovery. She had an uncle, Danh, brother to Ngoc and Phuong. A reluctant soldier forced into uniform by Tran. Simpson sneered at Kelly's accounts of Danh's feeble black-market activities. In contrast, Simpson was enthusiastic about Phuong, calling her 'Cassie', congratulating Mick Kelly for identifying such a valuable 'asset'. He urged Kelly to cultivate Phuong at all costs, including ribald advice on how his captain might do that. Ned recalled Simpson's savage words about Phuong. Mick Kelly hadn't been the only one she'd deceived.

Many of Simpson's letters were unintelligible, containing references to places and names Ned didn't know. The pile of the correspondence she had read grew larger, and still Ned found no mention of her mother, Ngoc. Perhaps she'd been too young to be an asset.

Ned sat back from the table and drew a deep, shuddering breath as a new name appeared in the letters. Phuong and Ngoc's sister – the eldest of the family – a Buddhist nun named Linh. A whole dead family was coming to life in ragged letters, in the language of military expedience. But no mention of anyone named Nhu.

The nun, Linh, was involved in something called 'the Struggle' – Ned guessed it was an uprising of some kind in Huế. Simpson's letters about her became increasingly agitated. He reminded Kelly that all the nuns and monks were all 'Commie' sympathisers, and warned him to take action if necessary.

Ned picked up another letter and, her hand going to her mouth as she read, realised that it was the nun, not her father, who had finally taken action.

June 5, 1966

Mick

I'm sure little Cassie is upset. Not a pretty sight. Shame you couldn't get her out of there before that silly bitch set herself alight. But I know, I told you to watch the nun and you don't have eyes in the back of your head.

One more barbecue. How many does that make it now? Those monks and nuns up there need to wake up to themselves. They're not going to get rid of Ky this way. It's not 1963. Not a lot of sympathy for martyrs anymore. It's lost its shock value. They just look like savages. People are sick of it – here and back home.

I know you'll keep Cassie on the straight and narrow. She chose her side. She's probably just still a bit shocked. How about I organise some leave for you both? Da Nang? Bit of sea and sand will cheer her up.

Simo

'Are you OK?'

Sandra popped her head around the corner. Ned suddenly wished Sean was there. He'd offered to come but she'd decided to do this alone. 'It can be a bit confronting,' Sandra said, stepping to the desk and seeing the letter that lay there. 'Was she . . . ?'

'An aunt. My mother's sister. I . . .'

'The language can seem pretty raw, can't it. Nineteen sixty-six was a difficult time in Huế.' Sandra pronounced the name differently to the way Ned had been reading it. The 'h' disappeared. The word became 'Way'; it dipped in the middle. Something about the sound was familiar, though Ned couldn't pin it down.

'What's it mean – "the Struggle"?'

'It was a protest movement, against the Saigon government, General Ky, the corruption. Some monks and nuns in Huế self-immolated but in the end,' Sandra said, tapping Simpson's letter, 'he was right. The uprising ended.'

'My other aunt – Phuong, the one Simpson calls Cassie. She changed sides, didn't she?'

The archivist pulled over a chair. 'Yes. I hope you don't think I was snooping; we have to do a fair bit of reading to find the relevant materials.'

Nod nodded, relieved to let the woman take over.

'In late 1966, a few months after her sister Linh died, Phuong disappeared. There's nothing in the letters about it – I suspect that Major Simpson and Captain Kelly probably met face to face to discuss it.

'Then the next mention we have of Phuong is this . . .' Sandra slid a poorly reproduced document towards Ned. 'It's a little difficult to read, and I'm afraid it's somewhat disturbing.'

More disturbing than a nun dousing herself in petrol and going up in flames? Ned placed her fingers on the edge of it and glanced up at Sandra. The archivist looked like she should be doing story-time at the local library rather than dealing with these tales of horror.

'Tell me.'

'Huế was under siege for over a month during the Tet Offensive, in early 1968.'

Ned nodded. 'I know, my father and my mother were trapped there.'

Sandra tapped the letters. 'Simpson writes about that. But it wasn't until a few months after the siege had been lifted and the North Vietnamese Army had withdrawn that the mass graves started to be uncovered in Huế. Survivors of the siege reported that the NVA came with lists of names; there were disappearances, summary executions. The body of Nguyen Duc Tran – your grandfather – was eventually found in one of those mass graves.'

Ned looked at the document under Sandra's hand; no photograph. Was her grandfather's face in any of the albums at home? What did he look like? Grandfather? Monster? Victim?

'Later that year a maid who had worked for your grandfather came forward and made a statement to US Army Intelligence. She said she'd witnessed his execution.'

Somewhere in a wall cavity a workman was hammering metal on metal. The sound reverberated through Ned's skull.

'What happened?'

Sandra settled herself then rattled through the details, as if speed could blunt the malice.

'She said she saw Captain Kelly with your grandfather at the family home in the Citadel on the morning the Tet Offensive began, 30 January. The youngest daughter, Ngoc, was also there. The maid was getting water from a well in the backyard when she heard North Vietnamese Army soldiers come to the house. She hid and claims she saw your aunt, Phuong, dressed in an NVA uniform, drag her own father – your grandfather – from the house, give him a mock trial, convict him of treason and shoot him in the head. The maid fled, and assumed that Captain Kelly and Ngoc must have been executed as well.'

Ned sat silently, one hand gripping her wrist. An old gesture.

When they were kids Linh used to tease her about it – was she so lonely she had to hold her own hand?

Sandra picked up another document, the words *Phung Hoang* above a wild-looking bird on the cover sheet, the pages within it heavily censored.

'The Phoenix Program. CIA ran it – covertly – with South Vietnamese Intelligence.' Sandra looked up at the ceiling, seeming to quote from memory. '*To identify and neutralise Vietcong infrastructure using kidnap, torture and assassination.*'

Ned stared at the drawing of the bird. It looked like a vulture, not a phoenix.

'They picked up Phuong in late 1972,' Sandra continued. 'She was interrogated, admitted executing her father, but she denied seeing her little sister Ngoc or Captain Mick Kelly in Huế that day.' Sandra pointed to a note written on the cover. 'The interrogating officer ordered that Captain Kelly be located and interviewed for corroboration. There's no record of the result.'

After Sandra had finished speaking they sat together, silent. Simpson had hinted at something that happened during the siege. Something that, if it had been known, would have prevented Mick Kelly from blackmailing his way into a new life. Was this it? She looked at the dates on the documents. By the time the maid had come forward, Mick and Ngoc were in Australia, counting down the days to Ned's birth. Had they witnessed Phuong executing her own father? And if they had, why had Phuong let them live? The army's answer would be simple: Mick Kelly was a collaborator, a coward who saved his own skin while others were being dragged away to die in unmarked graves.

So why had Phuong denied seeing Mick and Ngoc? Her body told the tale of how long she had resisted her interrogators. But judging from the thickness of the file with the ugly bird on its cover, she'd talked eventually. Ned wondered what had done it – the cigarette burns or the broken bones.

Yet when the war was over and her side had finally won, instead of staying to enjoy the fruits of victory Phuong had come looking for Mick and Ngoc.

The hammering and drilling had gone quiet. Ned looked up, suddenly aware it was late. The rooms were empty and, from somewhere outside, the Last Post was playing.

'I'm sorry. You're closing,' she said and got to her feet, stiff and awkward from the hours spent sitting.

'It's all right. Take your time. I thought, when I was assembling this, you might . . .' Sandra finished in a rush. 'I made you a copy of the papers. Take them away, talk about it with your family.'

'No,' Ned said. 'I don't want it.' She picked up her notebook, wrote a name down and tore off the page. 'Send it to Detective Inspector Zervos,' she said, slapping the page down on the envelope containing the photocopies. 'South Region Homicide, New South Wales Police.'

FROM THE STEPS OF THE WAR MEMORIAL the view took in the vast sweep of Anzac Parade all the way down to the lake. On the opposite shore stood the old and new Parliament Houses. In theory, it meant that those who decided which wars to fight had a direct line of sight to the memorial for those who died fighting them. In practice, Ned wondered how often eyes were raised from the politics of the day to notice.

The small crowd who'd attended the Memorial's daily ceremony began to disperse, wandering off towards the car park, dabbing at eyes moistened by the playing of the Last Post. Snippets of their conversations reached her: it was ancestor worship, but instead of incense it was red poppies stuck beside names on the Roll of Honour. She quickened her pace, taking the last stairs two at a time until she was free of them.

Ned was hot, dusty and tired by the time she got to the old Ainslie Hotel. An original Art Deco fit-out and black-and-white photographs from the thirties were all well and good, but right this minute she'd have swapped them for a swimming pool. Collecting the key, she started to climb the stairs when she caught sight of Sean in the hotel bar, his back to the lobby. As she approached the bar doors she saw that his drinking companion was a young, Asian male. For a long moment her brain refused to cooperate, too filled with family death and debris to make any connections. Then she recognised him, remembered him from her first dinner with Sean, being introduced to him as Lily.

Sunny Liu was speaking. Sean was listening. Neither of them smiling.

Ned went to step back through the doors, but Liu looked up over his beer and clocked her. Sean turned, an open look of pleasure on his face as he stood and dragged up another stool.

'Lily, we've been waiting for you. Beer, wine or G & T?'

She'd spent hours reading about a family that had consisted of traitors, collaborators, spies, torturers and murderers – and one sad, suicidal nun. She was not ready to talk about it. And she didn't have to, didn't even have to be Ned anymore. She was some other woman, Lily, a woman with a sexy, shady boyfriend, a woman who hung around in bars talking bullshit with ease to dangerous strangers.

It was liberating.

Three drinks later, they were climbing the stairs back to their room.

'Coincidence?' she asked, knowing it wasn't.

'The Job, it doesn't stop because I want it to. He's got business interests here. Been wanting me to come down and . . .' He shrugged, looked suddenly tired. 'I'm sorry, Nhu. I should have told you.'

He ran his hands down her arms as she opened the door to their room. The static electricity, a build-up of dry heat and synthetic carpet, made them jump.

'Thanks for backing me up. I know it can't have been easy, after your day. How did it go?'

'How did it go . . .' she repeated slowly. 'Patricide,' she said, pulling her T-shirt over her head, tossing it onto the chair. 'That's the word, isn't it, for killing your father?'

'Nhu?'

She continued undressing, stepping into the shower, taps on cold and hard.

'My family are fucked – were fucked. Hard to get the verbs right, but what the fuck, they're all dead anyway.'

He watched, then silently undressed, joined her under the

streaming water and held her.

There was viciousness in her passion that was new; she bared her teeth and bore down on him. He met her as an equal, and she absorbed him, discovering echoes of themselves in each other's cries. She watched his face, the changes that flowed over him when he abandoned himself. Swore she saw the masks melting, leaving him truly naked, above her, below her, within her, his mouth soft and open, eyes unfocused. Laid bare. She began to love what was left.

Indochine.

The word shakes the house. Dark. Linh is sound asleep. Linh can sleep through storms, but Nhu can't. And tonight the storm is inside the house.

Mum and Dad don't fight, they don't yell, but tonight they're doing both.

Words fly faster than she can keep up with. Words she's never heard. Their voices, like strangers, shaping new sounds.

Mum's voice making bitter, harsh sounds like a currawong.

Way. They repeat the word. *Way.*

They slide along it. It dips in the middle. The word has peaks and troughs she's never heard before.

And another word coming from both their mouths, over and over. *Indochine.*

Something smashes.

Linh mutters in the other bed, rolls onto her back and snores. The cast on her arm, pristine and white.

The back door slams, the car starts.

Mum cries in the kitchen.

'Huế!'

Ned woke, the word on her lips. The same word, the way Sandra had pronounced it, on the lips of her parents. She knew it now, knew what it meant, *where* it meant. She'd had enough night terrors to know which ones were fantasies and which were the past elbowing their way back into the present.

The images of her dream replayed silently as she closed her eyes. Ned remembered the day now.

Linh falling off the monkeybars in the backyard. Mum taking them both down to Bankstown Casualty, cranky because she couldn't find Dad and had to negotiate alone with the nurses and doctors in her accented English. Linh had still been wearing that cast at Manly, the day her parents had died.

Sean lay on his stomach beside her, sprawled in a deep sleep. She shivered and slid alongside him, seeking the heat from his skin.

Ned woke gradually, listening to the shifts in Sean's tone as he worked. Calls to Sunny Liu and then to Swiss Fowles, in between coffee and croissants, flaky pastry scattered on the sheets. She shook her head, still fuzzy from the disturbed night, hearing yet another timbre to his voice when he spoke to her.

'You had a bad night,' he said.

And then it all came out: the details of what she'd read about her family in Huế and her memory of her parents' fight. He listened, arms wrapped around her, his chin on her head.

'Last night, when I came back and saw you with Liu . . .'

'I said I'm sorry, Ned, I had no choice. He's a big target. When he calls I —'

'No, it felt good. I got to forget about them all for a while. It felt great.' She wriggled around and looked up at him. 'That's how it is, isn't it? You're free.'

He stared back down at her, the laugh lines were gone, a frown creased his forehead.

'Nothing is free, Ned.'

SANTAS, LIGHTS, REINDEERS AND FAKE snow had already started appearing in the shops around Greenwich. In the days since Ned had returned from Canberra, her sister had become an absence in her life. Linh's preparations for the sabbatical and her lectures at the Buddhist centre meant they barely saw each other, let alone spoke. Which meant Ned didn't have to tell her about her decision to slip into a new skin at the UCs. With the crutch of work kicked away, Ned had realised just how much the Job had given shape to her life.

She did need to tell TC. She set off for Bankstown rehearsing her thank-you-and-farewell speech, taking in the crime scene on her way. Dust eddies were rising behind the orange excavators and the Hills hoists had been uprooted. No extension on the dig. Ned eased back into gear and turned down Rickard Road, wondering if TC had even tried to convince Zervos to take another look. Not her problem now. She checked the rear-view mirror but there was no sign of a skinny black man weighed down with plastic bags.

TC was already in Uncle Pho's when she arrived, sitting in front of a steamy bowl of fiery red soup.

They ticked off the niceties of conversation before TC turned to business.

'Any pennies drop with your aunt?'

Ned had tried to get MM to talk about the past. Instead, her aunt recounted her conquests: the artistic who'd painted her, the poetic who'd poeted her – even, Ned deduced, the policeman who'd apparently 'supported' her through the dark days after the murders.

Ned had even offered to read through the supposed memoir in case there was something in there, only to be told grandly, 'It's with my ghost writer, dear.'

'TC, if my father and his ex-lover/double agent/sister-in-law were having an affair, MM would probably be the last person on earth they'd have told.'

'Fair enough. So, who do you reckon might've known about her turning up here?' Her mentor was still working the case. She tried to be obliging, wanting to scream that she now knew more about Phuong than she wanted to.

'Brian Hall was Dad's mate. Maybe he told him.'

'Yeah.' TC nodded his agreement.

'How is he?'

'Stable. Out of intensive care. Still assessing the damage, speech is affected, but the memory – who knows.'

Ned leant back from the table and gave a polite smile to the young waitress, who slid a plate of chilled rice-paper rolls in front of her. The tang of chopped coriander rose from the pearly skin. She dipped the neatly wrapped package into the dark, nutty sauce, concentrating on coating the end as she asked her question.

'The initial murder investigation – Mum and Dad's – anyone ever suspect Dad's old army buddies? You know, think they might've settled a score?'

Ned bit into her roll. Cool, fleshy skin gave way to the crisp bite of mint and the salt smack of prawn.

'Simo made an impression, I see.' TC was drowning a thin piece of beef, still pink. 'Suspects, though? Not as far as I know.'

There was no easy way to start the conversation but once TC had run out of questions about Phuong, she had no choice.

'I need to get back to work, TC.'

'There's no rush, little buddy.' TC dropped his chopsticks into his bowl. Bad form, letting them poke up like that. They looked like incense sticks, funereal. Linh had made her stop years ago.

'Maybe not for you.'

'If it was up to me, I'd have you back yesterday but . . .'

TC didn't have to spell it out. Each day the news from the ICAC inquiry delighted Sydney with increasingly lurid tales of police misconduct. The occasional barrister and solicitor were sighted making the walk of shame into the inquiry, coat over the head, newspaper in front of the face, but they were distractions from the main game. It was the cops that everyone wanted to see hung out to dry. For the bosses it meant that arse-covering was the only game worth playing. Zervos and Morgenstrom would be keeping her at a distance until the Coroner delivered a verdict.

'Once this is over, you can come back.' TC tried to sound positive.

'You can't go back. It's not a cliché, TC, it's true. I've decided to make a new start. Somewhere different, somewhere —'

'Not the UCs, Ned. That fucking Murph and his sideshow . . .'

His vehement response was unexpected. She was still formulating a reply when she saw a familiar figure approaching their table. Before Marcus Jarrett even opened his mouth, Ned saw the anger in the muscles knotting his throat, the clenched fists.

'Not off your tucker, then?' Jarrett asked, tilting up the edge of her plate then letting it fall back to the table with a plastic clatter. Ned grabbed at the rolls before they slid off the plate. TC slid his chair away from the table, got to his feet.

'Hope you toasted him, at least? Raised a glass in his memory, eh?' Jarrett was eyeballing TC.

'What the fuck are you talking about?' Ned snapped.

'He hasn't told you, then?' Jarrett looked down at her. 'About Mabo.'

'What? TC?'

'He died, Ned. A week or so back —' TC began.

'Died?' Jarrett interrupted. 'Fucking *murdered*. Someone poured kero all over him and set him alight. He was still smouldering when they found him.'

The odour of meaty broth turned her stomach; the white rice-paper rolls were fleshy and corpse-cool beneath her fingers. Ned was on her feet, out the door, leaving TC and Jarrett to raise their voices and right the chairs.

South Terrace wasn't so much fresh air as hot air with a different smell. Somewhere a durian was giving off its death scent. She slid down the glass wall, squatted on her haunches, head in hands, feeling sweat ooze under her fingers, roll down her back, down her neck, pool between her breasts. The world buzzed like a storm of blowflies.

'Sorry, Neddie, I was going to tell you.' TC squatted beside her. 'I tried to find him but no one had seen him.'

The threat of throwing up passed. She picked up a discarded newspaper, fanned herself, moving air over sweat-coated skin. Stared straight ahead.

'What happened?'

'Looks like he was sleeping rough, down under the railway pylons in Woolloomooloo. Some sick bastard . . . He's not the first warb it's happened to, been a task force on it, but homeless deros – not easy. If they're not fighting each other, someone's bashing 'em or the weather gets 'em.'

'But Woolloomooloo!' Ned began. 'How did he end up in —'

TC shook his head – a tiny movement, but enough to warn her to stop. Warb-dumping, that fine old tradition the force pretended didn't happen. With Patrol Commander Morgenstrom running scared of Indigenous deaths in custody, the practice had been revived.

'So that's it?' Jarrett's voice came from above like judgment, his buffed, black suit shoes before her. 'Just another dead coon. Thank fuck it wasn't in your cells, eh?'

'No, I just said – there's a team looking at the murders.' TC was back on his feet.

Jarrett stepped in closer, TC didn't step back. 'Come on, we all know what's going on. Someone from here dumped him there – just when you needed to speak to him.'

'You're fucking offside there, mate,' TC growled.

Their voices grew louder, two large two men standing toe to toe. A group of curious shoppers and shopkeepers looked on, uneasy as the argument intensified. Ned braced against the wall, slid up to her feet, saw Dawn in Marcus Jarrett's jutting chin, steady eyes.

'Blackfellas die all the time in this country,' Jarrett snarled. 'But when they die so conveniently, I get suspicious – and so should you.'

Ned shifted her gaze to TC. She'd told him to pick up Mabo, insisted he see to it, not Toy. Nausea threatened her again. Not TC.

'We can find out who took him into town,' Ned said to Jarrett.

'*If* he was taken.' TC turned on her, voice raised, anger flushing his pate.

'Not like he took a taxi,' Ned fired back.

'And who'd stick their hand up for it now?' TC snapped. They shared a look of mute understanding.

'We can check the rosters,' she said, seeing pity and contempt at her gullibility pass across both faces. 'Zervos might think what Mabo had to say is worth a bit more —'

'Dead or alive,' said TC, 'still just a warb's rambling.'

'So that's that,' Jarrett said, wiping his hands together.

'You think it's a coincidence?' Ned pressed TC.

TC turned his palms up, the flash of anger extinguished, or hidden. 'I honestly don't know what you want me to say. Warbs die.'

The sound of running feet preceded a young uniform constable pulling up, red-faced.

'Oh, it's you, boss. Um, we had a report . . .' He looked sceptically at Jarrett. 'Two men fighting.'

His partner had held back a little, speaking into his portable. 'Bankstown Foot Patrol One, re two men fighting outside Uncle Pho's. All quiet here, no further action.'

Someone else was approaching through the crowd, the

unmistakable slap of shoe leather on pavement.

'Jeez, hasn't anyone got anything bloody better to do than —' TC said as Toy nearly ran over the top of them, braking his momentum on TC's arm.

'Boss, you didn't answer your pager and the restaurant said you'd left.'

'Yeah, well now you've found me, what's —'

'Another body. Bodies . . . down at the Stacey Street site.'

'What?'

One word, three voices.

'Lalor, the site manager, just rung up – they found more bones.'

Marcus Jarrett looked skyward, cupped his hands around his mouth and bellowed, 'They're going to hear you now, uncle.'

Deja vu. Only this time, Marcus Jarrett joined TC, Toy and Ned on one side of a pit. Zervos and his men ranged along the other, like a bunch of gangland undertakers; rows of polished Italian leather shoes lined up along the lip of dirt, the elegant cut of each suit leg broken by the bulge of an ankle holster.

Below them a skeleton, torn up and scattered by the excavator but still recognisable, stark white against black dirt. Not mummified this time. Not a shred of skin or cloth clung to the bones.

'Old. Very, I'd say.' Gumby looked up at his audience. 'Pure chance they hit it. The driver was digging in the wrong spot – probably wouldn't have found them otherwise.'

'How unfortunate for him,' Jarrett said.

Ned tensed. Gumby continued, oblivious.

'This deep, it predates the building by a long stretch. Three femurs so far, a skull, bits and pieces. Need to get it into the lab to be sure, but I'd take a punt from the wear on these teeth that it's one for the museum not the morgue.'

'Not a crime scene, then?' Jarrett asked, eyes hidden behind sunglasses.

'Well, I mean, the bones'll be examined of course.'

'Of course.' Jarrett sounded dangerously polite.

'It's a grave, obviously.'

'Well, obviously – it's a hole in the ground full of dead bodies, isn't it?'

Even Gumby couldn't miss the fury, cold though it was. 'What I mean —'

'Oh shut up, Gumby, before you dig yourself any deeper.' Zervos cut short the growing discomfort. 'There are procedures to be followed here, Mr Jarrett, and we're well aware of them.

'Learnt a lot, have you? Can tell the difference between a crime scene and a burial site just like that?' Jarrett snapped his fingers.

Zervos assumed the stance, hands on hips, suit coat flipped back. All he needed was a gun on his hip. 'What are you —'

'You're so bloody sure this isn't a crime scene, you haven't even looked.'

'The age of the remains —'

'No crimes back then, eh? Just ancient history.'

'Plenty, I'm sure – but none I can do anything about.'

'Acknowledging them would be a start. Coroner's Act says *violent or unnatural death*, yeah?'

'What the fuck? Maybe it's before *our* time. Oh no, that's right – your lot lived in paradise, didn't they? No murders. No wars. Listen, I don't have time to debate politics with you —'

'Nah, too busy solving crimes, aren't you. How's that going, by the by? My mum?' Jarrett jabbed a thumb in Ned's direction. 'Pity her dad's already dead; you could've done him for Mabo as well.'

Ned stared down at the bones elbowing out of the dirt.

'Listen, it's a courtesy that you're even here,' Zervos continued.

'You're doing me no fucking favours, mate. I'm here as legal representative of the Metropolitan Land Council.' Jarrett folded his arms, legs apart, immovable.

'Then enjoy yourself. You'll be getting a wet arse out of it.'

Insistent thunder was overlaying the rumble of traffic. Zervos flicked his head and his cast of suits moved off, silent and well trained. 'Gumby, you know the deal. Get a tarp or something on this lot. It's going to start chucking it down any tick.'

Lalor had been hovering on the fringes. He followed Zervos.

'What do you mean, you don't know how long? I've got men and machines lined up for tomorrow – what am I meant to do with them?' Lalor's voice carried.

'What do you care? All government money, isn't it? It's their bloody law – see them about compo.' Zervos slammed the car door and was gone, leaving TC, Toy, Jarrett and Ned at the edge of the gouge in the earth.

Gumby climbed out and went off to rummage through the back of his van. TC and Toy followed. Beyond the fence, in the over-crowded car park of Bankstown Square, shoppers wheeled trolleys to their cars, glancing skywards as the thunder persisted; no ear-splitters, just continual, low-level grousing.

Jarrett hadn't moved. Ned stood, awkward and silent, the weasel words of sympathy lodged in her throat.

'Had much to do with Zervos?' she asked, to fill the space. 'Not really a people person.'

'No, he's not, is he,' said Jarrett.

They stood quietly. As the afternoon darkened, clouds boiling over from the south and the west cast a sea-green tint. The first large drops of rain began to fall. Jarrett didn't move.

'What happens now?' Ned asked. 'Will they leave them here?'

'I'm not running this show,' he said pointedly.

'Neither am I. Collateral damage.'

Marcus Jarrett looked up, a swift, sharp stare, then nodded towards TC. 'He told me your dad ran this site back in the day.'

'Yeah.'

'Guess your dad wouldn't have wanted any delays, either.' He motioned to Lalor, who was stamping back to the site office. 'The other woman who . . . died. She was your aunty?'

Too polite to say *murdered*.

He stared at her. Long and slow this time.

She nodded.

'Violent bloke, your dad?'

'Never to us but he was a soldier, so I guess.' She shrugged.

Had Vietnam been there all along? The soldier with dirty hands from a dirty war. Inert until it erupted one night, overwhelming a woman who'd blighted his past and another who threatened his future.

The rain quickened, beating dirt away from a small semicircle of white, revealing the brow of a tiny skull.

'Never knew my dad,' Jarrett said. 'Mum told me he died in a car accident when I was just a bub. Only found out through the Royal Commission, hung himself in prison, up in the Territory.'

'I'm sorry, Mr Jarrett.' Those weasel words again.

'Marcus.'

Ned accepted the gesture by meeting his eyes.

'He was doing life, my dad. Murder. Beat a woman to death. Drunk, both of them,' Jarrett continued. 'You don't get to pick your family, Ned. But you do get to decide whether or not you'll try to forgive 'em.'

'There's another option, Marcus,' Ned replied. 'You can make a new one.'

Gumby returned with his tarpaulin. Ned and Marcus helped him unfold it, weighting it down on the edges with bricks and rubble. At her feet, in the dirt and bones, lay the motive for Dawn Jarrett's murder. Dawn – the piece that didn't fit – did now. Two murders. Two motives. One grave.

My brothers, my sisters. Mabo's voice rippled beneath the nag of traffic and storm.

The thunder expanded into a series of shimmering cracks.

NED LEANT AGAINST THE RAILINGS under the bridge. A Circular Quay-bound ferry chugged past farting black smoke; the harbour seemed solid, shifting quicksilver under an overcast sky. One storm had broken at dawn and Sean had arrived with it, carrying its scent, shaking its heavy drops into her bed. Now another was manoeuvring into position over the Blue Mountains as she waited for him to pick her up, to go and see Swiss Fowles.

The rock 'n' roll rhythm of the trains shook steel overhead, a dissonant harmony with the random clash and boom of cars and trucks hitting the joints of the road deck. Flocks of schoolboys from St Aloysius queued up for buses by Bradfield Park or joined the girls from Loreto trailing backpacks up to Milsons Point Station. Ned sensed the last days of school in the boys' raucous laughs and in the girls' uniforms, hitched high to show off tanned legs.

The UCs office ended up being closer than she'd thought, only seven Ks from the city, handy to Bondi, Coogee, the airport. Seemed a contradiction in terms, such an unstructured bunch having an office, but even UCs needed somewhere to put in the overtime forms. Made sense, keeping them close to the city's heartbeat. Drugs made serious money, and serious money was still within orbit of the harbour, the eastern suburbs, the Cross, the quiet wealth of the north.

Sean drove into an industrial park in Rosebery. Severe, spare design was complemented by abstract desert plants: cacti and razorblade grasses that looked designed rather than grown. It was an anonymous industrial suburbia – monochromatic concrete boxes with tinted windows, and driveways that led to underground electronic doors. Sean turned down beneath a unit bearing an innocuous name and the vague promise of import/export opportunities.

Inside there was a makeshift gym in one corner, a TV cabinet surrounded by bean bags and unmatched lounges in another, a bar between them, a pair of bunk beds and a kitchen along one wall with an industrial-size barbecue set up beneath an extraction fan. A few desks and computers were a cursory nod to a workspace.

It was empty of people.

'Out on a job,' Sean said, leading the way up a short flight of stairs to a glassed-in office.

They entered without knocking. Swiss Fowles was holding a one-sided phone conversation that involved him swearing at whoever was on the other end. The silver mane was tied back today, in sleazy advertising-guy style. Ned measured what she knew about him. Four years of legend followed by two weeks in person at Goulburn. She'd heard the war stories of the supercop shot on an undercover drug deal back in the late seventies, left alone to die on a bush track up at Ingleside, crawling for hours before finally finding help; returning to work, hair sent pure white by shock. It was epic. It had also probably sent him mad, she'd decided after watching him humiliate and deride his trainees for two weeks. Suffering didn't necessarily ennoble the sufferer – it made some of them sadistic.

He hung up, looked briefly at her, then glared at Sean.

'What the fuck's she doing here?'

'We talked about this.'

'Yeah, and I said no. So fuck off.'

Sean sat down and nodded Ned into the other chair.

'We need her,' he said calmly. 'I've already introduced her.'

'You what?' Swiss was losing it. 'Who the fuck to?'

'Liu. She handled herself well.'

'I told you after that piss-poor effort in Goulburn, she's not cut out for it.' Swiss slapped the desk.

Ned had had enough of being talked about like she wasn't there. 'Piss-poor effort? Least my hair's still the same colour, mate. Directing police to draw guns on one another – give you a thrill, does it?'

'Too rough for you, was it, Detective? Planning on crying EEO? Sexual harassment? Racial discrimination?'

Swiss leered at her, reminding Ned of the old school rules. *We play rough. Want to play? Then don't cry when you get hurt.*

'I reckon you wanted to teach me a lesson,' Ned said.

'I like to think that everyone learns something from everything that happens on the UC course. Why do you think you were chosen, Detective Kelly?'

'I think you were trying to fuck with my head. See what would happen.'

'And what did happen, Detective?'

'I died.'

'We all die, eventually. How and when is something we try to exercise a little control over.'

Sean slapped his hands together. The sound cracked through the room. 'I'd like to knock your heads together.'

Swiss turned on him, snarling. 'What's up, mate? Don't want to root her on your own time?'

Ned went cold.

'Swiss, shut the fuck —' Sean was on his feet.

'We don't carry passengers here, Murph. You want to fuck her, go ahead, but I'm not paying you to do it.'

Both men were red-faced, on their feet and exchanging spittle. She could fight her own battles.

'You can jam your job, you twisted, mind-fucking prick.' Stuff burning bridges, she was going to blow a few things up on her way out. 'Can't play with crooks anymore so you fuck with your colleagues and call it training, eh? Only way you can get it up now?

I bet you had a fat that was pulling your face out of shape when —'

Sean had her by the arm and halfway down the stairs before Swiss had made it around the desk.

Outside in the parking area, a varied selection of vehicles, from the shabby to the sharp, had arrived while they had been arguing in the soundproofed office. She recognised the panel van and the Celica that Sean had used. A van with an electrician's decal on the side pulled up. The door slid open, revealing radios and video monitors inside. The drivers of the cars spilled out into the space – Swiss Fowles' bargain basement of human accessories for every criminal occasion. A last car drew in, a station wagon. Someone opened the rear door and a large German shepherd leapt out and began tearing about. The driver's-side door opened and she recognised the big boofhead as it emerged, the broad, red neck and blunt-cut grey hair.

Their departure was a blur of UCs offering drinks to Sean, and the sound of the barking dog reverberating through the factory space. Over by the bar she caught a brief glimpse of Sergeant Ugly, tilting back a beer and watching as Sean reversed out of the car space with a squeal of tyres.

It was a mostly silent trip back over the bridge. Hunters and Collectors on the stereo filled in the gaps. Ned stared hard out the window, blinking her eyes dry. Sean eventually broke the silence as they drove down Greenwich Road. An oil tanker was at anchor at the terminal, lit up like Luna Park. The Plimsoll line rode high above the water, nearly all pumped out.

' "A fat that was pulling his face out of shape" – you know, Ned, that's an image I could have really done without.'

'Was he right? Do I have to work with you to see you?'

The silence went on a beat too long.

'I see.'

The sense of an ending was physical; it opened up inside her.

She tried to imagine them, in real life, not this weird hiatus. She couldn't. Gut instinct told her they'd be in a car – just like this – snatching time between the end of one thing and the beginning of something else.

'No, I don't think you do.' Sean pulled over and turned off the ignition. The ship's pumps vibrated in the quiet of the early evening. 'Nhu, my life's complicated . . .'

'Your life's complicated, whereas mine, right now, is simplicity itself. Poor Murph. Any minute you're going to tell me your wife doesn't understand you.'

'Oh, but she does, only too well.'

Ned studied him and wondered what it was she saw. A smile – suppressed, rueful? She wondered when she'd arrived at this point, how she'd become some pathetic 'other woman' whining about the wife. This wasn't what she wanted.

'You deserve each other,' she said, opening the door, stepping out onto the grass.

'Nhu, it's not like that. I'm sorry, I know it's not easy for you right now.'

Sean followed her quickly, a hand on her shoulder. The car looked abandoned, doors open, headlights blazing. His hands ran down her arms, took her palms in his, squeezed them.

'That's why I thought if you came to the UCs, it'd be somewhere new, take your mind off everything. You had a taste of it in Canberra, didn't you? If we were working together, we could spend more time together. I could be around more . . .'

'And not have to do it in your own time. Been a bit of a strain these last weeks?'

His grip on her hands was momentarily too strong, too tight, but slackened before she registered any pain.

'God, Ned. Do I have to spell it out? Haven't you worked it out yet? I wanted to be with you. I *want* to be with you.'

'When it's convenient.'

On a roll now, she was unstoppable. Clarity was cruel. It hurt that Swiss had been the one to put it into words. But Swiss wasn't here, and now she needed to hurt someone. She started walking up Greenwich Road towards View Street.

'Now you're just being childish.'

His voice was tight with anger, a sound she hadn't heard before. She turned to look, curious.

'*Childish*? I'm sorry, I keep forgetting who you're meant to be. Mentor? Lover? Friend? Workmate?'

'Look, I thought it would help, OK? My mistake. Won't happen again.' He kicked the passenger-side door closed as he said it.

'Go home, Murph,' Ned said. 'I don't need your help.'

SEAN MURPHY HAD MADE NED'S exclusion from the Job bearable. But only now, after she had excluded him, was she realising just how powerful a distraction he had been. And only now that it was impossible did she fully comprehend just how much she'd wanted the life he embodied. She'd killed Lily herself. Right there in Swiss Fowles' office, more effectively than the empty gun in a cold Goulburn car park. All that was left now was Ned – was *Nhu*.

Waking in the early hours from a sleep of gnawing need rather than rest, a silent pager under the pillow, she contemplated her degeneration into clingy mistress. She had a lover she enjoyed and, if she was honest, a situation as convenient to her as it was to him. *Convenient. Enjoyable.* Passionless words. Not worthy of a scene. But she'd smashed it up anyway. Swiss's words had been cruel but she could handle cruel – she'd trained on Ugly. It was because his words had also been true. She'd seen the end coming and all she could do was to make sure she got there first.

So sleep was too short and the days too long and too empty. She tried to avoid the nightly news and ICAC's constant refrain of corruption, detectives, barbecue sets. Linh would pretend to ignore it, reading the *Herald* in silence, its ICAC articles branded with a cartoon cop carrying a sack of money.

MM made no such pretence, lapping at the scandals like a greedy cat. 'Do you know him?' she repeated, as yet another cop ran the press gauntlet into the commission. Some gave the cameras the hard

stare that worked so well in the interview room but had less impact
in the open air.

So Ned escaped; she ran and swam, lost herself in movement.
Rising early, she'd pass her sister's room, excluded by the faint
murmurings and sweet smoke of Linh's dawn rituals. One morning Ned had peered through the crack in the door, feeling like a
five-year-old. Linh sat cross-legged on a cushion, her straight back
to the door, her hands moving, hidden by her body. A bell sounded.
A vase of flowers and sticks of incense sat beneath a portrait of the
beaming Dalai Lama. Ned wondered how her sister reconciled this
stuff with science.

When Zervos finally phoned, Ned had gone past the point of
pride. Zervos, however, wasn't just going to sign off on her return to
work; he was insisting, politely, that Ned come into his office, hear
the evidence that would go to the Coroner. He made it sound like a
favour, even extended the offer to Linh. But Ned caught the steel in
his words and knew it was an order. Making sure no loose cannons
were rolling around his brief. If Zervos was the final hoop to jump
through in order to be put back on full duties – to get back to the
Job – then she'd roll his bloody cigarettes for him if she had to.

Linh had refused the invitation. Ned left the details on the hall
table and went in alone, taking the train into the city and walking down to the dilapidated building on Campbell Street. The Hat
Factory, an old, converted industrial brick box with dodgy lifts and
dim lighting. Ned didn't know if it had ever produced hats, but it
had certainly produced a lot of detectives. Standing one street back
from the concrete brutalism of the new Sydney Police Centre, the
Hat Factory recalled a time when Detective Sergeant Rogerson had
stalked the corridors instead of haunting the headlines. When he
still commanded equal parts of respect and fear, volunteering his
evidence from the witness box at Darlo District Court and having
it believed, not having it drawn under duress and mocked at ICAC.

Zervos's office was shabby, but that was a badge of honour down here. These tacky corridors had been the heart of the old school, with its inner sanctums: the Breakers, the Stick-ups, the Gamers. The CIB had been broken apart before Ned had joined up, and from the look of the packing cases and empty filing cabinets she'd passed in the hallways, Homicide would soon be shifting somewhere shinier, free of the old ghosts, of the badness that had seeped into the brickwork.

TC was in Zervos's office when she arrived. The Homicide inspector, in his subdued dark suit and half-glasses, could have passed for a Macquarie Street specialist, one who took on the terminal cases. He looked designed to deliver bad news.

'I was hoping to see your sister as well, Detective Kelly.'

'She's got other demands on her time today.'

'Pity. Well, before you start back at Bankstown I thought we should make sure there are no misunderstandings.' He tapped the large envelope with the crest of the Australian War Memorial on it. 'You clearly know the history between your father and the deceased woman, Phuong.'

Ned nodded.

'You may not be aware that your father was deeply in debt at the time of his death. Two mortgages – the house in Bankstown and the property on the northern beaches. The business looked sound enough but his personal finances . . .' Zervos raised a dark eyebrow, letting Ned absorb the implication.

She had no idea how Bushrangers had paid its owners. Commissions? Percentages? Money on completion of the job? If Dawn Jarrett was threatening to delay the building project, had that put financial pressure on Mick Kelly? To a Homicide detective, debt was a persuasive motive for murder.

'Our brief is almost complete. We don't expect an open verdict.'

Ned knew what he was saying. Unlawful killing by a known person would be the result. The Coroner would find Mick Kelly had a case to answer – but there would never be a trial to test the evidence.

'What's left to complete?' Ned asked, trying for the detached calm of a professional. A detective who could be trusted to return to her job, unencumbered by her past.

'We intend to speak to Brian Hall as soon as he's sufficiently recovered,' Zervos continued.

'Why Hall?'

'Your father and Hall were partners and old friends. When you and Detective Inspector Charlton interviewed him,' Zervos glanced at TC over his glasses, 'you were not in possession of all the facts about these matters.'

Footsteps squeaked along the linoleum corridor outside. The door opened and one of Zervos's suits showed Linh in. Ned closed her eyes and braced for what was to come. She'd been relieved when Linh had refused to come. Her sister had been too quiet of late. Ned didn't believe it was due to acceptance.

'Miss Kelly, I'm glad you could come. I was just telling your sister that —'

'And I just came in to tell you that you're wrong,' Linh said with disgust. 'My father was not a murderer.'

Ned took a breath, opened her eyes, watched her little sister with something approaching wonder. Equal parts of love and fury seemed to animate her as she stood, staring down the Homicide detective.

'With respect, Miss Kelly, your father had killed before. He had war experience, as your sister discovered from her research.'

Zervos slid forward the envelope from the War Memorial. Linh ignored both Ned and the envelope. Ned hadn't told Linh about Canberra. She hadn't told Linh about anything for a while now.

'Miss Kelly, you were a child. You loved your dad, and that's all natural and exactly as it should be. But you didn't know him.'

'I know he was murdered. Who did that – or don't you care? Too busy loading – that's the right word, isn't it? – loading a man who can't defend himself.'

Linh had been paying attention to ICAC, Ned realised. Like everyone else, she'd learnt a whole new vocabulary.

Zervos closed the file and spoke to Ned. 'It might be better if we do this later, when your sister is a little more composed.'

'Satisfied?' Linh hissed at Ned.

'It's better we know the truth,' Ned began.

'Is it? I used to have parents. I used to have memories of them, good memories, and you've spoiled them. Now I have victims, bodies, evidence, motives, but I don't have *them* anymore. They're really dead now.'

'Linh, it's murder, there's no choice. It overrides your feelings, my feelings, it's —'

'Your sister's right,' Zervos cut in. Ned wished he hadn't. 'You're involved, but this stopped being about you years ago.'

Linh turned and walked out. Ned followed her, all the way down the dingy corridors, with their flimsy office walls and dank stairwells, out onto the street. A group of warbs were sunning themselves outside a homeless shelter next door. They watched with interest as Linh flung words at her.

'You don't really care who killed Mum and Dad, do you?'

'Linh, I just needed to know the truth.'

'Well, I didn't.'

She gestured with her hand for Ned to stay put and marched down the hill, past the chuckling warbs and out of sight around the corner.

Ned climbed back up the stairs, not sure why, not sure where to go or what to do next. From the stairwell, she heard Zervos's voice in the hallway.

'I've seen enough murders and enough families coping with it, TC.'

'Yeah, well, everyone's different.'

'Maybe, but any counsellor knows talking about the dead is an important part of the grieving process. And for children – hell's bells, they needed to have *some* kind of relationship with their parents. But here, there's nothing. The old bird cut those kids off.'

Ned stepped out from the stairwell, silencing Zervos with her presence.

'Linh?' TC asked.

'She's gone.'

'Perhaps you should go after her,' Zervos said, flat voice, flat eyes.

'And get her a counsellor? Bit late in the day, don't you think? I came back to see if you'd finished.'

'Actually, there is one more thing. Any pets when you were growing up? Cat, bird – a dog, maybe?'

For an instant she wanted to hit him. She wished she was TC's size. She wanted to damage him. The same cold, rational violence she'd summoned while waiting for Baxter in a laneway, a police baton in her hands.

TC's hand came down on her shoulder, tethered her.

'No, we didn't have any pets. Why? Would it have helped in the grieving process, do you think?' she said sarcastically. Linh's rage had left her reckless. 'And what about the Kelly murders? Did you even look at —'

'I don't know if anyone promised you anything about that. If they did, they shouldn't have,' Zervos said, glancing at TC. 'Nothing new came up. The case remains open.'

Ned watched him leave, noiseless on the tatty linoleum. Pets. Asking her about fucking pets.

'Her nails,' she called out suddenly. Focus on the facts, she instructed herself, ignore the rest. You're a professional. 'Did you check the samples under her nails?'

Zervos paused, hand on the door handle. 'No match.'

All that family history stored in twisted little lines. Whoever it was lurking under Phuong's nails, it wasn't Mick Kelly. And Zervos hadn't volunteered the information.

'So, whose is it?'

'We'll be asking Brian Hall to volunteer a sample when he is well enough. It's possible he knows more about your parents' murder, as well.'

Ned's skin felt charged, the hairs along her forearms upright. Brian Hall. Zervos hadn't volunteered that piece of information either. When he'd said they'd interview Hall again, he made it sound like Hall was a witness, someone to tell them about Mick Kelly's money worries, not a suspect.

What would Hall tell them? She wanted to hear him. She wanted to know what was happening without waiting to be told.

'So, I'm right to go back to work?' Her need was stronger than her pride.

'Talk to your boss about your shifts, nothing to do with me.' Zervos shut the door to his office hard enough that the flimsy interior walls shook like the set of a cheap TV soap opera.

Her relief was coloured with anger. 'Counsellors? Relationships with the dead? *Pets* . . . What the fuck was that all about?'

'He's doing a degree at uni – criminal psychology, psychiatry something-or-other,' TC said.

'Wanker.' She got it now. She was homework, probably a case study in his essay on kids and 'the grieving process'.

'Ambitious,' TC corrected, as they started down the stairs together. 'Not planning on setting up a couch and a clinic. He wants to be Commissioner.'

TC's shoulders slumped. He'd accepted her request to return to Bankstown without a hint of 'I told you so'. That was what Ned called management. Zervos was part of the new breed and, degrees in hand, they were leaving the old guard behind.

'Just as well,' she said. 'If that's an example of his touchy-fucking-feely side, his patients would be leaping out of windows like lemmings.'

NED RODE A MONDAY MORNING train to work, stuffy, standing room only. Sweat was trickling down her spine by the time they crossed the bridge. The carriages emptied out at Wynyard and Town Hall as the city offices filled up. By the time she changed lines at Central she had a seat to herself and could open out the *Sydney Morning Herald*. Sarajevo was still under siege and militias were snatching food from the starving in Somalia, but the front page had the important news: Princess Anne was set to marry a sailor.

Bankstown Police Station looked smaller. The same faces would be shoplifting from Big W, nicking cars, breaking into houses, belting one another up at pubs, on footpaths, in kitchens or lounge rooms. Mean little crimes.

Shiny red strips spelt out *Merry Xmas* over the front desk, hung high enough to make it difficult for any disgruntled customers to grab them and garrotte someone. The Ds office smelt of fast food and stale cigarette smoke. Cleaners hadn't been through yet, though nothing short of arson would eliminate the essential scent of maleness that permeated every detectives' office Ned had ever set foot in.

The usual white noise of activity masked the need for any real communication. Her workmates greeted her with hasty, superficial comments and distracted nods tossed in passing. Hard to say who was more embarrassed by her presence, them or her.

'Hey, Neddie!'

'Lookin' tanned.'

'Been up the coast?'

Toy was locked in a one-way phone conversation, Figgy had his head in a word processor, and TC was in his fishbowl. It looked larger now that he was the only one in it. He looked up from the overnight CIRs and smiled, warm, expansive, genuine.

'Good to see you back, little buddy. Glad you changed your mind.'

'So, Toy didn't get Zervos to adopt him?' Deflect.

'Working on it.'

Silence.

'So.' She broke it.

'So,' he echoed.

Another silence, one she couldn't fill with anything personal yet. Maybe one day, in the pub, under cover of the hubbub and the encouragement of alcohol.

'Have you heard anything from Zervos about Brian Hall? Have they interviewed him?'

TC shrugged. 'If they have, they haven't told me.'

'Is he still in hospital? Is he —'

'Ned, not your job.' Kind but firm. 'Thought you could spend today catching up. Your pigeonhole's overflowing.'

She'd rather have got stuck into something – anything, as long as it got her out of the station, out of her own head. Instead, she emptied her pigeonhole onto her desk and began sifting. Please-explains from the Exhibits sergeant, requests from the DPP for further statements, a handful of witness subpoenas and a pile of ring-backs, messages and results on calls she'd made when she'd still had a role in the murder inquiry all those weeks ago.

Toy dropped past her desk on his way out to the DAL. 'Caitlin reckons I should put something in writing. To Zervos. Whatchya think?'

Caitlin. Detective Constable Running Sheets. Seemed Toy had got further than Figgy. She didn't look up.

'Dunno, Toy – reckon you can afford the suit?'

She made a start on the exhibit notices.

Figgy sat down a few minutes later. 'Wondered if you'd put in a good word for me – with Murph? I could do with a change and they rort the overtime and allowances in there.'

'Ask him yourself.'

'Yeah, I will, but just thought . . . seeing as you two are —'

'Figgy, fuck off.' She knew he'd gone when the aftershave faded.

The morning ground past and the office emptied, until only Ned and her mail were left in the outer offices, TC left in his. She made a start on her pigeonhole. Call-backs, too late now. Crunched and binned. Envelopes containing results of the business searches she'd ordered weeks earlier: the contractors who'd provided the brickies; the security firm on the site – SecSure, a Bankstown firm and a family show, by the look of all the Marshallsons on the list; the company that had owned the units under construction, Erimar Pty Ltd. The two directors were E. Vass and M. Shields, and the contact listed was a local solicitors' firm – Humphreys, Huie & Holt. Holt was still about; Ned had run across him in court, leading her to wonder if solicitors were recruited on the basis of talent or alliteration.

Not her case anymore. She stuffed the records into an inter-departmental envelope for Homicide. The brief was closed. If these were duplicates they could bin them; otherwise Detective Constable Running Sheets could file them.

TC passed her desk and dropped a fat folder in front of her. 'Take a look at this and liaise with Marcus Jarrett, OK? Keep us sweet with the MLC.'

It was an interim report on the skeletal remains found at the building site. It featured a cast of thousands, a clue to the power struggles that must have taken place out there in the dirt. Throw in interest from local council and local members – state and federal – it must've been a fully fledged shit fight.

The folder bulged with maps, graphs and charts, photographs of uneven ground pegged out into grids by white twine, neatly labelled images of rock and dirt and 'disarticulated human skeletal material' – bones. She skimmed over the jargon, lighting on the fragments she could absorb.

> Remains of:
> 6 adults (4 female, 2 male)
> 5 children (females, between 4 and 8 years)
> 2 infants

Like a shopping list.

A forensic dental specialist noted the teeth wear indicated a predominantly 'pre-contact' diet, concluding the remains were 'pre-historic'. Pre-historic. Before history. Couldn't get much older than that. Sounded like they'd always been bones, never fleshed or fully alive, just things lying there, passive and patient, waiting to be discovered and tallied and tagged.

A paragraph jarred; she re-read it. The first layer consisted of 'cultural material': cigarette butts and bandaids, bottle tops and tin cans, even a couple of apparently imperishable condoms. *Cultural material.* A modern garbage dump lay above the bones.

The lower layers revealed no signs of shell, stone, or plant or faunal remains. The archaeologists concluded this lack of pre-historic 'cultural material' indicated that this had not been a habitation site. No middens – mounds of shell and bone – to mark a home. The dead had come here – or been brought here.

Ned had passed middens on her runs through the stands of angophora by the harbour. Instinct drew her, as it had drawn those before her, to certain spots where she'd rest against a gentle sweep of sandstone, warm in the afternoon sun, above some little golden crescent of sand. Special places where, when she looked down at her feet, the remains of thousands of years of oyster feasts flecked the dirt.

She turned back to the file. No oysters here. The disarticulation and scattering of the skeletal materials were put down to animal disturbance. Some smaller bones were absent but, remarkably, only one significant piece was missing: a skull belonging to an infant. No marks to show a deliberate severing. Predation after death. Dingoes and babies, an Australian motif.

Phones rang out at the desks nearby but Ned barely registered them. Feet pounded up the staircase and a door on the level below slammed shut. From the meal room, hoots of laughter marked a punch line.

She kept reading, coming finally to the causes of death – violent and unnatural, all of them. A mix of blunt trauma injuries, mainly skull fractures, though the adult bones showed splintering and striations consistent with the use of firearms. Antique weaponry left distinctive marks.

The file was cold and slippery with photographs. She walked it back to TC's desk, but his office was empty. Behind the door was the archive box, her parents' names on the side. He still had it. The dead shared space in this office, waiting on justice. There'd be no justice for the unnamed and unknown dead. The dead stayed dead while the living counted the cost.

'Caught up, little buddy?' TC was at the door. 'Feel like a bit of burglar's clerking after lunch?' He settled into his chair and unpeeled a kebab. The aroma of onions and garlic blossomed from within the foil.

'Did you ever catch up with Mabo?' she asked, putting the brief on his desk. The old warb had been right. His people had been there all along.

The kebab paused halfway to TC's mouth. He smoothed out the plastic bag and put it back down. Hummus and oil drizzled over the lip of the pita bread.

'You worried about briefing Jarrett? You don't owe him any explanations. Just let him have a look at the brief —'

'Did you ever tell Zervos what Mabo said? About there being more bodies, about Bill Jarrett finding them back then?'

'Ned, let it go,' TC said gently. 'They turned up. Black Charlie was never going to be any help.'

'Did you see him?' She held her ground and his gaze, felt her eyes filling with tears. Mabo had deserved to be heard. Not dumped.

'Had a look for him, couldn't turn him up, so I asked the night shift to keep an eye out,' he said, lifting up his kebab, averting his eyes. 'He slipped through the net, Ned. It happens.'

She had to stop herself from nodding in compliance; respect for rank and authority was so ingrained. She owed TC. He'd brought her back without a post-mortem about Murph. She owed him her loyalty, her trust, not cheap suspicion. She picked up the pile of break-and-enter reports, turned and left the office.

The letter from Glebe was waiting in the mailbox when Ned got home. She sat on the front step, swatting away mosquitoes, and read the formal notification to Nguyen Thi Phuong's next of kin to come and claim her body from the morgue. The house was locked and silent behind her; no sign of MM or Linh. Ned gazed at the letter, shook her head, then stood up and got in her car.

The southbound lane of the bridge was crawling, as the evening current affairs reported that a bunch of Cambodian boat people in mandatory detention could finally be deported. If Phuong had turned up today she'd never have made it past Port Headland. In contrast, ICAC was providing stand-up comedy, with Neddy Smith asserting that being a thief didn't automatically make him a liar.

The closer Ned drew to Glebe, the further Phuong receded before her.

Despite the warm evening, a figure in a heavy coat was trundling a shopping cart filled with plastic bags past the shuttered doors of the morgue's loading bay. The dusted-off little grocery trolley she'd planned to give Mabo was still rattling around in the back of her Mazda. She sat in the car, hands gripping the steering wheel as the figure stumped away down the footpath in Arundel Street. His cart had a wobbly front wheel and kept lurching to the right as if it were trying to leap out into the road.

When her tears came, Ned was helpless to stop them. They rolled down her cheeks; her nose began flowing and her throat tightened. Mabo had had a crappy life and a terrible death and she'd done bugger all about either. TC had asked the night shift to keep an eye out for him and he'd ended up dumped in town. Away from his old haunts. He wouldn't have known where to go, where to avoid; wouldn't have known that in the city, even a warb who had nothing offered something to a sadistic bastard whose sport was setting them alight. Mabo made it dead warb number five in the past two years.

She rooted through her glove box for something to blow her nose with. The old warhorses told stories of bodies, live and dead, being shifted between police patrols by coppers too lazy to do the paperwork. Ned had laughed at the tale of the Water Police launch turning its spotlights on a pair of uniforms, catching them in the act as they tried to push a dead'un from the high-tide mark back into the water. No badness, just shonks. Stories from the old school, that pre-dated the development of forensics, the sort of thing that couldn't happen now.

Despite knowing where to go, who to see, even what forms to ask for, Ned wasn't at ease in the morgue. She'd guided the grieving through this maze before, relatives reclaiming their dead from the bureaucracy of unnatural death. No matter how kind, how helpful she'd been, she knew their memories would be forever tainted by the steel and smell of this place, their mourning doubly wronged by death and suspicion. But Ned wasn't in mourning, she didn't need a guide, and Phuong didn't feel like family.

Antiseptic clutched at her throat. Like a good hotel, the morgue had a night shift. Ned recognised the attendant on duty, the same man who'd escorted Marcus Jarrett to view Dawn's remains. He gathered together the documentation that would release the body to a funeral home and witnessed Ned's signature.

'Did you want to see her?'

'I've seen it,' she answered, too quickly, only noticing the *it* after the word was gone.

'Detective Kelly doesn't do the dead.'

She started at the sound of Marcus Jarrett's voice behind her. In that flash she saw him, gently kissing the terrible skin of his mother. He stepped up beside her, identical paperwork in his hands, in the name of Patrick Arthur Murray.

'You're looking after Mabo?' she said stupidly, avoiding the truth of Jarrett's words.

'No family.' He handed the papers to the attendant, who gave them a cursory look before stamping and stapling.

The silence was stretching thin. Ned scanned her memory for any pubs within walking distance, even a café – somewhere to suggest they go to, to talk, to put off returning to Greenwich for a little longer.

'I've got the brief, the first reports on the . . .' She hesitated for a moment; in her mind she was calling the Bankstown excavation reports 'the bone brief', but doubted Jarrett would appreciate the title. 'On the remains found on the site.'

Jarrett started for the back door. 'Send it to the office and I'll read it,' he said.

The back entrance to the morgue was well lit, with security cameras mounted above all the entrances. The door locked behind them with a series of electronic clicks, leaving them alone on the sloping footpath. The faint nausea that was her companion at the morgue began to recede. She didn't want to come back here again.

'I'll do that tomorrow,' she said. 'Any news about Mabo from Homicide?'

Jarrett expelled a breath, as if he'd been subliminally holding it in the morgue. He looked tired, puffy under the eyes. Slumped shoulders.

'Nah. They say things like "ongoing", "series", "pattern". But I don't see them setting up a stake-out around Woolloomooloo any time soon, do you?'

'He shouldn't have been there,' she said quietly.

'No. He shouldn't. Plan to do anything about that, Detective?' His body had grown taller; shoulders back, jaw thrust forward.

'I'm going to find out who,' she said, feeling her own jawline rising.

He shook his head and laughed. 'I'll believe it when I see it, Detective Kelly.'

He turned to leave, then stopped, opened his briefcase and pulled out a sheet of paper.

'You can add this to your brief, if you like. It's as good as a confession.'

Ned took the piece of paper, a photocopy of a page from *The Historical Records of New South Wales*. A paragraph was highlighted, a Government and General Order issued by Governor Philip Gidley King, dated 1 May, 1801.

From the wanton manner in which a large body of natives, resident about Parramatta, George's River, and Prospect Hill, have attacked and killed some of Government sheep, and their violent threat of murdering all the white men they meet, which they put into execution by murdering Daniel Conroy, stock-keeper in a most savage and inhumane manner, and severely wounding Smith, settler; and as it is impossible to foresee to what extent their present hostile menaces may be carried, both with respect to the defenceless settlers and the stock, the Governor has directed that this as well as all other bodies of natives in the above district to be driven back from the settlers' habitations by firing at them.

By the time Ned finished reading it, Jarrett was gone.

'DID I *WHAT*?' SENIOR CONSTABLE Davis looked at Ned as if unsure whether he ought to laugh at her or give her a mouthful. She'd had much the same response from every member of the night-shift crew when she'd asked if they knew how Mabo had ended up in Woolloomooloo.

'We're taking it up the arse from ICAC, IA and bloody Royal Commissions, Detective,' he'd said, turning back to write up the car diary for his shift. 'Don't need our own fucking workmates trying to stir up shit as well.'

Marcus Jarrett's derision had niggled at her. Finding out who'd dumped Mabo in town couldn't be that hard.

So she'd started with the station pads but there was nothing about Patrick Arthur Murray on the occurrence pad, that daily record of significant events. Then again Mabo, drunk and troublesome, would not have been classified as significant. The telephone message pad was a less filtered record but again, there was no trace of Mabo. No call from a member of the public to remove a drunk from the road, or attend to a man yelling abuse. If an incident had occurred that had led someone to dump Mabo in Woolloomooloo instead of the cellblock, it hadn't been recorded.

The most likely suspects, she'd reasoned, would be the night-shift crew. Seven nights straight patrolling quiet streets, long hours between jobs, just driving about, watching, waiting. Didn't take long to drive to town in the early hours. The night shift had rotated so the cops she needed were now back in daylight and scattered over various duties. Davis had been the last one. No one was confessing to anything.

Homicide had even less to say about their investigation into the dead warbs. The constable she spoke to was brusque, sounded pissed off that he'd been lumbered with such an uninspiring case. No witnesses, no suspects, and victims no one missed.

Ned hung up, the Ds office buzzing around her. Though she had sunk back into the rhythm of the Job, for the first time she'd found herself watching the clock, dreading the time to go home, yet unwilling to kick on with the team, fearful of the late-night drinks and inevitable sharing of confidences.

Toy pushed past her desk, braying about an arrest, an interview, a confession. He'd grown cocky since his brush with Zervos and his team. Ned had discovered an unexpected solidarity with Figgy in wanting to deck the young trainee detective.

She picked up the phone again, as much a reflex action to block out Toy as anything else. Automatically she dialled the number she knew by heart and, despite feeling like a stalker, asked the same question. 'Is Mr Hall up to having visitors yet?'

The warbs weren't the only brief Homicide had been close-mouthed on. So she'd sidestepped them. If the interviewers wouldn't tell her what had happened, she'd ask the interviewee. Zervos had reckoned that Hall knew more about Mick and Ngoc and Phuong than he'd let on. She had a right to know what that was.

So far she hadn't got past the nurses' station, but today the answer was different.

'Mr Hall's not here anymore. He's moved to a rehab hospital. If you hold on I can tell you where.'

Selway Private Hospital turned out to be an old Strathfield man-sion that still looked more like a large private home than a place the broken came to be reassembled. Ned had checked on visiting hours but nothing else. She wasn't asking permission this time.

She looked confident and was directed down a hallway.

Brian Hall was one of four men propped up in wheelchairs in a room that looked out over the back garden. They were all motionless but their eyes followed Ned as she approached. On the television the gaudy wheel of an afternoon game show spun round and round.

The stroke had smudged one side of Brian Hall's face. The eye leaked over the cheek. Lips dripped down towards his jaw. He gurgled at Ned. Once an instrument of speech, his mouth was now an obstacle.

'Dek'tiv – Dek'tiv elly.'

Repetition lent the sounds some clarity but she didn't feel like much of a detective. His face was incapable of showing the effort involved in communicating, but it was audible in the swallowed 'l' that lodged in the back of his throat like phlegm.

'Mr Hall,' Ned began. It had seemed easy when she'd planned it. Rock up, grill him, make him tell her what he knew. She bet that Zervos or one of his sergeants wouldn't have hesitated.

The art of the interview. The technical stuff was easy; the skill of open questioning, always asking why, where, when, how, never 'Did you?', 'Are you?' Never giving the option of a yes-or-no answer, always compelling an explanation. But the stuff that you had to find inside – that was harder. It took conviction to stand without pity in front of a slack-mouthed man, whose spittle fell back on him like sticky rain, and keep pressing for the truth.

The first of these skills was pointless. She couldn't even understand him. Hall was making a series of popping sounds, his eyes scanning back and forth as if seeking an interpreter to unlock his words.

The second skill, she began to doubt she had.

Then she heard a familiar voice approaching and felt the instant shame of a child discovered, red-handed, doing wrong.

'Nhu!' Linh stopped in the doorway, a tall woman at her side.

Ned suspected the astonished look on her little sister's face matched her own.

Linh had been a regular visitor. That much was clear from her familiarity with Dianne, Brian Hall's wife, but even more so from the light in Brian's eyes when Linh leant down and kissed his cheek. Whether Linh had been instrumental in keeping Ned at bay was less clear.

The sisters had gone into the garden, sought shelter at a picnic table under an umbrella. There was no breeze. The hot air of the late afternoon was trapped by the unit blocks overlooking the hospital.

'What are you doing here, Nhu?' Linh sounded tired.

'Same thing you are.'

'I doubt that. Please leave them alone.' The note of pleading caught Ned by surprise.

Through the large window Ned could see Dianne Hall leaning over her husband. She took his hand in hers, kissed the knuckles.

'Has he told you anything? About them?'

'I haven't asked.'

Ned wasn't sure if it was disappointment or disgust that coloured her sister's voice. She looked back to the window. Dianne Hall had disappeared.

'The Homicide Squad want to speak to him again, Linh,' Ned said hastily, as Dianne came out into the garden and down the path towards them.

'We know,' Linh said, with the certainty of someone who knew whose side she was on.

Dianne Hall joined them, a motherly hand pressing Linh's shoulder as she began to speak. 'It's good you came, Noo. Brian wanted to see you, to tell you – no, Linh, it's OK.'

'You know the Homicide Squad want to —' Ned began.

'Yes, yes,' Dianne said, as if this was a minor irritant distracting her from something more important. 'Tomorrow morning sometime. Brian wanted you girls to know what he'll be telling them.'

'But Dianne, I —' Linh objected.

'If Noo hadn't come, I'd have had to go to her, Linh.' Dianne turned a pair of sad, pale eyes on Ned. In better days she'd have been described as handsome, hearty even. Now her cheeks were hollowed and her clothes hung off her. 'Brian wanted you both to know.'

Linh made to get up; Dianne's hand on her forearm stayed her movement, her voice gentle. 'He's been wanting to tell you, Linh, but you wouldn't . . .' Linh dropped back into her seat, allowed Dianne to take her hand as she continued to speak.

'Brian wanted you both to know. Mick was no murderer.'

An intake of breath and then a smile lit up her little sister. It reminded Ned how long it had been since she'd seen one.

Ned scrutinised Dianne's face. Of course she'd say that. The Homicide Squad were coming tomorrow and if Mick was no murderer then her husband couldn't be one, either. Not even if it was Brian Hall's DNA under the victim's fingernails. She bit back the words and listened.

'Brian knew about Phuong. Mick was trying to help her. Despite their past, well, she was in bad shape. Mick . . .' She hesitated.

'What?' Linh sat forward.

'He . . . he loved Phuong.'

Ned saw Linh absorb the blow.

Love. The woman said it like it could only be exculpation for murder, not its cause. Ned knew what love was capable of. Her palms tingled.

'What about Mum?' Ned broke her silence. 'They were sisters.'

'He was hiding her from your mother. . . .' Dianne put her other hand on Linh's. 'She found out that time you broke your arm . . . Ngoc couldn't find Mick, and it all came out. Phuong had disappeared, Mick was frantic. He even went to the police but she was here under a false name, so . . .' Diane blushed. 'Mick said the cops were bastards.'

'He reported her missing?' Linh was suddenly energised. 'No one knew who she was, or that she was here. If she disappeared, who would know? If Dad killed her, why would he report her missing?'

It hurt to see the hope in Linh's face. The Halls were playing with them. If Mick Kelly had reported Phuong missing there'd be a record, and that record would have come up.

'Why didn't Brian tell the police, tell *me*, all this before?' Ned asked.

'He thought he was doing the right thing. He told Mary Margaret and she . . .' Dianne shifted in her seat, uneasy. 'He gave her the diary and the papers too.'

'What?' Ned said sharply. 'What papers, what diary? When did he . . . ?'

Ned remembered Stan Lucas's hard blue eyes as he told her he'd seen Hall leave the site with a box of papers the morning after her parents' murder. But MM didn't have any papers. She'd searched, Zervos had searched – they'd both found nothing.

'It was Mick's diary from his time in Vietnam, some papers, letters from Phuong. They were in his office on the site. Brian didn't want the police to, you know . . .'

The raw truth about murder. All the secrets spill out. Had Brian Hall realised this faster than most and acted to protect his dead mate's secret? Or was it more than just an affair Hall had been hiding? There was only his word – his wife's word – for any of it.

Then Linh spoke up, her voice quiet. 'Was he going to leave us? For her?' Her pain so naked, Ned looked away.

Ned had suspected her father of so many terrible things – war crimes, murder – that an affair seemed inconsequential. Through it all Linh had been steadfast, unshaken in her belief in her parents. Maybe she could bear the thought of them being murdered; maybe she could even bear the thought that her father might have been a killer. But too late, Ned realised that Linh couldn't bear the thought that he might have been about to leave them for his lover. Like everyone, Linh had a space, a small, dark little place, in which she dreamt the worst about the dead.

'He said Mick loved Phuong, he loved Ngoc, he loved you all. I don't know . . .' Dianne began to cry.

A litany of love that left Linh's question unanswered.

'FANCY A RUN OUT TO ARCHIVES?' Ned was at her desk attempting to get to grips with a fraud Toy was trying to palm off when TC loomed up beside her. She looked up but he was already heading back to his office. She followed.

'Thought you might want to have a look, before you take it back. I'm popping out to lunch. Just make sure you get it back there before four.' He closed the blinds and the door behind him, leaving her alone with the archive box containing her parents' murder brief.

The lid came off easily, the papers loosened by recent use. Everything Ned knew about their deaths she had absorbed from being told by other people; she could no longer distinguish how she had learnt the things she knew. Now the facts were all at her fingertips.

A black-and-white photo showed the gun that had shot her parents, lodged under the back wheel of the car. Tossed there? Abandoned? Dropped? Accidental?

Here were the forms that charted the murder weapon's journey through the bureaucracy of a criminal investigation. Exhibit Room to Fingerprints, Fingerprints to Ballistics, Ballistics to Exhibit Room again. Was it still there, causing some Exhibits officer irritation, or had it been disposed of? Its travels had been recorded, as had the results. Freshly fired. No prints. The striations of its barrel, as unique as the whorls on a fingertip. Serial numbers ground off. Common make: Smith & Wesson, the six-shot. Big brother to the five-shot she carried.

Her hand hovered above the forensic reports then turned them over, unread. Nothing there that she didn't know – really know – from the taste in her mouth and the damp sweat on her forehead. The photos passed, slick and unseen, through her fingers.

Instead, she looked at the statements. They were numerous, filled with stilted police-speak: *patrolling south when I heard something . . . where I saw a handgun under the rear driver's-side wheel of the vehicle . . . Detective Edwards arrived and I told him something . . . conveyed Exhibit Number 76/8291 to the Fingerprint Branch where I handed it to Detective Martins . . .*

Mind-numbingly pedantic fragments recorded the unfolding scene, the foot search that had found nothing, the witnesses who had seen nothing, the gun that had revealed nothing.

Then there were the statements coaxed from real people, the neighbours she had no memory of and who, in turn, seemed to have had little knowledge of them. Caricatures of Ngoc, *a good mother, difficult to understand, shy, quiet,* of Mick, *a hard worker, busy,* and two little girls, *cute, well-behaved;* the whole thing a *tragedy.*

Brian Hall's statement was longer and, though he hadn't lied, it was just a sketch – there was no colour.

The army's contribution to the brief was a testament to how a wealth of detail could contain so little information. If any backgrounding had been done, mate to mate, off the record, then that's where it had stayed.

A large envelope was at the bottom of the pile. The papers inside were few but thick, lodged in firmly. Ned tweezered them out with two fingers. Children's paintings. They belonged on the side of a fridge, curling up at the edges. She flipped the envelope back up and saw a neatly typed label featuring a hospital logo, a date, a doctor's name, Linh's name and hers. She looked again – her name a childish signature at the bottom of one painting, Linh's on the other. But no recall, no sense of ever having made those shapes, applied that paint, chosen those colours. A large yellow circle surrounded by white rays. A black circle within it. She'd drawn a sun. But it had happened at night.

The back seat of Dad's car, staring up through the open window, eyes full of the moon rolling yellow and fat along telegraph wires.

The bump into the driveway.

Home.

The air rips apart.

Dad's head blows open.

Red bleeds into yellow.

Fragments fly.

Things wet and warm, soft and sharp, pelt against her face.

Far off there's screaming.

The car idles.

A metallic stink of hot muffler and meat.

Forehead and cheeks, chin and neck, heavy and wet.

Her eyes are shut, lips sealed, but she can still taste it – salty but not like the sea – in the back of her throat.

Ned retched.

Gripping the side of the desk, resisting the punch of memory.

She'd spent her childhood being thrust back there unwillingly. A slammed door could send the world black. A pedestrian looming up by the car could split the air like a shot. Her mouth would flood with a vile sensation. Adrenalin, she learnt later – that sour, terrible taste. But knowing it was adrenalin couldn't destroy the knowledge that her mouth had once been filled with her father's fatal wounds.

Nightmares were normal. But falling through holes, wide-awake, landing on the back seat of Dad's car, living it again and again – that was not normal. She'd sealed those holes before she knew they had a label – post-traumatic stress. Goulburn had cracked them open once more. Sean Murphy had pushed her through at the point of a gun. Big moon. Dad's head. Red eclipse – but she'd clawed her way back.

Now she was back there again. This time falling through a crude kid's painting she had no memory of creating. She forced herself to swallow, not to spit. Listened to her breath, wrestled it into a slower rhythm. Made herself study the image on the desk: cardboard, paint, images, evidence.

It wasn't a sun. She'd painted a moon, a big, fat moon, made yellow by the streetlights. The moon and a black space where her father's head had been. But she hadn't painted anything red. No blood. It'd been dark. She'd felt it, smelt it, tasted it, but she hadn't seen any blood. Just the moon and the night and the explosion of light. Only in her memories had she dreamt the moon red.

She looked at Linh's painting and flinched. The cardboard was stiff with red paint.

Two stick figures were stacked up inside a box on wheels – a car, a kid's image of a car. Inside the car was red, all red. Outside all dark. Thick layers of black paint. Ned stroked it, consoling the little girl who'd painted it. As she did, she felt a shape underneath, off to one side of the car. She held it up to the light. The paint was applied so thickly that no light shone through. She turned it over and saw pencil indentations outlining the car and the stick figures sitting inside. But Linh had also drawn another figure, outside the car. She'd pressed heavily on the pencil then painted over it, burying it under black paint.

Had Linh seen the killer? Ned remembered the bump over the kerb, a figure on the footpath, but Linh had drawn someone – arm raised, pointing. There was no mention of it in the brief.

Ned flicked the papers of the brief back in line. All different sizes and thicknesses, their edges sticking out at angles. What had she expected to find? A clue that older and wiser heads than hers had missed? Instead, all she'd found here was a hint of the horror Linh carried with her, re-awakening nightmares of her own she'd spent years learning to forget.

She turned the pile of papers on end, tapped them into shape. The corner of one statement jutted out.

A name, a rank, typed in; a signature carefully penned above.

She tugged the page from the pile. A banal statement from a police cadet, stilted, one paragraph, transporting the murder weapon to the Fingerprint Branch.

Her spine grew cold.

A police cadet.

Like all cadets, this one had been assigned the most menial and boring of tasks, maintaining the chain of evidence on an exhibit. But still, she could imagine the momentary thrill of being trusted to handle an exhibit for a double murder. No ordinary exhibit either – the murder weapon itself.

Surely that was a first?

First kiss, first child, first murder. Things you'd always remember. And even if you had become so jaded that you'd forgotten – well, meeting the daughter of the murder victims would surely remind you.

Ned stared at the document and the signature.

So why hadn't Sean Murphy ever told her?

SEAN MURPHY'S WAS NOT THE only name Ned recognised as she went through the police statements again. Ugly had worked at Banks-town forever, so his signature turning up at the bottom of MM's statement was more of a reminder of his ubiquity than a shock. It was Sean's signature on the exhibit form that was causing her shirt to stick to her sweaty back while she turned and scanned, turned and scanned through the brief, sorting papers into two piles. It was the smaller pile – statements, forms and running sheets – that she picked up and photocopied. She packed the brief up, then changed her mind and made copies of the paintings, flipping Linh's over to capture the underside, playing with the contrast controls until it caught the faint outlines of the pencil scores.

TC must have known the bombshell waiting for her in that box. Knew she'd see it. Although she almost hadn't, almost put it all back in the box, unnoticed. Would he have told her? Or let her return the box and never mentioned it again?

Chance. He'd left it to chance.

Suspicion grew, like an insect bite: at first a feathery brush against the skin, then a growing, burning, consuming need to scratch. She hefted the brief onto her hip; the contents slid and settled. The past was committed to paper and boxed. It had weight and texture. She hurried. There was plenty of time to make it to archives before they closed, but she wanted to spend some time there, scratching at her itch.

The only car left was the Commodore station wagon, too sluggish for Figgy, not flash enough for Toy. Ned couldn't care less. She got in and backed out into Fetherstone Street. TC was strolling back from the direction of the railway station, a solidly built bloke in a business suit at his side. The suit was talking intently, TC's head bent towards him, nodding. He didn't notice her. She shoved Massive Attack's *Blue Lines* into the cassette player, and chilly licks and paranoia blew through the car. Her hands trembled on the steering wheel, palms tingling and hot. The past in a box beside her.

Police Archives. A paper morgue where the brief would be interned again, maybe back into the same square of dustless space it had occupied during its patient wait. Just one box in one row among all those rows of love, hate and blood. Justice, or the want of it, filed away, yellowing with age.

Ned handed the box over to the dust-coated sergeant, who checked each item against his list before signing his name to the activity report.

'I'd like to have a look at a few more things,' she said, interrupting his closure of books and straightening of ledgers. 'Same brief. Occurrence pads, telephone message pads.'

He sucked his teeth, and she waited for him to ask on whose authority the request came. Instead, he said, 'Where? When?'

'Bankstown, September and October 1976.'

'You're lucky – only started archiving the pads that year,'

He opened a gunmetal-grey cabinet, revealing a stack of large, blue-bound books, gold lettering on their spines, marbled edges glistening like oil on water. He found the year he wanted and opened it up. The indexes were handwritten, the scripts all different but all bearing the same attractive pride in penmanship. Those old station sergeants knew how to write.

'Just Bankstown? Or you want the sub-station, Revesby, as well?'

'Yes, both.'

Ned raided the drink machine for a cold can while she waited for the papers to be brought down. She'd been played. Lied to. If not in words then in what had not been said.

Shadows flitted down rows of the archive, cops biding their time till retirement, away from the front line. The echo of uneven footsteps dragging across the warehouse floor drew closer. An all-too-familiar sense of dread enclosed Ned. She hadn't expected him to be here. Last time, he'd been pushing paperwork around at the vehicle holding yard.

Ned looked up. Baxter was pushing a trolley piled with boxes of spring-binder folders her way. Her Banquo's ghost. She doubted she was anything much to him.

He had the caved-in look of an alcoholic, the skin colour of someone who sat in bars when he wasn't working in sheds like this. He must be thirty, but looked so much older.

He still limped.

'You've got till four unless you want to come back tomorrow,' he said, checking his watch. The last three fingers on his left hand had set crooked. When he looked up, recognition flickered over his face.

'New.' He sounded bored. 'You've copped a shit job here, then.'

Ned bumped into him more often than she liked on her travels through the back-end of policing. Baxter never mentioned Linh. Never had since the day he'd sliced her.

'Yeah. Well, can't all be glamour, can it?' she replied.

The police world was small and they'd established a professional blankness when they had to deal with each other. But though she knew the worst of him, he didn't know the worst of her. She resented that inch of moral high ground the bastard had over her as a result, the way these encounters always left her squirming with shame.

Word was that he was angling for a pension. Ned hoped he got it soon – for her sake.

Baxter limped away and Ned turned to the trolleys he'd left behind.

There was a day's work here. She decided to start with the

Bankstown records and work backwards from the date of her parents' murder.

The occurrence pad that sat on all police station counters was still the official running commentary on significant events. But she'd only gone back through a couple of days when she found a large gap in the records. At first she thought she'd missed a file, or that Baxter had left a file out. She got down on her haunches and hunted through the folders.

Then she saw it.

Inserted in an early September folder, a notice from the Royal Commission into Aboriginal Deaths in Custody. *Records removed.*

She checked the telephone message pads – same gap, same form. The Commission had wound up last year, but how long it would take for the papers to return was anyone's guess. She sat back on her heels.

This was the backwash from the death in custody at Bankstown that had made Inspector Morgenstrom so leery. Pins and needles from her cramped position forced her to straighten up.

Ned pulled another box from the trolley. Revesby occurrence pads. She opened the folder, started scanning the record of events in Revesby in September 1976. The quiet little sub-station generated fewer records. Parking complaints, the occasional bust, a bit of excitement with school kids taking an inter-school footie fracas onto the platform at Panania railway station.

She stopped.

Black flies buzzed before her eyes, stuffed her ears. Hot and cold tremors ran through her tendons.

She took the sheet out of the folder. Moving by feel towards the photocopier, she hit the copy button dumbly over and over before realising the power wasn't on. Then, propped up against it, the hum and whirr of its start-up cycle vibrating through her hips, she read the entry again.

Sleepy sub-stations. Same back then as they are now. A leisurely pace, a good spot for young officers, probationers, cadets, to learn the ropes, how to do things, practise making occurrence-pad entries like the one in her hands.

STATION Revesby	NSW POLICE FORCE OCCURRENCE PAD	Form 2945 D. West NSW Government Printer
ENTRY NO. DATE, TIME	DETAILS	RESULT
34/9 11.30 p.m. 30 Sept 1976	**MISSING PERSON INQUIRY** At about 9.50 p.m. Mr Michael Kelly attended Revesby Police Station to report a missing family member. The person was described as his sister-in-law but when pressed for details of her name, date and place of birth Mr Kelly stated that he was not certain what name the woman was using as she had only recently arrived in the country. He was unsure of her legal status and did not want to create problems for her. The station contacted the night car and spoke with Det. Sgt Urganchich by radio for further advice. Report not taken at this time due to lack of detail. It is not clear if the person is actually missing. Mr Kelly stated he was concerned as she had missed an appointment. He was advised to make further inquiries and contact Det. Sgt Urganchich when he had more details. S.J. Murphy Cadet	Det. Sgt Urganchich contacted by radio for advice. Mr Kelly advised to obtain details of the missing person and contact Bankstown Detectives if he wished to report the person missing. N.F.A. at this stage. S.J. Murphy Cadet

PHOTOCOPIES OF THE PAINTINGS LAY side by side on the kitchen table, the bold primary colours of the originals flattened into black and white. Crude, childish images lacking the joy such paintings should contain.

'Do you remember us doing them?' Ned asked.

Linh nodded slowly, as if the memory was unfamiliar.

'If you'd asked me about it, I don't think I would've. But seeing them – it brings it back. It was before Mary Margaret came to pick us up. We were still at the hospital. I remember the doctor bringing in paints – I guess he was a doctor. I remember thinking I'd better not get any paint on his white coat.'

'I can't remember it. Not at all. Nothing.'

'You were still . . .' Linh began.

Catatonic. Another word she'd learnt much later. The period of her life that it applied to was gone. Another of nature's survival mechanisms: not speaking, not talking. But the evidence of this painting, her name scrawled at the bottom, showed she had been trying to communicate something.

'You were still in shock.'

Ned cherished her sister for choosing the kinder word. Parents dead in body, sister dead in spirit, Linh had been utterly alone in the world, sitting in a hospital waiting to see what would happen next. Knowing it was beyond her control didn't stop Ned feeling the guilt of abandoning Linh back then.

'Where did you get these?'

'From the brief – Mum and Dad's brief.'

Linh stepped away from the table, wary, drawing in on herself.

'What? Why were you . . . ? What did it say?'

'Briefs don't "say" anything. They're a conglomeration of things – bits and pieces, evidence. The evidence speaks, or at least it's meant to. These were in the brief, part of it.'

'Evidence? These?'

'I suppose they thought it was a way in – a way to interview us. See what we'd seen.'

Linh looked back down at the table. 'I remember them asking questions – lots of different people, asking the same questions again and again.'

Ned put another photocopy out. The underside of Linh's painting.

'What's —'

Linh's hand clamped over her mouth, face drained. No time to make it to the bathroom. She swung around and threw up in the sink.

'So you did see someone?' Ned asked.

Out on the back deck, a glass of scotch apiece, the last of the Dimple that Sean had brought round, too long, too much knowledge, ago. Linh had her feet tucked under her on the sun lounge, a small shape in the dark, discernible by the clink of ice in her glass.

'I think I was trying to remember what happened. I wanted to remember, I wanted to see. A shape – a figure outside, on the footpath – passed in front, then a flash, and the windscreen shattering, screaming, then a flash – the noise, my ears . . .'

Ned hugged her. Linh sipped from her glass.

'I kept imagining I could see who it was, wishing I could see. But it was just a flash, a shape. Noise.'

'It's OK. Could you see – was it male, female?'

'Big. But then, I was little. Everyone was big back then.' Linh eyed her. 'What else was in the brief, Nhu?'

She couldn't tell her. Not yet. Ned didn't know if she could tell anyone. Once, she'd have gone straight to TC, for advice, to bounce ideas.

'You've seen something, haven't you? Found something.' Linh's voice quickened. 'You're different. What is it?'

'Maybe nothing. I need to check on a few things. I didn't – don't – want to tell you, not yet. I don't want you to get your hopes up, just in case —'

'In case what?' Ned heard the effects of the scotch in the way Linh laughed, a laugh on the cusp of tears. 'What could be worse than what already is?'

'Giving you the hope that it isn't true.'

'But you . . . .' Linh knelt forward on the lounge, wobbling, grabbed her sister's face in her hands. 'You don't believe it anymore, do you? You don't believe he killed them?'

The occurrence pad confirmed her father had tried to report Phuong missing. Was he covering up her disappearance? The faces and voices of the last weeks jumbled her thoughts. Her sister's hands on her skin. Mabo's hand on her arm, spinning her in circles, telling her Bill Jarrett had told Mick Kelly about the bones. Kelly had said he'd do something about it. Had he? Those missing pages of Bankstown records ached.

Linh's hands tightened. 'You don't believe it anymore, do you?'

Ned shook her head, slow, unable to find words.

They sat quietly together as Linh finished the bottle. The silence was companionable for the first time in a long time.

Ned looked up at the sky, picked out the Pleiades. The nest of stars played hide and seek in her peripheral vision, dissolving whenever she tried to stare at them. Below, in the narrows between Manns Point and Balmain, a prawn trawler drifted with the tide, throwing spots of light across the black water. •

There was only one authentic emotion Ned felt she could follow, only one thing she felt she owed the dead. It wasn't a matter of love.

It was a matter of truth. It meant starting all over again, with the evidence. She left her sister snoring gently on her bed and headed back into town, passing two booze buses between Greenwich and Glebe. The Christmas party season was in full swing. The faces of the police were washed blue and red by the rotating lights of their patrol cars. Alien and malign in their reflective vests, fluoro light wands in hand, they were marshalling cars into waiting lines, sorting the guilty from the innocent.

Ned held her ID up to the security cameras at the back of the Glebe morgue, pushed the door open when the locks clicked off and went to the administration desk.

'I'd like to see the PM results on Nguyen Thi Phuong.'

Ned took the report into the police room – a spartan place, grubbier and seedier than elsewhere, rank with the smell of stale cigarettes from an overflowing ashtray and, as she discovered trying to empty it, from an overflowing garbage bin. The night cleaners didn't come in here. Ned checked the photocopier for power and paper before settling down to read.

The scientific language was mostly meaningless to her. She skimmed to the summaries, the blow to the head, the broken neck, pictures of the scalp peeled back, the skull on show, a spider web of fractures, diagrammatic, lacking the meaty tinge of recent life. The injury had been inflicted by a brick. It would've killed her eventually. But someone had snapped her neck, put her down like an animal. Was it to spare her suffering, or just to make sure of the job?

She read on, pausing at a term, *nulligravida*, searching her memory for its meaning. Typical of the words that Deakin liked to use, expected professional cops to understand. The meaning hit her like a reprieve. Tears sprang to her eyes. Phuong had never borne a child.

It had never been said – not to her face, anyway – and she didn't know if she alone had thought it. But since the lies of the past had started to spill out, Ned had caught herself looking at Linh, her little sister, so small, so physically different from her, and wondering. Wondering what other secrets her parents might have been keeping. So much of what she had believed had already been demolished. But Phuong had died childless.

The DNA profiles of the family were clipped together with a photocopied document from the War Memorial Archive. The document showed a list of names, of Nguyens, similar to the one Ned had made in her notebook in Canberra. But there was one extra name in this list, sitting on the line beside her grandfather, Tran, and above the children, Linh, Phuong, Danh and Ngoc. It was the name of her grandmother. *Nhu.*

Ned imagined Ngoc, alone in a new land, nursing the little girl she named for a grandmother who would never hold her. She turned the list of the dead face down and picked up the next folder, a record of the scars and marks of Nguyen Thi Phuong. Up close, out of context, they were like some kind of tribal scarification. The contradictions of evidence and emotion flowed about her. Mick Kelly had tried to report Phuong missing. But Mick Kelly had dirty hands. Maybe he'd used them on other pieces of 'human intel', but not on Phuong. Ned remembered those hands on her back, pushing her on the swing at the park: big hands, safe and secure, controlled power in the push as she arced up towards the tops of the trees. Then she saw those hands holding a cigarette to the flesh of a stranger. Her fingers leapt from the photos as if from a flame.

Another set of images demanded her attention: pathetic, ragged legs, smashed at the shins, no feet. A wound on the right thigh was described, almost missed due to the damage to the legs. It was a dog bite, deep, inflicted at or close to the time of death, unhealed and untreated. Several dog hairs had been recovered from the clothes, and testing was underway to recover DNA, maybe establish a breed. The science was still so new, so exciting, that scientists could only anticipate results, but 'old' science concluded the bite had been inflicted by a large dog.

The report noted that although the causes of death of the two women were totally dissimilar, they were linked by the place and time of burial and by dog bites. Dawn Jarrett had a similar bite on her right forearm.

Zervos's question rang through the silent morgue.

Any pets when you were growing up?

REDFERN PARK WAS CHURNING. Lots of teenagers, lots of kids. There was an almost carnival atmosphere, if you liked your carnivals large, tough and edgy. Marcus Jarrett had been busy when Ned rang that morning, giving her two options: meet him here or try later in the week.

If she waited she'd lose her nerve.

She tacked through the crowd, dodging round the trunks of towering palm trees, feeling uncoordinated and agonisingly self-conscious. Voices blurred, calling out to one another. Cuz, sis, bro, aunty, uncle. In this vast family, she was nameless and alone. Giant Moreton Bay figs, their aerial roots dropping like dreadlocks from their wide, thick canopies, hosted large, animated groups sitting around their buttressed trunks. The figs grew in everything round here – out of the cracks in footpaths, seedlings even took root in the roof guttering of the red-brick commission houses nearby.

Tawny now in early summer, Ned's skin matched many of the people she passed. She was even darker than some – those whose ancestries probably included Irish Kellys like hers, but whose genes had bequeathed freckles, red hair and blue eyes.

The gap was more subtle than just skin. Wider. The cock of a head, a stranger's gaze, assessing, guessing, dismissing. The laughter and loose body language among friends and family, arms draped over shoulders, hips tilting easily to accommodate a child weary of standing, fingers threaded through fingers, feet planted proprietarily on the ground.

It was a crowd of locals, even if some of them had travelled for miles from places with more vowels than consonants in their names. They were still locals in the true sense of the word. A car cruised past, blasting the throbbing beat of Yothu Yindi's 'Treaty' into the mix.

Up the front, near the stage, suits dominated. Lots of them, talking into their sleeves and sporting spaghetti-wired earpieces like delegates at a deaf convention. A car with an Australian flag on its bonnet turned in, pulled up close to the stage. From a distance she saw a man climb out – tall, dark-haired, dark-suited. Prime Minister Keating. Could've been a D. Fraud Squad, from the slick cut of that suit and sleek cut of that hair. Did he feel as uncomfortable as she did? Or did those layers of spaghetti-eared sleeve-talkers insulate him?

Local speakers, dancers of various ages and sizes, came and went. Eucalyptus smoke curled through the crowd. She did a double-take when Phil Walker was introduced, a middle-aged man in a suit, a little soft and fleshy, a little bald.

Ned tried to imagine Dawn, middle-aged and plump like her sister Aunty Pat. Dawn wouldn't have grown soft. She'd have stayed wiry and driven, maybe pausing to celebrate Eddie Mabo's posthumous victory then searching out a new battle. The crowd had chattered through most of Phil Walker's speech then resisted the temptation to pour applause on him at the finish. Yeah, he'd fit right in down there in Canberra. The Tent Embassy might have been the closest Dawn ever got to Parliament, but Ned reckoned she'd be remembered longer.

If the PM had been expecting a mute, meek audience then he was in for a disappointment. Too many words over too many years had delivered him a cynical crowd, grudging with their respect.

They weren't reluctant to voice their thoughts, either. Ned followed the voice of a particularly vigorous heckler, entertaining the crowd with his annotations. The Prime Minister was five minutes into his speech by the time she found Marcus Jarrett in the shade of a tall palm. He'd removed his tie and suit coat but kept his sunglasses on. His head moved in her direction but that was all the acknowledgment she got.

'Tough crowd.'

'Depends who you reckon it's aimed at,' Jarrett said. 'This mob want more than words and a few banners.'

A cloud of white hair floated in a group of elderly women; Ned recognised Essie Freeman, down from Tuncurry. A flock of children darted past like larrikin lorikeets, swooping off towards a Moreton Bay fig, tumbling over the large woman propped up in the folds of its massive trunk. Aunty Pat Jarrett let them bounce on and off her as she watched the stage, arms folded, sceptical, the familial echo of her nephew.

Ned was close enough now to see a shiny patina of sweat on the PM's usually cool, pale complexion. Parliament must seem tame in comparison. She watched him glance up from his notes, gauging the mood of the crowd. He pressed on.

'*The starting point might be to recognise that the problem starts with us non-Aboriginal Australians. It begins, I think, with that act of recognition. Recognition that it was we who did the dispossessing . . .*'

A few cheers greeted that. The noise level dipped a little, leaving the voices of the children exposed as the PM spoke on.

'*We took the traditional lands and smashed the traditional way of life. We brought the diseases. The alcohol. We committed the murders . . .*'

Whistles and cheers began in earnest, genuine surprise on a few faces. The children picked up on it. Ned joined in the clapping. It took a unique set of circumstances for an admission of murder to be greeted with applause. Jarrett remained still, arms crossed over his chest.

'Don't know why he's using the past tense,' he said.

The PM was growing more confident, riding the momentum of the crowd, delivering the next lines to sustained applause and vocal acknowledgment.

'*We took the children from their mothers. We practised discrimination and exclusion. It was our ignorance and our prejudice. And our failure to imagine these things could be done to us.*'

'Good speech.' Ned leant over, shouting into his ear to be heard. 'Generous audience.'

He shrugged, but she noticed his arms were loosening a little.

'Can't imagine it's a vote winner,' Ned said. 'Why's he doing it now?'

'Politicians – better off trying not to think about them too much,' Jarrett responded, shifting his weight, and clasping his wrists behind him as if to avoid applauding by accident.

The heckler started up again. 'Get out of our country! Get out of our country!'

A few people around him told him to shut up.

'Come on – you said you wanted to talk?' Jarrett turned and headed away from the stage.

'We want justice, we want justice, we want justice!' The heckler's chants faded as she followed Marcus to the rear of the crowd.

'So, what's your news? Not a crime scene, then?'

'More like an archaeology doco. But like he just said – it was murder.'

'Won't see an inquest.'

'Violent and unnatural death,' she said. 'No one left to charge, though.'

'It'll be a curiosity. It's already a sideshow,' he said. 'No one seems to want to use the word "massacre".'

The Prime Minister was winding up.

'*We cannot imagine that we will fail. And with the spirit that is here today I am confident that we won't fail. I am confident that we will succeed in this decade.*

'*Thank you very much for listening to me.*'

There were stomps and cheers, enough to match the heckles and catcalls that peppered the audience. There was laughter too, as kids rode the buzz to the front of the stage, muscling away TV cameras and radio microphones to grab at his hand. The politician was smiling, laughing, pausing for photo ops. His relief looked unfaked. The cloud of lamb's-wool hair moved through the kids; Essie grasped his hand, wiping away tears. Aunty Pat got to her feet, shook her head and walked away with the heckler.

'Do you think it made a difference?' Ned asked. 'Him being a Bankstown boy, the grave . . . ? He was being pretty . . .' She searched for a word. 'Honest.'

'Words are easy.' Jarrett shrugged. 'Let's see his legislation, then I'll tell you if any of this was worth hearing.'

'Just wondered if he'd seen the reports. They shot them – some of them, anyway.' Ned stopped, aware of the guilt leading her to claim a Vietnamese ancestry she'd long ignored in order to say *they*, and mean *not me, not mine*.

'Winged them.' Jarrett watched the politician enjoying the calls of *'Bravo, Paul'*, ignoring the furious cries of *'About time'* and *'Give us back our land!'* 'Then finished them off with the rifle butts. Supplies still an issue then, never knew when the next ship would turn up. Weren't going to waste bullets.'

Ned sucked in a breath. The crowd swam – a constellation of faces, round and broad, narrow and sharp, black as space and freckled Irish, orbiting her, morphing into terror in an instant; the cheers becoming shrieks, skulls collapsing inwards under the butt of a gun, the children's screeches cut short with a wet crunch of bone. She concentrated on drawing in fresh, cleansing air and not throwing up.

'That missing skull never turned up, did it?' he asked.

She shook her head, pretended to shield her eyes from the sun, keeping them closed, concentrating on each breath.

'Usually they took the men's heads. Warriors like Pemulwuy – it was evidence of the death sentence. This was a little kid, though, and all the other heads were there.'

'They think . . . maybe . . . an animal,' she got out.

A tiny body, abandoned because there was no one else left to bury it. A dingo worrying at the corpse, rewarded with a mouthful of flesh and bone.

'Could be in a museum somewhere or taken as a trophy,' he continued. 'Soldiers liked collecting souvenirs to take back home, something to —'

She just managed not to splash his suit pants when she vomited into the rows of agapanthus.

Getting out of the park was a blur. Then Ned was in a cool, dark space, lying on a leather lounge, air sweeping over her face from an oscillating pedestal fan. She looked up at a pressed-metal ceiling; the rosettes and cornices seemed freshly restored. Marcus Jarrett came in, a tall glass of clear, sparkling liquid in one hand, a plastic bucket in the other.

'Which one do you want?'

The success of keeping down the lemonade and the effect of the sugar got her upright. Jarrett was fiddling with the stereo.

'Sorry about this,' she said. 'Stuffing you around. You meant to be somewhere?'

'It's OK. Got a weak stomach for a copper or is it just that politicians make you chuck?'

A bunch of humiliating memories made a quick victory lap.

'Bit of a hangover,' she lied. 'Sorry. I hope I didn't . . .'

'Nah – missed me, missed the car, the carpet. Pretty housetrained for a projectile vomiter.'

'Sorry.' No need to tell him she'd had lots of practice.

'You don't have to keep saying sorry, you know.'

She rolled the empty glass between her hands. He pressed play and instantly the big brass chords of the opening track of *Soro* roared out at the volume she usually played it alone in the car.

He turned it down. 'Must've been vacuuming last time I had this on.'

'No, please. I love this album.'

He looked over his shoulder at her, surprised, then smiled. Momentarily, Dawn Jarrett stood there. He turned the volume up slightly, his body rocking gently to the beat.

'*You're* into Salif Keita?'

'Love this album. That song at the end, "Sanni Kegniba", it's beautiful.'

'Like the moody ones, eh?'

'Yeah. The atmosphere. Sanni the Beautiful dies. Makes me wonder why.' She halted before she embarrassed herself with the story she'd invented around that track. The translated lyrics were enigmatic; the pain in Keita's voice wasn't.

Marcus Jarrett grinned at her. 'Music detective, too? Was it murder? Never off duty, eh, Ned?'

'He's got a bit to say about tradition, Salif Keita.' She didn't elaborate, didn't talk about Mali, about what happened to women there, about the traditions that killed them. She felt a flush of irritation – at herself for tiptoeing around him, at him, at all the elephants in all the rooms.

'Yeah? Never looked at the lyrics. It's the rhythm, the vibes, I'm into. Good dance music.'

His smooth progress across the room hinted that he knew a few moves. He mouthed the chorus, eyes crinkled, head thrown back. Dawn Jarrett's son.

'I don't think my dad did it, Marcus.'

He stopped, stared at her for a few beats, then sat down while she told him why.

Once she started, the words came without hesitation. She said it aloud for the first time, knowing it to be true. He listened. The music playing in the background made it easier, the familiar tracks rolling one after the other. By the time she'd finished telling him about Brian Hall, about the records she'd found, about the records she hadn't found, by the time he'd cross-examined and she'd handed over a copy of the Revesby occurrence pad, 'Sanni Kegniba' was dissolving in a waterfall of notes from the *kora*.

'You put a lot of faith in this guy Hall?'

'I thought maybe he was just trying to exculpate himself, with Dad as a bonus, but the entry at Revesby backs him up. Bill Jarrett reckoned my dad was going to do something about the bones at the building site, but then something happened – something side-tracked him. Well, now we know what that was. Phuong happened. She'd turned up in Australia, probably turned his life upside down, then disappeared. No wonder he was sidetracked.'

'What are you expecting to find in the Bankstown records?'

'See if Dad reported anything there. Anything at all, about the building site, about Phuong. It'd be around the date of the Revesby entry, or earlier. Something on one of the pads?'

Marcus studied the paper in his hands.

'Can you get access?' she asked. 'Through the ALS?'

'Access won't be a problem. I was representing some of the families at the Commission,' he said dryly.

Narrow and insensitive. That must be how he saw her. She didn't want to ask if someone was representing his family, too. Everywhere she turned she bumped into death, brushed thoughtlessly against someone else's grief.

'I'll see what's there. May I keep this?'

'Yes, I made a few copies.'

'Familiar name here. Small world, eh?'

She nodded, stiff.

'No point asking Sergeant Urganchich anything about it.' Marcus met her eyes again.

She shook her head.

'And you? You'll chase up this Cadet Murphy? See what he has to say?'

Didn't trust her voice to tell him, not just yet. She nodded instead.

'The morgue's releasing Mabo today,' Marcus said suddenly. 'I'm arranging his funeral – probably middle of next week.'

It wasn't much of an invitation, but she accepted it anyway. 'Let me know when.'

He looked closely at her.

'Got someone you can talk to about this? Family? Friend?'

You. The realisation was abrupt. *Just you.*

If he read her silence as a negative he didn't pursue it. Didn't offer to fill the breach, be the one to listen. He just handed over her bag, heavy with the weight of her firearm. She got to her feet.

'Feeling OK? Not about to up-and-under again, are you?'

'Just hung-over. Empty stomach, too much sun, need a . . .' Black aspro, she was going to say. 'A Coke, bacon-and-egg sanger – I'll be fine.'

'Black aspro and grease, eh?' Marcus nodded. 'Kill or cure.'

She could've felt more like a clown but it would've taken a red nose and silly shoes to do it.

IT WAS STILL EARLY AFTERNOON, but at the homeless shelters down Woolloomooloo way it was mealtime. A bowl of casserole, a bread roll and hope of a bed for a lucky few. Ned was told she was welcome to ask questions, as long as she pulled her weight in the kitchen first. She wasn't sure how long it would take Marcus Jarrett to check the Bankstown records, but she was determined that next time they saw each other she'd be able to meet his eye and know she'd tried to find out something about how Mabo had died.

She moved slowly from table to table, topping up mugs with cordial, asking the same question.

'My friend – the man who was burnt – did you see who brought him down here?'

On her third circuit someone finally answered. He was no dirtier or more damaged than the rest. His only distinguishing feature was his hair, unwashed and matted into dreadlocks behind his head, providing a permanent pillow wherever he went. He was the last one left at his table. He chewed slowly; only had a few teeth left and they were probably sore.

'You a copper?'

'Yes. But I'm here on my own. I want to find out who brought the dead man here.'

'And then?'

'And then try to make them take some responsibility for what happened.'

'Take responsibility – you a Sallie-Ann as well as a copper?'

'No,' she laughed. 'Just a copper.'

'Pity,' he said. 'At least the Sallies are useful.'

The prints on his fingers stood out, inked in dirt. He crumbled the last of his bread roll into acceptable form and dribbled it into the casserole juice, tilted the plate up and gave it a good licking.

'Sallies do stuff, see,' he went on. 'Now, if you said you were going to do this bloke over, or even sling me something, then maybe . . .'

Twenty dollars didn't buy firm evidence. Natty Pillow-Head wouldn't even give his name and he had no address.

'White Holden Commodore. One of those aerials with the twirly bit at the bottom – just like all cop cars have, even if they don't have the sign up. But he wasn't no D, this bloke. Seen enough cops drinking in uniform – stick out like dog's balls. Big grey-haired bastard, no neck, ears on his collar. Saw him get the little guy out of the back door; he didn't see me. Little blackfella was wobbly. Didn't stick around.'

The description wasn't much, but when you recognised the figure it was describing, it was everything.

It was only a short drive from Woolloomooloo. Ned pulled into a familiar parking space and went once more into the morgue. The admin staff had started giving her sly looks as if they suspected her of macabre obsessions, but eventually they handed over the PM report she asked for.

It was brief but it gave his name, Patrick Arthur Murray, and his age, forty-one. He'd been beaten. Burnt. The worst of the fire had died down by the time someone had investigated the flickering light at the end of the alley. The accelerant had been poured over his torso. All those clothes he wore, the layers, soaked in kerosene. He'd been a wick.

The report couldn't say if he'd been unconscious when he caught fire. He'd certainly been in no shape to run, roll, seek help.

Little blackfella was wobbly.

Jesus, Ned hoped he'd been out of it.

The photos from the scene showed Mabo's fists curled, his arms raised into the pugilistic stance the dead assume when fire cooks their flexors and shrinks their tendons. He looked like he'd been fighting off death. But he'd have already been dead by the time his limbs rose in combat.

Had Linh, her aunt, looked like this – once it was over? After she'd sat down to pray, poured petrol all over herself and dropped a match? The burning lotus, in the end, was just charred flesh and twisted limbs, and horribly dead.

Mabo's recorded alcohol level was high. Ned hoped it was high enough to anaesthetise him. No other drugs. Stomach contents: whisky. No wonder he was wobbly. Mabo was a meth man, fruity lexia in a cardboard box if he was flush.

Ugly had ensured he'd get into the back of a car without stacking on a blue.

There was activity in the loading bay as she left. A government contractor was unloading a body bag onto a gurney and bumping it up the ramp into reception. A funeral director's hearse was parked alongside, its driver smoking a cigarette and waiting his turn. Voices were calling out names and numbers, a body checking in, another checking out, each step along the way marked with documents and numbers. She heard one name through the hubbub.

'Murray, Patrick Arthur.' The driver of the hearse checked his papers.

'Last chance to say goodbye,' an attendant said as he passed Ned.

She followed him through the thick, plastic doors before she could give herself time to think about it.

The cold air pressed down on her shoulders like a pair of hands. Gurneys were lined up, each one with a body bag on it, various shapes and sizes deforming the bags, hinting at the various torments inside.

The attendant wheeled one trolley out from the row, straightened it up, then checked the serial numbers on the papers in his hand against the tags and documents on the bag. The outline of the body was oddly shaped – Mabo's limbs jabbing the bag into angles. In a quick movement, the attendant unzipped the top of the bag, flipping the cover back to expose the face.

The smell and sight were like thunder and lightning striking simultaneously. Even fresh from refrigeration, burnt flesh was pungent. Ned's mouth filled with fluid and she longed to spit. She didn't want to take another breath through her nose, she didn't want that smell soaking into her sense organs.

Mabo's face was flaccid, the dark skin charred in places, but the skull intact. Without those runny-egg eyes and life to animate the thin features, he looked much older. He didn't look peaceful. That was another of the lies we told to comfort ourselves, Ned thought. He just looked dead.

She made herself swallow the bitter froth in her mouth. A rage as cold and as calculating as revenge fell over her. Her hands, gripping the rail of the gurney, began to hum, the vibration coming not from the dead man but from the night when her baton had sung in her hands. She would find out who'd done this and if there was no justice to be found, then she would make them pay.

NED COULDN'T FACE BANKSTOWN – not yet. There were things she wanted to do there but not while TC and the rest of them were rattling around. She drove home, got through the front door and immediately called in sick. TC expressed concern that sounded as stilted as her excuse. The empty house in the afternoon light brought back memories that felt older than a few weeks. Sean in her bed, with all the time in the world.

At the door of her room she stopped. The usual clutter and mess. Her dirty clothes were dotted around the floor beside the laundry basket where she'd lobbed them, the bed unmade as she'd left it that morning. But her perfume bottles were on their sides. Someone had opened the bottom drawer. The one that stuck. The one filled with winter clothes she wasn't using.

She moved fast through the house. The usual targets of a bust were still in place: TV, video, stereo. She looked for entry points. Glass doors to the deck, locked; Linh's windows, open but the insect screens still bore cobwebs – no sign of entry; MM's old timber sash window, too heavy for MM to open and so usually closed, was ajar. Ned spun about, scanning the room, a wardrobe door not fully closed, a corner of a silk scarf hanging over the lip of a drawer. Her heart rate doubled as she replayed her arrival home – clattering into the hall, speaking on the phone, the sound of a car accelerating away down View Street as she hung up.

She replaced the phone, the number to North Sydney Police Station only half dialled. There'd be no prints. She knew that with a sick, gut instinct. Coppers wouldn't leave prints. It was someone looking for something, something specific, and she had no idea what it could be.

Ned ran hard and fast through bushland and street, trying to replace the smell of Mabo's burnt flesh with the sharp, clean astringency of crushed gum leaves and dirt, seaweed and salt water. The uneven ground of Greenwich Point, rising and falling over sandstone outcrops and knotted tree roots, forced her to think and feel through her feet, left no room for anything else.

She ran on, up through Smoothey Park, over the suspension bridge and down the hill to Berry Island, pausing at the rock carving on the flat sandstone shelf that looked back towards Greenwich. The large sea animal had been carved by people who'd clung on for barely a year after the First Fleet turned up. Smallpox. Piles of bodies rotting on the water's edge, no one left alive to bury them. The chiselled outline of the animal was faint, eroded by time, but in its belly were fresh wounds. Four large holes, roughly cemented over, marked the spot a park bench had occupied for decades.

Sweating and breathing hard, she ran back past Wollstonecraft Station, down the ramp and into Smoothey Park. The sun was dropping low; she was squinting into the glare, almost on the footbridge before she saw him and stopped.

He'd already seen her.

Sean slid his sunglasses up and smiled.

Her body greeted the sight of him with a deep, carnal leap. It was honest. But it wasn't love. It wasn't that generous. Had they felt like this – her father and Phuong? A tactile gnawing, or something less hectic, more heartfelt?

She'd lost count of the days since seen she'd seen him. No calls. No messages on the pager. Then suddenly here he was. Waiting. She thought about the window ajar in MM's room. Distrust contended with desire as she walked towards him.

'You're hard to catch,' he said.

'You seem to have managed.'

The shadows were long. His stretched across the footbridge. She stepped onto the bridge and into the elongated outline of his body.

'Thought you might've called me.' He leant back against the railing, body open.

'I've been . . .' Busy, she was going to say. How pathetic. 'Thinking.' Not much better.

'Ah.' He slipped his sunglasses back down, turning to join her, staring down at the creek below. 'Now there's a beginning that never ends well.'

'Didn't say I'd been thinking about you.'

'Nhu.' He said her name with care. 'You don't have to do this alone.'

In the last of the warm sun, with magpies running up and down their scales, she wanted to believe him, to excise those signatures, those documents.

'So, what's the verdict? Feel like I'm fourteen years old, hanging around the park after school.'

'Bit closer to forty than fourteen, Sarge.'

'Steady on! Didn't pick you as an ageist,' he laughed. She couldn't see if it reached his eyes.

'Bit like Old Father Time, aren't you – know everyone, everyone knows you – like you've been around forever. Must feel like it, sometimes?'

'Ned?'

She felt him move closer.

'What's up? What's happened?'

'You remember much about your cadet days, Murph? Or was it all too long ago?'

'Cadet days?' He sounded genuinely surprised.

Good at his job – sounding genuine.

'Guess it must've been pretty boring. All the shit jobs, the paperwork?'

'Like you said – a long time ago.'

Was he trying to keep an edge out of his voice? With the sun behind him, his sunglasses shielding his eyes, he was unreadable. Far below, the creek was in flow from overnight rains, noisy for its size.

'You never mentioned you worked at Banky, way back then.'

'Back when?'

'Late '76.'

'I've worked all over Sydney.'

'Yeah? Saw a lot of double murders, did you? As a cadet? Got a bit blasé about them?'

He didn't answer, just fixed black glass eyes on her. An expert. At deception, at maintaining a cover story. Wasn't likely to crack. She could reveal all her cards and he'd still be an unwritten slate.

Ever present, ever helpful, so supportive. Always turning up when she needed him. Ned wanted to get the evidence, the forms and papers, slap him around the face with them, make him respond. And then? Watch him shrug and say, *So?*

'I saw the brief – some familiar names there,' she went on. 'Surprised none of you mentioned it.'

'What are you carrying on about?' His body language shifted, only then did she realise it had been stiff. He folded his arms, hip against the rail. 'You've seen some old brief and —'

'Not some old brief – my *parents'* murder.' Her hands snapped into fists at her side.

'OK,' he said, voice steady. 'Sorry, I just don't know what I'm meant to have done.'

'You don't remember?'

'Remember what? You know how many briefs my name crops up in over the years? Thousands. You're right – police cadets got every shit paper-shuffling job going. You think I remember them all?'

'Maybe not. But I reckon you'd remember the interesting ones. Murders? Your first murder?'

'Nothing's interesting by the time it turns into filing. I don't mean to sound callous, but to you it's *the* brief – to me it was probably just more bloody paperwork that some headkicker reckoned was insignificant enough to be dealt with by the guy at the bottom of the shit heap.'

'No memory of it, eh?'

'Late 1976, let's see. My life in late 1976 . . . I was the newly married eighteen-year-old father of a screaming baby, husband of an hysterical, homesick, child bride, trying to work out how the hell we were ever going to be able to afford to move out of my dad's garage. Honestly, until I joined the main game, got into 21 Division, the Job was nothing but shitty paperwork, school crossings and pissy complaints about noise, dogs and parking.'

A breeze picked up. Up this high, the trunks of the eucalypts swayed visibly. Disorientating. Another train-load of commuters began their walk across the footbridge towards Greenwich. It undulated beneath her.

'I don't know what you want me to say, Nhu.'

He reached towards her, a hand to her cheek. She drifted out of reach.

'When you came down to Goulburn —'

'Nhu, we've been through —'

'You pulled a gun on me – in a car —'

'I didn't know who I was doing that job with.'

'On – you did a job *on* me, Murph.'

'And if I'd known anything about you – about what had happened – I'd never have done it.'

'So you say.'

'I don't know what you're seeing here, what you're making out of this – or why.'

Fact was, neither did she. She didn't know what to make of

it – not really. Maybe it was pride after all. Didn't like them all knowing more about her and her past than she did.

'Why are you here, Murph? Got so much time to waste that you can just hang around parks on the off-chance I'm going to run by?'

'You don't make it easy, you know that, Nhu? You make it really hard, to get close, to help.' He pushed away from the railing.

'Why should I? It's not like we're a happily-ever-after story, are we?'

'Oh. Decided that already, have you? Didn't think I might have a different take?' She had no trouble reading the anger on his face even with his sunglasses down.

'Come off it, Murph.'

'My kids are growing up and I've hardly seen them. I can't stop working – even when I'm not, I'm thinking about it. Thinking about who I'm meant to be, where I'm meant to be, what life I'm meant to be living. But I'm never where I want to be – and right now that's with you.'

'What was Ugly like back then, Murph?'

'What! Why are we talking about him? Didn't you hear what I just said?'

'I heard – I just don't believe you.'

'Neddie, why don't you ask TC about Ugly? They go back – he was TC's mentor, got him his start in Homicide.'

He sounded reckless, provoked. She doubted he was. The bridge began to vibrate, someone running towards them – fast. Sean stepped forward, between her and the approaching dog. Nero was overjoyed to see him, barely pausing to snarl at her, contenting himself with shoving his wet nose into her crotch, leaving a trail of drool across the front of her running shorts.

'Strudel!' Sean said. The dog dropped like it had been squashed, belly to the ground, nose to paws.

Police dog handlers all had a single word their dogs responded to, to break off an attack, before the offender was shredded.

'Shouldn't you have that thing on a leash?'

The dog was nailed to the ground at his side, alert, ears pricked, eyes locked on Sean.

'Ned, there's things you don't understand about this job yet . . .'

'Oh, I'm learning all the time about this job, Murph. You've already taught me heaps.'

He made a quick movement, had her hands in his before she reacted. 'I wanted you to work with me because I wanted to be with you.' She shook off his hands and stepped back. He spoke quickly, intense. 'I know. I know what it sounds like but it wasn't like that. With everything that's been going on, I wanted you to learn that sometimes you have to trust someone – really trust someone.'

'Learn how to trust someone? You? Trust is earnt not learnt.'

'And you need to give people a chance to earn it. I won't beg you, Nhu. You need help – call me, any time.' He held up his pager. 'Always on, always with me. Like I said – always working.'

MARCUS JARRETT'S VOICE ACCOMPANIED NED on the drive out to Bankstown that evening. She'd turned on the radio and heard him being interviewed about the Prime Minister's speech in Redfern Park. He spoke like a statesman, ignoring the reporter's cues to reduce the story to the level of personal grief.

'*My mother was just one in a long line of those murdered defending their land. It started well before her and it continues today. Dawn Jarrett sought not only truth but justice. Maybe some truths were told today, but justice will only come with land rights.*'

Marcus was giving his mother a final gift, the dignity to be immortalised as one in a line of fallen warriors rather than a sad, singular victim.

Ned turned the radio off when the story switched back to the latest shenanigans from ICAC and drove the rest of the way in silence. She rehearsed what she'd say to the station crew, hoping for familiar faces, perhaps her pool partners from Court Five – people who liked a chat but lacked curiosity.

Her luck was in. A brawl had sparked up at the Viking Tavern at Milperra. It had been renamed since the bikie massacre in 1984, but blues up there still drew a good response. Cops didn't rely on lightning not striking twice. The station sergeant asked if she'd mind the shop and dashed upstairs to grab a cuppa before the winners and losers were dragged in to bleed all over his charge-room floor.

Ned flicked back through the filed occurrence sheets. Not

looking at the night shift this time, but the late shift, the cops who should have been packed up and off home by 11 p.m. She found it. Urganchich had covered a late shift on the night Mabo died, volunteering for overtime when the rostered sergeant had gone home sick. Ugly and Mabo, like some kind of universal constant.

The station sergeant returned, steaming cup of tea in hand, and Ned went out to the muster room. The car diaries were filed in their pigeonholes – like the pads, a good indicator of a night's work. The condition of the vehicle, any dings, dents and scratches, was carefully noted; like a game of pass the parcel, if you signed out a car without noticing a new mark, then you wore it. A separate docket book recorded fuel: where, when and how much. The car diaries could tell you a lot about a night shift – assuming they were filled in.

The unmarked cars in the Ds office were taken home at night, but Inspector Morgenstrom's white Holden Commodore wasn't. His car had become the special-orders vehicle while he was on leave. The sergeants had been using it to run errands, carefully masked in the diary as official business. Ned almost laughed when she found the entry – Ugly having had no choice but to sign the book. He'd put petrol in the car, at the Police Centre. A terse entry, resentment captured in his small, tight signature. At 3 a.m. when Mabo had been smouldering in a lane at Woolloomooloo, Ugly had been at Surry Hills, barely a kilometre away, pumping petrol into a police car.

How furious, when he got into the city and realised the car was almost empty.

How tight, not to throw a few bucks in it to get back to Bankstown.

How arrogant, to think it wouldn't matter.

Morgenstrom's car was parked in the Inspector's space in a dark corner of the yard. Ned collected the keys and went out. She opened the boot, leant in, nose to the carpet. She ran her fingers over the carpet, rubbed them together. Slightly oily. Sniffed. Kero.

'Neddie?' She jumped, straightened, hand dropping from her nose like she'd been caught picking it. TC stood close behind her.

'TC.' She didn't even try her carefully constructed excuses on TC. Instead she stated the obvious. 'You're working late.' She slammed the boot closed. Let him make the running.

'What are you doing here, Ned?'

'Had a look at the brief. You were right, nothing much there I didn't already know.'

Silence fell between them like darkness. Their first chance to talk since she'd been to archives. First chance to see if he was going to tell her – about Sean, about Ugly. About their connection to her parents' brief.

'I've already looked, Ned. There's nothing to prove anything here. I spoke to the night crew about it.'

At first she wasn't sure what he was talking about, then she realised. Mabo.

'Ugly took this car into town —'

'And I spoke to him about it, he told me to get fucked. If the night crew know anything, they're not saying. There's nothing.'

There's a witness, she wanted to hiss. Wanted to shove her fingers under his nose. But she'd told TC about Mabo. She wasn't telling him about Natty Pillow-Head.

'Go back, don't you? You and Ugly?'

'What's that supposed to mean?'

A question answered with a question.

'Made a good mentor, did he? Twenty-one Division and Ugly. Quite an education.'

'Neddie, I don't know what you've been told —'

'I only know what people tell me, but so much of it's turning out to be crap.'

'Ned, let it go.' He spoke slowly, deliberately.

'Why?'

'Because you can't win this one. Pick your battles, Neddie. Be patient.'

She turned around to leave, and he didn't try to stop her.

Ned did a few laps around the block, then parked up the street from the police station.

She'd been waiting about fifteen minutes when TC came out, crossed the road and got into his unmarked car. He didn't look around, didn't check for watchers or followers. Brakelights came on, headlights, then he pulled out and drove away. She waited another five minutes. With her hand over the radio glow she allowed herself the luxury of listening to the news. Filling in more time, forcing herself to wait a little longer.

The arrival of the brawl participants provided the diversion she needed to get back in. From the noise coming out of the charge room it was same blue, different venue, the presence of the cops welding former enemies into allies. She climbed the stairs to the sergeants' room and closed the door on the sounds of war.

The four desks were theoretically shared, but, possession being nine-tenths of the law, Sergeant Urganchich had claimed sole tenure of one by uninterrupted occupancy. Other sergeants came and went, Ugly stayed on at the corner desk, ashtray piled high. The non-smoking policy was also theoretical in here. The accretion of years of paperwork and day-to-day record-keeping spread in all directions. The desk itself was standard departmental. Grey metal, shonky locks. The two drawers opened easily.

She rifled through the contents: tab stubs, lighters, paperclips, property docket books, pens, pencils, flyers, leaflets for a dry cleaner, one for a kennel, take-away menus, a wholesale pet food supplier, an escort service. Just crap. She slammed the drawer in frustration, then started on the desk.

More crap, mostly work-related. Forms to check, indexes to write up, two trays full of folders and briefs, fact sheets and statements for slim little sins in thin manila folders. She dug into the bottom of the tray – unfiled briefs, five years old. Ugly didn't believe in out-trays. A few old copies of *Police News*, a newsletter from the German Shepherd Dog Council of Australia. More flyers, advertising dog shows, puppies for sale. They looked homemade – photos cut out, stuck on a piece of A4 and photocopied. She smoothed out the least crumpled.

Five head shots of dogs were placed around a central photo of a woman and a dog posing, ribbons around the dog's neck, hind legs stretched out behind it, as if ready to leap. Each portrait had a different name, but each name had a common thread. There was Jungfrau Rising Son, Jungfrau Grandeur Kiel, Jungfrau Koenig Kestrel. The pamphlet boasted that Jungfrau Kennels could trace their dogs' bloodlines back to Jungfrau Freundlich Schönheit, a bitch imported from Germany in 1972. Five-time Best in Breed, outstanding Supreme Champion, and so on. Ned went back through the drawers, pulling out the leaflets. Names of dogs, dates, charts, bloodlines, family trees – they were like some exotic European royal family. Bloody dogs had a more extensive family tree than she did.

She looked at the pictures again. The quality of the photocopy was poor. The woman's face was a smudge under blonde hair. Ned squinted, guessed it was Erika – Mrs Ugly. You certainly wouldn't use her husband for advertising.

The portraits around the woman just looked like dogs to Ned. Handsome, savage dogs like Nero, who could no doubt trace his bloodlines right back to 1972. That meant they had a twist of DNA, changing minutely from generation to generation but tethering them all to Jungfrau Freundlich Schönheit. The bottom of the leaflets showed the business name: *E. Vass, trading as Jungfrau GSD Kennels Pty Ltd*.

E. Vass. Where had she seen that name before? The Ds office was one floor up, the clashing of cell doors one floor below. The name hovered at the edges of her memory then returned. The reports in her pigeonhole after she'd come back to work.

E. Vass and M. Shields. The names of the directors of Erimar Pty Ltd. The company that Bushrangers had been building a block of flats for in 1976.

The wheel turned a fraction.

It was the work of an instant. One idea leading intuitively to another. The Ds office was empty, the cupboard unlocked. She pulled out two exhibit bags. Using a tissue she picked out butts from Ugly's ashtray. Half-a-dozen of the freshest, dropped into the bag, sealed. Only when she turned it back over and confronted the blank boxes – the demands for details she couldn't fill in – did the futility of it overwhelm her.

Case name? Nguyen/Jarrett – guaranteed to attract attention.

Officer in charge of the brief? Her name or TC's? How long would that subterfuge last? Especially when she asked them to check the results against the samples under Nguyen Phuong's nails.

Offender or suspect? Here she'd insert the name of a serving officer . . . Who was she kidding?

She slumped at the desk, defeated. Official channels. DAL would suss out something was amiss before the morning tea break. She didn't have the skills. She'd learnt to do things by the book. With two bags – one filled, one empty – by her side, she drove home. Jumping from cassette to cassette, rejecting each in turn, until in frustration she settled for the radio and the angry voices of late-night talkback.

Tomorrow was the last sitting day of ICAC. A blessed bloody break until February. But until then ICAC was the late-night callers' topic of choice, and what a lot they had to work with. Cops selling drugs? A caller with a thready voice confirmed it, knew cops who did it, had bought shit from them.

'*Go to ICAC? No way, mate. Must be kidding – don't want to join Sallie-Anne Huckstepp at the bottom of a lake.*'

That released the hounds. From the '*I hate highway patrol – who doesn't?'* brigade, through to the *'They're all little Hitlers on a power trip'* gang – via the *'Too busy lining their own pockets to catch the rapists and robbers'* mob. They were all out there tonight, the haters, sleepless in Sydney.

Rolling down shiny streets, rain-slicked tarmac bright beneath streetlights, she passed buttoned-up houses with their verandah lights on and their rooms in darkness. An occasional single light burned in an upstairs window, or in the face of an otherwise blank block of flats. Ned pictured an angry mouth twisting into a telephone receiver, fist clenched, alone in the night.

A red light gave Ned the chance to rummage in her bag for another tape. Not looking to see what it was, she jammed it in and tilted her rear-vision mirror to deflect the headlights of the four-wheel drive behind her. Disposable Heroes of Hiphoprisy replaced the anger of talkback with some equally angry hip-hop. Beating her hands against the steering wheel, she sang her own version of the chorus.

The lights changed and she turned right, sweeping down the hill towards River Road and Greenwich. Once she was off the main roads, the streets got darker. The rain started up again, random pulses of brilliant sheet lightning sheered across the eastern skyline. Her windscreen wipers were having trouble keeping up with the downpour.

Storm cells, those pockets of intense weather that ripped haphazard paths through the suburbs, were a signature of a Sydney summer, like jacarandas in November and gardenias at Christmas. She slowed down, anticipating the steep, sweeping downhill right-hander, the blackness of the bushland gully on her left.

The four-wheel drive was tailgating. The lights behind her flashed, blinding even with her mirror tilted to night view. She swore, drifting into the left-hand lane, calculating he'd have overtaken her before the climb back into suburbia and the parked cars of Longueville. The headlights seemed to be floating with her, drawing closer.

It was instantaneous, the shift from irritation to fear, coinciding with the sensation that her front wheel had clipped the kerb. The steering became loose, the start of a skid. She made herself take her foot off the brake, back off the accelerator – try to drive through it, not fight it. Sensations returned of that day in the skid pan, at the Police Academy, a trainee copper with a driving instructor by her side, talking her through the fishtailing, floating motions of a sliding car.

Lights reared up on her right, the running board of a Land Cruiser hovered for measureless time beside her as she felt her car slowly coming back to her. The bulk of the door filled her driver's-side window then accelerated past in the time it took for her to draw breath. Red and blue light punched through the darkness. A police car came barrelling down the hill from Longueville towards her. The Land Cruiser accelerated away as the police car sliced through the teeming rain, no sirens. It whipped past her in the dip. She craned her neck to watch it fly up the hill, the tail end sliding out on the camber of the bend, realising it was hell-bent on getting somewhere else.

With her car back under control, Ned's body staged a rebellion. She clung to the wheel, shaking, her bowels liquid, imagining the sound of the Mazda crashing down the gum-tree-dotted slope, metal crunching, glass shattering, saplings cracking.

She looked at the packages beside her, wanting to believe she'd just had a run-in with a dickhead driver but scared to her core that she hadn't.

SLEEP WAS HARD TO FIND. Ned closed her eyes but headlights dazzled her. She opened them and possibilities raced through her mind. The Crime Squads used Land Cruisers, so did the DEA. She hadn't seen one at the UCs, but it might have been out on a job.

Did Ugly have one?

At dawn, she found herself sitting on the edge of the bath staring at the toothbrush Sean had left there. She was cold and stiff from too long in the one position.

The DAL had skin samples from under Phuong's nails. It had samples of dog bites on both women's bodies. And she was staring at Sean Murphy's toothbrush, and wondering what story his DNA could tell.

The young cadet learning to write occurrence pad entries had spoken to her father about Phuong. Then, the young cadet pushing papers about had handled the gun that had killed her parents. He'd lied to her – not in words, but by omission. She reached forward, snatched up the toothbrush and dropped it into a paper bag. Only once she'd done it, did she begin to tremble, to tell herself it was as much to clear as to convict him. She placed the paper bag down on her bed, beside the two exhibit bags – Ugly's cigarette stubs in one, her running shorts with Nero's dried slobber in the other.

Ned leant back against the bed head, arms wrapped around her knees, rocking as she tried to come up with the right words. She had obtained evidence. Illegally. Now she had to ask if Ben Torres was willing to risk his career at the DAL by doing a favour for an ex-girlfriend. But the phone in his office rang out and kept ringing out for half an hour. When someone finally picked up, it was to tell her Ben had taken an early weekend, a triathlon somewhere up north; he'd be back Monday.

She was still sitting on her bed, staring at the bags when her pager sounded. Heart pounding, she picked it up, fumbling at the controls.

But it wasn't Sean.

It was a message from Marcus Jarrett.

I have your document. My office. ASAP.

The ALS office was humming, pre-court conferences as the clock ticked down towards 10 a.m. Ned was shown into Jarrett's office past hostile eyes and sharp remarks about queue jumping.

'I heard your interview,' she told him. Not wanting to appear too needy. 'Last night. You were . . .'

'Yeah. Lots of dignity, not too much anger. Angry blacks scare the punters.' He started packing his briefcase with legal files. 'I don't have much time. I'm due in court this morning. What are you going to do with this?'

He jabbed at a document lying on his desk.

STATION Bankstown	NSW POLICE FORCE TELEPHONE MESSAGE PAD	Form 187B D. West NSW Government Printer
INFORMANT DETAILS	MESSAGE	ACTION
89/9 11.55 a.m. 22/9/76	I need to see the police at the building site on the corner of Stacey Street and Rickard Road. One of my workers has uncovered bones which appear to be human remains.	Bankstown CIB informed. P. Styles Pro/Const.
Mick Kelly Bushrangers Builders 796 045	P. Styles Pro/Const.	Attended, informant spoken to. Animal bones only. NFA. Det. Sgt V. Urganchich 6 p.m. 22/9/76

Even though she held it in her hands, Ned had to keep re-reading the telephone message to fully believe it. Something had been niggling her, something she hadn't been fully aware of. Why had her father driven past Bankstown Police Station and gone down to Revesby to report Phuong missing? Because Mick Kelly had already had dealings with Bankstown police. With Bankstown Ds. He wouldn't have known that Revesby was just a sub-station, accountable to the big station up the hill, sharing resources. No wonder he'd left Revesby empty-handed. No wonder he'd avoided Detective Sergeant Urganchich at Bankstown and instead reported Phuong missing at Revesby.

NFA. A favoured acronym. No Fucking Action.

Pretty succinct description of 1976 around Bankstown.

Animal bones. Mick Kelly had seen war, corpses, battlefields – he'd have known the difference between animal and human remains. He hadn't been trying to cover them up; he'd been trying to report them. Just like he'd tried to report Phuong missing.

They'd missed both entries on the pads back in 1976 and she knew why. The answer lay on one of the running sheets she'd copied from the brief. Detective Sergeant Urganchich had signed off that he had checked all the local pads for any mention of the Kellys. Tedious task. Good job for a local. Proactive, probably done before anyone even asked for it. The Homicide Squad would've been more than grateful to tick that piece of donkey-work off the running sheets.

'You going to hand it all on to Zervos? Should make for an interesting inquest,' Jarrett said.

It was a straightforward, reasonable question, demanding a straightforward, reasonable answer. A clear set of goals. A plan.

She didn't have one.

'I don't know.' Once she handed this over to Zervos she'd be reduced to a victim again – observing the crime scene from the wrong side of the police tape.

'ICAC?' Jarrett suggested, snapping the locks closed on his briefcase.

ICAC. She hadn't thought of it, but it made sense.

An old, cold case. Corrupt police. Ugly was corrupt. Had to be.

But covering up the discovery of human bones back in 1976 made him – what? A lazy cop who hadn't wanted to do anything about an Aboriginal grave-site. ICAC could accuse him of that and he'd claim that all he'd been doing was covering his arse, not wanting anyone to know he'd written off Kelly's report as NFA. It was all a long time ago and that's what lazy cops did, they covered their arses – it didn't prove much else.

'ICAC,' Jarrett repeated. 'Or do you have a problem with that?'

She knew how going to ICAC would shape the rest of her career. Even if it was murder. Even if it was family.

'No, it's just – what have we got? What can we tell them? It's too early.'

Jarrett shook his head. '*You don't get to decide what is and isn't significant, Mr Jarrett.*' He mimicked her lecturing him, here in this very office, what felt like years ago.

'I just think there's more I can do before I hand it over.'

Standing in Jarrett's office, under his sceptical gaze, Ned couldn't say exactly when she had decided that Erika Urganchich and E. Vass were the same person. But she was convinced now. And that would tie Ugly to the building back in 1976. So the same motive ascribed to her father as the builder – the financial cost of a delay – was just as strong if Ugly was the building's owner. But there were two directors of Erimar: E. Vass and M. Shields. If Erika had been fronting for Ugly, then it was likely M. Shields was fronting for someone else.

'Who are you trying to protect, Detective Kelly?' Jarrett's voice had grown cold. The man who'd moved to the beat of Salif Keita the day before had been replaced by the ALS advocate who didn't trust detectives.

'No one,' she bristled. She held up the document Jarrett had just given her. 'It's just this isn't enough. I need to —'

'It's enough for ICAC.' Jarrett picked up his briefcase, checked his watch. 'This isn't just about your family. If these documents clear your dad, well, bully for you. My mum's still dead and I want to know who killed her.'

She owed this man. He was halfway to the door when she started to say the rest, about Erimar, about her suspicions that E. Vass was Ugly's wife, about the DNA from Ugly and his dog, her hopes that Ben would run the forensics. She told him she needed more time, wondering as she said it if what she really needed was to keep moving, keep digging, because she was afraid of what she'd find when she stopped and put the pieces together. But she didn't tell him about Natty Pillow-Head seeing Ugly with Mabo, and she didn't tell him about Sean.

Jarrett retraced his steps, a crease in his forehead, taking it in, weighing it up.

'Illegally obtained DNA,' he said, shaking his head, 'Inadmissible. Hopelessly tainted.'

'I know, but it wouldn't be for court. Those samples, they can get them all again with warrants, in an investigation. But it would prove to us that we're right.'

He set down his briefcase, sat on the edge of his desk, fingers drumming the wood as he thought.

'You can't involve the DAL. That'd compromise everything.'

'Then a private lab . . .'

'Ned, drop it. Unless you want to be responsible for all DNA evidence being excluded at a trial down the track.'

He was thinking like a lawyer but the mention of a trial made her heart race with possibilities. Jarrett's phone rang. He answered it, curt; someone needed a conference in the cells at the Police Centre before court. He hung up and turned back to Ned, a long appraising look.

'You've got the weekend,' he said finally. 'Work out what you want to do, but just don't fuck anything up. No more illegal evidence gathering. On Monday we go together to ICAC with what we've got. Or I go alone.'

Ned followed him out of the office and onto Abercrombie Street, the noise of the morning peak hour preventing further conversation. Jarrett strode off towards the city, leaving Ned to consider what she hadn't told him and why. If he'd known how she'd linked Ugly to Mabo, he'd have taken this straight to ICAC and nothing she could have said would have stopped him.

She also hadn't told him that while she'd been standing in his office, explaining the connection between Erika and Erimar, saying it out loud, she'd realised the company name wasn't just a random collection of letters. *Eri*mar – *Eri*ka. Which left *Mar*. There were many possibilities. Either of her aunt's names – Mary Margaret. Could be a man's name. Mark, Martin.

Or another name. One she'd heard for the first time weeks ago. Sean Murphy's wife, the French exchange student who'd never gone home. Marianne.

NED HAD NEVER BEEN SO RELIEVED to be on an afternoon shift – even one with Figgy. Traffic was light on the trip to Bankstown, but she found herself checking in her rear-view mirrors, even making a few anti-surveillance sweeps down one-ways. But the only four-wheel drives she saw were filled with mums and kids.

She'd toyed with the idea of going to Erimar's solicitors to confirm that E. Vass was Erika, try to identify M. Shields. But Ned knew what solicitors were like with their clients; they'd tell her to bugger off – or worse, ring Zervos to complain. Instead, she had the street directory open, bookmarked with a Jungfrau Kennels leaflet.

Picnic Point reminded Ned a bit of Greenwich. It was a peninsula formed by a bend in the Georges River. Surrounded by bushland, it was hard to believe Bankstown was fifteen minutes up the road. Henry Lawson Drive followed the course of the river, land falling away from the road to the waterfront, the homes shielded by trees and long driveways, boats moored in front of many. A handful of older cottages, fishing shacks and family fibros still hung on, but most had fallen to architect-designed glass and columns.

Jungfrau Kennels didn't advertise at street level. Ned missed the number the first time – good size for the postman but not for a driver flashing past. Beyond the steel gates, the driveway ran between a corridor of tall gums then dipped down the rise, the roof of a house below just visible. Entry was via a buzzer in the brick wall, overlooked by a security camera. She hadn't counted on the camera and turned her head away as she buzzed.

Ned was confident the gates would stand up to the assault of the two large German shepherds hurling themselves against them. Nevertheless their sustained fury as she waited for a response began to shred her nerves. They leapt at the gate, attempted to dig through the concrete beneath it. She eyed off the angle at the bottom, assuring herself there was no way they could slide beneath it. Ugly wouldn't risk his dogs to the traffic – or risk a law suit from savaged neighbours.

'Vik?' The voice on the speaker-phone was barely audible above the snarling and barking.

Vik. So Ugly wasn't at home. The tension across her shoulders ratcheted down a notch and she turned her face back towards the camera lens.

'Um, hi. Yeah, look, I would've called first but I was passing by and I thought, hey, why not drop in. I —'

'Not interested.' A woman's voice.

'No, no, no – I'm not selling anything. I want to buy a dog. A couple, actually.'

She hadn't been sure how to approach Erika, but one look at Castle Urganchich had convinced her that just getting through the front door would be a challenge. She'd take this one step at a time. First get in, then see what sort of woman Erika Urganchich was.

'What? You want to buy a dog?'

'Yeah. Look, it's a little difficult to hear you. Um, can I —'

'Now's not a good time – come back later.'

'Oh, look, I'm here now. It'll just take a few minutes – please, I'm down from Coffs for the day, don't know when I'll be back in Sydney. I've heard so much about the Jungfrau bloodlines.'

There was a long pause. Ned began to think that Erika Vass-Urganchich had gone. Then she heard a whistle. The dogs responded as if on strings, bounding down the driveway and out of sight. The gate rolled back. By the garage, on the top level, waited the woman from the pamphlets. She made a cutting gesture with her hand and the dogs dropped to the ground, heads on paws.

'They are fantastic,' Ned gushed to Erika. 'You must feel so safe.'

'All in the training. Can you train dogs?' Erika spoke much as Ned imagined she trained her dogs. Clear and direct, no extraneous civility.

'Er, no. But they're not for me.'

Ned followed Erika in through a side entrance, keeping up a stream of bright chatter about a nonexistent brother and sister-in-law returning from a posting in Saudi, mysterious about the nature of it, implying wealth, a need for security in their new home.

Erika led her down two flights of stairs to a room that filled the lower floor of the house. There was a full-size pool table and a professional-looking bar at one end, an open fireplace with large, white leather lounges and armchairs at the other. Glass sliding doors looked out into a wide backyard flanked by bushland that ended at a jetty where a half-cabin cruiser was moored. The backyard was the heart of Jungfrau Kennels. It looked more like stabling for horses than dogs – enclosures, pens and runs. Their occupants, black and tan and handsome, were in various extremes of excitement, stirred up by their companions from the front gate. The two loose dogs sat staring in through the glass doors, eager to burst through. Buckley's and none, Ned thought. That's how much chance there was of ever creeping up on this place to execute a search warrant.

Erika needed little encouragement to talk about her dogs. Ned sensed the woman was glad to have something to occupy her, glancing a little too often at her watch but making no effort to hurry her guest off. They looked at trophy cabinets piled with silver and crystal, at ribbons, framed and hung. It was like a museum; Ned admired the photos on the walls of dogs posing, puppies gambolling, a muscular fair-haired man, arm in arm with Erika.

Affectionate. Carefree. The years had left their mark on Ugly.

The fashions changed but the dogs looked consistently fine and fierce.

At one end of the room was a bar that could have opened for

business; it had draught beer and a top shelf that would put a lot of the pubs she knew to shame.

The phone rang and Erika made a hasty apology, almost lunging for the handset. The conversation was muffled, and seemed to consist of Erika repeating 'No' and 'I don't know'.

Ned at first pretended to be absorbed by the large glass display case that dominated the back wall of the bar. But she soon found herself genuinely riveted. Instead of the rugby guernsey or the cricket bat with team signatures she expected to see, this one displayed a leather vest with *Bandidos* arched across the shoulders, above a cartoon character in a floppy sombrero. The bottom of the vest was ripped, the leather stained dark around the rent. Erika rejoined her just as Ned realised what she was looking at, too late to hide her reaction.

It was a trophy from the Milperra Massacre, when the Bandidos and the Comancheros had opened up on each other with shotguns at the Viking Tavern back in 1984.

'Wow. Amazing . . .' Ned hoped horror and wonder looked the same.

Erika's response was lost in the canine eruption outside. The dogs had disappeared from the glass doors. Seconds later a buzzer sounded through the house. Ned studied the bar more closely while Erika answered the speaker.

The framed colours were obviously the prize of the collection, but now that she knew the theme, a lot of what she'd passed over as kitsch took on significance. There was the usual array of knuckledusters, nunchakus and knives, but these were mounted, with small plaques beneath them. From a distance it seemed they had dates and names. There were smaller items, framed – a handwritten letter, crumpled and dirty, a cigarette lighter, a ring – impossible to put in context. The framed front page of a newspaper showing the Granville train disaster with the blood-smeared New South Wales Police shoulder badge set on top needed no context.

'No, he's not here.' Erika's voice carried but whoever she was talking to came back crackled and distorted; Ned couldn't make out what they were asking.

Ned knew Ugly probably wasn't the only cop to souvenir things. Soldiers did it too – hadn't MM sniffed in disgust at Mick's souvenirs? But the scale of Ugly's collection was audacious. Bikie colours. That wasn't a souvenir, that was evidence. She looked down and saw her arm was resting on a bar mat with the words *Viking Tavern* on it.

'I said he's not here . . . I don't know, try work.' Erika sounded agitated.

To one side of the bar was a small skull, the lower jaw missing. It rested on its crown; the cavity filled with matchbooks and novelty lighters. She reached out to touch it, to confirm the ghastly thing was plastic, a synthetic novelty of some kind. Her fingers leapt away from the raw rough texture of bone.

'I'd rather you wait till my husband —'

This time Ned heard the response.

'. . . *have a warrant . . . open up or . . . force.*'

Cops at the gates. Like a roo in a spotlight, Ned was momentarily paralysed.

'Give me one moment, I'll bring in the dogs.' Erika turned to Ned. 'I think you should —'

'I'm sorry, yes, of course,' she mumbled.

Erika seemed to be on autopilot, handing Ned a leaflet from a pile at the door, not reacting to the shaky hand that received it. Passing the security screen, Ned glanced at the featureless black-and-white fuzzy outlines captured by the camera. No hint who they were. She forced herself to breathe in calm, regular patterns. Erika signalled the dogs down and opened the gates. Ned walked up the long driveway towards the four men in suits walking down.

The one in front was a solidly built bloke in a business suit. Ned felt she'd seen him somewhere before. As she drew closer the sense grew stronger. Round-faced, thinning sandy hair, freckle-dashed face – he'd been talking to TC; she'd seen them together as she drove off to the archives.

The men drew level, the solid bloke and two others kept on going, their eyes flicking over her as they passed. The fourth one stopped. Of course. She would have, too. Someone leaves a house you're executing a warrant on – of course you stop and have a chat, get their details.

'Just one moment, Miss.'

This one was polite at any rate.

'I'm going to have to ask you a few questions.' He flashed a badge. An interstater, and an ID she hadn't seen before. 'I'm from the Independent Commission Against Corruption. Can you please tell me what you were doing here?'

ICAC.

Marcus must've decided not to wait for Monday. If this was the response, then they were taking it seriously. And after what she'd just seen in there perhaps Marcus had been right after all. Time to put up. She reached into her back pocket, pulled out her ID.

'I'm Detective Kelly, Bankstown Detectives. You'll find what you're looking for in there, on the bar. I guess Marcus Jarrett sent you?'

The flash of her police ID was all it took for the nice guy who called her 'Miss' to be replaced by a headkicker.

'What the fuck are you doing here, and who the fuck is Marcus Jarrett?'

'**I TOLD YOU – I WENT THERE** to see if Erika Urganchich was the E. Vass whose company, Erimar Pty Ltd, owned the block of flats being built in 1976 by Bushrangers. I thought if I could link her to the building, then I could link Sergeant Ugl . . . Urganchich, as well.'

They'd been at it, off and on, for a few hours, though Ned hadn't scored a trip into town, to ICAC headquarters. She guessed that Erika had.

After the short, sharp exchange on the driveway with Detective Curlewis, the conversation between Ned and various stony-faced representatives from ICAC had continued back at Bankstown. The solid bloke she'd seen with TC was the boss. Robertson. He hadn't asked any questions. Just listened and looked.

It became clear that ICAC had no idea what she was talking about or why she'd been at Ugly's place. She had no idea why they'd been there, either, and they weren't about to enlighten her.

She'd handed over her copies of the telephone and occurrence-pad entries, and the running sheet Ugly had submitted. She'd told them about Mabo and the kero in the back of Morgenstrom's car and the car diary that linked Urganchich to it. She told them there was a skull on Urganchich's bar. She hadn't told them she'd planned to try and run a few illegal DNA tests. In turn, they asked her when she'd last seen Urganchich.

'Ever see him anywhere other than here at Bankstown?'

'No, I don't socialise with the man.'

'Sure about that? Never seen him at another police establishment?'

The UCs. She'd seen him there. Her face felt hot.

'I did see him. At the UCs office, I saw him.'

'You applied for undercover work, Detective.' Not a question.

'I was thinking about it, but changed my mind about them and they changed their mind about me.'

'Why'd you change your mind?'

'I didn't think the lifestyle was for me.'

'Why'd they change their mind about you, do you think?'

'You'd better ask Swiss Fowles – Detective Inspector Fowles.'

'You and Detective Sergeant Murphy have been having an affair.'

'Why ask if you know?'

'What has Detective Sergeant Murphy told you about Sergeant Urganchich?'

'You might be surprised to know we didn't spend much time talking about him.' No reason to be narky, other than an instinct to be uncooperative.

'Past tense, Detective? The affair over, is it?'

'That would be my business.'

With a sense of disbelief she heard herself. Only this morning she was bagging up Sean's toothbrush, wondering if his wife was M. Shields, and now she was playing silly buggers with ICAC. She needed to stick her head under a cold shower.

'So you didn't spend much time talking about Sergeant Urganchich – but you spent some time. What was discussed?'

'Detective Sergeant Murphy said the UCs sometimes borrowed a dog from Sergeant Urganchich, for personal protection.'

'For personal protection.'

'That's right.'

'Did he say they used the dogs for any other reason?'

'No.' She looked at the questioner. 'What other reason would they want a dog for?'

Like every other question she asked, it went unanswered. She didn't know if they'd taken note of anything she'd told them until she saw Morgenstrom's car disappearing down Fetherstone Street on the back of a full-lift tow truck.

ICAC had hit Bankstown and Erika at the same time. TC's office was filled with suits again – but these weren't like Zervos's men and TC wasn't welcome. The door opened and closed but the blinds remained shut. The station staff hadn't taken long to work out who the target was. ICAC had taken over the sergeants' room, turned Ugly's locker, desk, drawers and files inside out and upside down, bagged the lot, then widened the net.

No one in the station was saying much about anything. Voices were too loud when they had to communicate, exaggerated calm mixed with barbs about dogs – not the ones who wagged their tails but the kind who gave up their workmates. Eyes met then slid away. All wondering, *Why are they here? Who brought them down on us?* A scum of suspicion settled.

The investigators started with the sergeants, then worked their way down the ranks. Interviewing each person, some longer than others, some brought back for further questions. TC was holed up in the Patrol Commander's office with a brace of suits and an unhappy-looking Morgenstrom, who'd been called in off leave – straight from the tennis court, by the look of him. He was going to be even crankier when he found out about his car. Meanwhile, phones kept ringing, jobs kept coming in. The wheel kept turning. Friday night in Bankstown simmered.

'Fuck – glad to get out of that place.' Figgy rolled his shoulders and settled in behind the wheel. 'So, what did they ask you?'

'Ugly, Ugly, Ugly,' Ned said. 'You?'

'Same. When'd I last see him, where does he hang out off duty – that sort of thing. What's he done, ya reckon?'

'Buggered if I know. Thought you might have a clue.'

'Me? Why me?'

Paranoia was infectious.

'Just thought, blokes' locker-room chat, you know.'

'Oh.' Figgy was slightly mollified. 'Wouldn't be in his shoes. He's a lazy shit but there's no badness in him.' Figgy shook his head. 'Poor bugger. Won't matter what he's done. Once they get you, they'll make sure something sticks.'

'Yeah.' She stared out the window. *No badness? Poor bugger?* Would that really be how they'd react? Ugly as victimised copper? What if he'd killed?

Figgy had all the insider gossip from the police grapevine.

'Ugly's brother, or cousin, or something – anyway, bloke's one of those back-room types in the Liberal Party, a mover and shaker. Word is ICAC have got it in for the Libs and the cops. First they knocked off Greiner, then they go after Roger, now they're killing two birds with one stone, giving the cops a kicking and using Ugly to get stuck back into the Libs.'

Ned let Figgie talk as he drove; all he needed was an occasional noise to show she was awake. All she needed was time to try and make sense of what had happened.

Mundane jobs kept them out of the station for most of the night. Eliminating registered owners of Toyota Nissans from an armed hold-up inquiry filled in the hours. By the time they reached the married couple with four kids under six and baby seats strapped into the back of the white station wagon, Figgy's mood had turned toxic. They picked their way down the hallway, booby-trapped by baby-walkers, trikes and plastic toys.

'Jeez, with that many rug rats to feed, he'd have to rob banks just to make ends meet,' Figgy snapped on the way out.

'Priceless, aren't they?' Ned knew the replies by heart by now.

'Cost a bomb and keep on costing.' He slammed the door, gunned the engine. 'If you're smart you'll stay single, and if you really feel the need to breed then don't try doing it on a copper's wage.'

Figgy's detailing of his economic woes – his mortgage, two kids and a wife who'd unexpectedly announced that number three was on the way – took them up to knock-off time. When Ned volunteered to finish off the pads and crime reports, he peeled off home.

It was nearly midnight when Ned climbed the stairs.

TC had reclaimed the fishbowl but didn't wait for her there. He burst out and met her halfway across the deserted office, a desk between them.

'What the fuck did you think you were doing?'

'You were wrong, TC. Reckon I can win this one.'

'You've got no idea what you're dealing with.' His fists clenched.

'Ever been to his place, had a drink at his bar – under his bloody Bandidos trophy cabinet? Seen the skull on the bar? Small, like a baby's. Like the one missing from that massacre site.'

'No.' The muscles at the sides of his mouth quivered.

'Ugly took the report from my dad about the discovery of those bones back in '76. He wrote it off.'

'There are things going on here . . .' TC leant over the desk, uncurled his hands, pressed them flat on the tabletop. 'Have you heard from Murph?'

'What? No.' She wasn't going to be deflected. 'Why'd they come after Ugly? It wasn't because of my info – they looked blank when I told them.'

'Dunno.'

'Come off it. I saw you and Robertson a couple of days back, he was telling you something. What've they got on Ugly?'

'It doesn't matter what they've got, because they haven't got *him*.' TC's shoulders slumped. 'He's hit the toe.'

She sat down, weary beyond all reckoning. The crackle of the police radio was white noise in the background.

'What's going on, TC?'

'I don't know the details, I'm not meant to know. You can't know. It's an ongoing operation and you don't fuck around with an ICAC investigation, Ned.'

'Must be serious for him to do a runner,' she said.

'Go home, Neddie. Just keep your head down, OK? Stay out of their way. And Murph – stay clear of Murph for a bit. Promise me.'

TC had aged in a day. Bags under his eyes, jowls drooping, but he stared at her like one of them was about to drown. She wasn't sure which one.

'Can't promise that, TC. Not when I don't know why.'

MM'S BEL CANTO TRILLING WOKE Ned from the heavy sleep she'd earnt courtesy of a bottle of scotch and a solitary vigil on the deck. Her pager had sat beside her, mute. The alcohol hadn't been enough to keep the dreams at bay. She'd woken shaking from a nightmare, her hands wet with sweat, buzzing from the memory of the baton. Not the usual dream. This time it'd been a hooded figure, tied to a chair. She'd beaten him, until the chair toppled over, the hood came off and Sean's crushed face bled onto the floor.

The sun was already high and hot, leaving her clammy and dry-mouthed on top of the sheets. A head-pounding shower helped a little but standing up was still a vertiginous event as she shuffled into the kitchen.

Linh was nowhere to be seen.

MM was entertaining a grey-haired woman Ned had never laid eyes on before. The coffee plunger still had some dregs in it and there was half a croissant on the platter. She helped herself to both with a mumbled 'Morning' to the stranger.

'My niece, Newie,' MM said, bringing a hand to her mouth, a gesture of faux secrecy that even the cheap seats would see. 'She's a detective, you know.'

'Nice to meet you, Newie,' the woman said. 'I'm Grace Milligan. I've been helping your aunt with her memoir.'

'You have?' Ned nearly dropped her mug.

'I'm just dropping over the latest draft. Almost ready for the publishers.'

'I see . . . um, that's great. Been looking forward to seeing – reading it.'

'Well, I'd appreciate any comments you have, Newie.' Grace handed Ned a card and stood up. 'I really should be off. It's been lovely meeting you finally. I've heard so much about you.'

'Yes, of course . . . No, MM, you stay there. I'll see Grace out.'

On the safety of the front verandah, Ned confessed. 'I thought this – the book, you – were all part of her imagination.'

'I can understand that,' Grace said with a slow smile. 'We started the project some years ago. Your aunt's . . . *decline* has been gradual, but more noticeable in the last few months.'

'Is there much in it, about my parents? About what happened to them?'

'Your aunt was rather focused on the art, you know, the music. There was only a little about their deaths.' Grace looked embarrassed. 'I know it's been in the news again lately. It must be very difficult for you.'

'It is. There are things about my dad, his military service, that we were never told. Did you rely on MM for the information about him? Were there any of his notes, letters – a diary?'

'No, no, nothing like that. Mary Margaret really didn't have much to say about her brother. It was more about her dealings with the police after she came back to Australia to look after you girls.'

'What dealings?'

No doubt about it now – Grace was embarrassed.

'Your aunt had a bit of a . . . *fling* with a policeman after your parents' murder. He was very kind, helped her deal with some of your parents' effects when she was clearing out the house. I've made a few changes to that section – I'm hoping she won't notice.'

'What changes?'

'Well . . .' Grace flushed, playing with her car keys. 'She wrote about finding a skull, in your parents' house. It was a child's skull, a baby's. She thought it must've been a war souvenir. Something her brother had brought back from Vietnam. This policeman, her friend, disposed of it for her – never told anyone. It was the kind of anecdote that just jarred, you know, with the rest of the book. Not the right tone. Not necessary.'

'Did she name this policeman?' Ned wasn't sure if it was the cicadas beating the air around her head or the hangover.

'Handsome, blond, she said – but then she'd hardly describe him as unattractive, would she? Your aunt is rather proud of her . . . liaisons, but she can also be surprisingly discreet. Seems he was married and a little on the young side.'

Ugly. Blond, married – that fit. He'd taken MM's statement. He had a baby's skull on his bar. But he wasn't that much younger than MM.

The pain in her head was excruciating.

It couldn't be . . . Christ, Sean would've been eighteen and MM would've been pushing forty. He'd been here – MM would've recognised him, remembered him. Had he fallen through the gaps in her memory? Or were they both keeping it from her?

Ned shook her head. The heat oozed around her.

'You don't look very well, Newie. Can I —'

'No, I'm fine, bit of a migraine . . . Um, did MM ever say what happened to everything from the house at Bankstown?'

'I did ask. She said it was all put in storage; didn't offer me access and changed the subject. I'm not sure if she kept the stuff or got rid of it.'

Saturday nights in Bankstown unfolded with a predictable rhythm. In honour of Figgy's frugality, they bypassed Uncle Pho's in favour of half-price, half-cold Macca's in the station meal room. Ned couldn't be bothered arguing, tuning out the shared moans of the afternoon crews about the cost of child-rearing in the Shire.

No one talked about Ugly.

The evening deepened, bringing with it a couple of prowlers

worth a quick spin with lights and sirens, then a hold-up alarm at the RSL which wasn't and a stick-up at a servo on the highway which was. Knock-off time was eleven and as the hour drew near, Ned began clockwatching.

It was the time of night when things began to heat up. Booze, blues and bouncers. Those who got punchy when they got drunk had usually done so by 10.30. Ned and Figgy were backing uniform up at a brawl at the sports club when the shift sergeant, Caroli, called them back to the station.

Caroli took them into the sergeants' room and shut the door. After ICAC's visit, Ugly's desk was bare. He wasn't going to need it again.

'Getting a few calls – didn't want to broadcast it.' He cocked an eye at Ugly's desk. 'In the circumstances.'

'What kind of calls?' Ned was wary. Figgy was looking at his watch.

'Noise complaints —'

'What!' Figgy let rip.'Fuck, Carlo, it's nearly knock-off and you want us to go and do uniform jobs?'

'What's it got to do with him?' Ned said, nodding at the empty desk.

'Noise is coming from his place.'

'So what?' Figgy was immovable. 'Get the night car to —'

'Because I'm giving *you* the job, Detective Constable, and the longer you stand here whingeing about it the later you're going to be.'

When all else fails, pull rank.

'Fuck. Fine, but if this runs into OT, I expect you to sign for it. Where is this joint?'

'I know,' Ned said. 'What is it, Sarge? What sort of noise?'

'Dogs. Been howling for the last hour or so. Won't shut up.'

'Dogs,' Figgy repeated, disbelief on his face. 'Fucking dogs. This just gets better and better.'

'Is there anyone in the house?' Ned asked Caroli.

He shrugged. 'Dunno.'

Ned understood why the neighbours were complaining. Sustained, bloodcurdling howls. As one dog drew breath, others had already plugged the gap. A wall of sound. The hairs on her arms rose like hackles. The moon, riding high, wide and bright, only added to the atmosphere. A sensor light had come on when they pulled up, but no other lights showed beyond the gates. No dogs greeted them. Too busy out the back.

'Check the neighbours first, eh?' Ned suggested.

Five minutes later they compared notes: light on downstairs in the early evening, dogs had started up about 10 p.m when all was in darkness; the dogs barked a lot when people came near the house but never like this. Ned opened up the car and pulled out one of the batons. Figgy looked at her, eyebrows raised.

'Dogs,' she said. 'Big dogs.'

Figgy pulled out the second baton. Ned pressed the buzzer, without much expectation. It remained unanswered. Didn't summon any dogs, either. She looked at the wall – smooth, no footholds, gates similarly designed.

'I can give you a leg-up,' Figgy offered.

'I'd like you on the same side of the wall, if it's all the same.'

They drove the car onto the footpath, flush against the boundary wall. From the roof of the car to the wall was not far, though the drop over it into the garden felt further than it looked. They didn't discuss how they planned to get out. Caroli had put them on a back channel of the police radio. Figgy exploited the privacy to communicate to him their progress, along with exactly what he thought of the sergeant.

The top level of the house was dark. The howling was louder now, rising from the kennels down the back. No one answered their knocks, and there was no buzzer on the front door. Probably considered redundant with the security gate and the guard dogs. Everything was locked. Ned braced for the scuttle of paws, expecting dogs to explode around the corner at any moment. She shifted the baton in her grip, carrying it in the ready position.

Her palm buzzed warm with the memory, the crack of metal on bone. She worked saliva into her mouth. They peered through windows. No lights.

'Look . . .' Her whisper lost beneath the wailing. 'No appliance lights.' In her torch beam the microwave, the digital clock radio, both blank.

They found the switchbox, halfway down the slope, along the sidewall of the house. The mains switch was off. Without speaking they slid their batons through the belt loops of their jeans, drew their revolvers, snub noses pointing at the ground, safeties off, torches off.

Figgy thumbed his portable, got Caroli back at Bankstown. 'A bit of fucking backup would be highly fucking appreciated,' he said into the radio, before turning the volume down and shoving it in his back pocket.

They moved forward, ducking under a side window, listening. Impossible to hear anything above the dogs' lamentations.

Should be barking, not howling – must know we're here, must smell us, she said, aloud or to herself, she couldn't tell. Her skin was too tight, each hair, each follicle stood independent of the next. Sound became gelatinous under the assault of ceaseless cries.

They had come all the way down the slope at the side of the house and were now level with the bottom floor. Around the corner would be the deck, the glass doors that led into Ugly's bar and pool room. They stopped, breathed, exchanged a look, then moved together. Ned went low, Figgy went high, leading with their guns before they both dropped down onto the grass by the steps of the back verandah.

Two shapes lay on the decking. Flat on her stomach, Ned craned her head up, far enough above the edge of the deck for the shapes to resolve. Two dogs. Ugly's guard dogs, lying on their sides. Inches away from them. Sleeping? Not these dogs. Drugged?

She nudged Figgy's leg. 'Dead?'

His shoulders lifted and fell.

The tall glass doors behind the dogs were slick, black glass, impenetrable without light. Figgy pointed back at the switchbox – motioned for her to wait.

Ned rehearsed the flash of light in the night, braced for the instant, for the moon to turn red.

The lights came on in the house. Not many. Not bright, but enough for a star of shattered glass in one of the sliding doors to sparkle.

Ned could see the two dogs clearly now. They were sprawled, tongues lolling, glassy-eyed, tops of their heads blown off.

Figgy slipped onto his stomach beside her and side by side they elbowed their way to the front of the deck and peered up.

In the room, in front of the starburst of glass, was the pool table. A low, rectangular lamp hung above it, lighting up the baize. Its green glow bathed the white shirt of a man slumped over the table. His legs dangled, buckled and ungainly. A dark, shiny stain splashed across his back.

'Fuck.' Figgy fumbled for the radio, called up the cavalry.

At the other end of the room a second lamp by the fireplace shone over the leather lounge and a blonde woman who was lying across it. Erika Urganchich was facing the window. Too still for sleep. Eyes and forehead wide open. A dark arc was sprayed across the pale leather.

'We have to check.' Ned said it.

'She's had it.'

'The bloke, his ankle . . .' A telltale bulge at the ankle that broke the line of his trouser leg.

Ned made herself rise from the safty of the earth. She scuttled across the deck, tried a door, felt it give and glide open. She flattened against the interior wall – solid, reassuring against her back. Protection. Her stomach, her face, felt soft, vulnerable and exposed. They kept the pool table between themselves and the night outside as they traversed the room.

The man's back was to the deck, the web of fractured glass lined up behind him – at its centre the perfect circle of a bullet hole. He had a surprised, goggle-eyed stare – caught mid-shot – the balls scattered where he'd pitched forward, cue in hand.

Ned touched his neck, her fingers repelled by the clammy dead skin. Curlewis, the ICAC investigator who'd fronted her in the driveway a little over twenty-four hours ago.

They moved across the room to the lounge, keeping low, using the furniture as cover. Now that they were inside, she was hyper-aware of the darkness that pressed against the glass out there. Ned imagined the leather, the wood and stuffing flying apart like skin and bone and brain.

When they reached the lounge, Ned didn't bother touching her. The hole in the back of Erika Urganchich's skull was larger than the one in her forehead.

Ned strained to hear. Was it the whine of approaching police cars winding through the dogs' chorus? It grew closer, the skirling sirens lifting the dogs to even greater mourning.

'Let's get some fucking lights on out there,' Figgy muttered. He looked spooked, hitting light switches randomly.

'I'll get the front gate open,' Ned said.

She found the security panel that Erika had used to let in the ICAC blokes, saw shapes in the dark on the screen, heard voices of the afternoon shift crews through the speaker-phone.

Figgy swore as the floodlights came on outside.

Ned swung around, looked out into the backyard, which stretched out beyond the deck and down to the water's edge. On the pathway that ran between the kennels lay another body. Something about its bulk, even at rest, told Ned who it was.

They edged their way back outside then, keeping close to the dog pens, approached the body. The dogs moaned as they passed.

The man lay on his back. His lower jaw and one side of his face was missing but enough remained – Sergeant Vik Urganchich. A gun in his out-flung hand. Not a police-issue revolver, this was boxy and modern, its barrel lengthened by a silencer. Ned saw another shape a few feet away. Another dog. One with a damaged ear.

The surviving dogs intensified their howls. Ned's teeth ached, her head rang. She began to believe the dogs were weeping – wailing and gnashing their teeth. She half-expected to see them rending their pelts, piling ashes on their heads. She couldn't bear it. She spun about, made the motion she'd seen Erika make with her hand.

'STRUDEL!'

It was like they all died at once.

COLDEST TIME OF NIGHT, the hour before dawn. Ned sat by the river, mug of coffee in her hand, blanket round her shoulders, feet tucked under her. Shoeless. Physical Evidence had taken her runners to cast the soles in plaster, identify her tracks, eliminate them. Her socks were dew-damp. She sat at the picnic table. Nice spot beneath the trees, by the brick barbecue. Urganchich's half-cabin cruiser rode the rise and fall of the river at the end of the jetty. Comfortable creaks and squeaks grizzled from rope and timber.

A tinnie found adrift midstream had been retrieved by the Water Police and tied up at the jetty. Now a police launch was spotlighting the progress of the police divers. Not because they really expected to find anything but because it was another 't' to cross, another 'i' to dot. The working theory was that Ugly had come by tinnie, knew about surveillance, knew ICAC would have someone in his house, knew he could walk past his own dogs without them creating a stir.

Strudel.

She warmed her hands around the mug, staring across the Georges River. The moon had set. Somewhere out there in the darkness was Heathcote Army Range and the national park. Up and down the river new suburbs were carving up the bush, but here, there were no lights across the water, just a sandstone cliff face and scrub and gum. Invisible in the night but present. She sat with her back to the house and the arc lights, the tents, the flash of cameras and the activity of men and women in suits and overalls. The dead still lay uncovered, offering up their wounds for inspection.

Now that it was over, the images bubbled. The flash of white bone and grey matter, the raw red meat of torn flesh. Vibrating like a gently rung bell, she pulled the blanket tighter.

Someone had done a bakery run for hot pies. She'd eaten one then lost it quietly into the river a little while later. Now she sniffed the coffee. Her stomach warned her not to try it.

'Detective Kelly.' Zervos sat down, steam curling in perfect cartoon wisps from his mug.

'Sir.' She wanted to sleep. For a few days.

'Robertson told me about the job you did on Urganchich. Busy little detective aren't you, Kelly?'

He sounded almost affable. Ned tried to shake off her lethargy, unfolded her feet, stuck them onto the wet ground, tried to shock herself into something approaching alertness.

Robertson? It came to her. The boss of the ICAC team. He'd come not long after the cavalry had arrived. From a respectful distance, she, along with the rest of them, had watched him lean down and look his dead officer in the face. Then they'd all pretended not to watch him take himself down to the river, alone. The outline of his shoulders had betrayed him, silently weeping.

'Got quite a bit on the ugly bastard, didn't you? Wondering why you didn't pass any of it on.' Zervos's cigarette burned fiercely on each draw.

She didn't answer.

'Robertson's wondering too. Makes him suspicious, makes him think you don't trust your own force, and it puts us in a very awkward position. ICAC don't think much of us. Less now, seeing as one of ours has fucking murdered one of theirs.'

Zervos's rage sounded all the worse for the tight rein he had on it. This sort of anger had a long, slow-burning fuse. Any kudos he'd got from investigating Dawn Jarrett's murder was tainted now. He was making it clear who he held responsible, and it wasn't just the dead cop lying on the grass not too far behind them.

'I wasn't sure,' she said. 'I wanted to be sure before I —'

'*Sure?* Well, you sure now? One dead cop, one dead witness and a dead suspect. Murder-fucking-suicide. You wanted a result, Kelly, well this is it. But you won't get many fucking answers out of it.'

'Bit quick,' she murmured.

'What?'

'Murder-suicide. I mean, what if —'

Zervos stamped on his cigarette. 'Expert on bullet wounds too, are you, Kelly? Powder burn under what's left of his chin, residue on the gun hand. Bloke at the end of his tether – no friends, nowhere to go and no guarantee his wife wasn't giving ICAC every fucking dirty bit of business he'd ever been involved in.'

'And was she?'

A nerve twitched at the side of Zervos's right eye. He looked down and began rolling another cigarette. 'It was early days.'

'But you can still check his DNA, see if it's under Phuong's nails, check for his dog's DNA in the bites on her and Dawn Jarrett.'

'ICAC checked yesterday, after you enlightened them. Urganchich's profile was on record at DAL.'

'And?'

'Not him.'

The revelation winded her. Not Ugly. Not her dad. The owner of the DNA still in the shadows. Like M. Shields.

'Checking the dogs'll take longer, but what does that prove?' Zervos continued. 'The Urganchichs have been selling security dogs all over Sydney for years.'

'Erika – you going to check out whether she was an owner of Erimar?'

Zervos dragged on his cigarette, turning a length of it into ash. 'ICAC have gone through it already.'

'She was, wasn't she?' Righteous anger warmed her limbs.

'Connects his wife to the site.'

'And what about the partner – M. Shields? Who's M. Shields?'

'Old records take time.' Zervos flicked his cigarette out into the darkness of the river. It floated for a brief instant then disappeared.

'Everything points to Ugly and that building site. Don't try and tell me it doesn't. That telephone message – my dad reported those bones on the building site and Ugly just gave him the flick. And then the occurrence-pad entry – Dad tried to report Phuong missing but runs straight into Ugly again. Then, what – a week or so later – Detective Sergeant Urganchich is signing off on a running sheet that says there's no mention of the Kellys on any of the local pads. He —'

'He was a lazy cop who shonked a job.'

'The skull on his bar, that —'

'Getting it checked. It could be from the original site – again, that proves what? He didn't want to get tied up with Aboriginal land rights shit back then. From the look of his bar he collects murderabilia.'

'It gives him a motive to shut Dawn Jarrett down.'

'And Nguyen Phuong? What's his motive there, exactly? You reckon the owners of the building had a motive for knocking off Dawn Jarrett, well then, the builders had an equally strong one. Particularly a builder who'd got himself in debt buying a flash house on the beach and with a mistress to look after.' Zervos shook his head. 'There's still only one person with a motive to murder both women.'

Their voices were carrying; a couple of the Physical Evidence team stopped their sifting and bagging to stare at them.

'So why did Ugly do all *this*, then?' Ned's coffee slopped out as she flung her hand back towards the crime scene. 'Something big was closing in on him. You don't do something like this —'

'Something big *was* closing in on him, Detective Kelly. But it wasn't anything to do Dawn Jarrett.' Robertson's voice put an end to their clash.

Ned swung around, unsure how long he'd been standing there. 'Then what?'

'The operation is ongoing. As such we cannot —'

Zervos stood up and stalked away. Robertson's spiel was clearly not news to him.

The ICAC officer didn't say anything more but he didn't go either. He sat down, shoulders slumped.

'Your officer,' Ned began, almost leaving it at that when she saw Robertson's chin tremble. Nothing for it but the weasel words of sympathy mixed with apology. 'I'm sorry. He was dead when we got here, that's why we didn't move him.'

From the ICAC vantage point, especially tonight, Ned guessed there was little to admire about the New South Wales Police. But if Robertson thought they'd skulked outside, waiting in the dark while his officer had bled to death, well, she was denying him that particular grievance.

'Nat Curlewis . . . Curly,' he said. 'Came up from Adelaide for this.'

Somewhere in the suburbs, half a continent away, Ned heard it. The knock on the door in the dark.

'Any other suggestions?' Robertson asked.

'Huh?' She reeled herself back from the distant sounds of grief in the ether.

'It's not his DNA under her nails. It's not your father's. Any other suggestions?'

She brought her knees to her chest, hugged them. Just the cold, she comforted herself, as trembling pealed through her. Balancing on the picnic bench, her soggy socks leaving prints on the wood, she thought about the toothbrush in the paper bag on her bed. Easy to be brave when it didn't count. When no one else knew.

Trust me.

'Maybe,' she said.

IT WAS BROAD DAYLIGHT BY the time Ned finally drove out of Bankstown, but all the way home she saw Robertson's face in the half light of dawn, that silent, interrogative stare when she'd said the name. Sean Murphy. She rewound the last few tracks on *Soro*, opened her throat and echoed the singer's grief, cry for cry.

Greenwich Road embodied a lazy Sunday morning, dogs on leads, children in tow. Residents wandered along, sloppily dressed, collecting bread, croissants, milk, caught between bed and committing to the day. Newspapers tucked under their arms, still safely headlined with the news of Charles and Diana's impending divorce. Good thing, really. It made much better Sunday brunch fare than cops, corruption and murder.

From the front door, Ned heard laughter and the clink of crockery. MM was occupying the Shrine, entertaining again. She slipped inside and flopped onto her bed, weighing up how grimy she felt against how worn out she was. A swim would be good but the energy required had been spent. She ducked past the Shrine's half-open door and made it to the bathroom undetected. Water sloughed off the sour stink of fear that had dried on her skin. She washed her hair, digging her fingers into the scalp, massaging away the grip of tension. Then, wrapped in a light cotton kimono, she readied herself for a covert sprint to her room.

'Newie.' MM had heard the shower and was demanding attendance. 'Come in – I want you to meet someone.'

I'm fucking tired and want to go to sleep. 'Just out of the shower.'

'I've got a very dear friend here, Newie.' MM appeared, grabbed her niece by the wrist. 'You look perfectly decent, don't be ridiculous.' She pulled Ned through the door.

Swiss Fowles was sitting back in MM's plush red armchair, a smile on his face, his feet stretched out under the coffee table. For an instant Ned thought she'd fallen asleep at the wheel. Any second she'd wake up, blinded by the lights of a four-wheel drive, about to plough into a tree.

'Newie, this is my very dear friend, David. David – my niece. Newie you'll *never* know just how wonderful David was to me after your mother and father died.'

Swiss smiled even more broadly, shaking his head, modest.

'He – helped – you?' The words were a poor fit.

'Newie, your father left things in such a state. I'm sorry darling, but without David's *discretion*, oh, it all could have been *very* embarrassing.'

MM's mystery man. Not Sean. Not Ugly. Swiss Fowles – who hadn't taken his eyes from hers. She hadn't noticed before just how dark they were. Against his pure-white hair they looked all pupil. Never thought what colour the hair had been before it turned white.

'Well, why don't I get dressed and then . . . ?' She began to move back to the door. Nothing between them but a piece of cotton – all wrong. Him being here – all wrong. Being here now – worse than wrong.

'Nah, don't bother about that. We're all friends here, right?' he said, leaning forward as if suddenly uncomfortable in the seat. One hand reached behind, pulled a handgun from his belt. 'Ah, that's better. Uncomfortable bastards, aren't they, Newie? You don't mind do you, Mary Margaret?' He laid it flat on the coffee table, flicked the barrel with his finger. It spun. Dull grey whirling against the French-polished wood.

Not police issue. Elongated barrel. Silencer fitted. Second one she'd seen. Ugly, using a silencer for a suicide – funny about that.

And turning off the power – when had Ugly managed that? Had Curly been playing pool in the dark? The barrel spun along with her thoughts.

'Of course not, David. Newie's always leaving hers about, aren't you, dear?'

'Don't take it to the shower though, eh?' Swiss grinned, halting the rotation with a fingertip. 'Sit down.'

MM was in her element. Ned recognised the signs. Always garrulous when she had a bloke to preen for, especially old flames. She was reminiscing now, all the detail she'd long denied Ned: how kind David had been in her time of need, how he'd taken that terrible thing out of the house at Bankstown, that war relic. 'A skull, darling! A baby's! And so discreet, never told anyone.' As MM spoke, Swiss set the gun spinning again. Hypnotic.

'Why are you here?'

'Newie! David, I do apologise – reminds me of her father sometimes.'

'Mary Margaret, you don't have to apologise to me.' He picked up the gun, cradled it in one hand. 'I just came by to catch up with my dear friend. Thought I'd better read this book, seeing as though I'm in it.'

MM fluttered and giggled. 'David. You *know* I'd never cause you any embarrassment. How is she?'

'She left me, Mary Margaret,' he said, his eyes never leaving Ned's face. 'Imagine. Gave her everything. Gave up *you* for her.'

'David, I'm so sorry. How terrible,' MM cooed.

'Eighteen years, me and Marie. You don't just walk out on someone after eighteen years without an explanation, do you?' He stared at Ned. 'Have to have a reason, right?'

E. Vass and M. Shields. Marie. Ned could still see Erika lying on a leather lounge at the base of a rainbow of drying blood. Had Erika told ICAC about the directors of Erimar? E. Vass and M. Shields.

'Oh David, I'm so sorry. But my darling, it wouldn't have made a difference – not then. I had my life, you were *squisito* but you were a young man with your entire career ahead of you, and I had mine. *Era destino, il mio prezioso.*'

'Well, that's why we've asked your ghost writer over for morning tea, haven't we, Mary Margaret?' Swiss cupped the gun butt in one hand, covered it with his other, patting it like it was a kitten curled into the palm of his hand. 'No need to hide our *affare di amore* now, is there?'

'Oh, David,' MM giggled.

Instinct told Ned that a wide knowledge net was a safety net. 'There's more than one draft,' she said. 'Publishers have got one and —'

'Oh no, darling, I've been working with Grace in *strictest* confidence. You know what publishers are like – lawyers telling you what you can and can't say. Grace is on her way over. I can't get onto Linh, though,' MM pouted.

Relief loosened Ned's limbs. Grace Milligan was on her way but Linh was safe. MM was flitting from subject to subject. Distractions, opportunities could present themselves, would present themselves. Be ready.

'Yeah, Linh's at uni,' Ned said, moving casually behind the lounge. Overstuffed, it would muffle a shot – but not stop it. 'Doing me a favour actually, took some DNA samples I didn't want to run through the DAL into some friends of hers. Scientists love a challenge. You know how it is, David – sometimes you have a hunch, don't want to put it on the record till you're sure.'

His fingers flexed around the gun butt. Her eyes were fixed on his hand, ignoring the memory of bodies ripped open by bullets. Behind her back, her fingers assessing which of MM's crystal objets d'art on the dresser behind her would have the best heft, travel with the truest flight.

Outside, the sunny Sunday continued, croissants flaked and

coffee frothed. The sense of fracture deepened. Couldn't happen. Not here, not in Greenwich. In MM's shrine. Her fingers closed around the cool outline of a crystal dove. Adrenalin was an explosion contained by flesh and blood. Made you mad. Invincible. Ned tried another lie.

'Saw Erika the other day. She told me all about her and Marie. About Erimar.'

The charade ripped. A crash as Swiss kicked over the table. Ned's arm drew back. MM yelped.

'Drop it!' Swiss was on his feet, the gun held steadily on MM.

'David?' MM said, weak, confused. The table had scraped down the front of her legs, tearing open both shins. Blood bright and red poured out, starting to fill her shoes.

The cricket-ball-sized dove tumbled out of Ned's hand.

'Where is she?' Swiss demanded.

'She's dead.'

'Not *her*.' Swiss dismissed Erika with a wave of his gun. 'Marie – what's she saying?'

'ICAC can't shut her up,' Ned improvised. If he didn't know where his wife was, then Marie wasn't dead. Maybe ICAC did have her, or maybe she was just hiding. Swiss's sense of self-preservation was strong – strong enough to bring him here, armed. Ned wondered if it was strong enough to make him run as well.

'Bullshit,' he said.

'They want something – someone – now that Ugly's dead. You heard about Ugly?'

'Oh, I know.' He stared hard at her. 'Poor old Vik – those bastards at ICAC drove the poor bugger to murder and suicide. Fucking tragic – a martyr.'

MM had gone into shock, whimpering, dabbing at her ripped legs.

'Martyr? Nah, not for shooting a copper,' Ned said, shifting position again. 'Funny he only killed three of his dogs, though.'

'Four – four dogs. One of them only had two legs.' Swiss looked pleased with his word play.

'You were there.' Her mouth was dry. 'You tell me.'

She wasn't sure if the words came out or just hovered in her thoughts, along with an image of Swiss in the dark, following Ugly between dog pens. Adrenalin was pumping, building up in her muscles, in an iridescence bursting before her eyes. Sound distorted. Time was reshaping. She began to believe that she could take him, outpace a bullet.

'Well, maybe not a martyr then. But I know one thing Vik's never going to end up as, and that's a witness – him or his fucking missus.' Swiss smiled, wide, confident.

'The dead can still witness – you know that. You're smart.' Ned was edging back towards MM. Her aunt was pale, her eyes starting to flutter. 'This doesn't seem smart. You're —'

'Don't you fucking dare condescend to me about what's smart, you slant-eyed little slut.' He jutted the gun at her, motioned her back from MM. 'Tell me about this DNA of yours, or . . .' He cycled the gun back towards MM.

She moved back until she felt a table against her thighs. She risked dropping one hand behind her, searching blind.

'I've got samples,' she said. 'You, TC, Ugly, Murph – all of you. Getting profiles now, to see who Nguyen Phuong scratched the night she died. ICAC have already cleared Ugly . . .'

The gun dipped for an instant, as if her words had struck. He shook his head. Hard to say if he was exhausted like her, hung-over, still drunk, or on something else. Her hand closed around something smooth and rounded: one of MM's marble eggs.

'What a fucking treacherous little cunt you are. Told him, warned him, to stay away. Reckoned he'd handle you.' He laughed out loud.

Her own breath sonorous. Ned adjusted her grip on the marble, her palms vibrating.

'Wanted you out at the UCs, reckoned we'd keep an eye on you there. Then you go sample his DNA – that's fucking hilarious.'

'Is it?' she said. Her tongue felt thick.

'DNA's not going to show you what he did.' He started to roar with laughter. 'Should've asked him about the gun.' He stopped laughing; stared at her, eyes overly wide, pupils huge, gun rising back up. 'You should've asked him what happened to the prints on that gun —'

The air cracked. A painful, ear-ringing explosion. Swiss spun, gun clutched in his hand, its barrel tracing an arc as he turned. The air split again and again, like planes bursting the barrier, sucking the breath out of her. Swiss crashed into the sideboard, lifeless but still upright before sliding clumsily to the floor, dragging Lladró and Wedgwood figurines down on top of him.

Smelling cordite, Ned panted, braced for more noise, braced for the night to burst open, for the moon to rise again, yellow bleeding into red. Through the doorway she saw a raised gun. A fist around the butt, index finger curled around the trigger, second hand clamped around the wrist, supporting the gun arm. Classic police-drilled shooting position.

Sean Murphy barely seemed to be breathing, his eyes and his aim locked on Swiss.

Each breath was jagged, sheer pain. Not enough air coming in. Light-headed. The marble egg slipped out of her fingers. She bent forward, hands going to her waist. Wet. Her hands were wet. She looked down. The robe was soaked through, dark, sticky.

Then the burning began. Everything else grew cold but between her waist and her neck, there was fire. She was on her knees. Heavy footsteps, boots, running, closer – the floorboards bouncing beneath her knees. Soundless.

She toppled forward, felt the couch against her forehead. MM's head was resting just in front of her, not moving, her hair the scent of an over-ripe peach. A perfume from her childhood, from that day in the hospital when MM had come, hugged two little girls to her and wept. The fragrance saturated her senses. Firelight flickered.

Ned lifted her head, focused on the doorway, on the gun, the hands locked around it. Sean Murphy's gaze slowly turned towards her, the gun travelling with it, maintaining his aim.

Ned closed her eyes, slipped through the fire and into the ice.

DAWN JARRETT GOT A GOOD send-off. A memorial service in Sydney Town Hall, lots of speakers, large photo on an easel, Dawn grinning down on the great and the good who'd gathered in her memory. Phil Walker spoke, seemingly without any sense of shame. So did the Premier, the Mayor and some of Dawn's old crowd, greyer but no less angry. The PM was there in a pre-recorded speech that was played on a big screen.

Ned saw it on the television hanging over her bed. She'd missed a few funerals. Curly's had been all flags and pipe bands and tears in an Adelaide cathedral. Dawn's had been private, up in Tuncurry, before the memorial. Family only. Mabo's had been the smallest, out at Rookwood in a plot bought and paid for by Marcus Jarrett. Ned hadn't asked about Ugly or Erika or Swiss.

All those burials while she lay and healed. A nicked lung. A couple of shattered ribs. Lucky, the doctors insisted; bit more to this side and it would've been her spine, bit higher her heart, bit lower – well, all sorts of problems when bullets rip up bowels and intestines. They assumed she'd be interested. She wasn't. It was enough to be able to heal.

She slept thick, drugged, dreamless sleeps, slipping back through fire and ice in the moment before she surrendered.

Waking brought moments of confusion. Wrapped in stiff, scratchy sheets, alive to the permeating stink of antiseptic and sounds that ricocheted along carpetless corridors. She'd lie awake with eyes scrunched closed, trapped in that moment from so long ago, scared to open her eyes on a world with such sharp, unlovely edges, where it felt like Mum and Dad had always been dead.

After a few days they let in Robertson.

'How much do you remember?'

Everything and forever.

She sipped her water through a straw, the novelty of being allowed to drink fluids again still fresh.

'Swiss waving a gun around. Swiss hitting the sideboard. Seeing Sh . . . seeing Detective Sergeant Murphy in the doorway with a gun. Not much after that.'

Robertson nodded. Same blank, gathering stare. She sipped, tasted plastic, waited to be told.

'Shooting investigation team found you were struck by a bullet from Detective Inspector Fowles' weapon.'

Made it sound like the gun had performed this feat without assistance. She stared back like she'd never imagined any other possibility, felt the suture knots drawing the seams of her skin together.

'Reflex, after he was shot. Squeezed off four rounds – semi-automatic. Three went high. You were fortunate.'

'Yeah, so I've been told.' She remembered the barrel of Sean's gun, swinging towards her, the space inside fathomless. The house dancing. 'Who else was there?'

'SPG. Detective Sergeant Murphy had called for backup.'

'I see.' She didn't. 'Guess I was lucky he turned up, then? And thought to bring along his mates. Why was that?'

Robertson shook his head. 'I told you, there's an ongoing operation.'

'Anyone left alive for you to work on?'

Robertson stared out the window. Need-to-know basis. 'Operatives still in the field, at risk. Limits what I can say.'

'I thought murder inquiries were about getting to the truth.'

'This wasn't a murder inquiry, Detective.'

'No? Dawn Jarrett, Nguyen Phuong, Mabo, my mum and dad . . .'

Robertson turned back from the view but still avoided her gaze. 'Homicide have that in hand. But any inquest on the Jarrett and Phuong murders will need to protect the identity of our informants.'

'Must be a fucking big job.' Still in too much pain to fill her lungs, she couldn't fill the words with power. He had made no mention of Mabo, of her parents. That box in archives would already be coated in a fine film of dust.

'What about Ugly?'

'The wound to Sergeant Urganchich may not have been self-inflicted.' Robertson was looking at the flowers, reading the cards.

She drew in another mouthful of water. Like rain on dry ground, it vanished without trace. 'M. Shields – Marie Fowles?'

Robertson didn't look up, studied a card. 'Yeah.'

'Saying much?'

'Enough.'

'And Murphy?'

Her question hung in the air, the sounds of the hospital grew louder, a trolley passing beyond the door, the clatter of metal.

'Shooting team found that Detective Sergeant Murphy shot and killed Detective Inspector Fowles in the execution of his duty.'

Unfortunate word that – execution. A word like that got the mind wondering. About timing. About things left half-said.

Should've asked him what happened to the prints.

Swiss had been in mid-flight. She sipped more water.

'Get a result on the DNA?'

'The samples under Nguyen Phuong's fingernails belonged to Detective Inspector Fowles.'

Strange how you could hold your breath and not realise it. Ned sank back against the pillows. Pain ripping through each breath.

'Were you expecting another name?' he asked.

She shook her head, not sure if she was relieved or disappointed.

You got famous if you lived, a fancy funeral if you didn't. After Robertson, the visitors arrived in cohorts. The team from Headquarters turned up and talked about counselling, welfare, and time off. They were followed by the Police Association, who covered the same ground before sounding her out. 'Police shootings are dynamite,' they said, 'and in the current climate . . .' In other words, Murph was a hero with no option but shooting to kill, and it was her job to make sure the Coroner got that.

Old workmates from old stations came. Classmates from the Academy, the Ds course and the boys from Banky. Toy was round-eyed, wanting to know what it felt like to be shot; Figgy narrow-eyed, wanting to know how the pieces had come together to make a shape that included her, Ugly, Swiss, Murph and ICAC. TC had been quiet, even a little gaunt, lost behind a bunch of flowers. He lingered behind.

'You gave me the brief, but you never told me they were in it – Ugly, Swiss, Murph. Why?'

'I thought maybe Murph had told you.' He shrugged, twisting the cellophane wrap around the flowers. 'And if he hadn't, well, that was between you and Murph.'

'You all go back, don't you? To Ugly.' That was what Sean had said.

'Vik trained a lot of young Ds, late sixties, early seventies. He was the best around. He *was* 21 Division. Got me my start in Homicide, got Swiss his at the Druggies.'

'And Murph?'

'After my time. Vik was out in Bankstown by then. But he got Murph a run in 21 when he finished his cadetship. Never looked back – Drugs, Vice, then the UCs.'

'Mateship. Wonderful thing, isn't it?' she said, seeing the path smoothed from cadet to trainee detective by a grateful senior detective with pull. Murph must've learnt early how the old school operated – and had been rewarded.

The cellophane crackled like electricity.

'Seen Murph?' Ned asked.

'He's acting inspector at the UCs.'

'Shoot the boss – get promoted. Better watch your back, TC, Figgy's ambitious.'

'Neddie . . .'

'Hasn't been in. No flowers, nothing. Why do you think that is, TC? Why'd you tell me to stay away from him? Why did you tell me it was a fight I couldn't win?'

TC came back to the bed. Voice low. 'Neddie, ICAC are all over everyone at the moment – especially out there at the UCs. Rumour is, it started out there. A tip-off. UCs were using Ugly's dogs to shake down targets – rip them off, sniff out their stash, then steal their drugs and their dough.'

Nero, the UC. So much for protection.

Something else TC told her came back. *Swiss just thinks he runs the UCs . . . And Murph lets him.*

'Then the UCs need a whole new crew. How come they've left Murph in charge?'

TC shook his head, 'Neddie, like I said, it's all rumours. We're eating ourselves alive out there.'

LATE. THE CORRIDORS QUIET, NURSES busy with records at their night stations, snores coming from rooms. Ned was walking up and down the long hallways, finding reassurance in achieving this simple act, measuring her growing confidence that walking and breathing were normal things, that going home the next morning was real. At the top of the corridor she turned and started back.

With a soft hiss the lift opened at the nurses' station. A figure came out, stood for a moment to get his bearings, looked left and right.

Once, her skin had seemed independent of her, anticipating his touch, rising to his voice, his scent. Now it encased her, dormant and spent.

She walked towards him, steady, upright, the low burning in her side reminding her of the cost. He met her halfway, outside an empty TV room where the set hummed low with unwatched news. She turned in to the TV room. Neutral ground, not her room; she wasn't letting him get that close.

'You're looking better,' he said.

Awkward, hands behind his back, elbows out. Played it well. Made her wonder if she'd ever seen anything that was real.

'Better than when?'

In the pale TV light, he looked grey. 'Jesus, Nhu . . .' He slumped into a seat, elbows on knees, hands cradling his head. 'I thought he'd killed you. I thought it was all for nothing.'

'All what?' She wanted to sit but didn't want to cede the advantage.

'I don't know what I'm going to do – it wasn't meant to end up like this.'

'Ended up OK for you. Boss of the UCs. Commissioner'll probably stick a medal on your chest.'

She was starting to see spots, her torn skin straining against its seam.

'Nhu, I wanted to come, but the Shooting team and ICAC . . . witness contamination. I shouldn't be here now.' He raised his head.

It was a good look. Grief. Remorse. It would be easy to believe him. He got to his feet, walked closer. Ned turned away, grunted, the movement mashing her ribs. She sat down, a hard, straight-backed chair.

'What was going on out there at the UCs, Murph? You, Swiss, Ugly, his dogs?'

'You shouldn't know this!' He ran his fingers through his hair, paced away from her, limbs jangling. 'Robertson wouldn't have told you. Bloody TC. If he knows . . . If it gets out, I'm fucked, I'm so fucked.'

Sean looked like he had at Goulburn, playing at being someone he wasn't. Ned concentrated on taking regular, steady breaths, riding the slip and slide of pain along her ribs.

Then it was the old Murph – quick, decisive, graceful movements – who dropped back in front of her, squatting at her feet, hands resting on her knees. Close. She smelt him. Citrus and salt.

'I worked on them, Nhu, on Ugly and Swiss. For ICAC. I wired up and I taped them.'

We never fuck over our own. Each other's all we have. His hands had been on her shoulders in Goulburn, warm like they were now – tactile, intimate.

'Why? Why would you do that to them?'

'They were putting everything – all of us – at risk. Greedy bastards, ripping off dealers that we'd been working on.'

His eyes raked hers, searching. For what? Understanding? Forgiveness? Belief?

'And when did you find out? You ran the UCs in all but name.'

'Nhu, I'm getting close to Sunny Liu, to his dad.' Sean spoke quickly, quietly, as if to draw her closer, deflecting from her question. 'That's how I heard he had contracts out on our people. They didn't know they were coppers but it wouldn't have mattered if they did. Swiss and Vik, they were going to get someone killed.'

'And so you thought I should join the UCs too?'

The UCs office, Ugly, his dog downstairs, she and Swiss abusing each other, Murph orchestrating them all. Her breathing became more rapid, her ribs sharpened along each intake.

'Nhu, no!' He looked horrified, his hands gripped her knees. 'It wasn't like that. I wanted to keep an eye on you. Once all this shit started bubbling up from the past, I thought that you coming to the UCs – you'd put pressure on them. I thought they'd start talking about what happened, back then, and I could tape them.'

'Yeah? Swiss was just starting to talk about the past – you heard him. But you didn't tape him, did you? You shot him. What *did* happen to the prints on the gun? On the gun that killed my mum and dad? The gun you took to Fingerprints, Cadet Murphy?'

His fingers loosened. Something rippled over his face. Regret? Anger? Other people's feelings were never really revealed in their faces, Ned decided. You end up seeing what you expect – or want – to see.

'I was eighteen, Nhu.'

'Mick was thirty-eight, Ngoc was twenty-seven, I was seven, Linh was six.' It was a mantra. He took her wrists gently. On his knees now, pleading.

'I was a kid. Jesus, Nhu, you think there are heavies around now? These blokes, back then, they were gods, they *were* the law. They didn't ask you, they *told* you, and you did what you were told and didn't ask questions.'

'Is that what you did?' She tilted closer. His eyes were over-bright. Tears. Unbelieving, she drew back. Gasped at the stab of pain the movement caused her. Twisted her wrists from his hands, pushed him away.

'Nhu, don't —'

'Who killed them? Swiss?'

'Nhu —'

'Ugly?'

'Please, Nhu, don't —'

'You?'

'No!'

His denial rebounded around the sparse little room. Ned heard the squish of distant footsteps, a nurse returning down the corridor. The world outside this grim little room went on.

'But you know, don't you?' Ned pressed, her breath coming in sharp gusts.

'I don't know.'

'I don't believe you.' Her chest was burning. Tears of pain.

'I don't – I don't know. I tried to find out. I wanted to make it right. It was a mistake, I was so young.'

'Oh fuck, oh fuck, oh fuck . . .' She rocked back in her chair, crossed her arms in front of her face, sought solace in mindless repetition.

'Nhu, don't. We're all entitled to one mistake, aren't we?' He reached for her, fingers stroking tenderly along her arms.

'Get away from me.' Unable to forget him in her bed, in her body, unable to trust anything she heard him say, anything she felt in response. She heard him getting to his feet, paper rustling, then something dropped onto her lap.

'I tried, Nhu. I wanted, after all this time, to make it up. Maybe one day.'

She sat there until the burning in her side had died from a flame to an ember. Until she had absorbed the grief afresh. She wasn't sure when he left, just that when she finally raised her head, she was alone.

In her lap was an envelope. Yellow interdepartmental, its journey through the service marked by locations and names hastily written and crossed out as it moved on. Back in her room, under strong light, she opened it.

Operation Jasper

Being a Joint Operation conducted by the National Crime Authority (NCA) and the Independent Commission Against Corruption (ICAC) targeting the theft and reselling of drugs by members of the NSW Police Service Undercover Unit and other members of the NSW Police Service.

Listening device obtained by virtue of Warrant no. AB 92/345/68 Issued at the Supreme Court, Sydney, on 4 November 1992 by Justice G.R. Brandon.

Transcript of a conversation recorded between Operative OJ4 and Detective Inspector David John Fowles, Commander, Undercover Unit, Special Operations Group, NSW Police Service.

Meeting #23

Date:	Sunday 14 December 1992
Time:	4.40 a.m.
Location:	Bourbon and Beefsteak Bar, Kings Cross
Present:	Operative: OJ4
	Detective Inspector David John Fowles: DF

First fifteen minutes of tape indecipherable – background noise, music, interference and static.

DF: The old man shot me once, now his kid reckons he's gunna do me again – only this time for good, you know.

OJ4:   You and Vik shouldn't have taken his gear, Swiss.

DF: We didn't know – I swear, Murph, we didn't know it was his. Fuck me, you think we'd have taken it if we knew it was old man Liu's? You'll smooth it, won't ya, Murph? See Sunny, tell him we'll get it back, throw in some more.

(Inaudible – background noise of people laughing.)

DF: Vik helped me. He was a good bloke. I know towards the end he was . . .

(DF crying, unintelligible.)

OJ4:   . . . can't help you now.

DF: But you will.

OJ4:   Sure, I can try. But if Marie rolls over to ICAC, nobody can fucking help you, mate.

DF: What can she tell? Only Vik knows, and you.

(Inaudible – music and background conversations.)

OJ4:   She's going to say you told her – told her how you ran Dawnie down.

DF: It was an accident. I wasn't gunna *hurt* her. Just frighten her a bit. Silly bloody black bitch tripped. Fucking accident, Murph – you know it was.

OJ4:   Marie says you knocked her, to shut her up so the building wouldn't be delayed. Reckons *(indecipherable)* going to say you told her before – looks planned, you know?

DF: Fucking bitch. Only did it for her so we'd have a bit extra in our kick. Fucking cunt. All she had to do was sign the fucking forms . . .

(Inaudible – arguing in background, loud music.)

OJ4:   ICAC won't care about that, mate. Marie says you planned it, right down to where you dumped her.

DF: Fuck me drunk. *Planned* – like fucking hell. It was an accident. I panicked. Mate, I tell you, I felt her go under, felt the car bump over her – I shit meself. She was a mess. I stuck her in the boot. I should've fucking just left the black bitch on the road, let someone find her.

OJ4: *(Inaudible)* . . . never understood why Vik let himself get tied up in such a fucking shit fight – thought he had more brains.

DF: Vik helped cos Vik was a good bloke, you know. Loyal. A-grader. She was in me boot for hours. I was just driving round, didn't know what to do, where to go. Then I call Vik and he says meet him at Banky and we'll pop her in concrete. Could've kissed him.

OJ4: Good plan. Just unlucky, eh?

DF: Fucking unlucky, Murph, all the way down the line. That fucking slopehead turning up out of the blue – who could've *(inaudible)* popping up *(inaudible)* office in the middle of the bloody night.

OJ4: Must've frightened the shit out of you.

DF: I thought I was going to have a fucking hearty, mate – what a fucking fright.
(Inaudible – background noise, people laughing, conversations, music.)

OJ4: . . . getting old.

DF: And what've I got to fucking show for it, eh? TJF mate, TJF.

OJ4: Yeah, well, I'd like to make it to forty, you know, but between you and Vik, and now Liu wanting your head on a stick . . .

DF: Fucking Liu.

OJ4: Yeah, you don't have a lot of luck with Asians, do you? *(Laughs.) (Inaudible – both talking over each other.)* She scratched you up pretty good.

DF: Fuck me. There I was, getting that black cunt out of the boot and bam! *(Inaudible background noise)* . . . like a fucking wild cat – scratching, clawing.

OJ4: Yeah, well, she was fucking VC, mate.

DF: Didn't know that at the time. No wonder we fucking lost that one, eh? *(Laughter.)* She had me down. Fucking kick *(inaudible – poor tape quality)* then Vik and the dog *(inaudible – laughter and music)* a brick – clocked her *(static)* finished her *(inaudible)* fucked, shattered, had to go and have a few . . .

Tape quality poor for fifteen minutes. Unable to transcribe until this point:

DF: You know better than to fucking ask that. Why bring up this crap?

OJ4: You want me to go see Sunny Liu, so I want to know. If old man Liu had the Kellys knocked, then *(indecipherable)* . . .

DF: You can be a real shit. You know that?

OJ4: Better a live shit than a dead dropkick who didn't ask enough questions.

DF: I don't know, Murph. Don't know who knocked them. Fucking ballsy enough to do it in the middle of the street, not ballsy enough to knock the kids *(interference)* . . .

OJ4: But if Liu —

DF: Listen, mate, I didn't ask. I didn't ask Vik and I sure as shit never asked Liu. *(Indecipherable – DF is slurring, becoming difficult to understand.)* . . . put up the money, lined up the company, got the girls to sign the papers. Thing got built, a few years down the track it gets sold and everyone's happy. Vik *(indecipherable)* going to miss the ugly bastard but *(indecipherable)* . . .

OJ4: *(indecipherable)*

DF: Leave it, Murph. Some shit you're better off not knowing *(indecipherable)* . . .

Tape finishes

Raw talk, cold facts and too many coincidences.

The date on the listening device warrant glared at her: 14 November. On Friday night – the 13th – Murph had been in Goulburn playing UCs with her in *Operation Tiger Lily*. He must have driven back from the Police Academy on Saturday morning and gone straight to ICAC. Getting an LD warrant on a weekend took clout. It took a big, bloody-baited hook.

Murphy had decided to betray his mates right after Goulburn. She and the past that she dragged along with her had scared him enough to run straight into the arms of ICAC.

Ned stood by the window, palm of her hand pressed flat against the glass. The Sydney skyline of blue and red neon blazed into the night across the harbour. She could see the distinctive shape of the hotel Sean had taken her to.

And ever since then he'd been at her side, at every turn of events, witness to every discovery. First-hand access to everything that happened, everything she'd thought, felt. Access to her.

Holding up his pager in Smoothey Park. *Always working.*

And while she had sat shoeless and shivering by the river in Ugly's backyard, Sean had been with Swiss at the Bourbon and Beefsteak. Wired and working. Betraying Swiss, recording one last conversation. Had he met Swiss there? Or had he been with him at Ugly's house? And how long had they sat in the bar afterwards, drinking and commiserating? Had Swiss gone straight from the bar to Greenwich? Or had he gone looking for Marie? Had Sean been with him or following him? And at Greenwich, how long had Sean been outside the door, listening?

She had read what he'd done to Swiss, but she still didn't know why. Guilt? A man trying to redeem the actions of a naïve young police cadet? Or the cold calculation of a professional liar with everything to lose, who was prepared to risk anyone and anything he had in order to protect himself?

Sean had held her and loved her, absorbed her tears and passion, stripped himself of his masks before her. She wanted that to be true. As true as the way he'd taken her to the UCs and thrown her at Swiss, just to see what shook loose.

Ned stood at the window, staring out into the night, imagined him returning to his wife, his children and the life in which she didn't exist.

IT WAS CHRISTMAS EVE WHEN Linh picked Ned up from the hospital and drove her down Greenwich Road. With the primary school closed, its inmates were free to patrol the streets, dreaming of the newer, better bikes they might find under a tree in the morning.

There were two cars parked outside the house. Ned recognised the aerials. Linh had barely cut the ignition before Zervos was opening Ned's door for her. Robertson hovered behind.

'Working Christmas Eve? That's dedication.' Ned inhaled the sweet white scent of gardenias growing by the Freyers' mailbox, the scent of Christmas.

'Good to see you up and about, Detective Kelly.' Zervos almost looked like he meant it.

'Welcome home.' Robertson poked a bunch of flowers in her direction, soggy wrapping paper from the Greenwich grocery store around the stems. Linh opened the front door and stood there, looking uncertain about staying but unwilling to abandon her sister.

'So, um . . . come in, I suppose,' Ned said.

They filed in, past the closed door to MM's shrine. Ned didn't want to look in there, not yet. MM wasn't coming home this time. No talk of waiting lists now. She had a bed in a dementia ward as soon as she was fit enough to fill it. Linh had dealt with it all while Ned had grown new tissue and sealed her wounds.

On the back deck, supplied with coffee, Zervos came to the point. There was a strong brief against Fowles by virtue of his DNA under Nguyen Thi Phuong's nails, and a good deal of circumstantial evidence against Urganchich through Erika, Marie Fowles and Erimar. There might even be enough to re-open the inquest into their parents' murder. The gun had been located, still sealed in an evidence bag, gathering dust at Ballistics. Just one among an array of weapons awaiting the chance to testify. It would be sent overseas for more DNA testing, but it was a slim chance. Ned read between the lines. The suspects all had had good reasons to touch it. DNA wasn't going to help.

'Shame no prints were ever found on the gun,' Robertson said, not turning from the view.

'Yeah, well, if wishes were horses . . . Professionals don't leave traces,' Zervos said.

'Don't leave their guns behind either,' Ned added.

Zervos shrugged. 'Called a throw-down. Not unusual.'

The injustice of it erupted from her. 'Five dead. Five!'

'Five?' Linh asked.

'I haven't forgotten about Mabo,' Ned said, turning to Zervos. 'I smelt kero in the boot of Morgenstrom's car.'

'There's an open inquiry into similar murders,' Zervos said quietly.

'Inspector Morgenstrom sometimes uses his vehicle to go shopping,' Robertson chipped in. 'He and his family use a kerosene stove when they go camping. See where this is going, Detective?'

She could. If Ugly had lived he'd have beaten it with a solicitor on L-plates.

'All this so those greedy bastards could protect their fucking shitty investment property.' Ned snarled. All that she'd lost, all that she and her sister had lost, burst out. She felt Linh's hand fold around hers. 'There's got to be more to it than that!'

Zervos lit his smoke, the flame flimsy in the bright sunlight.

'Urganchich and Fowles didn't own that building, or any of the others in Erimar's name,' he said. 'Erimar was fronting a money-laundering operation for the Golden Dragon triad. The wives' names just added another layer. Old man Liu bought Urganchich and Fowles years before and they were scared shitless of him, knew better than to let him down.'

'So, when Dad reported finding those bones, then started asking questions about Phuong . . .' Ned felt Linh's hand tight around hers. 'He was a problem.'

'Maybe,' Zervos agreed. 'Could be why your mum and dad were shot – but it still doesn't tell us who shot them.'

It crystallised. Why the brief couldn't really be made public. Why Sean had kept his position. Why pushing too hard to find out who pulled the trigger wasn't going to happen.

Sean had a 'relationship' with Sunny Liu to exploit. One that he could use to trade his way out of trouble because it might just deliver them the old man, a triad boss. Deep in the shadows a task force had probably been formed, ready to roll on to the next operation. ICAC had been tossed a few dead, dirty cops to satisfy them, but in the real world of policing, the hard men were already trading up to a bigger, better target. The wheel ground on.

Zervos was rising to his feet, nodding to Linh.

'Sorry we don't come with better news, Miss Kelly. Good to see you on the mend, Detective Kelly. Get a few more years under your belt, learn how to be a team player and there might be a spot for you in Major Crime.'

Linh paled.

Right now Ned couldn't imagine going back, but then she couldn't imagine doing anything else either. Unsure if her fear of who she was without the Job was stronger than her fear of the Job itself.

Zervos handed his coffee cup back to Linh.

'There's something I don't understand.' She looked up at the tall detective in his undertaker suit. 'Phuong scratched him – Urganchich. But how did she end up fighting with him?'

Ned saw Zervos glance at Robertson, and Robertson's small nod.

P. M. NEWTON

'Wrong place, wrong time,' Zervos said. 'We think she was waiting for your father in the site office. Late at night. Fowles and Urganchich wouldn't have expected anyone to be there. Certainly wouldn't have wanted a witness.'

In that instant Ned saw sadness settle on her little sister's features with a weight that aged her. All Linh knew was the furtive setting for an affair, Phuong waiting for their father in the middle of the night.

Ned had another story to tell. She'd read the transcript. Heard Swiss describe what happened. Knew that Phuong had died bravely, going to the aid of a woman she'd never even met. Ned finally had a story that might ease her little sister's grief.

Zervos went out to his car and Linh went to the kitchen. Robertson dawdled; if he'd had a shoelace he would have stopped to tie it.

She decided to put the man out of his misery. 'I know about Murph.'

'So I heard.' He sat down, pretence over.

'Just before Murph shot Swiss, Swiss said I should've asked about the gun – about the prints on the gun. I think he meant the gun used to murder my parents and I think he meant Murph. Murph was a cadet, he had custody of the gun, he took it to Fingerprints.'

Robertson was leaning forward, his hands locked together between his knees. 'Did Murphy say anything?'

She tried to think of his words, but it was implication not confession. 'Not in so many words, but I think he cleaned the gun – wiped it. Ugly or Fowles told him to and he did it.' She swallowed the bitterness.

Robertson's eyes were half closed. He rocked back and forward, unclenched his hands, stretched them, white-fingered, red patches where the blood had stemmed.

'He came to us. Unsolicited. Offered us this job. He played us. Fuck, I know he has. He played all of us. Never made sense before,

354

but it does now. Those tapes – the poor quality, the noise, the way it comes and goes – too bloody convenient. We hear exactly what he wants us to.' He walked over to the railing, stared into the middle distance. 'Even gave us Marie Fowles, right at the fucking end.'

Robertson turned away from the harbour, stared at Ned, as if to gauge the impact of his next words. 'They had an affair. Murphy and Marie Fowles. It was a few years back, but once he'd triggered this shit storm he went to work on her again – insurance probably. She went to him for help and he tucked her away somewhere safe, then let Swiss think she'd rolled over to us. Tipped him over the edge.'

Ned's skin tightened. The seam along her wound rippled like it was alive. Sean Murphy, manipulator of everyone he touched. Robertson was still watching her.

'Smart fella, eh?' She heard her voice but it belonged to someone else, someone harder, older, colder. A cop who could meet people for the first time on the worst day of their life and not believe a word she was told. 'What are you going to do about it?' She returned Robertson's stare.

'Nothing I can do. Can't touch him. He's valuable fucking bait for bigger fish. He'll stay put, keep working on the Lius.'

'After *this*? How? They must know he's a cop . . .'

'Liu's always known he's a cop – a bent one.' Robertson almost spat the words, slamming his fist onto the wood. 'Murphy reckons it's his cover story for the job. Bullshit. He's bent. They all were. ICAC's just the beginning. Mark my words, Detective Kelly, the lid's coming off this place. Make sure you're on the right side when it does.'

NED BLAMED IT ON THE morphine. That's what she told herself as Marcus Jarrett drove her out to Georges River National Park on Christmas Day to release the ashes of Mick and Ngoc Kelly and Nguyen Thi Phuong into the river.

It had started with the coverage of Dawn Jarrett's memorial, the week before. Linh was curled up beside Ned on the hospital bed, the TV news showing Marcus Jarrett shaking hands with the Minister for Attending Funerals.

'Geshela, my teacher, he doesn't get graves, or people visiting them, bringing flowers and stuff,' Linh had said. 'After all, they're not really in there. It's like an empty suit of clothes.'

'Very zen. So what should we do with them?' With the pain held at bay by drugs, Ned was happy to let Linh make plans. 'Were Phuong and Mum Buddhist, or were they Catholic? I don't remember Dad ever declaring an interest.'

'I dunno – I'm studying Tibetan Buddhism, not Vietnamese. Mind you, I think they're both Mahayana.'

'Buddhists have brand names?' Ned giggled. 'I still don't get it, you know. You're a scientist. How can this stuff make sense?'

'Because it's scientific, I suppose.'

'Bells and smells – just Catholicism with more colour and movement.' The drugs had mellowed her tone and the events had breached both their reserves. Ned meant no harm and Linh found none.

'Well . . .' Ned saw the little crease of concentration appear between her sister's eyebrows and knew she was in for a

Linhxplanation. 'You know how in quantum mechanics it's said that by the very act of observing an object, the object is changed?'

'No, not really.'

'Well, Buddhist philosophy says much the same. That's what makes it so . . .'

'Enlightening?'

'Interesting.' Linh risked a gentle shove.

'I still don't get it – the chanting, the bell ringing?'

'I like rituals,' Linh said.

'But if you needed a crutch . . . you and the nuns always got along OK, why didn't you just —'

'Because the Buddha-nature means we all start out pure. I like that. I like it more than original sin. I like the idea of us all with perfection inside, not corruption. It might be deep inside, but it's there.'

'Nothing to forgive or be forgiven, eh?' Ned closed her eyes, the faces of those who needed her forgiveness before her.

'Just kindness and compassion.' Linh had snuggled closer, into her sister's undamaged side. 'It makes the world just that bit more bearable to be in.'

Ned rubbed her sister's hand between her own. Everyone needed a crutch – who was she to deny her sister's choice, even if she herself could take no comfort in it?

'Go ahead – whatever you come up with for the funeral's OK by me.'

So, Linh got busy. Reporting back to Ned's bedside as the event came together. She organised the removal of their parents' ashes from the memorial wall in the cemetery neither of them had ever visited. Ned shared her hurt when all efforts to locate Sean Murphy had been stonewalled, but not her delight when she announced that Marcus Jarrett had accepted her invitation.

'He sounded really pleased to be asked,' Linh had told her. 'Said he'd do the Welcome to Country.'

She'd also tracked down a bunch of monks to conduct the service. 'They're Gyuto,' she'd beamed.

'Nice,' Ned had said, no idea what that meant.

And against the odds, it was nice. More than that – it was right. On Christmas Day by the Georges River, the monks, big robust men with faces and smiles as broad as the Mongolian steppes, chanted in a strange, chesty drone like a choir of didgeridoos. Then they mixed the ashes of the dead together in an ornate metal urn. No divisions left.

Nothing to forgive or be forgiven.

The monks placed head-dresses – outrageous things like golden, cresting waves – onto their round, brown, bald heads, then decanted the earthly remains of three people bound by war and love and death and life into the water. And it was over.

Ned thought the ashes would spread out, gently dissolve into the stream and head out to the sea, but they were gritty, chunky, and sank swiftly. Dry-eyed, she peered into the river at the light layer of dust floating on the top. It would be a slow journey to the sea, any sharp edges worn smooth by the time they reached it. If there was anything left of the people they had been, they could choose their own way.

'Strong karma,' Linh said. 'The three of them have lots to work out. Take a lot of rebirths.'

That didn't sound like peace to Ned.

Marcus seemed moved by the ceremony, he and Linh sharing hugs and tears at the end. They looked at ease in one another's arms, lingering there beyond the courtesy funerals demanded. Ned wondered what had taken place while she'd been healing, tried to catch her sister's eye, but Linh busied herself opening eskies of food.

A large Lebanese family picnic was in full swing at the next barbecue. Old women in headscarfs and old men with water pipes had watched the ceremony from a distance. Now, while their young men played soccer and their wives and daughters dished out the food, they broke into smiles watching the monks fold up their golden cloaks, tie their red shawls around their waists and take to the field in enthusiastic competition.

Ned did her best to toss a salad with one hand as Marcus fired up the barbecue. The smoke of burning eucalypt leaves wrapped around her.

'Merry Christmas, Ned.' Jarrett's voice carried on the smoke.

As the afternoon light grew red, Linh set off to drop the monks back to wherever it was she'd unearthed them, leaving Marcus and Ned to drive back together. They came to the intersection of Stacey Street and Rickard Road. The roadworks had finally finished and a deep excavation hole yawned where the unit block had once stood. On the corner, marking what would one day be the boundary of the new car park, was a hump of fill. Newly planted ribbon-grasses were wilting in the stony ground. The heap was topped with a large piece of sandstone. Striped and stippled in reds and yellows, it glowed in the afternoon light. A metal plaque reflected the slanting rays of the sun.

'MLC put it up,' Marcus said.

It was too far away, the writing too small to be read by any of the occupants of the cars flashing past. The memorial to the men, women and children of the Bidjigal clan, shot and beaten to death by soldiers, was unlikely to be overrun with visitors.

'There's nothing here, though.' Marcus's smile hovered between smug and triumphant.

'What?'

'They were murdered here. Would you bury anyone at the place they were murdered? We've taken them back to a place in their own country. Back there, down by the river. Where they won't be troubled anymore. Safe in their own earth.'

JANUARY MEANT THE SYDNEY TEST. The cricket was like a cushion between the old year and the new. Ned drowsed in front of the TV wondering just how many more runs Brian Lara was going to score. The young West Indian had just clicked over his double century when Linh came in, large-eyed, and handed Ned a solicitor's letter. It sought instructions for continuing the rental of a storage unit in MM's name. She'd been paying for it since 1976.

From the outside it just looked like a double garage, one of a row of anonymous storage units in a shabby industrial estate near Bankstown Airport. Then Linh unlocked the roller door, let it ride up, and the past was suddenly solid before them. Boxes lined one half of the space, furniture stacked in the other. Walking in was a waking dream. A good one, not like the others. Ned ripped back one of the covers, revealing the lounge they'd bounced on till Mum would come in threatening minor violence. A corner of the kitchen table, buttercup formica, was just visible beneath the boxes piled on it.

Boxes. So many boxes. They opened a few but the task was monumental. In one, their father was contained in paper – letters, diaries, correspondence. Some typed up, army crest on top. Small, handwritten notebooks, with stained scraps of paper between the pages. Books with Mick's name scrawled inside. Envelopes filled with photos, their father in uniform with a woman who wasn't their mother – in front of the Eiffel Tower, at a café, in a park; Phuong in a miniskirt, chic and sexy in sixties Paris. Things written, photographed and recorded. Things set down. So unlike those things carried in the heart. It would take time to read it all – absorb it all, understand it all – if it was even possible to understand their parents from these left-behind bits.

Their mother occupied the unwritten spaces. If Ngoc had written a diary, it had not survived. Any letters she'd sent must have remained unanswered, or else she had not kept the replies. But her presence was all around them. Ngoc wearing that vibrant, abstract sundress, the clothes she'd made them, the record albums. Ned remembered standing at her side, bored, bored, bored, picking at the embroidered flowers on her mother's flared jeans while Ngoc flicked through racks of LPs.

It was the Ngoc who had taken shape and substance in Australia who pervaded this room. Anchored by the land, by her husband, her daughters, by a future that had stretched out in a comforting suburban banality. Mick and Ngoc had lived their lives in contentment, relishing the lack of events. Confident they'd live to know their daughters, not realising the need to leave clues.

Mick existed here as a soldier, a lover, a witness. But it seemed that he too had fallen mute on his return from war. No more diaries, no reason to record the regularity of family life beyond the familiar tokens of photos and the occasional card, a school report of Nhu's, an orange tree in crayons by Linh.

Linh uncovered an old record player. Ned lifted the plastic cover. An LP still lay on the turntable where Ngoc had left it. The edges undulated in black warped waves. Unplayable. Linh opened the cupboard below, found the empty sleeve. Black cover, black clothes, young black woman with a huge afro hiding behind a giant guitar that blazed red in the spotlight. Her music had filled their house. Ngoc imitating the rich voice, surging along its vast vocal range, Mick joining her on the deep notes; the Vietnamese woman from

Bankstown who struggled with her English soaring alongside the West Indian woman from London.

Ned walked between the angophoras, their flesh-pink trunks reddened in the late afternoon light. Layers of shell fragments lined the track that led down from the rock carving of the sea creature to the small curve of sand on the harbour shore below. She settled into an eroded wave of sandstone, the rock warm, glowing with the sunshine of numberless days like this one.

She took out her Discman. A new CD copy of an old vinyl album. She remembered being little, concentrating under Ngoc's supervision, tongue out, lifting the arm of the record player, aware of the needle's fragile power to play or destroy the music. Then there'd be the crackle, the anticipation.

She pressed play, and the music began, precise and CD-clean. The simple strummed guitar, then piano, then that unique voice, full and round and splendid. Joan Armatrading reverberated through her earphones, track following track, till Ned reached one she had forgotten she knew. Had forgotten the sound of Ngoc singing it to Mick in the dark, his answer as he joined her on the chorus. *Save Me.*

In the glowing afternoon, with the past a long way away, Nhu suddenly needed to hear their voices again. Not in memory but in life. Just one more time.

But the singer reached the chorus and sang on unaccompanied.

Her tears were silent, the grief of resignation. They dropped onto the dark red leather folder she held in her hands. Her father's diary. Battered and frayed. The leather worn. The original pages bore a neat hand: dates, places – Paris, Saigon, Dalat, Hué. But the writing had grown more harried, the pages often undated until they ran out and it became a collection of slips and scraps of notepaper, hotel writing paper, postcards and envelopes, some dirty and crumpled. She held them, attempting to understand the truth of the entries, already comprehending the real sorrow of it. She'd end up knowing more about who her parents had been, but not who they had become, or who they could have been.

Two tugs were nudging a tanker into place at the oil terminal, the deep resonance of their engines visible in the churn of white water around their blunt sterns. She lifted a folded piece of paper from the diary. The back of an envelope. It was torn along its edges, fragile, handwritten, stained with ochre marks that could have been fingerprints, dirt or blood.

Nhu Kelly buried her feet into the warm sand on the edge of Sydney Harbour and began to read.

ACKNOWLEDGEMENTS

I owe a great debt to Catherine Cole. Without her counsel this book may never have progressed beyond an unfocused hope. Thanks also to my first readers: Mary Anne Anastasiadis, Julie Newton, Chris Van Eijk, John and Libby Mueller, Penny O'Donnell, Alison Slocombe and Billie Villes. Special thanks to Douglas Newton.

You need luck for your manuscript to fall into the right hands and before receptive eyes; I am deeply grateful to Graeme Blundell for kick-starting that process. Thanks also to Bernadette Foley for her generosity.

To my agent, Sophie Hamley, and all the fine people at Camerons – 'thank you' is inadequate. The opportunities you have created for me, Sophie, along with your sterling advice and solid advocacy, has changed my life.

My publisher, Ben Ball, recognised intuitively what I wanted to accomplish with this novel and offered me his enthusiasm, encouragement and insightful editorial advice in achieving it. Jo Rosenberg has been a great champion of the book and ran up too many hours of sleep debt in the editing processes; thank you, Jo.

In our house, Penguin meant book. Thanks to all at Penguin for their welcome and for helping me onto the bookshelf: Deb Brash, Dave Altheim and Cameron Midson for their design work; Tracey Jarrett for wrangling duties; my publicist Liesel Maddock; Daniel Ruffino, Sally Bateman and Anyez Lindop from the marketing team; Louise Ryan, the key accounts team and the sales reps for connecting books to readers. Thanks also to proofreader Jon Gibbs.

To Sydney – all those who lived here once, those who live here still, and all who love this concrete midden by the sea.

BEAMS FALLING

On the inside, Detective Nhu 'Ned' Kelly is a mess. Stitched up after being shot, her brain's taking even longer to heal than her body. On the outside, though, she's perfect, at least as far as the top brass are concerned. Cabramatta is riding high on the new 'Asian crime wave', a nightmare of heroin, home invasions, and hits of all kinds, and the cops need a way into the world of teenaged dealers and assassins.

They think Ned's Vietnamese heritage is the right fit but nothing in Cabra can be taken at face value. Ned doesn't speak the language and the ra choi – the lawless kids who have 'gone out to play' – are just running rings around her. The next blow could come from anywhere, or anyone. And beyond the headlines and hysteria, Ned is itching to make a play for the kingpin, the person behind it all with the money and the plan and the power.

Beams Falling is the brilliantly compelling and gritty second novel by the rising star of Australian crime writing. A portrait of our recent past, it's also a compulsive and utterly authentic insight into the way both cops and criminals work.

'Newton raises the bar for Australian crime fiction.'
MEN'S STYLE

'It's precisely the unshowy tautness of [Newton's] books and character-rich, layered plotting that becomes their strength. As *Beams Falling* starts to really grip, about halfway through, it feels as if it has more substance than many of its showier competitors.'
THE AUSTRALIAN

'This is an exceedingly well written and convincing novel that excels in its characterisations and subtle plotting . . . a first-class crime novel.'
THE SUNDAY CANBERRA TIMES